Atlantis

Gerhart Hauptmann

Contents

ATLANTIS

BY

Gerhart Hauptmann

PART I

I

The German fast mail steamer, **Roland**, one of the older vessels of the North German Steamship Company, plying between Bremen and New York, left Bremen on the twenty-third of January, 1892.

It had been built in English yards with none of those profuse, gorgeous gold decorations in a riotous rococo style which are so unpleasant in the saloons and cabins of ships more recently built in German yards.

The crew of the vessel included the captain, four officers, two engineers of the first rank, assistant engineers, firemen, coal-passers, oilers, a purser, the head-steward and the second steward, the chef, the second cook, and a doctor. In addition to these men with their assistants, to whom the well-being of that tremendous floating household was entrusted, there were, of course, a number of sailors, stewards, stewardesses, workers in the kitchen, and so on, besides two cabin-boys and a nurse. There was also an officer in charge of the mail on board. The vessel was carrying only a hundred cabin passengers from Bremen; but in the steerage there were four hundred human beings.

Frederick von Kammacher, to whom, the day before, the **Roland** had been non-existent, telegraphed from Paris to have a cabin on it reserved for him. Haste was imperative. After receiving notification from the company that the cabin was being held, he had only an hour and a half in which to catch the express that would bring him to Havre at about twelve o'clock. From Havre he crossed to Southampton, spending the night in a bunk in one of those wretched saloons in which a number of persons are herded together. But he managed to sleep the whole time, and the crossing went without incident.

At dawn he was on deck watching England's ghostly coast-line draw nearer and nearer, until finally the steamer entered the port of Southampton, where he was to await the **Roland**.

At the steamship office, he was told that the **Roland** would scarcely make Southampton before evening, and at seven o'clock a tender would be at the pier to convey the passengers to the ship as soon as it was sighted. That meant twelve idle hours in a dreary foreign town, with the thermometer at ten degrees below freezing-point. Frederick decided to take a room in a hotel, and, if possible, pass some of the time in sleep.

In a shop window he saw a display of cigarettes of the brand of Simon Arzt of Port Said. He entered the shop, which a maid was sweeping, and bought several hundred. It was an act dictated by sentiment rather than by a desire for enjoyment. The cigarettes of Simon Arzt of Port Said were excellent, the best he had ever smoked; but the significance they had acquired for him was not due to any intrinsic virtue of theirs.

He carried an alligator portfolio in his waistcoat pocket. In that portfolio, among other things, was a letter he had received the very day he left Paris:

*   *   *   *   *

Dear Frederick,

It's no use. I left the sanatorium in the Harz and returned to my parents' home a lost man. That cursed winter in the Heuscheuer Mountains! After a stay in tropical countries, I should not have thrown myself into the fangs of such a winter. Of course, the worst thing was my predecessor's fur coat. To my predecessor's fur coat I owe my sweet fate. May the devil in hell take special delight in burning it. I need scarcely tell you that I gave myself copious injections of tuberculin and spat a considerable number of bacilli. But enough remained behind to provide me with a speedy *exitus letalis*.

Now for the essential. I must settle my bequests. I find I owe you three thousand marks. You made it possible for me to complete my medical studies. To be sure, they have failed me miserably. But that, of course, you cannot help, and, curiously enough, now that all's lost, the thing that most bothers me is the horrid thought that I cannot repay you.

My father, you know, is principal of a public school and actually managed to save some money. But he has five children beside myself, all of whom are unprovided for. He looked upon me as his capital which would bring more than the usual rate of interest. Being a practical man, he now realises he has lost both principal and interest.

In brief, he is afraid of responsibilities which unfortunately I cannot shoulder in the better world to come--faugh, faugh, faugh!--I spit three times. What shall I do? Would you be able to forego the payment of my debt?

Several times, old boy, I have been two thirds of the way over already, and I have left for you some notes on the states I have passed through, which may not be lacking in scientific interest. Should it be possible for me, after the great moment, to make myself noticeable from the Beyond, you will hear from me again.

Where are you? Good-bye. In the vivid, flashing orgies of my nocturnal dreams, you are always tossing in a ship on the high seas. Do you intend to go on an ocean trip?

It is January. Isn't there a certain advantage in not needing to dread April weather any longer? I shake hands with you, Frederick von Kammacher.

Yours, George Rasmussen.

*   *   *   *   *

Frederick, of course, had immediately sent a telegram from Paris, which relieved the son, dying a heroic death, from solicitude for his hale father.

Though Frederick von Kammacher had profound troubles of his own to occupy his mind, his thoughts kept recurring to the letter in his pocket and his dying friend. To an imaginative person of thirty, his life of the past few years is in an eminent degree present to his mind. There had been a tragic turn in Frederick's own life, and now tragedy had also entered his friend's life, a tragedy far more awful.

The two young men had been separated for a number of years. They had met again and passed a number of happy weeks together, enriched by a liberal exchange of ideas. Those weeks were the beginning of similar epochs in the career of each. It was at little winter festivities in Frederick von Kammacher's comfortable home that the cigarettes of Simon Arzt of Port Said, which Rasmussen had brought from the place of their manufacture, had played their role.

Now, in the reading-room of Hofmann's Hotel, near the harbour, he wrote him a letter.

*   *   *   *   *

Dear old George,

My fingers are clammy. I am constantly dipping a broken pen in mouldy ink; but if I don't write to you now, you won't get any news of me for three weeks. This evening I board the ***Roland*** of the North German Steamship Company.

There seems to be something in your dreams. Nobody could have told you of my trip. Two hours before I started, I myself knew nothing of it.

Day after to-morrow it will be a year since you came to us direct from Bremen, after your second journey, with a trunk full of stories, photographs, and the cigarettes of Simon Arzt. I had scarcely set foot in England when twenty paces from the landing-place, I beheld our beloved brand in a shop window. Of course, I bought some, by wholesale, in fact, and am smoking one while writing, for the sake of auld lang syne. Unfortunately, this horrible reading-room in which I am writing doesn't get any the warmer, no matter how many cigarettes I light.

You were with us two weeks when fate came and knocked at the door. We both rushed to the door and caught a cold, it seems. As for me, I have sold my house, given up my practice, and put my three children in a boarding school. And as for my wife, you know what has befallen her.

The devil! Sometimes it makes one creepy to think of the past. To both of us it seemed a splendid thing for you to take over our sick colleague's practice. I can see you dashing about to visit your patients in his sleigh and fur coat. And when he died, I had not the slightest objection to your settling down as a country physician in the immediate vicinity, although we had always poked a lot of fun at a country physician's starvation practice.

Now things have turned out very differently.

Do you remember with what an endless number of monotonous jokes the gold-finches that fairly overran the Heuscheuer Mountains used to furnish us? When we approached a bare bush or tree, it would suddenly sway to and fro and scatter gold leaves. We interpreted that as meaning mountains of gold. In the evening we dined on goldfinches, because the hunters who went out on Sundays sold them in great quantities and my tippling cook cooked them deliciously. At that time you swore you would not remain a physician. You were not to live from the pockets of poor patients; the State was to salary you and put at your disposal a huge store of provisions, so that you could supply your impoverished patients with flour, wine, meat and necessities. And now, in token of its gratitude, the evil demon of the medical guild has dealt you this blow. But you must get well again.

I am off for America. When we see each other again, you will learn why. I can be of no use to my wife. With Binswanger, she is in excellent hands. Three weeks ago, when I visited her, she did not even recognise me.

I have finished forever with my profession and my medical and bacteriological studies. I have had ill luck, you know. My scientific reputation has been torn to shreds. They say it was fuzz instead of the exciting organism of anthrax that I examined in a dye and wrote about. Perhaps, but I don't think so. At any rate, the thing is a matter of indifference to me.

Sometimes I am thoroughly disgusted with the clownish tricks the world plays upon us, and I feel an approach to English spleen. Nearly the whole world, or, at least Europe, has turned into a cold dish on a station lunch-counter, and I have no appetite for it.

*   *   *   *   *

He wound up with cordial lines to his dying friend, and handed the letter to a German porter to mail.

In his room, the temperature was icy, the window-panes frozen over. Without undressing he lay down in one of two vast, chilly beds.

At best, the frame of mind of a traveller with a night's journey behind him and an ocean crossing ahead of him, is not enviable. Frederick's condition was aggravated by a whirl of painful, partially warring recollections, which crowded into his mind, jostling and pushing one another aside in a ceaseless chase. For the sake of storing up strength for the events to come, he would gladly have gone to sleep, but as he lay there, whether with open or closed eyes, he saw past events with vivid clearness.

The young man's career from his twentieth to his thirtieth year had not departed from the conventional lines of his class. Ambition and great aptitude in his specialty had won him the protection of eminent scientists. He had been Professor Koch's assistant, and, without a rupture of their friendly relations, had also studied several semesters under Koch's opponent, Pettenkofer, in Munich. When he went to Rome for the purpose of investigating malaria, he met Mrs. Thorn and her daughter, who later became his wife and whose mind was now deranged. Angele Thorn brought him a considerable addition to his own small fortune. The delicacy of her constitution caused him, eventually, to move with her and the three children that had come to them to a healthy mountain district; but the change did not interfere with his scientific work or professional connections.

Thus it was that in Munich, Berlin, and other scientific centres, he had been considered one of the most competent bacteriologists, a man whose career had passed the stage of the problematical. The worst against him--and that only in the opinion of the cut-and-dried among his fellow-scientists, who shook their heads doubtfully--had been a certain belletristic tendency. Now, however, that his abortive work had appeared and he had suffered his great defeat, all serious scientists said it was the cultivation of side interests that had weakened his strength and led the promising young intellect along the path of self-destruction.

In his icy room in the English hotel, Frederick meditated on his past.

"I see three threads which the Parcae have woven into my life. The snapping of the thread that represents my scientific career leaves me utterly indifferent. The bloody tearing of the other thread"--he had in mind his love for his wife--"makes the first event insignificant. But even though I should still hold a place among the most hopeful of the younger generation of scientists, the third thread, which is still whole, which pierces my soul like a live wire, would have nullified my ambitions and all my endeavours in science."

The third thread was a passion.

Frederick von Kammacher had gone to Paris to rid himself of this passion; but

the object of it, the sixteen-year-old daughter of a Swedish teacher of stage dancing, held him in bondage against his will. His love had turned into a disease, which
had reached an acute stage, probably because the gloomy events of so recent occurrence had induced in him a state in which men are peculiarly susceptible to love's
poison.

It was a friend of his, a physician, who had introduced him in Berlin to the girl
and her father, and who later, when sufficiently acquainted with Frederick's secret,
raging love, had to take it upon himself to inform the enamoured man of every
change in the couple's address.

Doctor von Kammacher's scanty luggage did not indicate careful preparation
for a long trip. In a fit of desperation, or, rather, in an outburst of passion, he had
made the hasty decision to catch the *Roland* at Southampton when he learned that
the Swede and his daughter had embarked on it at Bremen on the twenty-third of
January.

II

After lying in bed about an hour, Frederick arose, knocked a hole in the ice
crust in the pitcher, washed himself, and in a fever of restlessness descended again
to the lower rooms of the little hotel. In the reading-room sat a pretty young Englishwoman and a German Jewish merchant, not so pretty and not so young. The
dreariness of waiting produced sociability. Frederick and the German entered into
a conversation. The German informed Frederick that he had lived in the United
States and was returning by the *Roland*.

The air was grey, the room cold, the young lady impatiently paced up and
down in front of the fireplace, where there was no fire, and the conversation of the
new acquaintances dwindled into monosyllables.

The condition of the unhappy lover, as a rule, is concealed from the persons
he meets, or unintelligible to them. In either case it is ridiculous. A man in love is
alternately transported and tormented by brilliant and gloomy illusions. In spite of
the cold, cutting wind, the young fool of love was driven restlessly out to roam the
streets and alleys of the port. He thought of what an embarrassing position he had

been in when the Jewish merchant had insinuatingly inquired for the purpose of his journey. In his effort not to reveal the secret motive of his ocean crossing, Frederick had stammered and stuttered and given some sort of a vague reply. He decided that from now on, in answer to intrusive questioners, he would say he was going to America to see Niagara Falls, Yellowstone Park, and visit an old collegemate of his, also a physician.

During the silent meal in the hotel, the news came that the ***Roland*** probably would reach the Needles at five o'clock, two hours earlier than was expected. Frederick took his coffee and smoked some Simon Arzt cigarettes with the German, who at the same time tried to do some business in his trade, which was ready-made clothing. The two men, carrying their luggage, then went to the tender together.

Here they had an uncomfortable hour's wait, while the low smoke-stack belched black vapours into the dirty drab mist that lay oppressively upon everything about the harbour. From time to time the sound of the shovelling of coal arose from the engine-room. One at a time five or six passengers came on board, porters carrying their luggage. The saloon was nothing more than a glass case on deck, inside of which, below the windows, a bench upholstered in red plush ran around the sides. At irregular intervals the bench was heaped with disorderly piles of luggage.

Everybody was taciturn. No one felt reposeful enough to settle in any one place for a length of time. What conversation there was, was conducted in a subdued, frightened sort of whisper. Three young ladies, one of whom was the Englishwoman of the reading-room, unwearyingly paced up and down the full length of the saloon. Their faces were unnaturally pale.

"This is the eighteenth time I have made the round trip," suddenly declared the clothing manufacturer, unsolicited.

"Do you suffer from seasickness?" somebody asked in reply.

"I scarcely set foot on the steamer when I turn into a corpse. That happens each time. I don't come back to life until shortly before we reach Hoboken or, at the other end, Bremerhaven or Cuxhaven."

Finally, after a long, apparently vain wait, something seemed to be preparing in the bowels of the tender and at the wheel. The three ladies embraced and kissed, and an abundance of tears were shed. The prettiest one, the lady of the reading-room, remained on the tender; the others returned to the pier.

Still the little boat refused to move. Finally, however, at nightfall, amid pitch-black darkness, the hawsers were loosened from the iron rings of the dock, a piercing whistle burst from the tender, and the screw began to churn the water slowly, as if merely to test itself.

At the last moment three telegrams were handed to Frederick, one from his old parents and his brother, who wished him a happy voyage, one from his banker, and one from his attorney.

Though Frederick had left neither friend nor relative nor even an acquaintance on the quay, yet, the instant he perceived the tender in motion, a storm assailed him, whether a storm of woe, misery, despair, or a storm of hope in endless happiness, he could not tell. All he felt was that something burst convulsively from his breast and throat, and seethed up, boiling hot, into his eyes.

The lives of unusual men from decade to decade, it seems, enter dangerous crises, in which one of two things takes place; either the morbid matter that has been accumulating is thrown off, or the organism succumbs to it in actual material death, or in spiritual death. One of the most important and, to the observer, most remarkable of these crises occurs in the early thirties or forties, rarely before thirty; in fact, more frequently not until thirty-five and later. It is the great trial balance of life, which one would rather defer as long as is expedient than make prematurely.

It was in such a crisis that Goethe went on his Italian journey, that Luther nailed his ninety-five theses to the church door in Wittenberg, that Ignatius Loyola hung his weapons in front of an image of the Virgin, never to take them down again, and that Jesus was nailed to the cross. As for the young physician, Frederick von Kammacher, he was neither a Goethe nor a Luther nor a Loyola; but he was akin to them not only in culture, but also in many a trait of genius.

It is impossible to express in words the extent in which his whole previous existence passed in review before Frederick's mental vision as the little tender sped beyond the harbour lights of Southampton, carrying him away from Europe and his home. He seemed to be parting with a whole continent in his soul, upon which he would never set foot again. It was a farewell forever. No wonder if in that moment his whole being was shaken and could not regain its balance.

Loyola had not been a good soldier. Else, how could he have discarded his arms? Luther had not been a good Dominican. Else, how could he have discarded his monk's robes? Goethe had not been a good barrister or bureaucrat. A mighty, irresistible wave had swept over those three men and also, for all the disparity between them, over Frederick von Kammacher, washing the uniform away from their souls.

Frederick was not one of those who enter this crisis unconsciously. He had been feeling its approach for years, and it was characteristic of him that he reflected upon its nature. Sometimes he was of the opinion that it marked the termination of youth and the beginning, therefore, of real maturity. It seemed to him as if hitherto he had worked with other people's hands, according to other people's will, guided rather than guiding. His thinking appeared to him to have been no thinking, but an operating with transmitted ideas. He put it to himself that he had been standing in a hothouse, and his head, like the top of a young tree reaching upward to the light, had broken through the glass roof and made its way into the open.

"Now I will walk with my own feet, look with my own eyes, think my own thoughts, and act from the plenary power of my own will."

In his valise, Frederick carried Stirner's "The Individual and his Own."

Man living in society is never wholly independent. There is no intellect that does not look about for other intellects, if for no other object than to seek confirmation, that is, reinforcement or guidance, at all events, companionship. That Frederick von Kammacher's new intellectual companion was Max Stirner, was the result of a profound disillusionment. He had been disillusioned in his deep-seated altruism, which until now had completely dominated him.

III

Dense darkness closed in around the tender. The lights of the harbour disappeared completely, and the little cockle-shell with the glass pavilion began to roll considerably. The wind whistled and howled. Sometimes it blew so hard that it seemed to be bringing the tender to a standstill. The screw actually did rise out of the water. Suddenly the whistle screeched several times, and again the steamer made its way through the darkness.

The rattling of the windows, the quivering of the ship's body, the gurgling whirr-whirr of the propeller, the whistling, squalling and howling of the wind, which laid the vessel on her side, all this combined to produce extreme discomfort in the travellers. Again and again, as if uncertain what course to pursue, the boat stopped and emitted its shrill whistle, which was so stifled in the wild commotion of the waters that it seemed nothing but the helpless breathing of a hoarse throat-- stopped and went backwards--stopped and went forwards, until again it came to an uncertain halt, twisting and turning in the whirling waters, carried aloft, plunged down, apparently lost and submerged in the darkness.

To be exposed to impressions of this sort for only an hour and a half is enough gradually to reduce a traveller's nerves to a state of torture. The proximity of that awful element the surface of which marks the limits of the one element in which man is capable of living, forces upon the mind thoughts of death and destruction; all the more so since the water's tricks seem so incalculable to the landman that he sees danger where there actually is none. Another thing hard for the man accustomed to unhampered movement to bear is the close confinement. All at once he loses his illusion of freedom of will. Activity, the thing that in the eyes of the European endows life with its sublimest charm, cannot in the twinkling of an eye turn into absolute passivity. Nevertheless, despite these novel, distressing experiences, de- spite throbbing pulses, over-stimulated senses, and nerves tautened to the snapping point, the situation is by no means lacking in fascination.

Thus, Frederick von Kammacher felt a flush of exaltation. Life was straining him to her breast more closely, wildly, passionately than she had for a long time.

"Either life has again become the one tremendous adventure, or life is noth- ing," a voice within him said.

Again the tender lay still. Suddenly it groaned, churned the water, sent out huge puffs of hissing steam, whistled as if in great fear, once, twice--Frederick counted seven times--and started off at its utmost speed, as if to escape Satan's clutches. And now, all at once, it turned, swept into a region of light, and faced a mighty vision.

The **Roland** had reached the Needles and was lying tide rode. In the protection of its vast broadside the little tender seemed to be in a brilliantly lighted harbour. The impression that the surprising presence of the ocean greyhound made upon Frederick was in a fortissimo scale. He had always belonged to that class of men--a class which is not small--whose senses are open to life's varied abundance. Only on the rarest occasions he found a thing commonplace or ordinary, and was never blase in meeting a novelty. But, after all, there are very few persons who would be dull to the impressions of an embarkation by night, outside a harbour in the open waters.

Never before had Frederick been inspired with equal respect for the might of human ingenuity, for the genuine spirit of his times, as at the sight of that gigantic black wall rising from the black waters, that tremendous facade, with its endless rows of round port-holes streaming out light upon a foaming field of waves protected from the wind. In comparison with this product, this creation, this triumph of the divine intellect in man, what were undertakings like the Tower of Babel, allowing that they were not isolated instances and had actually been completed.

Sailors were busy letting the gangway-ladder down the flank of the **Roland**. Frederick could see that up on deck, at the point where the ladder was being suspended, a rather numerous group of uniformed men had gathered, probably to receive the new passengers. His state of exaltation continued, even while everybody in the tender's saloon, including himself, suddenly seized with haste, grasped his or her hand luggage and stood in readiness. In the presence of that improbability, that Titan of venturesomeness, that floating fairy palace, it was impossible to cling to the conviction that modern civilisation is all prose. The most prosaic of mortals here had forced upon him a piece of foolhardy romance compared with which the dreams of the poets lose colour and turn pale.

While the tender, dancing coquettishly on the swelling foam, was warping to the gangway-ladder, high overhead, on the deck of the **Roland**, the band struck up a lively, resolute march in a martial yet resigned strain, such as leads soldiers to battle--to victory or to death. An orchestra like this, of wind instruments, drums and cymbals was all that lacked to set the young physician's nerves a-quiver, as in a dance of fire and flame.

The music ringing from aloft out into the night and descending to the little tender manoeuvring in the water, was designed to inspire timid souls with courage and tide them over certain horrors attendant upon the moment. Beyond lay the infinite ocean. In the situation, one could not help representing it to oneself as black, gloomy, forbidding, a fearful, demoniac power, hostile to man and the works of man.

Now, from the breast of the **Roland**, tore a cry rising higher and louder, upward from a deep bass, a monstrous call, a roar, a thunder, of a fearfulness and strength that congealed the blood in one's heart.

"Well, my dear friend **Roland**," flashed through Frederick's mind, "you're a fellow that's a match for the ocean." With that he set foot on the gangway-ladder. He completely forgot his previous identity and the reason of his being here.

When, to the wild tune of the brass band, he stepped from the upper rung upon the roomy deck, and stood in the garish sheen of an arc-light, he found himself between two rows of men, the officers and some of the ship's crew. It was the group of uniformed men he had noticed from below. He was astonished and delighted to behold so many confidence-inspiring masculine figures. It was an assemblage of magnificent specimens of manhood, all, from the first mate down to the stewards, tall, picked men, with bold, simple, intelligent, honest features. Moved by a sense at once of pride and of complete trust and security, Frederick said to himself that after all there was still a German nation left; and the singular thought flashed through his mind that God would never decide to take such a selection of noble, faithful men and drown them in the sea like blind puppies.

A steward picked up his luggage and led the way to a cabin with two berths, which he was to have to himself. Soon after, he was sitting at one end of a horse-shoe-shaped table in the dining-room. The service was excellent, and the few passengers from the tender ate and drank; but it was not very lively. The main dinner was over, and the little company from the tender in the great, low-ceiled, empty saloon, were each too tired and too engrossed in self to talk.

During the meal Frederick was not aware whether the mammoth body was moving or standing still. The faint, scarcely perceptible quiver seemed too slight to be a sign of the motion of so huge a mass. Frederick had made his first sea voyage when a lad of eighteen as the only passenger on a merchantman going from Hamburg to Naples. The thirteen years since had considerably weakened the impressions of that trip. Moreover, the luxury of this ocean liner into which he had strayed was something so new to him, that all he could do at first was scrutinize everything in astonishment.

When he had drunk his customary few glasses of wine, a sense of peace and comfort stole over him. After their long irritation and tension his nerves succumbed to a pleasant tiredness, which pressed upon him so healthily and imperatively that he felt almost sure of a refreshing night's sleep. He even made the firm resolution-- in his condition scarcely necessary--that for this night bygones should be bygones, the future the future, and the present, without regard for past or future, should belong unqualifiedly to rest and sleep.

When he went to bed, he actually did sleep for ten hours, heavily, without stirring. At breakfast in the dining-room, he asked for the passenger list, and with a wild leap of his heart read the names for which he had been looking, Eugen Hahlstroem and Miss Ingigerd Hahlstroem.

IV

He folded up the list and glanced about. There were about fifteen to twenty men and women in the saloon, all engaged in breakfasting or giving their orders to the stewards. To Frederick it seemed they were there for no other purpose than to spy upon his emotions.

The steamer had already been travelling for an hour on the ocean. The dining-room took up the full width of the vessel, and from time to time its port-holes were darkened by the waves dashing against them. Opposite Frederick sat a gentleman in uniform, who introduced himself as Doctor Wilhelm, the ship's physician. Straightway a very lively medical discussion began, though Frederick's thoughts were far away. He was debating with himself how he should act at his first meeting with the Hahlstroems.

He tried to find support in self-deception, telling himself he had boarded the **Roland**, not for the sake of little Ingigerd Hahlstroem, but because he wanted to see New York, Chicago, Washington, Boston, Yellowstone Park, and Niagara Falls. That is what he would tell the Hahlstroems--that a mere chance had brought them together on the **Roland**.

He observed that he was gaining in poise. Sometimes, when the adorer is at a distance from the object of his devotion, the idolatry of love assumes fateful proportions. During his stay in Paris, Frederick had lived in a state of constant fever, and his yearning for his idol had risen to an unendurable degree. About the image of little Ingigerd Hahlstroem, a heavenly aureole had laid itself, so compelling in its attraction that Frederick's mental vision was literally blinded to everything else. That illusion had suddenly vanished. He felt ashamed of himself. "I'm a ridiculous fool," he thought, and when he arose to go on deck, he felt as if he had shaken off oppressive fetters. The salt sea air blowing vigorously across the deck heightened his sense of emancipation and convalescence and refreshed him to his inner being.

Men and women lay stretched out on steamer chairs with that green expression of profound indifference which marks the dreaded seasickness. To Frederick's astonishment, he himself felt not the least trace of nausea, and only the sight of his fellow-passengers' misery caused him to realise that the **Roland** was not gliding through smooth waters, but was distinctly pitching and rolling.

He walked around the ladies' parlour, past the entrance of an extra cabin, and took his stand under the bridge, breasting the steely, salt sea wind. On the deck below, the steerage passengers had settled themselves as far as the bow. Though the **Roland** was running under full steam, it was not making its maximum speed, prevented by the long, heavy swells that the wind raised and hurled against the bow. Across the forward lower deck there was a second bridge, probably for emergency. Frederick felt strongly tempted to stand up there on that empty bridge.

It aroused some attention, of course, when he descended down among the steerage passengers and then crawled up the iron rungs of the ladder to the windy height. But that did not trouble him. All at once such a madcap spirit had come over him, he felt so happy and refreshed; as if he had never had to suffer dull cares, or put up with the whims of a hysterical wife, or practise medicine in a musty, out-of-the-way corner of the country. Never, it seemed to him, had he studied bacteriology, still less, suffered a fiasco. Never had he been so in love as he appeared to have been only a short time before.

He laughed, bending his head before the gale, filled his lungs with the salty air, and felt better and stronger.

A burst of laughter from the steerage passengers mounted to his ears. At the same instant something lashed him in the face, something that he had seen rearing, white and tremendous, before the bow. It almost blinded him, and he felt the wet penetrate to his skin. The first wave had swept overboard.

Who would not find it humiliating to have his sublime meditations interrupted in such a tricky, brutal way? A moment before, he felt as if to be a Viking were his real calling, and now, inwardly shaking and shivering, amid general ridicule, he crawled ignominiously down the iron ladder.

He was wearing a round grey hat. His overcoat was padded and lined with silk. His gloves were of dressed kid, his buttoned boots of thin leather. All these garments were now drenched with a cold, salty wash. Leaving a damp trail behind, he made his way, not exactly a glorious way, through the steerage passengers, who rolled with laughter. In the midst of his annoyance Frederick heard a voice calling his name. He looked up and scarcely trusted his eyes on seeing a large fellow in whom he thought he recognised a peasant from the Heuscheuer Mountains, a peasant with an evil reputation for drunkenness and all sorts of misdeeds.

"Wilke, is that you?"

"Yes, Doctor, I'm Wilke."

The little town in which Frederick had practised was called Plassenberg an der Heuscheuer, that is, Plassenberg by the Heuscheuer Mountains, a range in the county of Glatz where excellent sandstone is quarried. The people of the district loved Frederick both as a man and a physician. He was the wonder-worker who had performed a number of splendid cures and he was the human being, without pride of caste, whose heart beat warmly for the good of the lowliest of his fellow-men. They loved his natural way with them, always cordial, always outspoken, and sometimes harsh.

Wilke was bound for New England to join his brother.

"The people in the Heuscheuer," he said, "are mean and ungrateful."

Shy and distrustful at home, even toward Frederick, who had treated him for his last knife wound on his neck, his manner here, with the other passengers crossing the great waters, was frank and trustful. He was like a well-behaved child chattering freely.

"You didn't get the thanks you deserved, either, Doctor von Kammacher," he said in his broad dialect, rich in vowel sounds, and recounted a number of cases, of which Frederick had not known, in which good had been repaid by evil tattle. "The people around Plassenberg are not fit for men like you and me. Men like you and me belong in America, the land of liberty."

Elsewhere, Frederick would have resented being placed in the same category as this rowdy, for whom, he recalled, the police were searching. But here he felt no indignation. On the contrary, he was pleasantly surprised, as if by an unexpected meeting with a good friend.

"The world's a small place," said Frederick, passing over the theme of ingratitude and the land of liberty, "the world's a small place. Yet I am surprised to see you here. But I'm wet to the skin, and have to go change my clothes."

On his way to the cabin, on the promenade deck, he encountered the blond captain of the *Roland*, Von Kessel, who presented himself to Frederick.

"The weather is not quite up to mark," he said by way of excuse for the little mishap on the lower bridge. "If you enjoy standing in front there, you'd better put on one of our oilskins."

Now that the vessel's movement was more accentuated, the cabin, in which Frederick changed his clothes, was a problematical place of abode. The light came from a round port-hole of heavy glass. When the wall with the port-hole in it rose and turned inward like a slanting roof, the sunlight from a rift between the clouds in the sky fell upon the mahogany berth opposite. Sitting on the edge of the lower berth, Frederick tried to steady himself, holding his head bent to keep from striking against his upper berth, and frantically endeavouring not to follow the receding movement of the wall behind. The cabin was rolling in unison with the vessel's movement. Sometimes it seemed to Frederick as if the port-hole wall were the ceiling, and the ceiling the right wall; then again as if the right wall were the ceiling, and the ceiling the port-hole wall, while the actual port-hole wall, as if inviting him to jump, shoved itself at right angles under his feet--during which the port-hole was wholly under water and the cabin in darkness.

It is no easy matter to dress and undress in an oscillating room. That the vessel's motion could have changed so markedly within the one hour since he left the cabin, astonished Frederick. The simple operation of drawing off his boots and trousers, finding others in his trunk, and putting them on again became a gymnastic feat. He had to laugh, and comparisons occurred to him, which made him laugh still more. But his laughter was not heartfelt. Each time he received a knock, or had to jump to regain his balance, he muttered exclamations and instinctively contrasted all this with the comfortable waking up from sleep in his own house. Groaning and labouring, he said to himself:

"My whole personality is being shaken through and through. I was mistaken when I supposed that I had already got my shaking up these last two years. I thought fate was shaking me. Now, both my fate and I are being shaken. I thought there was tragedy in me. Now, I and my tragedy are bowling about in this creaking cage, and are being disgraced in our own eyes.

"I have a habit of pondering over everything. I think about the beak of the ship, which buries itself in each new wave. I think about the laughter of the steerage passengers, those poor, poor people, who, I am sure, scarcely have a gay time of it. My sousing was a treat to them. I think of the rapscallion, Wilke, who married a humpbacked seamstress, ran through her savings, and abused her daily--and I almost embraced him. I think of the blond Teuton, Captain von Kessel, that handsome man, somewhat too insipid-looking and too thick-set, who is our absolute lord and whom we trust at first glance. And, finally, I think about my constant laughing and admit to myself that laughing is a sensible thing only in the rarest circumstances."

Frederick continued a conversation with himself in a similar strain for a while, and cast bitter, ironical reflections upon the passion that had brought him on this trip. He had actually been robbed of his will; and in this condition, in that narrow cabin, surrounded by the ocean, it seemed to him as if his life, and his foolish impotence, were being held up to the rudest ridicule.

When Frederick went up again, there were still a number of persons on deck. The stewards had fastened the steamer chairs to the walls, some of them having slipped and left the occupants, ladies and gentlemen, with the blue marks of their fall. Refreshments were being served. It was interesting to see how the stewards, carrying six or eight full cups, balanced themselves over the heaving deck.

Frederick looked about in vain for Hahlstroem and his daughter.

In walking the full length of the deck several times, examining all the passengers with the utmost care and circumspection, he noticed the pretty young Englishwoman, whom he had seen for the first time in the reading-room of the hotel in Southampton. She was wrapped in rugs and furs and snugly settled in a spot shielded from the wind and warmed by the two huge smoke-stacks. She was receiving the attention of a very lively young man sitting beside her. Each time Frederick passed, the young man scrutinised him sharply. Suddenly he jumped up, held out his hand, and introduced himself as Hans Fuellenberg of Berlin. Though Freder-

ick could not recall ever having met him before, the good-looking, dashing young
fellow succeeded in convincing him that they had both been present at a certain
evening affair in Berlin. He told Frederick he was going to the United States to
take a position in a mining region near Pittsburgh, Pennsylvania. He was a wide-
awake young man and, what is more, a Berlinese, and had great notions of his own
importance. Frederick's reputation in Berlin society inspired him with tremendous
respect. Frederick responded to his advances courteously, and allowed him to recount all the latest Berlin news, as if he himself had not left the German capital only
a week before. He realised he could depend upon Fuellenberg's garrulousness for
every item of interest.

It quickly became evident that Hans Fuellenberg was an amiable, giddy-headed
young buck, knowing well how to deal with the ladies. When Frederick called his
attention to the fact that the Englishwoman was casting impatient glances toward
him, visibly eager for his return, he complacently winked his eye as if to say:

"She won't run away. And if she does, there are plenty more."

V

"Do you know, Doctor von Kammacher," Fuellenberg said suddenly, "that little
Hahlstroem is on board?"

"What little Hahlstroem do you mean?" asked Frederick coolly.

Hans Fuellenberg could not contain his surprise that Frederick should have
forgotten little Hahlstroem. He was sure of having seen him in the Kuenstlerhaus
in Berlin when Ingigerd danced her dance there for the first time, the dance that
then aroused admiration only in the artist world, but later became the sensation of
all Berlin. He described the affair.

"The pick of the Berlin artists were standing around the room and on the stairs
in informal groups, leaving the centre of the floor clear. Even Menzel and Begas
were there. A special exhibition was to open soon, and the walls were hung with
a collection of Boecklin pictures. The name of the dance was 'Mara, or the Spider's
Victim.'

"I tell you, Doctor von Kammacher," the young man went on, "if you didn't see that dance, you missed something. In the first place, little Ingigerd's costume was very scanty, and then her performance was really wonderful. There are no two opinions about it. A huge artificial flower was set in the middle of the room, and the little thing ran up and smelt of it. She felt all about the flower with closed eyes, vibrating as if with the gauzy wings of a bee. Suddenly she opened her eyes and turned to a rigid statue of stone. On the flower was squatting a huge spider! She darted like an arrow to the farthest corner of the room. Even in the first part of the dance she had seemed to float without weight in the air; but the way sheer horror blew her across that room made her seem like nothing but a vision."

Frederick von Kammacher had seen her dance the dreadful dance, not only at the matinee in the Kuenstlerhaus, but eighteen times again. While Fuellenberg was trying to express his impression with "great," "tremendous," "glorious," and similarly strong epithets, Frederick saw the whole dance over again with his mind's eye. He saw how the childlike body, after cowering and trembling a while in the corner of the room, approached the flower again to the accompaniment of music played by a tom-tom, a cymbal, and a flute. Something which was not pleasure drew her to it. The first time she had traced her way to the source of the perfume by sniffing fragrance in the air. Her mouth had been open, the nostrils of her fine little nose had quivered. Hans Fuellenberg was correct in his observation that her eyes, as she held her head back, had been closed. The second time, she seemed to be drawn against her will by a gruesome something, which alternately aroused fear, horror, and curiosity. She held her eyes wide open, and now and then covered them with both hands, as if in dread of seeing something hideous.

But when she came quite close to the flower, all fear suddenly seemed to drop away from her. She hopped for joy and laughed--she had been needlessly alarmed. How could a fat, immobile spider squatting on a flower be dangerous to a creature with wings? This part of her dance was so graceful, so full of droll, bubbling, child-like merriment, that the audience laughed tears of delight.

Now, however, a new phase of the dance began, introduced in a thoughtful strain. Having danced herself to satiety and intoxicated herself with the flower's perfume, Mara, with movements of agreeable fatigue, made as if to lay herself to rest, but delayed here and there to brush from her body something like the threads of a spider's web, at first serenely and pensively, then with growing disquiet, which communicated itself to the onlookers. The child paused, reflected an instant, and apparently was about to laugh at herself because of the fears that had arisen in her soul; but the next minute she paled with fright, and made a dexterous leap, as if to free herself from a trap. Her blond hair tossed back in Maenadic waves turned into a flaming stream. Her whole appearance evoked involuntary cries of admiration.

The flight began. And now the theme of the dance was Mara's entanglement in the threads the spider wove about her, which gradually choked her to death. No dancer has ever executed such an idea with equal skill and fidelity.

The little creature freed her foot from the meshes, only to find her neck entwined; she clutched at the threads about her throat, only to find her hands entangled; she tore at the cobweb, she bent her body, she slipped away; she beat with her fists, she raged, and only enmeshed herself the more tightly in the horrible skein; finally she lay fast bound. During this last phase of the dance, her artist audience stood there rigid, breathless, suffocating with a sense of horror.

It was not until nearly the end that Frederick von Kammacher felt that his fate was forever linked with this girl. The feeling grew stronger during the few moments that remained before the conclusion of the performance. The poison of infatuation came from the expression of her face. He noted precisely how it forced its way into him and how his whole being suddenly grew sick. When little Ingigerd Hahlstroem once more opened her eyes with a look of abysmal dismay, and fastened them in helpless inquiry upon the spider, calmly drinking her blood away, an inner voice seemed to command Frederick to become her compassionate knight, saviour, and protector.

VI

Since, in Fuellenberg's opinion, Frederick von Kammacher was not sufficiently interested in the dancer, Ingigerd Hahlstroem, he mentioned several other recent Berlin celebrities also on the *Roland* on their way to the United States. There was *Geheimrat* Lars, a man well-known in art circles, who often cast the deciding vote in purchases of works of art by the government. He was going to America to visit museums, private and public, and study the art situation in general. There was Professor Toussaint, an eminent sculptor, some of whose monuments had been erected in several German cities, chiefly Berlin, works done in a wishy-washy Bernini style.

"Toussaint," Fuellenberg, who seemed to be fairly loaded with Berlin gossip, explained, "needs money. He needs the money that his wife spends and the social season in Berlin swallows up. He and his wife and his wife's maid are all travelling free on his reputation. When he lands in New York, he won't have enough in his pocket even to pay his hotel bill for three days."

Fuellenberg pointed out the sculptor, Toussaint. He was lying in a steamer chair, rising and falling in unison with the **Roland**. As Frederick turned to look at him, he noticed an odd man without arms being led across the deck by his attendant, who grasped him by his collar and carefully dragged him through a small door close by into the smoking-room.

"That man's a vaudeville star," Fuellenberg continued with his descriptive catalogue. "He will appear in New York with Webster and Forster."

Some stewards came oscillating across the deck to serve the chilly passengers with bowls of hot bouillon. After Fuellenberg had seen to it that his lady was duly served, he deserted her and went with Frederick to the smoking-room. Here, of course, loud talking and tobacco smoke prevailed. The two gentlemen lit their cigars. In one corner of the small room, some men were playing skat, and at several tables, German and English politics were being thrashed out. The main theme of discussion was the rivalry between America and Europe. Wilhelm, the ship's doctor, with whom Frederick had become acquainted at breakfast, came in from his morning inspection of the steerage, and seated himself beside Frederick.

"There are two hundred Russian Jews emigrating to the United States or Canada," he told him, "thirty Polish families, and about the same number of German families from the south, north, and east of Germany. Altogether there are nearly four hundred steerage passengers, among them five babies at the breast and fifty children between the ages of one and fifteen."

Doctor Wilhelm invited Frederick to accompany him the next day on his tour of inspection. He was a man of not more than twenty-six. He had a fair complexion and wore glasses. His manner was somewhat stiff. Ever since he had passed his examinations, two years before, he had been a physician on a vessel. Once he had taken the trip to Japan, once to South America, and several times to the United States. Frederick, of course, immediately thought of his dying friend, George Rasmussen, put his hand in his pocket, and presented his new colleague with Simon Arzt cigarettes.

The cigarettes furnished a starting-point to tell all about George Rasmussen; and when Doctor Wilhelm had learned everything about him, except his name, and then learned his name, too, the world again turned out to be a very small place. Doctor Wilhelm was a friend of George Rasmussen's. They had studied together, one semester in Bonn and one semester in Jena, and had belonged to the same club in Jena. The last few years they had even corresponded. Naturally, the discovery instantly brought the two physicians closer.

The tone in the smoking-room was that of jolly carousals in German **Bierstuben**. The men let themselves go, talked in loud voices, and gave rein to that coarse humour and noisy gaiety in which time flies for them and which to many of them is a sort of narcotic, giving them rest and ease for a while from the mad chase of existence. Neither Frederick nor Doctor Wilhelm was averse to this tone, which revived old memories of their student days, when they had become accustomed to it. Though to the average student the carousals, now taboo, may be an evil, physically and intellectually, they are the time and place, nevertheless, at which the phoenix of German idealism soars up from tobacco smoke and beer froth to wing its flight to the sun.

Hans Fuellenberg soon felt bored in the company of the two physicians who, in fact, had completely forgotten him; and he slipped away, back to his lady.

"When Germans meet," he said to her, "they must scream and drink **Bruederschaft** until they get tipsy."

Doctor Wilhelm seemed to be proud of the smoking-room.

"The captain," he said, "is very strict about not having the gentlemen disturbed. He has given absolute orders that women under no circumstances, not even if they smoke, are to be permitted here."

The room had two metal doors, one on the starboard and one on the port side. The person entering or leaving had to contend violently with the wind and the motion of the vessel. The stewards had mastered the art perfectly. Shortly before eleven o'clock, Captain von Kessel appeared. It was his custom to visit the room at about this time every day. After giving friendly or curt answers, as the case might be, to the usual questions regarding the weather and the prospects for a good or bad crossing, he seated himself at the same table as the physicians.

"A seaman was lost in you," he said to Frederick.

"I think you must be mistaken," Frederick rejoined. "I have had quite enough of a salt water sousing. I assure you, I am not longing for another."

A few hours before, a pilot-boat from the French coast had brought the latest news, which the captain proceeded to recount in a calm, quiet manner.

"A vessel of the Hamburg-American line, a twin-screw steamer, the **Nordmania**, running for only a year, had a mishap about six hundred miles out from New York. It turned back and reached Hoboken safely. The sea was comparatively calm, but all of a sudden a waterspout arose close to the ship, and a great mass of water burst over the ladies' saloon, crushing through its roof and the roof of the deck below and hurling a piano down into the very hold."

The other piece of news he told was that Schweninger was in Friedrichsruh with Bismarck and that Bismarck's death was being expected hourly. Though both Doctor Wilhelm and Frederick von Kammacher disapproved of Bismarck's exceptional anti-Socialist law and its consequences, they were filled with hero worship of the man, Doctor Wilhelm the more so, since the home of his childhood stood on the edge of Sachsenwald, scarcely an hour's ride from Friedrichsruh. He was choke-full, of course, of local Bismarck anecdotes and began to reel them off.

"Are you annoyed?" Bismarck asked his barber, when he came in one day with his moustache twirled upward in the new fashion of the race tracks. "A moustache trimmed and twisted like that to me looks as if it were terribly annoyed and for no reason."

VII

The international gong had not been introduced on the **Roland**. The trumpeter of the band sent two blasts across the promenade deck and through the corridors of the first cabin as a signal for the midday meal. The first blast entered with the howling of the wind into the close, noisy, crowded smoking saloon. The attendant of the man without arms came to conduct his master across the deck again. Frederick watched the armless man with great interest. He seemed to be extraordinarily brisk and quick-witted. He spoke English, French and German with equal fluency, and to everybody's delight parried the impertinences of a saucy young American, whose disrespectfulness did not yield even before the sacred person of the captain; for which the dignified skipper sometimes rewarded him by staring over his head like a lion over a yapping terrier.

The table in the dining-room was in the form of a trident, with the closed end at the rear and the three prongs pointing to the prow. Opposite the centre prong was a false mantel with a mirror, where was posted the elegant figure in blue livery of Mr. Pfundner, the head-steward. He was a man of between forty and fifty. With his white, artificially curled hair, which gave the impression of being powdered, he resembled a major-domo of Louis XIV's time. As he stood there, head erect, looking over the swaying hall, he seemed to be the special squire of Captain von Kessel, who sat at the end of the middle prong, in the capacity both of host and most honoured guest. Next to the captain sat Doctor Wilhelm and the first mate. Frederick, having found favour in the captain's eyes, was assigned a place next to Doctor Wilhelm. The ship was no longer tossing so violently, and the dining-room, in consequence, was fairly well filled. The last ones to enter were the card players of the smoking-room, who came storming in. At the closed end of the trident, Frederick saw Mr. Hahlstroem, but without his daughter.

Many stewards very quickly and deftly served a vast quantity of dishes. Wine was also placed on the table. Within a short while the corks were popping from champagne bottles in the vicinity of the card players. In a gallery the band played without interruption. There were seven numbers on the printed music programme, which bore the name of the vessel, the date, and a picture of negroes in evening dress and high hats plucking at banjos.

VIII

Still the forward part of the vessel and, along with it, the dining-room with all its dishes, plates, and bottles, with its gentlemen guests and lady guests and the steward-waiters, with its fish and vegetables and meats and drinks and brass band, were lifted high on the mountain top of one wave and plunged deep in the trough of the next. The mighty working of the engines quivered through the ship. The dining-room walls had to cope with the onslaught of the opposing element.

The electric lights were turned on full. The grey of the cloudy winter day did not suffice to illuminate the room, especially since what brightness there was outside was every instant shut off by the water splashing against the port-holes.

Frederick enjoyed the daring of it--to be dining in festivity to the accompaniment of frivolous music in the illuminated bowels of this monster, this ***Roland***. From time to time the mighty ship seemed on the point of encountering invincible resistance. A combination of opposing forces would rise up against the stem, producing the effect of a solid body, a veritable mountainside. At such moments the noise of the talking would die down, and many pale faces would exchange glances and turn to the captain or to the prow of the vessel. But Captain von Kessel and his officers were absorbed in their meal and paid no attention to the phenomenon, which for moments at a time brought the ***Roland*** to a quivering standstill. They never looked up, but kept to their eating and talking, even when, as often happened, tremendous masses of water hurled themselves against the walls, threatening to crash through what seemed like pitifully thin partitions for excluding that mighty, wrathful element, thundering and roaring with suppressed hate and fury.

During the meal Frederick's eyes were constantly drawn to Hahlstroem's tall figure. Though his hair was touched with grey, he was certainly still to be counted a handsome man. Next to him sat a man of about thirty-five, with a bushy beard, dark, bushy eyebrows, and dark, deep-set eyes, which sometimes darted a sharp, piercing glance at Frederick--at least so it seemed to Frederick. The man troubled him. He noticed that Hahlstroem graciously permitted the stranger to entertain him and pay him court.

"Do you know that tall, fair-haired man, Doctor von Kammacher?" the physician asked. In his confusion Frederick failed to answer, looking helplessly at Doctor Wilhelm. "He is a Swede. His name is Hahlstroem," Doctor Wilhelm continued. "A peculiar fellow. Earlier in his life he made a mess of your and my profession. He is travelling with his daughter, not an uninteresting little miss. She's been dreadfully seasick, and hasn't left the horizontal in her berth since we set sail from Bremen. That dark fellow sitting next to Hahlstroem seems to be something like, well, let us say, her fiance."

"By the way, what do you do for seasickness?" Frederick asked hastily, to conceal his dismay and turn the conversation.

IX

"You here, Doctor von Kammacher? I can scarcely trust my eyes." At the bottom of the companionway Frederick felt Hahlstroem tackle him, just as he was about to mount to deck.

"Why, Mr. Hahlstroem, what a peculiar coincidence! It's as if the whole of Berlin had agreed to emigrate to America!" Frederick exclaimed, simulating surprise with somewhat forced liveliness.

"May I present Mr. Achleitner? Mr. Achleitner is an architect from Vienna."

The man with the piercing eyes smiled with an air of interest, holding fast to the brass balustrade to keep from being hurled against the wall.

The door of a rather gloomy saloon opened on the first landing. It bore the misleading sign "smoking-room," misleading because the smokers never used it, far preferring the cosey little saloon on deck. A brown upholstered bench ran around the brown, wainscoted walls. Kneeling on the bench one could look out through three or four port-holes upon the seething and boiling of the waves. The entire floor space between the benches was taken up by a table finished in a dark stain.

"This room is a horrid hole," said Hahlstroem. "It positively makes me creepy."

A loud, trumpet-like, laughing voice called out from inside the room:

"I say, Hahlstroem, if this sort of weather holds out, neither your daughter nor I will keep the first day of our engagement with Webster and Forster. We're not even making eight knots. Perhaps I'll be able to manage. A big dose of salt water doesn't hurt me. To-day is the twenty-fifth. If we reach Hoboken at eight o'clock the evening of the first of February, I can appear for my act in perfect serenity at nine o'clock; but that frail blossom of yours can't. She will certainly need a few days to recover from the hardships of this trip."

The three men entered the smoking-room. Frederick had already recognised the voice as belonging to the man without arms, who, he learned later, from Hahlstroem, was a world-renowned celebrity. For more than ten years the bill-boards of every great city in the world had been displaying simply his name, Arthur Stoss, which alone sufficed to draw throngs to the theatres. His special art consisted in doing with his feet whatever other people do with their hands.

The first sight of him, of course, was repellent; but in the smoking-room on deck Frederick had got over his first repulsion and had become interested in his personality. Yet the situation in which he now beheld him was so novel, so remarkable, almost to the point of improbability, that he had difficulty in concealing his amazement. Arthur Stoss was eating lunch. Since this room was so little used and since a man forced to handle his knife and fork with his feet could not be permitted to eat in the public dining-room, they served Arthur Stoss with his meals here. To the three onlookers it had the value of an artistic performance to see how the actor managed to manipulate his instruments with his clean, bare toes--and that despite the pitching of the vessel--meanwhile, in the best of humour, uttering the wittiest remarks as bite after bite disappeared down his throat. He began to banter Hahlstroem and Achleitner, sometimes in rather caustic fashion, while exchanging glances with Frederick, as if he thought vastly more of him than of the other two men, who soon withdrew from his attacks to go on deck.

"My name is Stoss."

"Mine, Von Kammacher."

"It's very good of you to keep me company. That Hahlstroem and his henchman are disgusting. Though I have been an actor for twenty years, I can't stand the sight of such weedy weaklings, who don't do anything themselves and exploit their daughters. They have the effect of an emetic on me. For all that, he plays the great man. He has no talent, so he is going to boil soup from his daughter's bones. Yet he goes about nose up in the air. If he sees a dollar in the dirt and somebody of distinction is looking, he will let it lie. He won't pick it up. There is no denying he has an attractive appearance. He has the stuff in him for a very clever, fashionable swindler. But he would rather take it easy and live off his daughter and his daughter's admirers. It's astonishing how many people are willing to make asses of themselves. There's that Achleitner--look at the condescension with which Hahlstroem treats him and the lofty way Hahlstroem plays the role of benefactor! He used to be a riding-master. Then he got mixed up in some quack cure, a combination of Swedish gymnastics and hydrotherapeutics, and his wife left him, a fine, hard-working woman, now doing splendidly as head of a department at Worth's in Paris."

Frederick felt drawn up-stairs to Hahlstroem. The man's past as Stoss described it was at that moment a matter of indifference to him. But Stoss's remark about the asses some people are willing to make of themselves sent a fleeting red to his face.

Arthur Stoss grew more and more communicative. He sat like an ape, a resemblance impossible to avoid when a man uses his feet instead of his hands. When he had finished his meal, he stuck a cigar in his mouth, like any other gentleman. In him the likeness to an ape was accentuated by the breadth and flatness of his nose and the formation of his heavy jaws. He looked like a fair-skinned orang-outang. However, his high, broad forehead gave him the mark of the human intellect. He had no beard, that is, he had never in his life, probably, had to remove a hair from his parchmenty, freckled, yellow skin. His cheek bones were prominent, and his head unusually large. Though his general appearance made a most energetic, by no means effeminate impression, there still was something eunuch-like about it, the high pitch of his voice adding to this impression. While casting about for an opportunity to escape the monster's spell, Frederick was nevertheless deeply interested in him from a medical and anthropological standpoint. The man, without doubt, was an extremely instructive specimen of abnormality. His facies was that of an intermediate sexual stage.

"People like Hahlstroem," he continued, "are actually not worthy of the healthy limbs with which God endowed them. Of course, even if one has a figure like a statue by Myron, it is awkward if there is too little up here"--he tapped his forehead.

"That is what is the trouble with Hahlstroem. There is too little up here. Look at me. I don't say everybody, but at least nine out of ten, in my position would have succumbed as a child. Instead of that, I have a wife, I own a villa in the Kahlenberg Mountains, I support three children of my step-brother and an older sister of my wife, who was a singer and lost her voice. I am absolutely independent. I remain on the stage because I want to bring my wealth up to a certain point. If the **Roland** were to sink to-day, I could go down with perfect equanimity. I have done my work. I have invested my money at a high rate of interest. My wife, my wife's sister, and my step-brother's children are all provided for."

The actor's attendant appeared, to help his master to his cabin for his afternoon nap.

"My days are mapped out like a time-table," Stoss explained. "My attendant here, Bulke, served his four years in the German navy. With all the ocean crossings I have to make, I couldn't get along with a man who wasn't used to the water. I need a perfect water rat."

X

A little spell of dizziness came over Frederick when he went to his cabin to fetch his heavy overcoat. On deck it was very quiet as compared with the morning. Hahlstroem was nowhere to be seen, and Frederick seated himself on a bench near the entrance to the main companionway. With his collar turned up and his hat drawn over his forehead, he succumbed to the state of drowsiness characteristic of sea trips, in which, despite the heaviness of one's eyelids, one feels and perceives with a restless lucidity of the inner vision. Images chase through one's mind, a kaleidoscopic stream, shifting incessantly, going and coming, and finally reducing the soul to a state of torture. The sybaritic meal with its clatter of plates, its talking and music, was still whirling through Frederick's brain. He heard the vaudeville actor declaiming. The half-ape was holding Mara in his arms. Hahlstroem in all his height was looking on, smiling. The waves were rolling heavily against the tiny dining-room and pressing hard on the creaking hull. Bismarck, a huge figure in armour, and Roland, the valiant warrior in armour, were laughing grimly and conversing. Frederick saw both wading through the sea. Roland was holding Mara, the tiny dancer, on his right palm. Every now and then Frederick shivered. The ship careened, a stiff southeaster heeling her to starboard. The waves hissed and foamed. The rhythm produced by the rise and fall of the pistons finally seemed to turn into the rhythm of Frederick's own body. The working of the screw was distinctly audible. At regular intervals the stern would rise out of the water, carrying with it the screw, which would then buzz in the air, and Frederick would hear Wilke from the Heuscheuer saying:

"Doctor, if only the screw doesn't snap."

Finally, all the machinery of the vessel seemed to be turning in his brain. Sometimes one engineer in the engine-room would call out to another, and the clang of the metal shovels when the stokers fed the furnace penetrated to the deck.

All of a sudden Frederick jumped to his feet; he thought he saw a ghost, or a dead-alive corpse, reeling up the companionway and making for him. It was the clothing manufacturer whom he had met at Southampton, looking more like a man in his death throes than one already dead. He gave Frederick a ghastly glance of unconsciousness and let a steward support him to the nearest steamer chair.

"If that man," Frederick thought, "is not to be reckoned among the heroes, then there never have been any heroes in the world."

"Each time I cross," the clothing manufacturer had said, "I suffer from seasickness, from the moment I set foot on the ship until I leave it."

And what horrible extremes of suffering he had to go through!

Opposite Frederick, at the entrance to the companionway, stood a cabin-boy. From time to time at the signal of a whistle from the bridge, he would disappear to receive orders from the first or second mate, or whatever officer happened to be on duty. Often an hour and more would pass without the summons, and the handsome lad had plenty of time to meditate upon himself and his lot in life. Frederick felt sorry for him as he stood there on guard, bored and chilly; so he spoke to him.

He learned that his name was Max Pander and that he came from near the Black Forest. The next logical question to put to him was whether he liked his work. The boy answered with a resigned smile, which heightened the charm of his handsome head, but showed he had none too much passion for the seaman's calling.

"There is not much in travelling on steamers," he observed. "A real sailor belongs on board a sailing vessel. There is a mate of mine here on the **Roland**," he added in a tone of great admiration, "who is only eighteen years old and has already been on two long, dangerous trips on a schooner."

To Frederick, it seemed as if lasting passion for the sea--the sea, which was already making him miserable--must be a conventional myth. It was three o'clock. He had been on board only nineteen or twenty hours, and already found it a petty hardship. "If the **Roland** doesn't make better time," he calculated, "I shall have to go through the same difficulties of existence eight or nine times twenty-four hours. But I will get back to land and remain there, while Pander, the cabin-boy, will have to return across the ocean a few days after landing."

"If someone were to find you a good position on land," Frederick asked, "would you give up your position here?"

"Yes, indeed," said Pander, emphasising his reply with a decided nod of his head.

"A nasty southeaster," said Doctor Wilhelm, passing by beside the tall figure of the first mate. "How would you like to come to my room? We can smoke and have some coffee there without being disturbed."

XI

Walking along the deck below the promenade deck, one passed a covered gangway on both the starboard and port sides, into which opened various official rooms, including the officers' cabins, among them Doctor Wilhelm's, a comparatively spacious room, containing a bed, a table, chairs, and a well-equipped medicine closet.

The gentlemen had scarcely seated themselves when a Red Cross sister, who worked under Doctor Wilhelm's direction, appeared and gave a report, smiling as she did so, of a woman patient in the second cabin.

"In my two years of practice on a steamer, this is the fifth time I have had a case like this," Doctor Wilhelm said after the sister had left. "Girls who can no longer conceal the consequences of their mistake and are at loss what to do, take passage on a ship, when it is almost certain that the event they expect will occur. Such girls, of course, never suspect that they are typical on all sea trips, and are surprised when our stewards and stewardesses sometimes treat them with corresponding respect. I myself, of course, always do all I can for the poor creatures, and I usually succeed in inducing the captains not to make an announcement of the birth, in case there is one. Once a girl about whom we could not help giving notice was found hanging to the window sash in her lodgings near the harbour."

Over their coffee and Simon Arzt cigarettes, the whole woman question was unrolled.

"So far," said Frederick, "the woman question is nothing but the old-maid question, at least in the way women conceive it. The sterility of old maids sterilizes the whole movement."

Frederick developed his ideas. But tormenting visions of Mara and her admirer pursued him, and he discoursed mechanically, his reasoning on the woman question having become a matter of rote to him.

"The vital germinal spot of each reform in women's rights," he argued with apparent liveliness, blowing clouds of smoke, "must be the maternal instinct. The cells of the future cell-state, which will be a healthier social body, is the woman with the maternal instinct. The great women reformers are not those who would have women act just like men in all externals, but those who are conscious that all men, even the greatest, were born of women. They are the conscious mothers of the race of men and gods. A woman's natural right is her right to the child, and it is a most inglorious page in the history of woman that she has allowed herself to be deprived of that right. The birth of the child, in so far as it is not sanctioned by a man, is subject to the fire and brimstone of public scorn. And this scorn is the most pitiful page in man's history. The devil knows how it ever came to possess such awful, absolute dominion. Form a league of mothers, I should counsel women. Each member shall give token of her motherhood by having children without the sanction of a man, that is, without regard for so-called honour. In this lies woman's strength, but only if she takes pride in her child, instead of bearing it with a troubled conscience, in cowardice, concealment, and fear. Reacquire your proud, instinctive consciousness, which you are fully justified in having, of being the mothers of humanity; and having that consciousness, you will be invincible."

Doctor Wilhelm, who kept in touch with professional circles, was acquainted with Frederick's name and the outcome of his scientific career. His unfortunate bacteriological work was on his book shelf. Nevertheless, the name of Frederick von Kammacher had an authoritative ring, and association with the great man flattered him. He listened to Frederick's exposition intently.

The Red Cross sister entered again to summon Doctor Wilhelm to a first-class woman patient. The physician's small, close hermitage, in which Frederick was now left alone, gave him opportunity to reflect upon the meaning of his remarkable journey. The **Roland** was proceeding more smoothly, and while he sat there smoking cigarettes, a sense of comfort came over him, partly attributable, however, to the general effect of a sea trip on one's nerves. It seemed wonderful to him to be on this great transport of human cargo, to be driven onward to a new continent along with so many fellow-men, subject to the same weal and woe. And the cause of his presence on the ship was so curious! Never before had he had so strange a sense of being a will-less puppet in the hands of destiny. Again dark and light illusions mingled in his brain. He thought of Ingigerd, whom he had not yet seen; and when he touched the quivering wall of the low room, he was penetrated by happiness, that the same walls were protecting him as the little dancer and that the same bottom was holding them up.

"It's not true. It's a lie," he repeated half aloud, referring to the statement of the armless man, that Hahlstroem was exposing his daughter to dishonour and was exploiting her.

Doctor Wilhelm's return aroused Frederick from his dreams with a painful shock. Doctor Wilhelm laughed and continued to laugh, as he threw his cap on the bed and said:

"I've just dragged our little Hahlstroem and her pet dog on deck. The little imp has been giving a regular performance, in which her faithful poodle, Achleitner, plays the part, one moment of the beaten cur, the next moment of the spoiled darling."

Doctor Wilhelm's report made Frederick uneasy. The first time he had seen Mara, she seemed to him the incarnation of childish purity and innocence. But since then, rumours had reached his ears which shook his faith in her chastity and caused him many agonised hours and sleepless nights. He had even had an excellent opinion of her father, and that, too, was shaken.

Doctor Wilhelm, who also seemed to be extremely interested in Ingigerd, began to speak of Achleitner.

"He told me in confidence, he's engaged to her."

Frederick remained silent. That was his only way of concealing his profound dismay, now that the ship's doctor confirmed the supposition he had expressed at the dinner-table.

"Achleitner is a faithful dog," Doctor Wilhelm continued. "He is one of those men who have a canine sort of patience. He sits up on his hind legs and begs for a lump of sugar. He fetches and carries and lies down and plays dead. She could do whatever she wanted, and he would still, I think, be her patient, faithful poodle. If you'd like to, Doctor von Kammacher, we might go on deck and visit her. She's lots of fun. Besides we can watch the sun set."

XII

Little Mara lay stretched out in a steamer chair. Achleitner was most uncomfortably perched on a small camp-stool directly in front of her, so that he could look straight into her face. He had wrapped her up to her shoulders in rugs. The setting sun, casting its rays across the mighty heavings of the sea, glorified a lovely face. The ship was no longer tossing so violently, and the deck was lively with people sitting in chairs or promenading up and down. Some of the passengers had got over their seasickness, and there was a general air of revived animation and talkativeness.

Mara's appearance was somewhat conspicuous. She wore her very long, light hair flowing, and was playing with a small doll, a fact of which every passerby turned about to assure himself.

When Frederick saw this girl, who for weeks had been hovering in his soul, in his dreams, in his waking hours, who, as it were, had covered the rest of the world from his sight, or, at least, had cast a veil over it, his excitement was so intense and his heart beat so violently against his ribs that he had to turn away to keep his countenance. Even after the lapse of several seconds, it was difficult for him to believe that the enthralled, enslaved condition of his being was not noticeable to the people about him. But his excitement was by no means due solely to the fear of self-betrayal. It sprang from his passion, which, he suddenly realised, dominated him with undiminished strength.

"Papa told me you were here," the little miss said to him, adjusting the blue silk cap on her doll's head. "Won't you sit down with us? Mr. Achleitner, please go and get a chair for Doctor von Kammacher." She turned to Doctor Wilhelm. "Your treatment was summary, but I am grateful to you. I feel very well sitting here, watching the sun set. You're fond of nature, aren't you, Doctor von Kammacher?"

"Nur fuer Natur hegte sie Sympathie," trolled Doctor Wilhelm, swaying on tip-toe.

"Oh, you are impudent," Ingigerd reproved him. "Doctor Wilhelm *is* impudent, you know," she added to Frederick. "I saw he was the very instant he looked at me and the way he took hold of me."

"But, my dear young lady, so far as I know, I never took hold of you."

"If you please, you did--going up the stairs. I have blue marks as the result."

The chatter ran on for a while in a similar strain. Frederick, without betraying it, was on the alert for every word she uttered, noted every play of feature, watched for her glances, for the rise and fall of her lashes. He jealously studied the others, too, and caught every expression, every movement, every glance that was meant for her. He even noticed how Max Pander, the handsome cabin-boy, still standing at his post, held his eyes fixed upon her, a broad smile on his lips.

Ingigerd's pleasure in receiving the homage of three men and being the centre of general interest was evident. She plucked at her little doll and her odd, checked jacket, and gave herself up to coquettish whimsies. Her affected voice filled Frederick with the delight of a long, cool drink to a thirsty man. At the same time, his whole being was inflamed with jealousy. The first mate, Von Halm, a magnificent young man of twenty-eight, a perfect tower of a man, joined the group and was favoured by Ingigerd with looks and pointed remarks, which indicated to her admirers that this weather-tanned officer was not an object of indifference to her.

"How many miles, Lieutenant, since we left the Needles?" asked Achleitner, who was pale and evidently chilly.

"We're making better time now," Von Halm replied; "but for the last twenty-two or twenty-three hours, we haven't made more than two hundred miles."

"At that rate it will take two weeks to reach New York," cried Hans Fuellenberg, somewhat too forwardly, from where he was sitting a little distance away.

He was still flirting with the English lady from Southampton; but now, irresistibly drawn to Mara's sphere, he jumped up and left her, bringing the tone that was agreeable to Mara and all her admirers, except Frederick von Kammacher. The jolliness of the little group communicated itself to the rest of the promenade deck.

Disgusted with the orgy of banality, Frederick moved off to be alone with his thoughts. The deck, which in the middle of the day had been dripping with water, was now quite dry. He walked to the stern and looked out over the broad, foaming wake. He heaved a deep breath of joy at the thought that he was no longer in the narrow spell of the little female demon. Suddenly the long tension of his soul relaxed. Though he might have suffered a profound disenchantment, yet he felt as if he had taken a sobering bath, which left him a free agent, alone with his own soul. He felt ashamed of his instability. His passion for that little person seemed ridiculous, and he covertly beat his breast and rapped his forehead with his knuckles as if to awaken himself from a dream.

But, finally, the great cosmic moment of the slowly setting sun cast its spell over the young German adventurer.

A fresh wind was still blowing from the southeast, slanting the vessel slightly to the side where the sun hung over the horizon, turning the heavens in the west into a great, dusky conflagration. That sun, beneath which a slate-coloured sea was rolling in waves gently tossing foam--that sea, slate-coloured in the east and a cold, darkening blue in the west and south--that sky above, with great masses of clouds--these were to Frederick like the three mighty motives of a world symphony.

"Any one who is susceptible to them," he thought, "has no real cause to feel small, for all their awful majesty."

He was standing near the log, the long line of which was trailing in the ocean. The great ship was quivering under his feet. From the two smoke-stacks the wind was pressing the smoke down over the waves, and a melancholy procession of figures, widows in long crepe veils, wringing their hands in mute grief, drifted away backward, as if into the twilight gloom of eternal damnation. He heard the talking of the passengers, and represented to himself all that was united within the walls of that immense house, hurrying forward restlessly--how much hunting, fleeing, hoping, fearing. And in his soul, responding to the universal miracle, arose the great unanswered questions that seek to penetrate to the dark meaning of existence:

"Why?" "What for?"

XIII

He began to pace the deck again without noticing that he drew near Ingigerd Hahlstroem.

"You are wanted," a voice behind him suddenly announced. Seeing how he started, Doctor Wilhelm excused himself.

"You were dreaming; you are a dreamer," Mara called. "Come over here. I don't like these stupid men."

The six or eight gentlemen in attendance, with the exception of Achleitner, laughed and withdrew with a humorous show of great obedience.

"Why do you stay here, Achleitner?" Thus the faithful canine received his dismissal.

Frederick saw how the men withdrew together in groups at a little distance, whispering as they usually do when having sport with a pretty woman who is not exactly a prude; and it was with some shame, at any rate, with expressed repugnance that he took the stool still warm from Achleitner's body. Mara began to rhapsodise about nature.

"Isn't everything prettiest when the sun goes down? I think it's fun--at least I like it," she quickly substituted, when Frederick made a wry face at the remark. She spoke in sentences that all began with "I don't like," or "I despise," or "I do detest." In the face of that vast cosmic drama unfolding itself before her senses, she sat wholly unmoved and unsympathetic, displaying the overweening arrogance of a spoiled child. Frederick wanted to jump up, but remained where he was, pulling nervously at the end of his moustache, while his face assumed a stiff, mocking expression. Mara noticed it, and was visibly upset by this unusual form of homage.

Frederick had one of those idealistic heads set on broad shoulders characteristic of certain circles in the "nation of poets and philosophers." His ancestors had been scholars, statesmen, and soldiers. The general, his father, was in externals wholly the soldier; but beneath his uniform, his heritage from his own father, a renowned botanist, director of the botanical gardens at Genoa, actively manifested itself in a strong interest in science. Frederick's mother was a well-read woman, passionately fond of the theatre and an enthusiastic lover of Goethe and the poets of the romantic school. Her father, who had been prime minister of Wittenberg, as a student and even later in his career, composed poetry, which her adoring love for him had caused her to publish and several times revise and reprint.

Though Frederick had never been ill, there were times when he showed symptoms of a peculiar passionateness. His friends knew that when all went well, he was a dormant volcano; that when things did not go so well, he was a volcano spitting fire and smoke. To all appearances equally removed from effeminateness and brutality, he was subject, nevertheless, to accesses of both. Now and then a dithyrambic rapture came over him, especially when there was wine in his blood. He would pace about, and if it was daytime, might address a pathetic, sonorous invocation to the sun, or at night, to the constellations, particularly to the chaste Cassiopeia.

Since she had known him, Mara felt that his proximity was by no means lacking in danger; but being what she was, it piqued her to play with fire.

"I don't like people that think themselves better than others," she said.

"Being a Pharisee, I do," Frederick drily rejoined, and went on cruelly: "I think for your years you are extremely forward and cock-sure. Your dance pleases me better than your conversation." He felt much like a man berating his sister.

Mara silently studied him for a moment, a suggestive smile on her lips.

"According to your notions," she finally said, "a girl mustn't speak unless she's spoken to, and she mustn't have any opinions of her own. You look as if the only sort of girl you could love would be one that was always saying, 'I am a poor, ignorant thing. I don't understand what he sees in me.' I hate such nincompoops!"

Conversation came to a halt. Frederick half rose to leave, but she restrained him with a self-willed, pouting, "No." There was something childlike and honest in that pouting "no" which touched his soul and drew him down on the stool again.

"In Berlin, while I danced, I always had to look at you," she continued, holding her doll against her lips so that her little nose was a bit flattened. "The very first time I saw you, I felt something like a bond between us; I knew we should meet again."

Frederick started, though not for an instant deceived, knowing this must be an oft-used formula for establishing a relationship, and in essence a lie.

"Are you married?" he heard before he had fully recovered his balance. He turned pale. His answer was hard and repellent.

"It would be well, Miss Hahlstroem, if you were to examine me more closely before you treat me as one among many. So far, I don't believe in the bond that unites us. During your dance you looked not only at me, but at everybody else." He spoke with increasing coldness. "At any rate, it doesn't in the least concern you whether I am, or am not, married--just as little as it concerns me what repulsive personages, whom nothing but a depraved instinct can enjoy, you keep company with." He meant Achleitner.

Ingigerd gave a short laugh. "Do you take me for Joan of Arc?"

"Not exactly that," rejoined Frederick, "but if you would allow me, I should like to regard you as still a girl, a distinguished little lady, whose reputation cannot be too carefully guarded against the faintest blemish."

"Reputation!" sneered the girl. "You are very much mistaken if you think I ever cared for anything of the sort. I'd rather be disreputable ten times over and live as I please, than have a good reputation and die of boredom. I must enjoy my life, Doctor von Kammacher."

Frederick's teeth clenched. Outwardly composed, he was suffering the pangs of torture.

Ingigerd proceeded to reveal her life in a series of confidences of such shocking content as to be worthy of a Lais or a Phryne. Doctor von Kammacher, she said, might be sorry for her if he wanted to, but nobody was to make a mistake about her. Everybody associating with her was to know exactly who she was. In this she betrayed a certain dread, as one who would absolutely guard others as well as herself against the catastrophe of disillusionment.

When the sun had set, and Ingigerd, still with that suggestive, sensual, evil smile on her lips, had finished her hideous confession, Frederick found himself confronting the knowledge of a childhood so outrageous as to be worse than anything he had met with in all his experience as a physician.

Several times in the course of her narrative, Achleitner and her father had come to take her inside, but she had angrily driven them away. It was Frederick who finally helped her back to her cabin.

In his own cabin, without even removing his overcoat, he threw himself on his berth to think over the inconceivable story. He sighed, he gnashed his teeth, he wanted to doubt it. Several times he said aloud, "No!" or "Impossible!" and beat his fists against the mattress of the berth above. He could have sworn an oath that this time there had not been a single lie in Mara's whole shameless narrative. "Mara, or the Spider's Victim." Now, of a sudden, he understood her dance! She had danced the thing she had lived in her own life!

XIV

"I have set my all on nothing."

To the accompaniment of this refrain beating in his soul Frederick maintained an outer show of hilarity. He and the ship's doctor were drinking champagne. He had ordered the first bottle with the soup and had immediately drunk several glasses.

The more he drank the less he felt the smart of a certain burning wound, and the more wonderful the world appeared, full of miracles and riddles, surrounding and penetrating him with the intoxication of an adventurer's life. He was a brilliant entertainer, with an easy, happy way in conversation of popularising his rich store of knowledge, and with a light humour, which stood at his command even when, as now, grim humour crawled in the depths of his being, like evil reptiles. Thus it was that the captain's corner that evening fell under his spell, both of his jocular self and serious self.

Though he had lost his belief that science and modern progress alone possess the power to convey happiness, he extolled their virtues. As a matter of fact, in the festive gleam of the countless electric lights, excited by the wine, the music, and the rhythmic pulse beat of the moving vessel, it seemed to him at times as if humanity in a festal procession with music playing were sailing to the Isles of the Blessed. Perhaps, he said, science may some day teach man the secret of immortality. Ways and means would be found to keep the cells of the body young. Dead animals had been brought back to life by pumping a salt solution into them. He spoke of the wonders of surgery, always the theme of conversation when a man of the present, over his champagne and pate de foie gras, triumphs in the superiority of his age over all other ages. In a short while, he declared, chemistry would solve the social question, and man would forget what it is to worry about food. Why, chemistry was on the verge of discovering how to make bread of stones, a thing that hitherto only plants could do. Frederick continued in a similar strain, speaking by rote, and scarcely looking up, yet fascinating his listeners.

But in the midst of the whirl of self-intoxication, he thought with a shudder of bedtime, knowing he should not close his eyes the whole night. And what recompense was the brightest height of the clearest day for the hell of a single sleepless night, such as he had often spent within the last years.

After dinner, he went with Doctor Wilhelm to the ladies' parlour, from there to the smoking-room. Soon after, he went on deck, where it was dark and gloomy and the wind was again whining dismally through the rigging of the four masts. It was bitter cold, and snowflakes, it seemed to him, swept his cheeks. Finally, there was nothing for him to do but go to bed.

For two hours, between eleven and one, he lay writhing in his berth, sometimes for a short while falling into a troubled state between waking and sleeping. In both states he saw visions, now a wild dance of faces, now a single stark face, which tormented him and would not budge. Yet an irresistible impulse gathered in him to keep his mental eye open for the devilish play of supernatural powers.

He had turned out the electric lights, and in the dark, when the eye is unoccupied, one is doubly sensitive to the messages of hearing and feeling. He caught every sound, felt every movement, of the mighty ship, steadily pursuing its course through the midnight. He heard the churning of the propeller, like the labouring of a great demon condemned to slave for mankind. He heard shouts and calls and the walking of men when the coal-passers threw overboard the cinders from the huge boiler furnaces. On the trip to New York those furnaces consumed over a thousand tons of coal, and the casting away of the slag and ashes was left for the nighttime. Thus, to the relief of the man wrestling with sleep, his attention was drawn to the present and the things taking place in the ship's body.

Yet, when there was no sound or movement to distract him, his imagination succumbed to torturing thoughts of Mara and sometimes of his wife, with whose sufferings he occasionally used to reproach himself. Now that Ingigerd Hahlstroem had dishonoured his love for her, his conscience smote him all the more. His whole mentality seemed to have entered a state of reaction against the poison of his passion. A high fever raged in his veins. The thing that in this condition represented his "I" was engaged in a wild chase after the "you" of Mara. He picked her up in the streets of Prague and dragged her back to her mother. He discovered her in houses of ill repute. He saw her standing before the home of a man who had taken her with him out of pity and then had turned her away in scorn, and she stood for hours weeping outside his window. Frederick had by no means fully sloughed the skin of the conventional German youth. The old hackneyed ideal of virginity was in his eyes still surrounded by a sacred aureole; but no matter how often he discovered Mara in evil things, no matter how often he rejected her in his imagination, or tried with all the moral strength of his being to destroy her image in his mind, her face in its golden setting, her frail, white girlish body pierced through each curtain, each wall, each thought with which he strove to conceal the evil spirit that would not be exorcised either by prayers or curses.

Shortly after one o'clock, Frederick was tossed out of his berth. This time it was not one of those dream-like visions that had roused him with a start from a doze. The next instant he was thrown against the frame of the berth. It was evident that the weather had grown worse and the ***Roland*** was travelling in heavier waters of the Atlantic.

XV

A few minutes after five o'clock Frederick was already on deck. He seated himself on the same bench as yesterday, opposite the companionway leading down to the dining-room. His steward, a sympathetic, indefatigable young man from the province of Magdeburg, brought him tea and toast. It was a boon to Frederick.

Every few minutes the water dashed over the railing and washed the deck. From the penthouse over the door of the companionway, streams would suddenly come raining down, completely drenching Max Pander's little mate, who was now standing on guard. The masts and rigging were decorated with icicles, and rain and snow were falling alternately. It seemed as if the dreary grey dawn, with its uproar, with the whining, whistling, and howling of the furious wind in the masts and rigging, with the swishing and seething of the waters, wanted to prolong its existence infinitely, while the day refused to enter.

Warming his hands on his big tea-cup, he looked out over the ship's side, which every now and then seemed to sink perpendicularly. His eyes glowed. He felt as if they had sunk deep into their sockets. After the hardships of the last few days, especially the past night, it was natural that he should feel bruised, bodily and spiritually. He had a sense of vacancy and dull-mindedness, a welcome feeling, to be sure, compared with his sensations of the night, when the procession of images passed through his brain. Nevertheless, the strong, moist, tonic wind, the taste of salt on his lips refreshed him. He shivered a little, and sat with his head sunk in the upturned collar of his overcoat. Presently he began to feel pleasantly drowsy.

But he did not fail to perceive the full majesty in the turmoil of the waves and the struggle of the floating palace. There was beauty and strength in the steamer's fixed course, in the way it clove the rolling crests of the bottle-green waves, steady, tranquil, fearless. He admired the **Roland**, praised it, and was grateful to it as to a living being.

Next after him to appear on deck were three children, two girls and a boy, of from five to eleven. One of the helpful stewards fastened their chairs and most solicitously guided them to their seats, one at a time. Children are spoiled on steamers. There they sat, rocked to and fro, fearlessly looking out upon the solemn, awful rolling of the long waves, upon the horror of the tempest.

Shortly after seven o'clock, a slim man wearing the ship's uniform slowly approached Frederick. Frederick had noticed him the day before and been interested by his air of cool impassibility. He was smoking a cigarette and inhaling, as when Frederick had first seen him. Wearing an expression of profound apathy, he seemed to be completely absorbed in this occupation of smoking and inhaling. As if casually, he drew near Frederick's bench, touched his cap, and said:

"Doctor von Kammacher?"

"Yes."

"Here is a letter for you," he said, drawing it from his waistcoat pocket. "It came by the French pilot-boat yesterday. The reason I did not deliver it is, that I could not find your name on the passenger list. My name is Rinck. I am in charge of the mail on board."

Frederick thanked him. He was moved to see his father's handwriting. Rather for the sake of being friendly than from genuine interest at that moment, he asked Mr. Rinck what prospect there was of better weather. The sole answer was an unintelligible English word, a shrug of the shoulders, and a puff of cigarette smoke blown with gusto.

Frederick put the letter in his breast pocket, and he felt his heart beneath beat more warmly, less turbulently. He had to close his eyes to prevent a hot gush of tears. Doctor Wilhelm found him in this soft mood, and it occurred to him that perhaps after all Frederick had been tragically affected by the bitter close of his professional career.

"I slept like a bear," he said. And it was evident from the healthy colour of his face and his comfortable way of stretching and yawning that his night's sleep had thoroughly refreshed him. "But the weather is fiendish," he added, seating himself close beside Frederick.

"Congratulate you," said Frederick. "I didn't sleep a wink."

"Take some veronal. But whatever you do, come down now to breakfast with me. The best thing for you is to keep moving. So I advise you, after breakfast to come with me on my visit to the steerage. It will take your mind off things and may interest you. There are interesting types there, women, too. But before we go, we must make ourselves insect-proof. We'll puff powder on our clothes in my room."

XVI

The gentlemen had breakfasted--baked potatoes and cutlets, ham and eggs, broiled flounder and other fish, beside tea and coffee--and were entering the steerage.

Here, to keep from falling, they had to hold fast to the iron posts supporting the ceiling. After their eyes had grown accustomed to the twilight always reigning in the steerage, they saw a swarm of human beings rolling on the floor, groaning, whimpering, wailing, shrieking. The weather did not permit of the opening of the port-holes, and the exhalations of about twenty Russian-Jewish families, with bag and baggage and babies, polluted the air to such an extent, that Frederick could scarcely breathe. Mothers lying on their backs with open mouths and closed eyes, more dead than alive, had infants at their breasts; and it was fearful to see how the retching convulsed them.

"Come," said Doctor Wilhelm, observing something like a tendency to faint in Frederick's face. "Come, let us show how superfluous we are."

But Doctor Wilhelm and the Red Cross nurse, who accompanied him, had a chance, here and there, to do some good. He ordered grapes and a tonic for those who were suffering most. These things were obtained from the store-rooms of the first and second cabin.

With great difficulty they made their way from section to section. Everywhere the same misery, the same flight from want and infuriated persecution. Even the pale faces of those who were able to keep on their feet and had found a place to stand in that swaying shelf of misery, were marked by a hopeless, brooding expression of anguish and bitterness.

Among the hundreds of immigrants, there were some pretty girlish faces. To a few the fever produced by the unusual circumstances had imparted a bold, passionate charm. The glances of the physicians and these girls met. Such circumstances overstimulate the feelings and make them highly susceptible. Great stress, great danger cause the life of the moment to flare up more alluringly and also create a sense of profound equality among human beings. In the very midst of fear and tension, a boldness develops ready at any moment to make a leap.

Doctor Wilhelm pointed out to Frederick a Russian-Jewish girl of about seventeen. The expression of her face was sombre. Her features were most delicately chiselled, and she was as transparent as an image of wax. Doctor Wilhelm, observing the defiant air with which she glowered at Frederick, remarked that he must have conquered at first sight.

On passing farther, Frederick heard a voice bawl his name. It was Wilke, but a very different Wilke from the one he had met on deck the morning before. He was cursing and scolding at everybody and everything, while trying to raise himself from his mattress; a feat rather difficult for him to accomplish, because, in the first place, the rolling of the vessel in the steerage was fearful, and in the second place, he had evidently been trying to counteract the wretchedness of his condition by the imbibing of whisky. Doctor Wilhelm gave him a sharp berating. Wilke, very clearly, was a nuisance, perhaps even a danger, to everybody about him. In his intoxication he fancied he was being pursued. The rags from his open bundle lay spread on his mattress mixed with cheese and bread-crumbs, and in his right hand he held open a large pocket-knife.

Doctor Wilhelm had not been aware that he was dealing with a particular acquaintance of Frederick's. His admonitions were of no effect. Wilke shouted that his neighbours had robbed him, and so had the stewards, and the sailors and the captain. Frederick took his knife away from him, spoke to him in a military tone, and unceremoniously touched a scar on the rough fellow's hairy neck to recall to him the fact that he had already sewed one knife wound, from which he had barely escaped with his life. That worked, and Wilke seemed to be repentant. Frederick gave him some money, but not for whisky, as he told him, and added he would try his best for him, but only if he heard that he had been behaving like a decent human being.

XVII

The physicians ascended on deck again. On breathing in the ocean's pure breath after the foul odours of the steerage, Frederick felt as if he had escaped from a hideous, suffocating hell.

With difficulty they made their way across the wet, empty deck, ever and again washed by waves sweeping overboard. To keep their footing they had to cling to the railing. Not a soul was on deck. The ship, restlessly rolling and pounding, seemed to have been left to fight its fight alone. But this was an awful scene that relieved and refreshed Frederick.

He went to the ladies' parlour, there to read the letter from home, which he had nearly forgotten. A few women, who were not seasick, were scattered through the room, lolling in their chairs in a state of limp exhaustion. The saloon smelled of plush and varnish. It was decorated with a number of mirrors in gold frames, there was a grand piano, and the sound of footsteps was muffled by the soft carpet covering the floor. The prevailing colour was blue.

Frederick made himself comfortable in one of the blue arm-chairs, and opened the envelope. He found a letter from his mother also. But he was more anxious to learn his father's feelings and opinion of the step he had taken, and he read his letter first.

*　　　*　　　*　　　*　　　*

Dear Frederick,

I do not know whether this letter will find you, or where it will find you. Perhaps not until you reach New York, where it may arrive later than you. I should really like you to have your old father's and mother's greetings on your trip, which is something of a surprise to us. But we are used to surprises from you, since we have not had your unreserved confidence for a long time. I am a fatalist, and far from wishing to bore you with reproaches; but it is a pity that ever since you have been of age, so many differences have arisen in our ways of thinking and acting. A great pity, God knows. If only you had sometimes listened to me--but, as I said, there's no use to come limping after with "if only's" and the like.

My dear boy, now that fate has afflicted you so sorely--I told you from the very first that Angele comes of a diseased family--at least hold your head up. If you do, then nothing's lost. And I especially beseech you--don't take that nonsense of your failure with bacilli too much to heart. You know, I've already told you I think all the noise they make about bacilli is a hoax. Why, Pettenkofer himself swallowed the whole culture of a typhus bacillus without its hurting him.

For all I care, go to America. It may not be a bad idea and need not be a failure, I know persons whose lives were wrecked here and who went to America and returned millionaires, to be envied and fawned upon. I don't doubt that after all you have gone through, you have carefully weighed and considered the step you are taking. Dear Frederick, I beg of you, concentrate. The man who wants too much wants nothing. Above all, get rid of your philanthropic notions. You would never believe me when I told you that you uselessly sacrificed your money, your time, and your career to your philanthropic notions. And don't take up with Utopias, such as, for example, Socialism is, even at best. Bismarck is gone. The exceptional law against the Socialists has been repealed. Now we'll be seeing wonders from that pack of red internationals without a country. Did you read that some Anarchist dogs have again been throwing bombs--in Paris in a cafe not far from the Gare St. Lazare, right among a lot of innocent people, and seven or eight were killed. My dear boy, you were in Paris. For God's sake, in the discontented mood you are in, don't throw yourself in with such desperate elements.

Forgive me. It was a slip of my pen. But here in Goerlitz, far from the firing line, even a rational man, when he is troubled, begins to imagine things. With your talents you might have been an officer on a general's staff long ago.

God be with you. Write to us. I am convinced that with your great talents, you will strike root over there and make your fortune. Be on your guard against art and against side interests, from which a man cannot make a living. Do you know that the Grand Duke has made Botho his adjutant? It looks as if the boy might rise pretty high.

Have a good trip and sometimes think of your devoted father.

*   *   *   *   *

With a sigh and a short, almost inaudible laugh of great compassion and great bitterness, Frederick folded up the letter.

"'I don't know whether this letter will find you, or where it will find you,'" he repeated, and added mentally, "or how it will find you."

Then he sat still for a while, staring into space.

After a time he became observant of the American jackanapes, who had annoyed him in the smoking-room the day before. He was flirting with a young lady apathetically lounging in an easy-chair, a Canadian, Frederick had been told. He did not trust his eyes when he saw the American, who had been toying with a small box of matches, pile them up carelessly, and set fire to them in that inflammable room. A steward came up and modestly explained that it was his duty to ask him to refrain from what he was doing. At which the jackanapes dismissed him with "Get out of here, you idiot."

Frederick drew out his mother's letter, but before reading it, he had to meditate briefly upon the matter that took the place of brains in the young American's skull.

*   *   *   *   *

My Dear Son,

Your mother's prayers accompany you. You have gone through a great deal and suffered very much for one of your years. To let you hear something pleasant at the very start, I will tell you of the children. They are very well. This week I convinced myself with my own eyes that they have a good home with Pastor Mohaupt. Albrecht is splendid. Bernhard, you know, is more like his mother and always has been a quiet child. But he seemed more alert and more talkative. The life in the pastor's house and on the farm seems to please him. Pastor Mohaupt thinks both boys are by no means untalented. He has already begun to give them lessons in Latin. Little Annemarie asked me very timidly about her mother, but especially about you. She spoke of you often. I told the children there was a medical congress in New York or Washington, where they would at last make an end of that dreadful disease, consumption. My dear child, do come back soon to this dear old Europe.

I had a long talk with Doctor Binswanger. He told me your wife's trouble is hereditary. It was in her all the time and would certainly have cropped out, sooner or later. He spoke of your work, too, dear child, and thought you ought not allow yourself to be crushed. Four or five years of hard work, he said, would make up for your set-back.

Dear Dietrich, listen to your old mother and put your trust in our loving Father in heaven. I think you are an atheist. Just laugh at your old mother. But believe me, we are nothing without God's help and mercy. Pray sometimes. It won't do any harm. I know how you reproach yourself on Angele's account. Binswanger says you may have a perfectly easy conscience. And if you pray, believe me, God will remove every thought of guilt from your harassed soul. You are only thirty. I am seventy. From the experience of the forty years more that I have, I tell you, your life can still turn out so that some day you will scarcely have a recollection of all you are now suffering. You will remember the facts; but you will try in vain to recall the feelings of anguish with which they are now connected in your mind. I am a woman. I was fond of Angele. And yet I could observe you two together perfectly objectively. Believe me, there were times when she would have driven any man desperate.

*   *   *   *   *

The end of the letter was all motherly tenderness. Frederick saw himself at his mother's sewing-table by the window, and in his thoughts kissed her hair, her forehead, her hands.

When he looked up, he heard the steward remonstrating with the American and heard the American say in good German:

"The captain's a donkey."

The word had the effect of an electric shock. The next instant another pile of matches sent up a wavering flare in the gloomy, terrifying twilight.

Frederick mentally cut out the young man's cerebrum and cerebellum for an anatomical examination, proceeding strictly according to the rules of dissection, as he had so frequently done in actuality. He hunted for the centre of stupidity, which undoubtedly composed the American's whole soul, though his impudence, which he possessed in a rare degree, may also have had its seat in the brain. Frederick had to laugh. In his amusement he realised that little Ingigerd Hahlstroem no longer had any power over him, less, perhaps than, for example, the dark Jewess from Odessa, whom he had seen for the first time only a quarter of an hour before.

Captain von Kessel entered. He greeted Frederick with a slight nod of his head and seated himself at a table beside a lady, with whom he was acquainted, apparently. The American coxcomb and the pretty Canadian exchanged glances. She was languishing in her easy-chair, pale but coquettish. Frederick set her down as a woman of unusual southern beauty--straight nose, quivering nostrils, heavy, nobly arched eyebrows, black as her hair and the shadowy down over her fine, expressive, twitching lips. Her gestures had the weary grace of a Spaniard. She was laughing, and her long, slim form stretched on the chair shook. Her admirer, with a comic expression of seriousness, was again building a little pile of matches. In her weak condition she was unable to resist the impulse to laugh, and every now and then hid her face behind a black lace shawl.

It was an exciting moment when the American, in defiance of the Captain's presence, again made ready for his dangerous play.

Von Kessel, broad and ponderous and somewhat too short-legged, seemed out of proportion in the dainty parlour. He was speaking quietly with his lady. From the expression of his face it was evident that the weather was giving him cause to be serious. Suddenly the matches flared up. Now the captain's calm St. Bernard head turned slightly, and a voice said in a tone not to be misunderstood:

"Put that fire out!"

Frederick had never heard an order from a man's lips so incisive, so truly commanding, so fearful. The American turned pale and in the twinkling of an eye smothered the flame. The beautiful Canadian closed her eyes. But the captain, as if nothing had occurred, continued to converse with his lady.

XVIII

Soon after, Frederick was in the barbershop getting a shave.

"Wretched weather," observed the barber, wielding the razor with a sure hand, despite the dreadful tossing of the vessel. He seemed to be an intelligent man. Frederick had to listen to a second account of the **Nordmania**, of how the waterspout had plunged through the ladies' parlour and carried the piano down into the hold.

An ordinary German servant-girl of the peasant class entered. She looked healthy to the core and none too intelligent. The barber called her Rosa and gave her a bottle of eau de Cologne.

"That's the fifth bottle of eau de Cologne that I've given her for her mistress since we left Cuxhaven," the barber explained after she had left. "Her mistress is a divorced woman with two children. Her name is Mrs. Liebling. She is very nervous. Rosa hasn't a very easy time of it. For five dollars a month she has to be at Mrs. Liebling's beck and call morning, noon and night. She takes entire charge of the children. Soon after we left Cuxhaven, Mrs. Liebling came to have her hair dressed. You should have heard how she went on about that girl. The things she said against her. Not a spark of gratitude. She said the stupid, lazy thing wasn't worth the price of her second-class cabin."

Several times Frederick had heard the sound of quarrelling mingled with children's crying in the cabin opposite his. Once he had even distinctly caught the slapping sound of what must have been a box over somebody's ear.

"Does she hit Rosa?" he asked the barber.

"Yes."

Clearly, then, it was his neighbour of the opposite cabin in whose service the girl was.

Frederick enjoyed listening to the lively barber retail gossip, while he lay stretched out in his patented chair. It diverted his mind from troublesome thoughts. The barber, who had been sailing the seas for many years, was by no means of the ordinary type of his class. He delivered a short discourse on modern shipbuilding, the moral of which was, not to construct light steamers for speed.

"Altogether," he observed, "it's a pity to lay so much stress on record-making. How is a great big body with walls like a wafer to resist heavy seas for any length of time? And see what tremendous engines it has to carry and what an enormous amount of coal it consumes. But the *Roland's* a good boat. It was built in Glasgow in the yards of John Elder and Company. It has been running since June, 1881. The engines are compound steam-engines with three cylinders and 5800 horse power. They require one hundred and fifteen tons of coal every day. The boat makes sixteen knots an hour, and has a tonnage of 4510. There are one hundred and sixty-eight men in the crew."

The barber had all these details at his fingers' ends. In a tone of annoyance, as if the thing caused him personally a lot of trouble, he told that the *Roland* on each trip to or from New York dragged one thousand and three hundred tons of anthracite coal in its coal-bunkers. A slow trip, he insisted, was safe and comfortable, while a quick trip was dangerous and expensive.

The little saloon with its electric lighting would have been a very comfortable place to be in, had it only stood at rest. But unfortunately its walls were quivering to the pulse of the engines and the floor was rising and sagging to the swell and fall of the waves, which every now and then leapt against the port-hole with tiger-like fury. The flasks in the closets rattled.

"A heavier ship," said the barber, "built to go more slowly, wouldn't be pitching like this."

Next he spoke of a little person, who dyed her hair, a dancer. She had spent more than an hour in his chair, having him show her rouge and face powders, until finally he had displayed his entire stock of Pinaud and Roger et Gallet. The barber chuckled.

"On sea trips," he said, "a man has a chance of getting to know the queerest women." And he proceeded to recount a number of incidents, which, on his own word, he himself had witnessed. The heroine in each case was an erotomanic woman.

"Just ask our doctor," he said. He was of the old-fashioned sort of barber-surgeon, and in the capacity of surgeon had gathered the most scandalous portion of his experiences. "One of the worst cases," he went on, "was that of an American girl, who was found lying unconscious in one of the life-boats swinging from the davits. She was hideously abused by all the crew, one at a time, but they fixed it so that the whole blame could be laid on her."

Frederick knew that none other than Ingigerd Hahlstroem was responsible for the direction the barber's thoughts had taken. She had been sitting in the very chair in which he was now reclining. A current streamed from its upholstery into his body. His heart began to beat irregularly, ceasing for an instant, then leaping wildly. To his horror, he observed that Mara's power over him was not yet broken.

He jumped up and shook himself. He felt as if he must plunge into a hot and cold bath and let stinging douches run down his spine to wash him outwardly and inwardly clean and expel that foul poison from his blood.

XIX

The barbershop lay aft, and nearby one could look through glass panes upon the working of the cylinders and pistons. Frederick toilsomely clambered up to the promenade deck and crept into the overcrowded smoking-room. Though it disgusted him to be wedged into a small space with a lot of noisy men, he had come here in the desire to escape the wild orgy of his thoughts. Doctor Wilhelm had kept a place for him.

"The doctor tells me you were in the steerage, and a beautiful Deborah made a dangerous impression upon you," the captain said, smiling roguishly.

Frederick laughed. He ordered beer, and the conversation was jolly from the start.

In their corner the skat players were sitting over their cards. They were business men, all of apoplectic constitution. They had been drinking beer and playing skat ever since breakfast, in fact, except when they slept, ever since boarding the steamer. The conversation in the room was of no interest to them. Even the weather failed to elicit any questions from them. They seemed to be insensible to the tossing of the great vessel, or the dismal howling of the wind. The force of the roll was so tremendous that Frederick involuntarily clutched at the thing nearest to him. Up went the port side, down went the starboard. Up went the starboard, down went the port side. Sometimes Frederick felt as if port and starboard might plunge one over the other; in which case the **Roland's** keel would float above water, while the bridge, masts, and smoke-stacks would be submerged at a distance below the surface. And in that case all would be lost; but those skat players, it seemed to him, would go on playing undisturbed.

Hahlstroem's tall figure came creeping with bent head into the tobacco smoke. His clear, cold, critical eyes roved about looking for a seat. He paid no attention to the armless man, who jestingly shouted an ironic remark to him. With cool politeness he seated himself at the greatest possible distance from Stoss, drew a pouch of tobacco from his pocket, and filled a short Dutch pipe. Frederick's immediate thought was, "Where is Achleitner?"

"How is your daughter feeling?" Doctor Wilhelm asked.

"Oh, she's just a little upset now. The weather will be getting better, I suppose."

The whole company, which, of course consisted of the men either by nature or from frequent exposure proof against seasickness, now entered into the usual discussion of the weather.

"Is it true, Captain," somebody asked, "that last night we nearly collided with a derelict?"

The captain smiled, raised his brows, and made no reply.

"Where are we now, Captain? Was there fog last night? I saw some snow fall. And for at least an hour I heard the siren blow every two minutes."

But Captain von Kessel remained highly monosyllabic in everything pertaining to the management of the vessel and the prospects for a good or bad crossing.

"Is it true that there is gold bullion on board for the treasury in Washington?"

Von Kessel smiled and sent a thin wreath of cigarette smoke curling through his moustache.

"That would be carrying coals to Newcastle," remarked Wilhelm.

And now the great theme, the theme of themes, became the general topic of conversation. Each of the travellers, of course, straightway had a picture of his own fortune in mind, every cent of it, or else tried to make an accurate mental calculation. They all turned into calculating machines, while aloud comparing the capitals of the great American banking firms, the Bank of England, the Credit Lyonnais and the wealth of all the American millionaires. Even the skat players gave their attention for a few moments at a time.

America was then suffering from a business depression, a crisis, as the political economists dub it. The causes of the depression came up for discussion. Most of the Americans present happened to be Democrats, and they threw the blame on the Republicans. The Tammany Tiger was the subject of especial execration. It not only controlled New York City, the mayor of which was a creature of Tammany, but had also put its men into the most influential positions throughout the land. And every Tammany man knew how to shear his sheep. As a result, the American people were thoroughly bled. The corruption in the highest offices was said to be on a tremendous scale. Millions of dollars were appropriated to the navy, but if a man-of-war actually happened to be built, the thing was a great achievement, since the money, long before it was applied to its proper purpose, sifted down into the pockets of peaceful Americans, whose interest in the navy was of the slightest.

"I shouldn't care to be buried in America," cried Stoss, in his sharp voice. "It would be too dreary and boresome for me in my grave. I hate their spitting and their ice-water." The burst of laughter that greeted his remark encouraged him to further sallies. "Americans are parrots, incessantly chattering two words, dollar and business, dollar and business, dollar and business. Those two words have been death to culture in America. An American doesn't even know what it is to have the Englishman's spleen. Think of the fearfulness of living in a country called the land of dollars. We have human beings living in Europe. The Americans regard everything, even their fellow-men, from the point of view of the number of dollars they represent. If a thing can't be reckoned in dollars, they have no eyes for it. And then Carnegie and Company come and want to astonish us with their disgusting shopkeeper's philosophy. Do you think they're helping the world on by slicing off some of the world's dollars and then returning some of the sliced off dollars with a great flourish of trumpets? Do you think that if they do us the favour to give us some of their money, we'll throw overboard our Mozart and Beethoven, our Kant and Schopenhauer, our Schiller and Goethe, our Rembrandts, Leonardos, Michael Angelos, in short, all our wealth of art and intellect? What is a miserable cur of an American millionaire, a dollar maniac, as compared with all those great men? Let him come and ask us for alms."

XX

The captain invited Frederick to his cabin and asked him to write a few words in his album. On the way, he showed him the chart-room and the wheel-house, where a sailor was turning the great wheel at the directions of the first mate, whose voice came from the bridge through a speaking-tube. Frederick read the compass in front of the wheel and saw that the *Roland* lay west-southwest. The captain was in hopes of striking better weather by taking a more southerly route. The helmsman did not allow his attention to be diverted for the fraction of a second. He kept his bronzed, weather-beaten face with its corn-coloured beard turned unwaveringly toward the compass, and his sea-blue eyes fastened upon the west-southwest line. And the face of the compass, in its round copper case, notwithstanding the vessel's elephantine leaps and bounds, never deviated from the horizontal.

When they reached his cabin, the handsome blond German, whose eyes came of the same stock as the mariner's at the wheel, became more expansive. He insisted on Frederick's taking a comfortable seat and offered him a cigar. He spoke of his own life. Frederick learned that he was unmarried, had two unmarried sisters and a brother with a wife and children. The pictures of his sisters, his brother, his brother's wife, his brother's children, and his parents were hung symmetrically on the wall over a red plush sofa. They were sacred objects.

Frederick did not fail to ask his stereotyped question:

"Do you follow your calling because you have a decided preference for it?"

"Tell me of a position on land where I could command the same salary, and I'd exchange without an instant's hesitation. Seafaring begins to lose its charms when a man gets on in years."

The captain's guttural voice was extremely agreeable. It suggested to Frederick the sound of colliding billiard balls. His enunciation was perfect, absolutely free of a dialectic tinge.

"My brother has a wife and children," he said. Though there was, of course, not the slightest trace of sentimentality in his tone, it was evident from the gleam in his eyes how he idolised his nieces and nephews. He pointed out each one's picture and at the end said frankly, "My brother is an enviable man." Then he asked Frederick whether he was the son of General von Kammacher. He had taken part in the campaign of 1870 and 1871 as lieutenant of the regiment of artillery of which Frederick's father had been chief. He spoke of him with great admiration and reverence.

Frederick remained in the captain's cabin over half an hour. His presence seemed to give the skipper special pleasure. It was astonishing what a gentle, tender soul was hidden beneath the commanding exterior. Before disclosing a bit of that soul, he always puffed harder at his cigar and gave Frederick a long, searching look. By degrees Frederick discovered what magnet was tugging strongly at the blond giant's heart. He kept recurring alternately to the Black Forest and the Thueringian Forest, and Frederick had a mental picture of the magnificent man clipping his privet hedge in front of his cosey cottage, or walking among his rose bushes with a pruning knife in his hand. He could detect that the captain would far rather be living secluded in a sea of green leaves and green pine needles; and he felt convinced that it would have been delicious to him to submerge himself forever in the soft rushing of endless forests and dispense forever with the rushing and roaring of all the oceans in the world.

"Perhaps the night of all days has not yet come," said the captain, with a humorous expression. He rose and placed the large album in front of Frederick. "Now I am going to lock you in here with this pen and this ink, and when I return, I want to find something clever on this page."

Frederick von Kammacher turned the leaves of the mariner's album. It was unmistakable that the hope for a vegetable garden, gooseberry bushes, the chirping of birds, and the buzzing of bees was most intimately connected with this book. Under the pressure of dreariness and the grave responsibility for many a sea trip, it must expand the captain's soul to look over it, Frederick thought. It seemed to point to a time when, in the peace and security of his simple home, it would serve its turn by testifying to all the dangers its possessor had gone through, all his past struggles and hardships. In a sheltered haven it would afford pleasant retrospect, full of content.

Frederick's own quietistic ideal in the form of a farm and a solitary log hut occurred to him. But he was not living in it alone. The little devil Mara was sharing it with him. In embitterment he mentally climbed to still lonelier regions, and saw himself a hermit, who prayed, drank nothing but water, and lived on roots, nuts, and sometimes a fish of his own catching.

When the captain returned and he and Frederick had taken leave of each other, this is what he found in his book:

Borne aloft on wave and ocean,
Of thy master's course partaking,
Some day thou wilt cease thy motion,
Of thy master's rest partaking.
In the garden of his stillness,
To his manly deeds inspiring,
Thou wilt faithfully bear witness.
Thou art language well becoming
Him who daily danger faces,
Gratitude of souls proclaiming,
Whom he bore through cosmic spaces.
The signature was
"Frederick von Kammacher, Globetrotter."

XXI

Frederick, holding on to his hat with one hand and clinging to the railing with the other, descended from the windy heights of the captain's cabin to the promenade deck. When he passed the cabin of the first mate, the door opened, and Von Halm appeared in conversation with Achleitner. Achleitner was pale, and there was an anxious look in his face.

"I have rented the lieutenant's cabin for Miss Hahlstroem. I could not bear to see her suffering so in her own cabin," he called to Frederick.

The gale had increased. Not a passenger was to be seen on deck. Sailors were inspecting the life-boats. Huge masses of water seethed against the ship's side, cutting into its course obliquely. The waves made a mad leap into the air, hung there for an instant in the form of white corals, and fell like a thousand lashes on the deck, which was all awash. The breath of the gale tore the smoke backward from the mouths of the smoke-stacks and scattered it in the wild chaos in which heaven and sea were mingled. Frederick glanced down at the fore-deck. In his burning brain arose a thought of the Jewess and then of the scoundrel, Wilke. But the fore-deck was so swept by the seas that nobody could keep his footing there, except the lookout men, who were holding watch at the beak of the vessel, not far from the cat-head.

Between the door leading to the main companionway and the companionway itself was a square level space, about which a railing ran and in which a few people could stay and enjoy the fresh air without being drenched. When Frederick, on his way below deck, passed through the open door, he found a quiet assemblage of pale-faced passengers. One chair was still unoccupied. He seated himself in it, with the fanciful notion that he was joining a gathering of condemned men.

"That poor sinner there must be Professor Toussaint, the famous sculptor in need," Frederick thought, judging so from the man's slouched hat and great cape. Now and then the man exchanged a few words with a person sitting next to him, who might be *Geheimrat* Lars. Frederick had once met the *Geheimrat* at a dinner at the mayor's house, but he had only a faded recollection of his appearance. The clothing manufacturer had dragged himself from his cabin, heaven knows how, and was lying in his chair like a corpse. Besides these, there were two men conversing with each other, one small, rotund and scary-faced, the other tall and thin.

The tall one was showing the other a section of a submarine cable and letting the hard piece, intricately braided of hemp, metal and gutta-percha, pass from hand to hand. From his choppy, whispered sentences, the company learned that in 1877 he had worked as electrical engineer on a steamer laying a cable between Europe and the United States. The work on the high seas had lasted without interruption for many months. He had spent several months supervising the construction of the steamer itself in the yards, especially the riveting of its metal plates. He spoke of what is called the cable plateau at the bottom of the ocean, stretching from Ireland to Newfoundland, a strip of grey sand so named because it supports the main transatlantic cable.

The copper wires in the centre of the cable, he said, were called its soul, the rest of the mass, almost as thick as a man's fist and resembling a great hawser, served merely as a sheath to protect the soul. Frederick had a mental vision of the fearful solitudes of the ocean depths, with the monstrous metal serpent, apparently without beginning and without end, creeping over the sandy bottom peopled by the enigmatic creatures of the deep. It seemed to him as if such profound isolation must be gruesome even for the dead mass of cable.

Then he wondered why it was that mankind at each end of the cable had burst into jubilation upon the transmission of the first messages. Perhaps there was some mystic cause for rejoicing. The real cause could not possibly be that one was now able to telegraph "Good morning, Mr. Smith," or "Good morning, Mr. Brown," twenty times a minute around the earth's circumference, or that one could adulterate humanity's mind with newspaper gossip from the four quarters of the globe.

In the midst of these meditations, his chair slipped, and Frederick, in company with the electrical engineer, the dozing manufacturer, a lady physician, and a lady artist, was hurled against the banister, while the opposite row of passengers, including the *Geheimrat* and the professor, was hurled on top of them. It was a ridiculous incident, but Frederick observed that no one seemed to find it so.

They tried to arrange themselves in order again. One of the ever-industrious stewards appeared, and, as if to comfort them for their overthrow, passed about

Malaga grapes from the ship's inexhaustible store.

"When shall we reach New York?" somebody asked. The eyes of all the others instantly turned upon the questioner in amazement and alarm. The steward, usually so polite merely smiled an embarrassed smile and gave no reply. In his opinion an answer, one way or the other, would have been to challenge fate. The passengers felt much the same. Indeed, the idea that their feet would actually ever tread solid land again seemed in their present condition almost like an extravagant fairy tale.

The short, stout man, to whom the electrical engineer was chiefly directing his discourse, was conducting himself peculiarly. At short intervals he would look out anxiously into the uproar, turning his small, watchful eyes searchingly up to the tops of the masts, which never ceased to describe great arcs in the air (starboard to port, port to starboard!), and out into the monotonous rolling of the waves, swelling into ever higher and larger masses. His face was full of concern. Frederick was on the point of inwardly ridiculing the pitiful landlubber's cowardice, when he heard him say that scarcely three weeks before he had brought his schooner safely to New York from a three years' trip around the world, and intended to start out from New York on the same trip to last the same length of time. The little gentleman was the experienced captain of a sailing vessel. In the course of his fifty years, he had spent more than thirty on all the waters of the globe.

XXII

Frederick reflected upon the timid skipper, whose characteristics seemed to harmonise so poorly with the demands, active and passive, of his rigorous calling. He wondered what it is that permanently holds a man like that to his marriage ties and all the duties of his life. Then he arose to wander about the **Roland** vaguely.

The enforced idleness of a sea trip, especially in bad weather, induces passengers, when they have made the complete round of the vessel, to begin over again and go through the same circle. Thus, Frederick, after descending the companionway, ascending it, and descending again, found himself on the leather-seated bench in the smoking-room avoided by most of the smokers, in which the armless man had taken his meal the day before.

Hans Fuellenberg entered, asked whether he was not permitted to smoke a cigarette in the room, and began to grumble about the weather.

"Who knows how this thing is going to end?" he complained dismally. "Perhaps, instead of reaching New York, we'll have to be towed into port somewhere in Newfoundland."

Frederick was indifferent to the prospect. He noticed that young Fuellenberg cared for nothing except to produce an impression; and young Fuellenberg noticed that Frederick von Kammacher was not susceptible to the impression he tried to produce. He cast about for another theme of conversation.

"Do you know there are two priests on board? You should have been at Cuxhaven when they got on. The sailors were beside themselves. I hunted up the fellows, the sailors I mean, in the forecastle. How they did curse! It was fearful. The stoker told all the men of the engine-room. They said you could not get genuine seamen to think any differently--with priests on board something is bound to go wrong."

"How is your lady?" asked Frederick.

"My lady is retching her soul away, if she has such a thing as a soul. Two hours ago I helped her to bed. That Englishwoman is already a full-blooded American. Shameless, I tell you! Something tremendous. I rubbed her forehead with brandy. She partook of a goodly quantity, and then I unbuttoned her waist. She seems to take me for a masseur chartered extra by her munificent husband. The thing became boresome. And besides, in that pitching boudoir, my own soul began to rise up through my stomach, and the poetry went to the devil. She showed me the photograph of her devoted husband in New York. I think she has another in London." He was interrupted by the first call for dinner, which the trumpeter announced at the bottom of the companionway. The trumpet blast was lost without resonance in the heavy air and the bluster of the waves. "What's more," he concluded, "she sent for Doctor Wilhelm."

The dining-room presented a very dreary appearance. Neither the captain nor any of the officers of the *Roland* were present, the demands upon them in such bad weather being too severe to permit them to leave their posts. The tables had been provided with a wooden apparatus dividing them into small compartments, which prevented the plates, glasses and bottles from slipping any distance. Nevertheless, there was much breaking of crockery, and it required all the skill of the stewards to serve the dishes, especially the soup. From the kitchen and the china room every now and then came the sound of a tremendous crash. There were scarcely twelve people at table, among them Hahlstroem and Doctor Wilhelm. After a time the skat players, as usual, came bursting in, talking noisily and red of face. Their winnings were immediately transmuted into Pommery. Notwithstanding the fearful weather, the band was playing. There seemed to be something frivolous, almost challenging, in the playing of music when, at short intervals, the **Roland** would come to a quivering standstill, as if it had run upon a reef. Once the illusion was so strong that a panic arose in the steerage. Mr. Pfundner, the head-steward, brought this explanation of the horrified shrieks that had penetrated the dining-room above the noise of the raging waters, the rattling of the plates and the blare of the band.

At dessert Ḥahlstroem left his place at the other end of the room and, balancing himself with difficulty, came over to Frederick and Doctor Wilhelm, and asked permission to seat himself beside them. He seemed to have been drinking whisky, as he had dropped his natural shell of reticence. He spoke of hydrotherapy and gymnastic exercises, and called himself a quack. It was the gymnastics, he said, that had given his daughter the idea of taking up dancing. As if to challenge the others, he elaborated bold philosophic theories, dealing out one wild statement after the other, each of which would have been a trump sufficient to end the game for ten German Philistines. To believe his own word, he was a terroristic Anarchist, a white-slave trafficker, an adventurer always. At any rate, he espoused the cause of all who were Anarchists, procurers, or adventurers. He argued in all superiority, upon egotistic grounds, calling these the intellectuals, and all others, creatures without brains; in which his philosophy showed some similarity to Frederick von Kammacher's new philosophy, now that Frederick had entered upon a new phase of his life.

"America," said Hahlstroem, "is known to have been settled by rogues. Were you to spread a tent over America, you would have the most beautiful, the most comfortable penitentiary in the world. The natural form that survives and triumphs in America is the great rascal, the great Renaissance idiot. In fact, it is the one form that will triumph throughout the world. You'll see some day how the great American rascal will get the whole of Europe, including England, into his clutches. Europe is also dabbling a little in Renaissance ideals and Renaissance beasts. It is busily working away, so to speak, on its own rascalization. But America is in advance by ten horse lengths. Europe's Cesare Borgias sit in the cafes with ***Glockenroecken a la Biedermaier*** and give voice to their criminal genius in fairly innocent verses. They all look sickly, as if a barber had cupped all the blood out of their veins. If Europe wants to save herself, she has only one hope--to make a law by which it will be a crime to surrender an adventurer, an embezzler, a fraudulent bankrupt, the keeper of a disorderly house, a thief, or a murderer to America. On German, English and French vessels in American ports, such people have already been placed under the special protection of Europe. Then you will see how soon Europe will outdistance Uncle Sam."

The physicians burst out laughing.

"When did geniuses ever do anything morally? Even the creator of heaven and earth did not know how to. He produced an immoral world. Every high form of human intellectual activity has thrown ethics overboard. What would a historian be who, instead of making researches, would moralise? What would a physician be who would stop to moralise? Or a great statesman, who would toe the chalk-line of your middle-class ten commandments? As for an artist, when he moralises, he is a fool and a knave. And please tell me, what sort of a business would the church do if all of us were moral? There would be no church."

There was a cold gleam of audaciousness in the Swede's eyes. His utterances produced a strange impression. Even if he had pronounced fewer wild paradoxes, Frederick von Kammacher would have succumbed to his spell. He eagerly sought for resemblances between father and daughter, or, more accurately, he observed them without seeking. They were very evident to one who, alas, to his own torture, was carrying the daughter's picture alive in his soul. As long as the Swede spoke, he could not help wavering between repugnance and admiration, and he kept asking himself whether this man was really the sort of person that Arthur Stoss had described him to be, no gentleman, a weakling, an idle ragamuffin.

XXIII

As they arose from table and were ascending the companionway to the deck, Hahlstroem suddenly said to Frederick:

"My daughter is expecting you. We have a friend on board, Mr. Achleitner, a soft creature, but the possessor of much money, which he doesn't know the best way to get rid of. So he made it worth while for one of the officers to give up his luxurious cabin opening on deck to my daughter. Unfortunately, that gives him the right to make an unmitigated nuisance of himself sometimes."

When the men entered the comparatively roomy cabin on deck, they found Achleitner sitting on a rather unsteady chair, while Mara, carefully wrapped up, was lying stretched out on a couch. She instantly called to her father, please to remove Mr. Achleitner, who was boring her, and signified to Frederick that she had a special favour to ask of him. Hahlstroem and Achleitner obediently withdrew, and Frederick *nolens volens* had to seat himself on the camp-chair.

"How can I be of service?" he asked.

She put one of those inconsequential requests with which she liked to busy everybody about her. She did this, she explained, because if many people were not doing something for her, she felt neglected.

"But if you don't want to do it," she added--it was to get her a bottle of perfume, or something of the sort, for which a stewardess would have been the right person to ask--"but if you don't want to do it, then please don't. I should prefer it if you didn't. In fact, if I bore you, I would just as soon sit alone."

Frederick realised that this beginning was a foolish expression of embarrassment.

"I should like to be of service to you in anything I can, and you don't in the least bore me."

That was the truth. Alone with Ingigerd in her cabin, where the vessel's motion was less perceptible, he was sensitive to the full fascination of her presence. The pangs of the ocean crossing had given her sweet girlish face a waxen transparency. At her request the stewardess had loosened her hair, and it lay spread in a golden flood over her white pillow, a golden flood, the sight of which was highly disturbing to Frederick. Where was there an adornment for the head, a queen's diadem, which could exercise so powerful, so divine a charm? It seemed to Frederick as if that tremendous vessel, with its hundreds of human ants, were nothing more than the cocoon of this tiny silkworm, this delicately coloured, delicious little butterfly; as if the sixty naked helots down at the ship's bottom shovelling coal into the white heat under the boilers, were toiling and sweating merely to be of service to this childish Venus; as if the captain and officers were the paladins of the queen, and the rest of the crew her following; as if the steerage were rilled with blindly devoted slaves, and as if the **Roland** were proudly carrying a fairy tale from "A Thousand and One Nights" across the salt desert.

"Did I hurt your feelings yesterday by telling you my story?" she asked suddenly.

"Mine? No! You are the injured one in the life you have unfortunately led."

She looked at him with a sardonic smile, plucking a pink wad from the lid of a box of sweetmeats beside her. In her looks and smiles, Frederick felt her cold, wicked enjoyment. And since he was a man and knew he was impotent in the face of such fiendish mockery, a wave of physical fury mounted in him, driving the blood into his eyes and causing him involuntarily to clench his fists. His full-blooded nature occasionally had need of such frenzy. It was a phenomenon with which his friends were familiar.

"What is the matter with you?" whispered Ingigerd, plucking at the pink wad. "I am not afraid of a monk like you."

Her remark was not calculated to calm Frederick's passionate surge. However, he mastered his feelings with evident, redoubled exertion of his will power. Had he not succeeded in controlling himself, he might have more resembled a Papuan negro than a European. He might have turned into a beast in human form, and might have thrown overboard, as he himself clearly felt, more than was good of what both self-acquired and imposed culture had formed in him. He had no desire to turn into another animal in Circe's stables.

It was as if Ingigerd were the very incarnation of the evil Psyche, so few of a man's feelings were concealed from her. She knew what fight Frederick had just fought and she knew he had conquered.

"Oh, I wanted to become a nun once myself," she said, and began in a mixture of truth and fiction to prattle of a year she had spent in a convent. "I wanted to turn good, but didn't get very far. I am religious. Really I am. I can say so with a clear conscience. Anybody with whom I don't feel I could pray to God, is disgusting to me. Perhaps, after all, I shall end by being a nun, but not because I am pious." She did not realise how egregiously she was contradicting herself. "Oh, no! It wouldn't occur to me to be pious. I don't believe in anything but myself. Life is short, and nothing is coming afterward. A person ought to enjoy life. A person who deprives himself of a single enjoyment sins against himself, beside practising self-deception."

She was led to speak of her mother. Frederick was startled by the hatred, the vulgarity with which she referred to her.

"I could kill her," she said, "although, or just because she is my mother." Her face lost its purity of expression and assumed an ugly, repulsive look. "With papa it is different. But it gets to be an awful nuisance always to be dragging him about with me."

The stewardess came in. She spoke to Ingigerd in a loud, cheery way.

"Better here than down below, isn't it, Miss?"

She bolstered up her cushions, rearranged her coverings, and left again.

"The silly thing has already fallen in love with me, too," said Ingigerd.

"Why am I sitting here?" Frederick thought, and was about to attempt in all kindness to remove the cataract from the eyes of the foolish little creature. Why did great waves of pity keep sweeping over him? Pity for which she did not ask. Why could he not rid himself of the idea of innocence, of chastity, of the uncontaminated while in the presence of this child fiend? She seemed pure and unsullied, and each capricious movement, each remark of hers only heightened the impression of touching helplessness.

"All love is pity." This sentence of Schopenhauer's, which he held to be both true and paradoxical, flashed into his mind. He took one of her dolls in his hand, and tried in the kindly way that he had acquired with his patients to make Ingigerd Hahlstroem understand that one does not go through life unpunished in the belief that life is mere doll's play.

"Your dolls," he said, "are actually beasts of prey. Woe to you, if you don't realise they are beasts before they bury their claws in your flesh and rend you with their fangs."

She gave a short laugh without answering. She complained of a pain in her breast.

"You're a physician. Won't you examine me?"

"That's Doctor Wilhelm's business," Frederick answered brusquely.

"Well," she said, "if I am in pain and you as a physician can stop the pain, but don't want to, your friendship cannot amount to much."

Frederick did not turn a deaf ear to this correct reasoning. He had long before realised that her delicate constitution was with difficulty holding the balance between debit and credit. Each instant it was in danger of losing its balance.

"If I were your physician," he said, "I should send you to live for three years with a German country pastor, or an American farmer. I should not let you see anybody but the old pastor or the old farmer and his wife and their daughters. I should not let you go to see a play, let alone appear on the stage yourself. It is those cursed variety shows that have sent you to the dogs, physically and morally."

"I am a ruffian," he thought, "and there's medicine for her."

"Do you want to become a farmer?"

"Why?"

"Because you are already a pastor," she laughed.

The conversation was interrupted by the screeching of a cockatoo on a stand in the back of the cabin. Until then Frederick had not noticed it.

"What else will be turning up? Where did you get that beast?"

She laughed again.

"Please give me the beast. Koko! Koko!" Frederick arose and let the great, rosy-white seafarer clamber on his hand. "I like animals better than I do most people I meet," she said.

The bird kept screaming "Cockatoo!" until Frederick felt it fairly applied to him.

In the meantime the **Roland**, sinking into deep troughs and climbing over watery mountain crests in an ocean that was like a great machine regularly at work, had plowed its way into fog. The siren was bellowing.

"Fog?" exclaimed Ingigerd. Every bit of blood vanished from her face, which was already too pale. "But I am never afraid," she added immediately, took a bonbon in her mouth, and let the cockatoo nibble at it. The bird unfeelingly trod on the girl's beautifully heaving breast. She made it sing ***Stille Nacht, heilige Nacht*** and some well-known music-hall airs, and told stories of her menagerie.

Every instant Frederick had to perform some small service, and while she was giving an enthusiastic description of a little monkey from Java that she had once owned, he asked himself whether he was a physician, a nurse, a hairdresser, a chambermaid, or a steward, and whether Ingigerd Hahlstroem would not in the end reduce him to a messenger boy.

He yearned to be on deck in the open air.

Soon after, Achleitner entered with an anxious, questioning expression in his eyes, and Ingigerd dismissed Frederick most ungraciously. There was a look of hatred in her glance. But scarcely was Frederick outside in the fog with the knob of the door still in his hand, when it seemed to him as if ropes and chains, the chains of an enslaved man, were dragging him back to the girl's couch.

XXIV

"What is to become of me?" Frederick questioned himself. He scarcely heard Hans Fuellenberg's jolly shout of greeting as the young man reeled past. Hans Fuellenberg did not fail to observe whose door it was that Frederick von Kammacher had just closed behind him, nor that, as he stood there with the knob still in his hand, he seemed to be in a state of indecision and absorption.

The siren was sending up its deafening roar. It was that wild, fearful, ascending cry, as if torn from the breast of a monster bull, which he had first heard on the tender. There was something menacing in it, and at the same time something of an anxious warning. Frederick never heard it without applying menace and warning to himself. Likewise, the driving mist seemed to be a reflection of his soul; or his soul a reflection of the driving mist and also of the vessel, as it struggled onward into the unknown, unseeing and unseen. He stepped over to the railing and looked straight down the ship's side. There he could tell with what tremendous rapidity the ***Roland*** was cleaving the water.

"Isn't man's courage utter madness?" he thought. Could any one, from captain to the lowest sailor, prevent the propeller-shaft from snapping at any moment? The screw was constantly rising and buzzing in the air. Who could sight a vessel in time to prevent the collision that would inevitably smash in the thin walls of the great hollow body? Who could hope to avoid one of the many derelicts drifting in the fog almost submerged? What would happen if the might of the waves were to hurl that great lumped mass of wood and iron against the ***Roland's*** side? What would happen if the engines were to break down? If a boiler were to prove unequal to the uninterrupted strain put upon it? Then, too, icebergs were met with in those waters. And suppose the storm were to grow worse.

The things that European civilisation has accomplished are tremendous. The trouble is, the object to which the means are applied is not worthy of the means. The how is great. The wherefore receives only a stammering reply. So much is certain, that the life of the average man to-day is fuller of adventure and heroism than the life of a bold adventurer a hundred and fifty years ago.

Frederick went to the smoking-room on deck. He found the card players, Doctor Wilhelm, Arthur Stoss, Professor Toussaint and some more gentlemen gathered over their afternoon coffee.

"Hullo!" they shouted when he appeared in the doorway.

The room smelled strong of coffee and the pungent odour of tobacco. In the instant that Frederick held the door open, the wreaths of mist and heavy tobacco smoke met.

"What's the matter, gentlemen?" Frederick asked.

"Did you operate on the dancer," someone cried, "to remove that mole two inches from her backbone right over her left hip?"

Frederick turned pale, and said nothing. Had he uttered a single word, the result might have been a scandal, perhaps even a duel, out there on the high seas.

He seated himself beside Doctor Wilhelm and acted as if the shout of greeting and the unknown man's question had not referred to him. Doctor Wilhelm proposed a game of chess. Frederick accepted, and while playing, he had time to choke down his humiliation and resentment. He glanced about furtively to find the speaker.

"There are some people, Doctor von Kammacher," Arthur Stoss said in a raised voice, "who leave their decency in Europe when they travel to America, though that does not reduce the price of the passage."

The man at whom the remark was aimed left it unanswered.

"But, Mr. Stoss," said an elderly man from Hamburg, whose conscience in regard to the offence thrust upon Frederick was evidently clear, "we're not in a ladies' parlour, and we needn't take jokes amiss."

"I am not in favour of jokes," said Stoss, "that are made at the expense of persons who are near at hand, but not present, especially when a lady is concerned. I am still less in favour of them when they are coarse and indecent."

"Oh, Mr. Stoss," rejoined the man from Hamburg, "everything in its place. I have nothing against sermons, but we're having bad weather here on the ocean and this room is not a church."

"Besides, nobody mentioned names," another man said.

Here the American jackanapes joined in the cross talk.

"When Mr. Stoss is in New York," he said drily, "he will hold services every night at Webster and Forster's."

"Some American youngsters are celebrated for their cheek," Stoss countered.

"Directly after the celebrated Barrison sisters' appearance, after the song 'Linger Longer Loo,' Mr. Stoss will raise his hands to heaven and beg the audience to pray." The American spoke without moving a muscle of his face. He had the last word. The next instant the slim young fellow was outside the door.

Arthur Stoss had the pleasure of knowing he was a fool for his pains. But, like Frederick, he paid no attention to the thrust, or to the laughter it provoked.

"People are very much mistaken," he said, turning to Professor Toussaint, who was sitting beside him and to whom he had been introduced a few minutes before, "if they suppose that morality among vaudeville performers is laxer than among any other set of persons. It's an absolutely false assumption. A performer above the average, who must always be at the very height of his powers, has to practise moderation to the point of abstinence if he wants to remain on top. Does anybody suppose that a loose life is compatible with those startlingly bold feats that an acrobat does every day and tries to improve upon every day? Damn it! It's something to make your ordinary mortal marvel at. Why, to do any one of the many things we do, we have to practise asceticism and chastity, and patiently peg away day after day at hard, dangerous work. Your plain business man, who never omits his glass of beer, has no idea what it is like." He continued to sing the praises of vaudeville actors.

"May I ask what your specialty is, Mr. Stoss?" asked Hans Fuellenberg.

"A very easy specialty, once you know how. But if it should ever come to a duel between you and me, young man, you'd have to choose what eye or ear or tooth you'd be ready to part with."

"He's as good a shot as Carver," someone said. "He can take the middle right out of an ace three or four times in succession."

"Just like any other display of skill. But don't for a moment suppose, gentlemen, that even if a man has arms and doesn't have to hold the gun with his feet and pull the trigger with his toes, that he learns how to do it without sweating and self-denial and endless patience."

"Somebody said you play the violin like Sarasate," said Hans Fuellenberg.

"Not exactly. Nor need I, considering the way I was born. But I am fond of music and my audiences go wild over my playing."

Captain von Kessel entered. He was received with a general "Ah!" Through the door burst a great wave of sunlight.

"The barometer is rising, gentlemen."

The fog had lifted, and now the men in the smoking-room realised that the *Roland* was rocking no more than easily and comfortably and was making its way with majestic speed.

This acted like a charm. The captain left the door open and had Pander hook it back. A man, who had been lying asleep in a corner--in that half sleep which is the mildest symptom of seasickness--rose to a sitting posture and rubbed his eyes. Hans Fuellenberg and a number of other men hastened out on deck. Doctor Wilhelm and Frederick, who had lost the game, followed.

XXV

The two physicians paced the full length of the promenade deck. The air was mild. The ship was moving quietly, as if its great body took delight in pushing onward through none but low waves. It was surprising to see how gay the life on deck was. They were constantly raising their hats and making way for somebody. The stewards had carried the news of the good weather down to the passengers in their stuffy cabins, and all the seasick travellers had come crawling on deck. There was much talking and laughing. Each moment brought fresh surprise over the galaxy of merry women that had kept themselves stowed away in the *Roland's* interior. It was just an ordinary Saturday afternoon in January; yet suddenly an atmosphere of festivity prevailed not to be outdone by a Christmas eve.

Hans Fuellenberg passed by. He was cracking jokes for everybody's benefit and flirting desperately with his Englishwoman, who had recovered from her seasickness. She had found a friend, a woman in a fur cap and coat, with a magnificent crown of light hair, like a Swedish woman's. She seemed to be greatly amused by Fuellenberg's poor jokes and poor English. He had abstracted her muff and was alternately conveying it to his stomach, his heart, and--this very passionately--his mouth. The young American jackanapes was promenading with his Canadian, who looked very haughty and blase, yet much fresher. The delicate creature seemed to be shivering with cold, though she was wearing an elegant coat of Canadian sable, which reached to her knees. Frederick greeted the clothing manufacturer, whom his steward had helped up on deck. He had been lying in his cabin more dead than alive, and his steward had been feeding him on nothing but Malaga grapes.

Ingigerd was holding court on the port side in front of her cabin, the door to which stood open, it flattering her vanity to have the many promenaders see and envy the privilege she was enjoying.

"If it is agreeable to you, Doctor Wilhelm, let us remain this side of the Rubicon. That little girl slightly bores me. By the way, can you tell me how I came to bring down on myself that shout when I entered the smoking-room and that man's vulgar remark? To be sure, as a physician and free-thinker it's a matter of indifference to me."

"Oh," said Wilhelm, trying by an air of lightness to appease Frederick, "this is all it was. Fuellenberg probably saw you coming out of Miss Hahlstroem's cabin, and said something in the smoking-room. You know his mischievous way."

"I'll box his ears," said Frederick.

"The trouble is, the little girl is making herself generally conspicuous. The worst rumours are afloat about her. All men seem alike to her, whether stewards, firemen, sailors, or cabin-boys. And that greasy Achleitner! I assure you, all over the ship, in the forecastle, among the stewards when they polish the silver, and in the officers' cabins, they do nothing but titter and laugh at her and Achleitner and anybody falling under suspicion on her account."

"Don't you think that's slander?"

"Why, you and I are physicians. I don't care a fig one way or the other."

Frederick laughed. "I have set my all on nothing."

Suddenly he said:

"You're right. I'm of the same opinion. I must really throw overboard that old idealistic German Adam sticking in me like a Sunday afternoon preacher."

The two men laughed. Their mood turned merrier, chiming in with the general atmosphere of hilarity.

One reason for this predominating sense of happiness was the fact that all the passengers, after struggling with nausea and sleeplessness during those miserable, crawling, endless hours in the doleful grave of their cabins, had learned to appreciate the value of mere healthy existence. Merely to live, merely to live! That was the cry that rang in every step, every laugh, every word, drowning all care. None of those concerns which each of them had dragged on board, whether from Europe or America, now had the least might. Merely to live was to win in the great lottery. They knew sunshine follows rain, and they said to themselves, "If worse comes to worst, you will willingly put up with bread and salt and a hoe and a vegetable garden, and no one in the world will be a happier mortal than you."

Those promenading men and women were each glad of the other's existence. They loved one another and were ready without hesitation to commit all sorts of follies, deeming them mere bagatelles, which on solid land they would never have condoned in themselves. Their rejoicing was a crucible melting together all the barriers by which convention divides man from man. They experienced a sense of relief and liberation, and drew in deep breaths of this atmosphere of freedom.

At the captain's order, the band set up its music stands and instruments on deck amidships; and when the blithe strains resounded through the whole of the *Roland*, that was the climax of festivity. For half an hour it seemed as if the few clouds floating in the blue sky, the steamer, the people on the steamer, and the ocean had agreed to dance a quadrille.

For moments at a time the waves would form the droll, chubby-cheeked face of a jolly old man. All at once the dreadful old man of the sea had turned good-humoured. He even seemed to be in a jocular mood and displayed a certain clumsy vanity in letting his puppets, swarms of flying fish, dance their dance, too, in a circle about the *Roland*. Perhaps, at his bidding, a whale would soon be spouting. Indeed, within a few minutes, the immigrants on the fore-deck were shouting, "Dolphins!"

The gentlemen could not for any length of time avoid Ingigerd.

"Theridium triste, the gallows spider, you know," said Wilhelm, as they approached her.

"How so?" said Frederick, slightly startled.

"You know what a gallows spider does near an ant nest. It sits on the top of its blade of grass, and when a myrmidon passes below, it throws a little skein of cobweb at its head. The ant does the rest. It gets tangled up until it is absolutely helpless, and then the tiny little spider comfortably eats it up."

"If you had seen her dance," said Frederick, "you would be more inclined to assign her the role of the ant throttled by the spider."

"I don't know who," said Wilhelm, "but some poet says, the sex is strongest when it is weak."

Ingigerd was able to boast a new sensation, which she owed to Mr. Rinck, the officer in charge of the mail, a pretty little dog, a ball of white wool, scarcely larger than a man's two fists put together. The polar bear in miniature was barking wildly in its ridiculous thin falsetto at the great ship's cat, which Mr. Rinck was holding to its nose.

"With your permission, Mr. Rinck, we shall sleep well to-night," said Wilhelm.

"I always sleep well," replied the other phlegmatically. Close to the cat's soft, heavy, hanging body, his cigarette, as always, was burning between the fingers of his right hand.

The cat spat, the dog barked. The piping sound drilled Frederick's ears like needle pricks. Ingigerd laughed and kissed the little yelper.

Wilhelm began a conversation by telling of the tremendous amount of work Mr. Rinck had to do between Cuxhaven and New York.

"Just take a look here, Doctor von Kammacher," he said, opening a door nearby, through which one could look into a deep, square pit filled half way up to the top with thousands of packages of all sizes. "Mr. Rinck has to arrange all of these."

"Exclusive of the letters," Mr. Rinck supplemented phlegmatically.

"Theridium triste," thought Frederick. He seemed to himself like an ant trying head over heels to escape the spell of the little spider, whose golden cobweb in long, open strands was luring on its victims.

"That Rinck," said Wilhelm, as they resumed their promenading, "is a peculiar sort of chap. It is worth the while to get to know him. Twenty years ago he suffered hard luck from a woman of the same type as little Miss Hahlstroem. Men should never marry women of that type. Ever since, he has been indifferently facing every sort of death on all the waters of the globe, not to mention an attempt at suicide. You ought to hear him talk. It is very difficult to get him to do it, because he doesn't drink. You can't succeed until you have been on four or five trips with him. People speak a great deal of fatalism, but to most of them the idea is merely a paper idea. To Rinck it is not a paper idea."

The life on deck kept assuming a more and more unconcerned, mundane aspect. Frederick was astonished to see so many persons from Berlin whom he knew by sight. Professor Toussaint introduced himself, and led Frederick to his wife, who was lying stretched out in a steamer chair. Their attempt at what is called conversation resulted in a few sickly sprouts.

"I am making this trip at the invitation of an American friend," Toussaint explained somewhat condescendingly, and mentioned the name of a well-known millionaire. "Even if I receive orders over there, I will not allow myself to be persuaded into making America my home. Interest in art should be elevated--" The pale, aristocratic man with the care-worn expression went on to expatiate upon his hopes and troubles, while his wife, who was still beautiful, looked on with a blase expression of irony. Probably without being conscious of it, Professor Toussaint too frequently referred to the United States as the dollar land.

On the after-deck the passengers in unrestrained jollity, had begun to dance. It was Hans Fuellenberg, the ever vivacious Berlinese, who had taken the lead. Inspired by the Strauss waltz that the band was playing he had engaged the lady in the fur coat. A number of other couples followed their example, and there, under the bright sky, an informal ball was opened, which did not end until sundown.

When the musicians with their shining brass instruments were about to make their way inconspicuously below deck, the passengers detained them, and in the twinkling of an eye, a large collection was taken up. Thereupon the dance music began again, even blither than before.

XXVI

Doctor Wilhelm was summoned away, and after a while Frederick succeeded in taking leave of Toussaint and his wife. He remained alone. The clear heavens, the deep blue sea, smooth as glass, calmed as if by a miracle, the music, the dancing, the sunlight, and the dear, sweet, pacifying, all-forgiving letter of his mother--it was in his pocket--awakened in him a fresh, pleasant sense of vitality.

"Life," he said to himself, "is always this way or that, a moment filled with pain or pleasure, with darkness or brightness, with sunlight or heavy, black clouds; and according to the moment in which we view our past and future, these will darken or brighten. Should existence in the shining light possess lesser reality than existence in the dark?" "No, it should not," was the answer that came from everything within and about him, filling him with youthful, almost childlike joy.

Frederick had pushed back his slouched hat, had unbuttoned his light overcoat, and was standing with his arms crooked over the railing. He looked out upon the sea. He felt the pulse beats of the engines, his ears were filled with the pliant, melodious chords of the Viennese waltz; the whole world had turned into a brilliant, lively, sparkling ballroom. He had suffered and caused others to suffer. Now he embraced all those through whom he had suffered and who had suffered through him, and seemed to wed them in blissful intoxication.

At this point Ingigerd Hahlstroem passed by with the giant Von Halm. Frederick heard her say she did not dance, that dancing was an insipid pleasure. With that, he started away from the railing, went up to the Canadian, and in a peculiar, fiery German manner ruthlessly drew her away from the young American, who was completely taken aback. It was evident that the delicate, exotic woman, whose breast rose and fell convulsively, took pleasure in that strong conqueror's arm as they circled about in the dance.

At the conclusion of the dance, he found himself under the necessity of murdering French and English with her for a time and was very glad when he could gracefully deliver her over again to the jealous young American.

Stoss was being transported across the deck by his valet, who, as always, held him by his coat collar.

"My private overland and oversea express," he called to Frederick.

Frederick pulled up a steamer chair for him in a sudden impulse to chat with Stoss.

"If the weather remains like this," said Stoss, after his valet had carefully and skilfully seated him in the chair, "we can reach Hoboken some time on Tuesday. But only if the weather does remain like this. The captain tells me that when we are running under full steam, as now, we make sixteen knots an hour."

Frederick started. So Tuesday this life under the same roof with Ingigerd was to end.

Frederick had been profoundly humiliated by the coarse insult offered him in the smoking-room. He knew of no other way to escape the impression of it except by a sort of ostrich policy. For that reason he had passed over the incident lightly when speaking to Doctor Wilhelm. Once his feeling of delicacy, smarting like a sensitive nerve, had ceased to ache so intensely, he looked upon the scandal much as a somnambulist would look upon the thing that has awakened him and guarded him against a humiliating fall. For more than half an hour his passion for the little devil of a dancer had turned into disgust and repugnance, until now he suddenly had to admit once again that separation from her was inconceivable.

"That little dancer is a piquant wench," said Stoss, as if he had divined Frederick's thoughts. "It would not seem at all strange to me if an inexperienced man were to fall into her toils. I think she resembles one of the younger Barrison sisters, who sing 'Linger Longer Lucy, Linger Longer Loo.' A man must certainly don armour in dealing with her."

"I am completely at a loss to understand," lied Frederick, "how I ever came to fall under suspicion with that creature. She is of absolutely no interest to me."

"Good Lord, Doctor von Kammacher! Who doesn't fall under suspicion with her?" He laughed unblushingly. "I myself did."

Frederick suffered. He looked sidewise at the armless trunk, and his soul writhed in humiliation at the thought of his own ridiculousness.

Stoss went on to philosophise on erotics in general. He, the Don Juan without arms, read Frederick a lecture on the art of handling women. This led to his boasting, which detracted markedly from his quality of fineness. His intellect also shrank in direct proportion to the increase of his vanity. Something seemed to be working in him impelling him to impress people at all costs with his successes as a man.

A servant-girl led two children by. Frederick drew a breath of relief, for she diverted Stoss from his unsavoury theme.

"Well, Rosa," he called, "how is Mrs. Liebling?" It was his habit to obtrude himself upon everybody. From the gossip of Bulke, his valet, he had learned of Rosa and her cross. The difficult lady she served was the excitable person of whom the barber had told Frederick and with whom he was acquainted from certain impressions of his hearing. Rosa, who was carrying Ella Liebling, a girl of five years, on her crimson arm, looked pleased and laughed.

"She is not coming on deck. She's taken up with fortune-telling and table-turning."

Bulke, in whose eyes Rosa seemed to have found unqualified favour, took Siegfried Liebling, a boy of seven, from her hand and helped her place both children safely in steamer chairs.

"There is nothing to beat a crazy woman," Stoss declared. "That Mrs. Liebling actually called in Mr. Pfundner, the head-steward, to help her with Rosa"--the very Rosa, who unwearyingly and self-sacrificingly worked for her day and night, in good weather and bad. The worst to be said against her was that at utmost she was a little too ready with her tongue.

XXVII

The music was still playing, the sun was still shining from a slightly clouded sky. On the dry deck the travelling city, in the gayest, most superficial mood, was still dancing in the face of the infiniteness of heaven and sea. A steward came up to Frederick and presented the second engineer, who brought a message from Doctor Wilhelm asking Frederick to come to him immediately. The engineer led Frederick to the engine-room and down a perpendicular iron ladder. The warm, heavy smell of oil almost robbed Frederick of his breath. The downward climb seemed endless.

On all sides the engines were working. Frederick glanced at the gigantic cylinders, in which the compressed steam was moving pistons up and down like pump handles. The pistons communicated their motion to the big shaft running aft along the keel to the stern, and the revolutions of the shaft in turn produced the revolutions of the screw propelling the vessel across the Atlantic.

Oilers holding oil cans and waste clambered in and out of the rotating masses of iron with astounding sureness and boldness. To graze one of the fly-wheels, or to step one inch within the unguarded circle of their revolution, was to receive a deadly blow. Here was the heart and soul of the vessel, the real modern miracle of strength, the like of which no age in the past has been able to produce. An iron soul, a steely heart. It was as if one were descending below earth into the glowing workshop of Vulcan of old, the lame god, who did not demonstrate the full skill of his divinity until our times.

Still deeper down went the descent, to where, from numerous shovels handled by almost naked helots, coal was flying into the white heat under the boilers, into a row of gaping jaws of fire. Frederick felt as if he had reached the heart of a crater. It was a black shaft smelling of coal, slag, and burning things. Apparently it was lighted only by the constant opening of the furnace doors, spitting white heat. How was it possible for such a conflagration to be contained in the ***Roland's*** interior without reducing the whole to ashes? What a conquest to fight such a sea of fire, to keep it in check, and carry it through sea and storm; to manage that it should carry itself three or six thousand miles in the ocean in fair weather or foul, hidden away and absolutely innocuous.

Frederick panted for breath. The glowing heat of the abyss instantly brought the perspiration pouring out on his face and neck. He was so absorbed in the novelty of the impressions that he completely forgot he was surrounded by water about twenty feet under the surface of the sea. Suddenly, he became aware of Doctor Wilhelm's presence, and in the same instant saw a man entirely naked stretched out like a corpse, a white body on the black coal dust. The man had ceased to breathe.

In a second Frederick, now wholly the physician, had Doctor Wilhelm's stethoscope in his hand and was listening to the man's heart. His mates, blackened with coal from head to foot, were ceaselessly at work in the engine's unremitting service, shovelling coal, opening the furnace doors, and slamming them shut. They scarcely cast a glance at their fallen comrade, and that only when they stopped to gulp a glass of beer or water.

"It was hardly three minutes ago," said Doctor Wilhelm, "that he broke down. That man over there, the one who has just washed himself, is his successor."

"He was just about to throw coal into the furnace," explained the engineer who had called for Frederick, shouting at the top of his voice to make himself heard above the clanging of the shovels and the banging of the iron doors, "when his shovel flew out of his hand about twelve feet away and almost struck a coal-trimmer. He was hired in Hamburg. The moment he set foot on board, I thought, 'If only you pull through, my boy.' He joked about himself. He said, 'If my heart is good.' I was sorry for him. He wanted to cross the great pond, and that was his only way of getting over. He wanted, no matter how, to see his brother again, his only living relative, or somebody else. They hadn't seen each other for fourteen years."

"Exitus," said Frederick, after a prolonged investigation of the man's heart. Even a few moments after the stethoscope had been removed, one could see the ring it made on his bluish, waxen skin. His chin dropped. They put it back in place, and Frederick bound his jaws with his white handkerchief. "He had a bad fall," Frederick remarked. It may actually have been the unfortunate fall to which the helot owed his death. There was a deep bleeding gash in his temple from the edge of a large nut. "Probably a heart stroke," Frederick added, "the result of the heat and over-exertion." He looked at the dead man, then at his mates, naked, blackened, illuminated by the jaws of the glowing furnaces, and thought of the fifth commandment, "Thou shalt not kill." If we were to take the commandment literally, how far should we get?

The physicians mounted on deck, and several of the men picked up the victim of civilisation, the modern galley-slave, still covered with the sweat of his fearful occupation. With the handkerchief about his head, he looked as if he were suffering from toothache. They carried him up out of the glowing pit to the cabin set aside for dead bodies.

Doctor Wilhelm had to notify the captain. Nobody on deck, where the band was playing the last measures, was to suspect that a stoker had died. With the help of the Red Cross sister, they stretched him on a mattress, and within a short time a circle of the higher officials of the vessel, at their head the captain, and among them the purser and the physicians, were gathered about the corpse.

Captain von Kessel ordered the stoker's death to be kept secret, particularly requesting the two physicians not to mention it. Formalities had to be gone through, documents had to be drawn up and signed. This kept them busy until dark, when the first call for dinner was trumpeted across the deck and through the gangways of the first-class section.

XXVIII

Frederick went to his cabin and removed the grey suit he had worn in the purgatory of the stoke-hole. He put on striped trousers, a black waistcoat, and black frock coat. By the time he appeared in the dining-room, a lively procession of brilliant toilettes was already making its way there. Almost all the ladies of the first class came rustling in. Frederick from his seat observed that many of them had to stop for an instant at the doorway to pluck up their courage. Then, with a charmingly humorous smile, they would conquer their dread of seasickness, particularly threatening in the dining-room, and step over the threshold.

Save for the slight quiver that ran through the walls and ceilings of the whole vessel, its motion was scarcely perceptible. The music began, and the swarm of stewards in livery, who came hurrying in, could serve each guest with a full plate of soup without need of balancing.

"A full-dress dinner," said the captain with a contented glance about the room as he seated himself.

Fish was already being served when Ingigerd entered on the arm of the very ungainly and very ordinary looking Achleitner. At the sight of her absurd get-up, Frederick felt like sinking through the floor. The barber had piled her beautiful light hair into a fearful mountain of puffs, and about her narrow shoulders she wore a Spanish shawl, as if to represent Carmen--a very pitiful Carmen, who provoked jeers and jibes from one end of the table to the other.

"What deadly green stockings!" Frederick thought, as he choked down a piece of fish with the bones in it.

"Why in the name of sense does she wear those bronze slippers?"

"Some chalk, please, for the lady," said one man. "She is going to dance the tight rope for us."

Mischievous looks and remarks flew about the table. Both the ladies and the gentlemen choked over their fish or wine and had to hold their napkins to their lips. Not all of their remarks were pronounced **sotto voce**, and among the card players, who were again drinking champagne, the jokes aimed at Ingigerd and Achleitner were particularly loud and coarse.

Could Frederick believe his eyes? Terror shot to his heart. That sad little monstrosity was walking toward him--stood next to him in compromising intimacy--was saying poutingly:

"When are you going to pay me a visit again?"

Frederick made some inconsequential reply.

Necks in standing collars, bare throats encircled with gold chains and pearls turned toward the captain's table. Frederick could not recall ever having had an experience so painfully humiliating. Ingigerd saw nothing and felt nothing. Achleitner, however, seemed to be rather ill at ease under the perceptible cross-fire of the animated company, and tried to lead her away. Finally, she left the tortured man, saying:

"My, you're dull and stupid! I don't like you." At which the captain's corner burst into a prolonged laugh, which was a relief to everybody's but Frederick's feelings.

"I assure you," said Frederick, with a tolerable attempt at dry irony, "I don't know what I have done to deserve this distinction, or what I shall do to deserve it in the future."

Then they spoke of other things.

The clear weather and the prospect of a peaceful night filled the festive diners with undimmed gaiety. They ate, they drank, they laughed, they flirted, all in the delightful consciousness that they were citizens of the departing nineteenth century, with the probability of being citizens of the even grander twentieth century.

XXIX

After dinner the two physicians went to Doctor Wilhelm's cabin, where they sat together discussing the resultant of modern civilisation.

"I very much fear, very much, indeed," said Frederick, "that our world-wide means of communication, which mankind is supposed to own, really own mankind. At least so far, I see no signs that the tremendous working capacity of machines has lessened human labour. Nobody will deny that our modern machine slavery, on so tremendous a scale, is the most imposing slavery that has ever existed. And there is no denying that it is slavery. Has this age of machinery subtracted from the sum of human misery? No, most emphatically, no! Has it enhanced happiness and increased the chances for happiness? No, again."

"That is why every three or four men of culture," said Doctor Wilhelm, "are disciples of Schopenhauer. Modern Buddhism is making rapid strides."

"Yes," said Frederick, "because we are living in a world all the time making a tremendous impression upon itself. As a result, it is getting to be more and more fearfully bored. The man of the intellectual middle class is gaining in prominence, while he is more mediocre than he has been in any previous age. At the same time he is glutted and more blase. No form of idealism, no sort of genuinely great belief can hold its ground any longer."

"I admit," said Wilhelm, "that the great industrial corporation, civilisation, is parsimonious of everything except human lives and the best that is in the human being. It places no value upon them. It lets them rot. But I think there is one comfort. I think civilisation possesses this one good, that it breaks us away once for all with the worst savageries of the past. No inquisition, for instance, can ever be possible again."

"Are you sure of it?" asked Frederick. "Don't you think it is strange that alongside the greatest achievements of science, alongside Galileo, Kepler, Laplace; alongside the spectrum analysis and the law of the conservation of energy; alongside Kirchoff and Bunsen; alongside steam, gas, electricity, the blindest and most antiquated superstitions still survive, powerful as ever? I am not so certain that backsliding into the most horrible times of the *Malleus maleficarum* is impossible."

Doctor Wilhelm had rung for a steward, who now entered. Max Pander appeared at the same time.

"Doctor von Kammacher, I feel as if we must have some champagne. Adolph," turning to the steward, "a bottle of Pommery."

"They're making a big hole in the champagne cellar," said Adolph.

"Of course. The people are all celebrating their escape from drowning yesterday and day before yesterday."

Pander had come at the captain's order for the stoker's death certificate. The document was lying ready in the medicine closet. After Pander had left, Wilhelm told Frederick some remarkable incidents of the dead man.

"His name was Zickelmann. There was the beginning of a letter in his pocket. It was something like this: 'Dear mother, I have not seen you for sixteen years. I have forgotten how you look, dear mother. I am not doing well, but I must go to America to see you once again. It is very sad when a man has no relatives in the whole world. Dear mother, I just want to look at you, and I really won't be a burden to you.'"

The champagne appeared. Before long, the first bottle was replaced by the second.

"Don't be surprised if I am immoderate," said Frederick. "My nerves are in need of it to-day. I have to stupefy myself. Perhaps, with the help of this glorious medicine, I shall be able to sleep a few hours."

It was half past ten, and the physicians were still sitting together. The wine naturally produced a greater degree of intimacy between these two men, who were of the same profession and had already become fairly well acquainted with each other. It was very pleasant to Frederick to unbosom himself.

He said he had entered the world with too favourable a preconceived notion. In a spirit of idealism he had refused the military career for which his father had intended him, and had taken up the study of medicine, in the belief that he would thus be of most service to humanity. He had been deceived.

"The genuine gardener works for the garden full of healthy plants; but our work is devoted to a decaying vegetation sprung from diseased germs. That is why I took up the fight against mankind's awfullest enemy, the bacteria. I admit that the dreary, patient, laborious work, which bacteriology requires, did not satisfy me, either. I didn't possess the capacity to petrify, which is absolutely indispensable in an academic man. When I was sixteen years old, I wanted to become a painter. Over the dissecting table, I composed verses. The thing that I should now most like to be is a freelance writer. From all of which you can see," he concluded, laughing ironically, "that I have made rather a mess of my life."

Wilhelm refused to admit it.

"But I have," Frederick declared. "I am a genuine child of the times, and I am not ashamed of it. The greatest intellects of the day are all in a state of inner ferment. Every individual of significance is just as divided against himself as humanity on the whole. I refer, of course, only to the leading European races. I embody the Pope and Luther, William II and Robespierre, Bismarck and Bebel, the spirit of the American millionaire and the enthusiasm for poverty that was the glory of St. Francis of Assisi. I am the maddest progressive of my time and the maddest reactionary. I despise Americanism, and yet I see in the great American world-invasion, the dominion of the exploiter, something similar to one of the biggest works that Hercules performed in the Augean stables."

"Here's to chaos!" cried Wilhelm.

They touched glasses.

"Yes," said Frederick, "but only if it gives birth to a dancing heaven, or, at least, a dancing star."

"Beware of dancing stars," said Wilhelm, laughing and looking at Frederick significantly.

"What can a man do if his blood is on fire with that cursed poison?"

Under the influence of the champagne, the sudden confession seemed as natural to Wilhelm as to Frederick.

"'There once was a rat in a cellar hole,'" Wilhelm quoted.

"Of course, of course," said Frederick, "but what is to be done against it?" Then he turned the conversation to general questions again. "Why should a man keep himself intact when he has lost his ideals? I have made ***tabula rasa*** of my past. I have drowned Germany in the ocean. Is Germany really the great, strong, united Empire? Is it not rather the booty over which God and the devil--I was about to say the Kaiser and the Pope--are still wrangling? You will admit that for more than a thousand years, the unifying principle was the imperial principle. People talk of the Thirty Years' War as having disintegrated Germany. I should say it was the thousand years' war, of which the Thirty Years' War was only the worst excess, the worst paroxysm of that plague of religious dissension with which the Germans are inoculated. And without unity, Germany is a very queer structure. Its owners, or its inhabitants, don't possess it, except in a slight degree. And the believer with the tiara at Rome tugs and tugs at it, levying extortion under the threat of destroying the entire structure; until he is actually able to buy it back with the compound interest that has been accumulating. In that case nothing will be left but a heap of ruins. One could shriek and tear one's hair because the German does not see that in his basement there is an awful Bluebeard's chamber. And not for women alone. He has no inkling of what an arsenal of clerical instruments of torture lie there ready for use--clerical, because they lie ready for the infliction of horrible corporal martyrdom in the service of a bloody, fanatical, papistical belief. Woe, when the door to the Bluebeard chamber opens. They are continually picking at the lock. Then we shall witness all the sanguinary horrors of the Thirty Years' War, the degenerate slaughter-house cruelty of an inquisition."

"That's something we won't drink a toast to. Rather let us toast the healthy, cynically outspoken ideal of the American, the exploiter ideal, with its tolerance and levelling down."

"Yes, a thousand times rather," said Frederick.

So they drank a toast to America.

A second-cabin stewardess led in the Russian Jewess. The girl was holding a handkerchief to her nose and mouth. Her nose had been bleeding for an hour without cease.

"Oh," she said, retreating a step from the threshold back to the deck, "I am in the way." But Doctor Wilhelm insisted on her coming in.

It turned out that this was not the real mission on which the stewardess had come to see Doctor Wilhelm. She whispered a few words, unintelligible to the others, into his ear. He excused himself to Frederick, asked him to look after the Jewess, and left the cabin with the stewardess.

XXX

"You are a doctor?" asked the Russian Jewess.

"Yes," said Frederick.

Without wasting many words, he made her lie prone on the couch, inserted a tampon in her nose, and used other means to stanch the flow of blood. He had kept the door to the deck open to let the cigarette smoke out and the fresh, healing salt air in. The girl lay quietly on the couch; and Frederick thought it advisable to look through one of Wilhelm's medical books.

"So far as I am concerned, you may smoke," she said after a while, having noticed that Frederick absent-mindedly started to light a cigarette several times and then, recollecting himself, desisted.

"No," he said curtly, "I won't smoke now."

"You might at least offer me a cigarette," she said. "I am bored."

"That's proper," he said. "A patient should be bored."

"Oh, I am not a patient."

"Patientia is the Latin for 'patience,' my dear young lady. You are not a patient in so far as you are very impatient."

"If you let me have a cigarette, then I will say 'Yes, you are right.'"

"I know I am right, and there can be no question of your smoking now."

"But I want to smoke. You are impolite," she said, obstinately kicking up her heel.

Frederick ordered her to be quiet, and she let her foot drop again on the leather upholstery. He looked at her with an intentionally exaggerated expression of sternness.

"I am not your slave, do you understand? Do you think I left Odessa, where there is enough ordering about, to be ordered about by every stranger I meet?" she grumbled. "I am cold. Please shut the door."

"If you want, I will shut the door," said Frederick, getting up to do so with an air of resignation not altogether genuine.

In the morning in the steerage, Frederick and this Deborah had exchanged a glowing look of understanding. Now, although, or perhaps because, the wine was in his veins, he was eager for Doctor Wilhelm's return. His absence seemed to be unduly prolonged. For a time the girl lay silent. Frederick found it necessary to examine the tampon in her nostril. As he was doing so, he noticed tears in her eyes.

"What is the matter?" he asked. "Why are you crying?"

She suddenly began to beat him with her arms and fists, called him a sleek, heartless bourgeois, and wanted to jump up; but she had to succumb to Frederick's superior, gentle strength and return to her reclining posture. Frederick seated himself as before on an upholstered chair opposite the couch.

"My dear child," he said, very gently, "you are behaving queerly, slinging about those honourable epithets. But we won't discuss that. You are nervous. You are excited. You have no blood in your veins, and even if you had a stronger constitution, the condition of your nerves after the hardships of this trip, especially in the steerage, could scarcely be different."

"I'll never travel first class, never!"

"Why not?"

"Because, considering the misery in which the majority of human beings are languishing, it is a mean low thing to do to travel first class. Read Dostoievsky, read Tolstoy, read Kropotkin! We are being chased like animals. We are being persecuted. It doesn't matter where we die."

"It may interest you to know that I have read them all, Kropotkin, Tolstoy, Dostoievsky. But don't suppose you are the only persecuted person on earth. I am persecuted, too. We are all persecuted."

"Oh, you are travelling first class and you are not a Jew. I am a Jew. Have you the faintest idea of what it means to be a Jew in Russia?"

"That is why you and I are now travelling to a new world," said Frederick, "to America, the land of liberty."

"Indeed!" she sneered, "I and liberty! I know my fate. Don't you know into what hands I have fallen? I am the victim of vile exploiters!"

The girl cried, and since she was young and of the same delicacy of figure as Ingigerd, only of a very different race, a dark-haired, dark-eyed race, Frederick felt himself perceptibly weakening. His compassion grew; and he was well aware that openly expressed sympathy is the surest approach to love. So he again forced himself into a hard, repellent attitude of opposition.

"Now I am nothing but a physician representing another physician. What does it concern me, and how can I help it, if you have fallen into the hands of exploiters? Besides, all of you intellectual Russians are hysterical--a trait utterly repugnant to me."

She jumped to her feet and wanted to run away. To restrain her he caught first her right, then her left wrist. She looked at him with such an expression of hate and contempt that he could not but be sensitive of the girl's passionate beauty. Her face was of the colour that greensickness imparts. Her features were exquisitely delicate. In contrast, Ingigerd's face, with which Frederick fleetingly compared hers, seemed unrefined, even coarse. Here was the aristocracy of a too highly bred race, somewhat faded, to be sure, but at that moment all the more seductive.

"Ugh! Let me go, let me go, I say!"

"What have I done to you?" Frederick asked. For a moment he was genuinely alarmed, scarcely knowing whether he had not been actually guilty of a wrong against her. He had been drinking champagne and was excited. If someone were to enter now, what would he think of him? Even centuries before, had not Potiphar's wife, from whom Joseph fled, resorted to certain successful slanderous means? "What have I done?" he repeated.

"Nothing," she said, "except what you are in the habit of doing. You have insulted an unprotected girl."

"Are you crazy?" he asked.

Suddenly she answered: "I don't know." And in that instant the hard, hateful expression of her face melted, turning into complete submission, a change that went irresistibly to the heart of a man like Frederick. He forgot himself. He was no longer master of his feelings.

XXXI

This strange incident of meeting, seeing, loving, and parting forever had passed swiftly as in a dream. Since Wilhelm had not yet returned, Frederick, long after his visitor had fled, went out on deck, where the exalted impression of the starry heavens shining over the infinite expanse of the ocean, purified him, as it were. He was neither by nature nor by habit a Don Juan, and it astonished him that the unusual, surprising adventure seemed the most natural thing in the world.

The deck was empty. Another boy was on guard in Pander's place. The temperature had sunk to below freezing-point, and a thick coating of hoar-frost lay on the rigging.

As he stood leaning over the railing, he had a painful vision of the sum total of life and death within the eons of life on earth. His innermost being smarted with the pain of it. Death must have existed before the beginning. Death and death! That was the limit, he thought, of vast sums of trouble, hope, desire, enjoyment--enjoyment which forthwith consumed itself to make way for renewed desire, for illusions of possession, for realities of loss, for anguish, for conflicts, for meetings and partings; all uncontrollable processes bound up with suffering and fresh suffering and suffering again. It gave him some satisfaction to assume that now that the passage was so smooth, his Deborah and all her companions in suffering were probably lying wrapt in unconscious sleep, for a time relieved of the great madness of life.

While waiting for Doctor Wilhelm, absorbed in these reflections, Frederick involuntarily turned away from the edge of the deck, and became aware of a dark mass not far from the smoke-stack, cowering in a corner against the wall. The thing looked strange to him. On stepping closer he saw it was a man on the floor asleep, wrapped in his overcoat with his cap drawn over his eyes, his bearded head resting on a low camp-chair. Frederick was convinced it was Achleitner. Why was he lying there in the freezing cold instead of in bed? Frederick found the right answer. Not more than three paces away was the door of Ingigerd's cabin; and he was the faithful dog in three senses, the watchdog, the Cerberus, the dog crazed with the rabies of jealousy.

"Poor fellow," Frederick said aloud. "Poor, stupid Achleitner!" He felt genuine, almost tender sympathy; and over him came all the woe of the deceived lover, as we can trace it from Nietzsche and Schopenhauer down to Buddha Gotama, whose pupil, Ananda, asks: "Master, how shall we comport ourselves toward a woman?" Quoth the master: "Avoid the sight of her, Ananda, because a woman's being is hidden. It is unfathomable as the way of the fish in the water. To her, lying is as truth, and truth as lying."

"Sst! What are you doing here?" said Doctor Wilhelm, stepping up softly. He was carrying something in his hands carefully wrapped up.

"Do you know who is lying here?" said Frederick. "It is Achleitner."

"He wanted to keep his eye on that cabin," Wilhelm remarked cynically, "to limit the attendance."

"We must wake him up."

"Why?" said Wilhelm. "Later, when we go to bed."

"I am going to bed now."

"Come to my cabin first for a moment."

In his cabin the physician laid a human embryo on the table.

"She has attained her end," he said, meaning the girl travelling second class, who in his opinion had taken the trip for no other purpose than to rid herself of her burden and avoid disgrace. At the sight of the little object, Frederick did not know whether to be born or never to awaken to life was preferable.

He went out on deck again, aroused Achleitner, and led him to his cabin, resisting and mumbling incomprehensible words, though half asleep. Then, in dread of the agonies of insomnia, he went to his own cabin.

XXXII

He fell asleep immediately, but when he awoke, it was only two o'clock. The ship was still moving easily, and he could hear the screw working regularly under the water. Life in times of great physical crises is a fever, which travelling and sleeplessness enhance. Frederick well knew his own nature, and was alarmed when he saw himself robbed of the peace of sleep after so short a time.

But had his sleep actually meant peace? Lying on his back with wide, staring eyes, he saw vast nocturnal spaces of his soul opened up, where in bottomless depths another chaotic life had been born--a multitude of tormenting visions, in which things and persons most familiar had arisen in combination with things and persons entirely strange. He tried to recall his dreams.

He had dreamed he was wandering hand in hand with Achleitner among the dark smoke widows trailing backward over the ocean from the funnels of the ***Roland***, far, far away. He and the Russian Jewess together with great difficulty dragged the dead stoker, Zickelmann, up into the blue ladies' parlour; and by means of a serum, which he himself had discovered, he brought him back to life. He smoothed over a quarrel between the Russian Jewess and Ingigerd Hahlstroem, who fought and called each other abusive names. He was sitting with Doctor Wilhelm in his cabin, and, as Wagner once had done, was observing a homunculus still undergoing embryonic development in a glass sphere on which light was shining. At the same time Ingigerd's cockatoo was squawking in Arthur Stoss's voice and continually asseverating:

"I am already a man of absolutely independent fortune. I am touring simply to bring my fortune up to a certain amount."

Under the impression that he was recalling these things to his memory, Frederick was really dreaming again. Suddenly he started up, cuffing Hans Fuellenberg furiously and saying: "I'll box your ears." Shortly afterward he was in the smoking-room delivering a crushing sermon for the third or fourth time, morally felling to the ground the man who had desecrated his sacred relation to Ingigerd. But the captain came in, and said they had to bury the stoker. There was a dead man on board. When Frederick stepped from the smoking-room, he saw the corpse lying in the coffin. It was not Zickelmann, the stoker, but Angele, his suffering, neglected wife, in one of her hysterical attacks in which she lay in a trance. And it was not at the entrance to the smoking-room, but in Plassenberg in the Heuscheuer, in front of his comfortable house. Captain von Kessel was standing in the garden clipping a privet hedge. It was at night, but a full moon was shining bright as day over the lonely valley meadows in front of his house. Angele arose and Frederick went to lead her into the house. She resisted. Now the consciousness of his spiritual separation from her filled him with infinite sadness, a sadness more bitter and profound than any that had ever inspired him in his waking moments.

"I am a mother," said Angele, "but not by you."

He embraced her, weeping, and wanted to draw her into his house. She resisted gently, but firmly, and declared she was forbidden to enter. He saw her wandering across the meadows in the moonshine, slowly and wearily.

"Angele!" he cried. He ran after her.

"It is so hard for me," she said, "because life and not death has robbed me of you."

Frederick groaned aloud. A great stone seemed to be lying on his breast. He heard the rushing of waters. He saw the flood come leaping through all the valleys, over the tops of all the hills, wave upon wave, from all sides. The moon was shining. He saw Angele climb to a little skiff lying moored somewhere; and the tide carried away the skiff with her in it. The waters overwhelmed his house.

Again the wandering began, hand in hand with Achleitner and the smoke widows across the ocean desert. Again began that difficult dragging up-stairs and down-stairs of the naked, dead stoker, with the help of the young admirer of Kropotkin. The dispute between Ingigerd and Deborah, his sermonising of Fuellenberg and the man in the smoking-room repeated themselves, each repetition intensifying his torment. The homunculus in the glass sphere in Doctor Wilhelm's cabin appeared again. It developed with light thrown on it. In his anguish, in his impotence against that martyrising chase of visions, Frederick's persecuted soul, gasping for peace, suddenly rose in revolt, and he said aloud:

"Kindle the light of reason, kindle the light of reason, O God in heaven!"

He rose in his berth, and saw that Rosa, the servant-girl, was in reality holding a burning candle over him. She bent down slightly, and said:

"You are dreaming hard. Aren't you feeling well, Doctor von Kammacher?"

The door creaked. The servant-girl Rosa had left. The ship was moving quietly. Or was he mistaken? Was the *Roland* no longer proceeding so calmly and steadily as before? He listened intently, and heard the screw whirring regularly under the water. Monotonous calls penetrated from the deck. Then came the loud rattling of the cinders pouring overboard. Frederick looked at his watch. It was five o'clock. So three hours had passed since he had first awakened! Again, with a clatter and a thunder, a load of ashes slid into the Atlantic Ocean. Was it not the mates of the dead stoker, Zickelmann, who were throwing it overboard? Frederick heard the crying of children, thereupon the sobbing and whimpering of his hysterical neighbour, and finally Rosa's voice, trying to quiet Siegfried and Ella, who was a talkative little girl. Siegfried was fretfully begging to be taken back to his grandmother in Luckenwalde. Mrs. Liebling was scolding Rosa, telling her she was responsible for the children's behaviour. Frederick heard her say:

"You all trample about on my nerves. I wish the three of you were at the bottom of the sea. For heaven's sake, let me sleep!"

XXXIII

Notwithstanding all these impressions, Frederick fell asleep again. He dreamed that he and Rosa, the maid, and little Siegfried Liebling were in a life-boat, rocking on a calm, shimmering green sea. Strangely enough, there was a mass of gold ingots in the bottom of the boat, probably the gold ingots that the *Roland* was supposed to be carrying to the mint in Washington. Frederick was at the helm, and after cruising about a while, they reached a bright, cheery port. It may have been a port in the Azores, or the Madeira Islands, or the Canary Islands. At a short distance from the quay, Rosa jumped overboard and reached land holding Siegfried clear of the water. People received them, and they disappeared in one of the snowy white buildings at the harbour front. When Frederick landed, to his joy he was greeted on the marble steps of the quay by his old friend, Peter Schmidt, the physician he intended to visit in America. In response to curious questions, he always said that this was his main purpose in crossing the ocean. His delight at seeing him in a dream, in the setting of the white tropical town, after a separation of eight or nine years, was a surprise to himself. How was it possible that he had only occasionally and superficially remembered so magnificent a man, so dear a youthful companion?

Peter Schmidt was a Friesian. He and Frederick had sat together on the same school bench; later, they had spent two years together in the gymnasium at St. Magdalene at Breslau and several semesters in the universities of Greifswald, Breslau, and Zuerich. Owing to a combination of common sense, many-sided knowledge, and humanitarian enthusiasm, Peter Schmidt had exerted great influence on his friends. There was also an adventurous streak in his nature, inherited from his father, a Friesian colonist, who lay buried in a churchyard in Meriden, Connecticut.

"It is good that you have come," said Peter Schmidt. Frederick felt as if he had been long expecting him. "Your wife, Angele, just arrived in a skiff."

His friend silently led him to an inn near the harbour. A sense of security such as he had never before felt came over him. While he took a little luncheon in the dining-room, where the host, a German, stood opposite, twirling his thumbs, Peter Schmidt explained:

"The town is not large, but it will give you an idea of the country. You will find people here that are contented and have made their last landing."

It was taken as a matter of course that there, in that strange, silent city in the dazzling sunlight, the fewest possible words were to be spoken. Some new, mute inner sense appeared to make meanings clear. Nevertheless, Frederick said:

"I've always taken you for the mentor in unknown depths of our predestination." By which he meant to express his awe at his friend's mysterious being.

"Yes," said Peter Schmidt, "but this is only a small beginning, though enough to indicate what is hidden under the surface here."

Peter Schmidt, born in Tondern, now led Frederick out to the harbour. It was a very small harbour. There were a number of ancient vessels lying half-sunk in the water.

"Fourteen-ninety-two," said Peter Schmidt. That was the year the four hundredth anniversary of which was being much discussed by the Americans on board the *Roland*. The Friesian pointed to both the half-submerged caravels and explained that one of them was the *Santa Maria*, Christopher Columbus's flag-ship. "I came over with Christopher Columbus," he said.

All this was unqualifiedly enlightening to Frederick. Nor was there anything enigmatic in Peter Schmidt's explanation that the wood of those slowly decaying caravels was called *legno santo* and was used for fuel, because it contained the spirit of knowledge. Farther out to sea lay a third vessel, with a great, black breach forward on the port side.

"It sank," said the Friesian. "It brought in a great lot of people."

Frederick looked at the vessel. He was dissatisfied. He would have liked to ask questions about the unfamiliar, yet curiously familiar ship out there at sea; but the Friesian left the harbour and turned into a narrow, crooked street with a steep flight of stairs.

Here an old uncle of Frederick, who had been dead more than fifteen years, came toward him comfortably puffing at a pipe. He had just arisen, it seemed, from a bench by the open entrance to his house.

"How do you do?" he said. "We are all here, my boy." Frederick knew whom the old man meant when he said, "We are all here." "We fare very well," the old man, who in his lifetime had not been exactly favoured by fortune, continued, grinning. "I didn't get along so well when I was up with you in the dismal air. In the first place, my boy, we have the *legno santo*." With his pipe he pointed to the dark interior of his house, where blue tongues of flame were leaping on the hearth. "And besides, we have the Toilers of the Light. But I am detaining you. *We* have time, but *you* must hurry." Frederick said good-bye. "Fiddlesticks!" exclaimed his uncle. "Do you people down there still keep up that tiresome business of 'how-do-you-do' and 'good-bye'?"

Climbing higher up the street, Peter Schmidt led Frederick through a number of houses and inside courtyards. In one of the courtyards with many corners, reminding Frederick of certain ancient sections of Hamburg and Nuremberg, was a ship-chandlery bearing the sign, "The Seagoing Ship."

"Everything here looks quite ordinary," said Peter Schmidt, "but here we have all the ancient models." He pointed to the small model of an ancient vessel standing in the little window of the chandlery, among packages of chewing tobacco and leather whips.

Ships, ships, nothing but ships! The sight of this last vessel seemed to produce the beginning of a slight gnawing resistance in Frederick's brain. He knew he was looking upon an all-embracing symbol, which he had never before seen. With a new sense organ, with centralised clarity of thought, he realised that here, in this little model, was comprehended all the wandering and adventuring of the human soul.

"Oh," said the chandler, opening the glass door of the little shop, at which all sorts of wares hanging on the door swung to and fro with a clatter, "Oh, you here, Frederick? I thought you were still at sea."

Frederick recognised the chandler as George Rasmussen, whose farewell letter he had received in Southampton. He was dressed in a shabby cap and dressing-gown belonging to a confectioner long dead, whom he had known when a boy. Mysterious as it all was, there was yet something natural in this meeting with his friend. The little shop was alive with goldfinches. "They are the goldfinches," Rasmussen explained, "that settled in the Heuscheuer Mountains last winter, you know, and were fatal to me."

"Yes, I remember," said Frederick. "We would approach a bare branch or tree, and suddenly it would seem to shake itself and scatter thousands of gold leaves. We interpreted it as auguring mountains of money."

"Well," said the chandler, "it was precisely thirteen minutes past one on the twenty-fourth of January when I drew my last breath. I had just received your telegram from Paris absolving me from my debt. Back there in the shop, among other things, is my predecessor's fur coat, which--I am by no means complaining--infected me. I wrote you that if I could, I would make myself noticeable from the Beyond. Well, here I am. But even here everything isn't perfectly clear and plain, though I am feeling better, and we all rest in a pleasant sense of basic security. I'm glad you and Peter Schmidt have met. He counts for a lot here in this country.' You will meet each other above again, in New York, at the celebration of the four hundredth anniversary of 1492. Good Lord! Of what significance after all, is that little discovery of America?" Rasmussen in his strange disguise removed the miniature vessel from the show window. It, too, was called the **Santa Maria**. "Now, please be careful," he said. Frederick noticed that the old confectioner took one vessel after another of the same sort, but diminishing in size, from the first one. "Patience," he said, while still pulling more and more vessels from the entrails of the **Santa Maria**. The procedure caused Frederick no slight astonishment. "Patience. The smaller are always the better ones. If I had time, we should reach the smallest, the final, the most glorious work of Providence. Each one of these ships carries us not only beyond the boundaries of our planet, but even beyond the limited barriers of our senses. Each of them is adapted to carry us across the border. If you are interested," he continued, "I have other wares in my shop. Here are the captain's hedge-scissors, here is a plummet with which one can sound the lowest depths of the firmament and the Milky Way. Here are the tropics of Cancer and Capricorn. But you have no time, and I won't detain you."

The chandler closed the glass door on them; but they saw him with his nose flattened against the pane, mysteriously, as if he still had something to sell, holding his finger to his mouth, shaped like a carp's. His lips seemed to be framing certain words. Frederick understood *legno santo*, Toilers of the Light, and even what his uncle had said about "up with you in the dismal air." But Peter Schmidt thrust his fist through the glass door, pulled Rasmussen's embroidered cap off his head, took from it a little key, and beckoned Frederick to come away with him. They left the houses behind and stepped out into the open rolling country.

"The thing is," said Peter, "it will mean a lot of trouble."

And they ran and climbed for hours. Evening fell. They lit a fire, and slept in a tree rocking in the wind. Morning came. They took to wandering again, until the sun lay low on the horizon. Finally, Peter opened a small gate in a low wall. On the other side of the wall was a garden. A gardener was tying vines.

"How do you do, Doctor?" he said. "The sun is setting, but we know why we die."

On looking at him more closely, Frederick recognised the dead stoker in the man, whose face was illuminated by the rosy flush of the setting sun and wore a friendly smile, as he stood there in what was a strange garden, or vineyard, or fairyland.

"I'd rather be doing this than shovelling coal," said the stoker, pointing to the cords hanging in his hands, with which he had been tying up the vines.

The three of them together now walked a rather long distance to a wild section of the garden, where it had turned completely dark. The wind began to rush, and the shrubs, trees and bushes of the garden swished like breakers on the shore. The stoker beckoned to them, and they squatted on the ground in a circle. It seemed as if the stoker with his bare hand had taken a bit of burning wood from his pocket. He held it close to the ground, to illuminate a round opening, something like the burrow of a marmot or a rabbit.

"Legno santo," said Peter Schmidt, pointing to the glowing piece of charcoal. "Now, Frederick, you will get to see those ant-like little elves that are called *noctiluci* or night-lights. They pompously call themselves Toilers of the Light. But whatever their name, it must be admitted that they are the ones that take the light hidden in the entrails of the earth, store it up, and sow it in fields, the soil of which has been especially prepared; and when it has grown to its full size and has borne fruit a hundredfold in the shape of gold sheaves or nuggets, they harvest it and save it for the darkest of dark times."

And, actually, looking through a crevice, Frederick saw something like another world, with a subterranean sun shining on it. A multitude of little elves, the Toilers of the Light, were mowing with scythes, cutting stalks, binding sheaves, loading carts, and storing in barns. Many cut the light out of the ground, like nuggets of gold. Undoubtedly it was the gold meant for the mint in Washington that was haunting Frederick's dreams.

"These Toilers of the Light," said the Friesian, Peter Schmidt, "are the most stimulating to my ideas."

At this point Frederick awoke, while the voice of the stoker close beside him was saying:

"Many will soon be following me."

XXXIV

The first thing Frederick did on waking was to look at his watch. He had a dull feeling that he must have slept through the whole night and even the following day. He peered at the hands incredulously and held the watch to his ear to convince himself it had not stopped. No, it was still running. Consequently, since his last waking, only six or, at the utmost, eight minutes had passed.

This fact as well as the peculiarity and the vividness of his dream set him to marvelling. He could not recall ever having dreamed so coherently and logically. Are there dreams that are more than dreams? Was Rasmussen dead? Had his friend, keeping his promise, chosen this way to make himself noticeable from the Beyond? A strange shudder went through Frederick. In his excitement it seemed to him that he had been honoured with a revelation. He took his memorandum book from the net bag over his berth and jotted down the date and hour that the remarkable chandler had mentioned as the time of his death. "Thirteen minutes past one," he distinctly heard Rasmussen's voice saying, "thirteen minutes past one, on the twenty-fourth of January."

The **Roland** was tossing slightly again, and the great siren was bellowing. Its repeated thunderous cries, which indicated fog, the lurching of the vessel, the sign, perhaps, of fresh storms and hardships to be gone through, vexed and fretted Frederick. From the adventurous doings in his brain, he was transported to the no less adventurous doings in reality. Awakening from his dreams, he found himself locked into a narrow cabin, plowing through the high seas, on a vessel heavily freighted with the fearful dreams of many souls, and yet not sinking from the load of that cargo.

Frederick was already on deck before half past five. The fog had lifted, and from over the edge of a leaden sea of moderate-sized waves rose the dawn of a gloomy morning. The deck was empty, producing the impression of dreary loneliness. The passengers were all lying in their berths. None of the crew even were visible. It looked as if the mighty ship were pursuing its course wholly without human agency.

XXXV

Frederick was standing near the log-line, which dragged in the broad, churning wake. Even in the ghostly dawn, hungry gulls were following the ship, sometimes flying near, sometimes dropping back, ever and anon swooping down into the foamy wake with a mournful cry, as of condemned souls. This was no vision, and yet Frederick scarcely distinguished it from a dream. With his nerves unstrung, with his being still penetrated by the marvels of his sleeping life, which remained partially present to him, the strange heaving waste of the ocean seemed no less miraculous than his dreams. Thus the ocean had been tossing its mountains of waves beneath the blind eyes of millions of years, itself no less blind than those eons. Thus and not otherwise had it been since the first day of creation: "In the beginning God created the heaven and the earth. And the earth was without form, and void; and darkness was upon the face of the deep. And the Spirit of God moved upon the face of the waters."

Frederick shivered. Had he ever lived with anything else than a spirit and spirits, that is, with ghosts? And at this moment was he not farther removed than ever from what is considered immovable solid ground, from what is called reality? In his state of mind, did he not believe in fairy tales, sailors' superstitions, the Flying Dutchman, and hobgoblins? What was that ocean hiding in its infinite waves rolling under the low, grey sky? Had not everything arisen from the ocean? Had not everything gone down into its depths again? Had some power disclosed the submerged Atlantis to Frederick's mental vision? Why not?

He was passing through profound, enigmatic moments of a fearful yet pleasurable dread. There was the ocean, on which an apparently abandoned vessel, a small spot in infinity, was staggering forward with no visible goal ahead and no visible starting-point behind. There were the heavens lying heavily upon it, grey and dismal. There was Frederick himself, alone. Every animate creature in that solitude was transformed in his soul into visions, phantoms and apparitions. Man is always facing the unfathomable alone. That gives him a sense of greatness along with a sense of desertion. There was a man standing at the stern of a vessel, while the darkness of night was yielding to the dawn, bound by the invisible, glowing threads of his fate to two continents of the globe, and awaiting the new, less tormenting form of life that comes from the sun, a strange star millions of miles removed from the planet earth. All this was a miracle to Frederick, almost overwhelming him, as if he were imprisoned in marvels. In a sudden seizure of hopelessness that he would ever throw off the suffocating oppression of riddles and miracles, the temptation came upon him to leap over the railing. Close upon this feeling followed the timidity of a man with a bad conscience. He glanced about, as if in fear of discovery. He wiped his eyes and forehead with his hands, because it seemed to him that the dead stoker with the bloody wound had for a long time been sitting nearby on a coil of rope. His chest felt heavy, as if a load were dragging it down. He heard voices. He saw his wife, Angele, wringing her hands. Suddenly he thought he was to blame for her illness, that he was a criminal; and all his thoughts of Ingigerd Hahlstroem made him doubly despicable in his own eyes. His ideas grew confused. In a wave of absolute credulity, he thought the voice of his conscience was condemning him to death. He thought that his life was being demanded as an atonement, that he must sacrifice himself, or else the *Roland*, with all it carried, would sink.

At that moment Frederick heard a strong voice saying:

"Good morning, Doctor von Kammacher."

It was the first mate, Von Halm, on his way to the bridge. Before the healthy beauty of the human voice, the haunting visions instantly fled, and Frederick's soul was restored to sanity.

"Were you making deep-sea researches?" Von Halm asked.

"Yes," said Frederick with a laugh, "I was about to make a sounding for the submerged Atlantis. What do you think of the weather?"

The giant was wearing his sou'wester and oilskin. He pointed to the barometer. Frederick saw it had dropped considerably. Adolph, the steward, came in search of Frederick. Having failed to find him in his cabin, he was bringing him his zwieback and large peasant cup of tea on deck. Frederick seated himself on the same bench as the day before, opposite the companionway. He sipped the cordial drink and warmed his hands on the cup.

Before he had finished, the wind was again beginning to boom in the rigging of the four masts, and a stiff, obstinate wind was heeling the vessel to starboard. Frederick set to bargaining inwardly, as if he had to reckon with the powers on account of the new hardships to be gone through. He suddenly longed to be with Peter Schmidt in America. Since his dream, it seemed more and more important for him to see, and associate with, his old comrade again. He thought he was rid of Ingigerd, the more surely as she had played no part at all in the momentous Atlantis dream. The sooner the voyage with her ended the better.

XXXVI

By the time Frederick was taking his real breakfast with Doctor Wilhelm in the dining-room, at about eight o'clock, the whole mass of the vessel was again quivering and at short intervals again seemed to be running hard against walls of rock. The low-ceiled room in dismal gloom, dotted here and there by electric lights, was leaping in a mad dance, one moment riding high on the crest of a wave, the next moment plunging deep into an eddying trough. The few men that had ventured to table tried to laugh and joke away the situation, which by no means offered a rosy outlook.

"In the pit of my stomach I have the feeling I used to get as a child when I swung too high."

"Kammacher, we're in the devil's cauldron. There'll be things doing compared with which the things we've gone through aren't a circumstance," said Wilhelm.

From somewhere came the word, "Cyclone," a dreadful word, though it seemed to make no impression upon the steamer **Roland**, a model of determination, steadfastly cleaving the waves and tearing breaches in the mountains of water. New York was its goal, and it was hastening onward.

Frederick wanted to go on deck, but it looked bad there, and he remained on the upper step under the protection of the companionway penthouse. The level of the sea seemed to have risen, so that the warrior **Roland** appeared to be making his obstinate way through a deep defile. One could not help succumbing to the impression that each instant the defile would close overhead and settle the faithful vessel's fate forever. Sailors in oilskins were climbing about to make fast every loose thing. Great waves had already swept overboard. The salt water was trickling and flowing over the deck. As if that were not enough, the heavens were driving down rain and snow. The rigging was howling, groaning, booming, and whistling in every pitch and key. That severity, that awfulness of the elements, that eternal rushing and roaring and seething of great masses of water, through which the steamer was staggering forward as if in mad, blind intoxication, that mournful, raging tumult kept up hour after hour. By noon it had even grown worse.

Very few responded to the trumpet-call for luncheon. There were about ten men beside the woman physician and the woman painter. Hahlstroem seated himself at Frederick's and Wilhelm's empty table. The ladies' places were not far away.

"No wonder," said Frederick, "that sailors are superstitious. The way this awful weather dropped out of a clear sky is enough to make a man believe in magic."

"It may even grow worse," Wilhelm observed.

The women heard his remark, looked up, and made horrified eyes.

"Do you think there is danger?" one of them asked.

"Danger is always imminent in life," he replied, and added with a smile: "It is merely a question of not being frightened."

Incredible to relate, the band began to play as usual, and, what is more, played a piece entitled **Marche triomphale**. The effect on all was at first a slight shudder;

then nobody could resist a smile at the apparent irony of it.

"The musicians are heroes," said Frederick.

"In general," remarked Hahlstroem, "our grim humour nowadays is a great asset. If those musicians were to receive the order, they would play 'A Country Girl,' and 'My Hannah Lady,' in the jaws or the belly of a whale. If they didn't, they'd fare just as badly."

"O Lord, anything for a steady table, a steady seat, a steady berth! The man possessing these things seldom knows how rich he is," said Frederick, in a voice raised to a shout to make himself heard above the noise of the sea without and the music within. The men laughed, and the ocean, to add to their amusement, raised them up in the fog, the tempest, and the snow to the top of a wave ninety feet high. Everybody was instantly silenced. Even the orchestra played a frightened pause not indicated in the score.

On ascending the companionway after lunch, Frederick saw Arthur Stoss in the unfrequented smoking-room eating his meal in perfect equanimity and cheerfulness undisturbed by the weather. Frederick went in for a chat with the original, witty monstrosity. He was cutting his fish with a knife and fork held between the great toe and the second toe.

"Our old omnibus is jolting a bit," he said. "If our boilers are good, there is nothing to fear. But there's this much about it. If it is not a cyclone yet, it may still turn into one. I don't care. It looks more discouraging than it really is. What a man will do! To show the people in Cape Town, Melbourne, Buenos Aires, San Francisco and Mexico what a man with a firm, energetic will can accomplish, even if nature has not favoured him, he will plow through all the cyclones, hurricanes and typhoons of all the waters of the globe. Your business man sitting in the Winter Garden in Berlin, or the Alhambra in London, never dreams of all the things the performer giving his number must go through before he can merely stand where he is standing. He can't ever take it easy and let himself get rusty."

Frederick was feeling miserable. Although his dreams were still haunting his brain, and Ingigerd, or his sick wife, or the Russian Jewess was still present in his soul, he nevertheless felt that all sensations were becoming more and more submerged in the one sensation, that on all sides there was distinct menace of a brutal danger.

Hans Fuellenberg entered. His face was lifeless.

"There is a corpse on board," he said, in a tone implying a causal relation between the dead stoker and the raging storm. It was very evident that the spice had been taken out of Hans Fuellenberg's life.

"I heard the same thing," Stoss said. "My man, Bulke, told me a stoker died."

Frederick simulated ignorance of the event. Accustomed to observe himself honestly, he realized that though the fact was not new to him, Fuellenberg's statement of it had made him shudder.

"The dead man is dead," said Stoss, now attacking his roast with appetite. "We won't be wrecked on the dead stoker's corpse. But last night a derelict was sighted. Those corpses, the corpses of vessels, are dangerous. When the sea is rough, they can't be sighted."

Frederick asked for more information about derelicts.

"About nine hundred and seventy-five drifting derelicts," Stoss explained, "have been sighted in five years here in the northern part of the Atlantic. It is certain that the actual number is twice as great. One of the most dangerous of such tramps is the iron four-masted schooner, *Houresfeld*. On its way from Liverpool to San Francisco, fire broke out in its hold, and the crew abandoned it. If we were to collide with anything of that sort, there wouldn't be a soul left to tell the tale."

"You can't pass through the gangways," said Fuellenberg, "the bulkheads are closed down."

The siren began to roar again. Frederick still heard defiance and triumph in the cry, and yet something recalling the broken horn of the hero Roland in Roncesvalles.

"There is no danger yet," said Stoss to calm him.

XXXVII

Long after Stoss had been led away by his valet and tucked in bed for his afternoon nap, Frederick still remained in the unfrequented smoking-room. The place made an uncanny impression. Yet its very gloominess insured privacy; and in the gravity of the situation he had need to be by himself. He began, perhaps prematurely, to consider the worst eventuality. He thought it might be well to stand in readiness. Around the walls ran a bench upholstered in leather. Kneeling on it, he could look through the port-holes out upon the mighty uproar of the waters. In that position, watching the waves beat with inconceivable persistency against the desperately struggling vessel, he let his life pass in review before his mind's eye.

Grey gloom was closing down on him. After all, he felt that he yearned for life and was far from being as ready to die as he had occasionally supposed. Something akin to regret came over him. "Why am I here? Why did I not stop to consider and summon all my rational will power to keep me from this senseless trip? For all I care, let me die; but not here, not in a desert of water far from mother earth, immeasurably far from the great community of men. This seems to me a particularly awful curse. Men on solid land, in their own homes, men among men, have not the least notion of it." What was Ingigerd to him now? A matter of indifference. Shaking his head, he admitted that he now had only the narrowest concern for himself. What a beautiful hope to escape that brutal fate and land on some shore! Any fragment of land, any island, any city, any snow-clad village was a garden of Eden, an improbable dream of happiness. How extravagantly grateful he would be in the future merely to tread dry land, merely to draw breath, merely to see a lively street! He gnashed his teeth. Of what avail a cry for help here? How could a man find God's ear here? If the extreme thing were to happen, and the *Roland* with its mass of human beings were to founder, one would see things that would prevent the man that had seen them, even if he escaped, from ever being happy again.

"I would not witness it," thought Frederick. "I would jump overboard to avoid the sight of it. And while that would be happening, none of my friends and relatives would be thinking of me at all. 'The steamship *Roland* sunk' appears as a head-line in the newspapers. 'Oh!' says the reader in Berlin, the reader in Hamburg, and Amsterdam. He takes a sip of coffee, puffs at his cigar, and comfortably settles back to a taste of more details of the catastrophe, whether observed or fabricated. What a hurrah for the newspaper publishers! A sensation! More readers! That is the Medusa into whose eyes we look, and who tells us what the genuine value of a cargo of human lives is in the world."

Frederick attempted in vain to battle against a still-life picture, which the *Roland*, valiantly struggling onward, with its siren almost stifled in the storm, showed him at the bottom of the sea. He saw the majestic vessel in a coffin of glass. Across its decks swarms of fish swam hither and thither. Its cabins were all filled with water. The large dining-room, with its panels of walnut, its tables, and leather-upholstered revolving chairs, was filled with water. A big polyp, jelly-fish, and red, mushroom-like sea-anemones had penetrated into the very gangways along which the passengers were now walking. And to Frederick's horror, the liveried corpses of Pfundner, the head-steward, and his assistant stewards were slowly floating about in a circle. The picture would have been almost ridiculous, had it not been so grue-some and had it not so certainly lain in the realm of the possible. Think of all the things divers report! All the things they have seen in the cabins and gangways of submerged steamers; inextricably knotted masses of human beings, passengers or sailors coming toward them with outstretched arms, upright, as if alive and as if awaiting them. A closer examination of the clothes of those guardians and adminis-trators of a lost estate at the bottom of the sea, those strange ship-owners, business men, captains, pursers, those fortune-seekers, money-seekers, embezzlers, adven-turers, or whatever they might be, showed that they were filled with polyps, crus-taceans, and all sorts of ocean worms, enjoying their stay there as long as something remained beneath their shredded garments except gnawed-off bones.

Frederick beheld himself down there, too, one of those decaying phantoms, months old, wandering about in the ghastly abode of the sunken *Roland*, in that horrible Vineta, where each man passed his neighbour mutely with a frightened gesture, each seeming to carry in his breast a congealed cry of anguish, which he expressed with bowed head and outstretched arms, or head thrown back and open mouth. Or else he was hideously crawling on his hands, or wringing his hands, or folding them, or spreading out his fingers. The engineers in the boiler-room seemed still slowly, slowly to be controlling the cylinder and driving-wheel; yet differently than before, since the law of gravity seemed no longer to be in force. One of the engineers was doing his work in a peculiarly twisted way, like a man asleep caught between the rim of the wheel and the piston-rod covered with verdigris. Freder-ick descended on his ghastly tour down to the stokers, whom the catastrophe had surprised in the midst of their occupation. Some were still holding their shovels in their hands, though unable to lift them. They themselves were floating, while the shovels to which they clung did not stir from the bottom. All was over. They could not kindle the fire into a white glow, and so could not keep the mighty steamer in its course. In the steerage the sight was so horrible to behold, with men, women and children of all nationalities huddled and tossed in thick, dark heaps, that even a cat-shark, which had made its way through the chimney of the stoke-hole and then through the engine, did not feel sufficiently courageous or hungry to mingle in the gathering. ***Noli turbare circulos meos***, these people, too, seemed to be saying. All were thinking strenuously, absorbed in the profoundest meditation--they had plenty of time for profound meditation--upon the riddle of life.

In fact, they seemed to be placed there merely for the purpose of reflecting. Those men and women wringing their hands or spreading their fingers, or walking on their hands, or even standing on the tip of a single finger, while grazing the ceiling with their feet, were all thinking. Professor Toussaint alone, who came floating toward Frederick in the gangway, seemed to be acting differently. With his right hand raised, he seemed to be saying: "An artist may not rust. He must air himself. He must seek new conditions of life. If he doesn't receive the honour he should in Italy, he should simply go to France, like Leonardo da Vinci, or even emigrate to the land of liberty."

"I want to live, live, nothing else," thought Frederick. "In the future, like Cato the Elder, I would rather walk a year on foot along a way that I could cover in three days on a steamer."

To avoid the hideous companionship of the blue, swollen thinkers, he left the gloomy, funereal smoking-room, and, with aching head and leaden limbs, dragged himself on deck, where the wild scurrying of the storm and the chaos of snow, rain and salty clouds of foam tore the weight away from his soul.

XXXVIII

In the space at the head of the companionway Frederick came upon the same company as the day before, sitting close together in steamer chairs--Toussaint, the timid skipper of the sailing vessel, the woman artist, the woman physician, the tall electrical engineer, and a man who had not been there the day before, an American colonel. He was a handsome specimen of the highest type of his widely spread species. He was engaged in a conversation on the number of miles covered by all the railroads in the United States, and his statements concerning their extent set fire to the European chauvinism of the electrical engineer. They forgot the weather in their debate. Each party to the dispute named an incredible number of miles and vaunted the advantages of the railroads in his native country.

"We are running at only half speed," said Toussaint to Frederick. "Isn't it strange how suddenly the weather changed?"

"Very," answered Frederick.

"Of course," Toussaint continued with a pale grimace intended for a smile, "I don't understand anything about cyclones, but the seamen say this storm is cyclonic."

"It may be called a cyclone," said the timid little skipper of the sailing vessel. "If it were striking us astern instead of ahead, it would not be so bad. As it is, the *Roland* at the utmost cannot make more than three miles an hour. Were I on my schooner and had the same storm blown up so suddenly, we should not have had time to furl a sail. We should have been lost. Thank the Lord, it is better on modern steamers. Nevertheless, I feel more comfortable on my four-master, and the devil knows, I'd like to be on it now."

Frederick could not help laughing.

"As for the *Roland*," he said, "I would rather be, let us say, in the Hofbraeuhaus in Munich. Your four-master has no greater charms for me than a cabin on the *Roland*."

Hans Fuellenberg came lounging in and told them a wave had swept away one of the life-boats on the after quarter. At the very same instant an arched mass of water came flying slantwise over the port bow.

"Oh!" everybody cried.

"Magnificent, beautiful," said Frederick.

"That's cyclonic," the woman artist repeated.

"Believe me," they heard the colonel say again, "the stretch from New York to Chicago alone"--

"That was a Niagara Falls," said Toussaint.

The wave, dropping into the ventilators and chimneys, had fairly bathed the vessel. It was cold, too, and the *Roland* was continuing its obstinate, praiseworthy trip under a crust of ice and snow. Icicles were hanging from the rigging. Glassy stalactites formed about the chart-room and everywhere on the railings and edges of things. The deck was slippery, and it was a perilous venture to attempt to make one's way forward. But when Ingigerd's cabin door opened and her long light hair rumpled by the wind appeared in the slit, Frederick instantly made the venture. She drew him into her cabin, where he found two children keeping her company.

"I invited them to stay with me because it's fairly comfortable in this cabin."

The seriousness of the situation had extinguished in the girl all coquetry and capriciousness. Frederick almost forgot what he had suffered on her account and in what fatal dependence he had been upon this creature only a short time before.

"Tell me, is there danger, Doctor von Kammacher?" she asked.

His evasive answer seemed to make no impression upon her. He was astonished to see how energetic and resolute she was, in contrast with her behaviour of yesterday, when she played the spoiled, suffering, helpless child. She begged him to go try to find her father.

"In case anything happens, you know, it would be well not to be so far away from him."

"What do you suppose will happen?"

Without answering this, she asked him to stop at cabin 49 on the way and tell Rosa to come up.

"My little guests keep clamouring for her. If she doesn't come up for a while, I can't keep them quiet. Then she can serenely go back again to her silly, sentimental mistress. What do you think of a man like Achleitner?" she continued. "He is lying on all fours in his cabin, crying and groaning, 'Oh, my poor mother! Oh, my poor sister! Why didn't I obey you, mamma!' and so on. Just fancy, a man! Poor fellow!" she added, her tone changing. "It's enough to move a heart of stone." She held fast to the bedstead, not to be thrown into a corner like a splinter, and shook with laughter.

The mountain of stones under which Frederick had buried the little sinner, Ingigerd, was at that moment removed, and love stood there with unparalleled might. Such genuine bravery and genuine humour, combined with so much tenderness, he had never credited her with. Nervous and tired as he was, he felt irresistibly drawn to her, felt his will slipping from him. But a little, and he would have thrown himself to the floor and kissed the small feet in slippers.

Frederick's amazement waxed when all of a sudden she wanted to cross the deck and go below to comfort that donkey Achleitner. Frederick would not allow her. He was ashamed of his previous attack of fright, called himself a miserable coward, and got himself under perfect control. In this attitude he played the role of a severe mentor, Ingigerd's responsible guardian and protector, strict, but fatherly and good-natured. Though she laughed at him, it by no means displeased her to let him have his way.

XXXIX

Frederick's kindliness to Ingigerd's little wards made it unnecessary to summon Rosa. He asked the children their names, and they were soon chattering confidingly with their new uncle. Ella Liebling, a girl of five, to whom Ingigerd had given her doll, was sitting at one end of the couch, a cover wrapped about her legs, while Siegfried had established himself comfortably on the bed. With a spiritless expression for a child, he was playing a rather monotonous game of cards with an imaginary partner.

"Mamma is divorced," Ella explained. "Papa was always quarrelling with her."

"Yes," said Siegfried, pushing his cards aside, as if waking up from a trance, and bending over to Frederick, who was sitting beside Ella, "mamma once threw a boot at papa."

"But papa is strong," said Ella. "He once picked up a chair and knocked it down and smashed it to pieces."

Though Ingigerd was suffering from nausea, she had to laugh.

"Those children are great sport," she said.

"Papa once threw a bottle against the wall," Siegfried went on, "because Uncle Bolle was always coming to see us."

And so the children continued, like little wiseacres, to discuss in detail the theme of "happy marriages."

"Rosa says mamma is to blame because papa left us," observed Siegfried.

"I think so, too," said Ella. "I think mamma's to blame."

"Rosa said mamma doesn't do anything but read novels."

"Rosa says," Ella chimed in, "that if mamma were not always lying in bed, she would feel much better."

And "Rosa says," "Rosa says," went on for a long while. The former non-commissioned officer and lackey of the vaudeville star, Bulke, came towing Rosa across the deck in the same way as he did his master. Both looked red and contented. Frederick asked what the prospects were for the *Roland*.

"Oh, everything's all right," Bulke laughed, "if only something else doesn't turn up."

"Bulke," said Rosa, "take Siegfried on your back."

Bulke proceeded to do so, while Rosa lifted Ella to her crimson arm.

Now the children begged to remain where they were, although before they had been annoying Ingigerd by constantly crying for Rosa.

"Let them stay," said Ingigerd.

Rosa thanked her. "They are really best off here," she said. "All they take for supper is some milk and a roll. I will bring it right away."

"What is that on your arm?" asked Frederick. It looked as if a beast had been clawing at her.

"Oh, nothing," she said. "My mistress doesn't know what she is doing. She's out of her senses from seasickness and fright."

XL

For five hours the cyclone raged unmercifully. At ever shorter intervals, gust on gust in increasing fury hurled itself against the vessel.

With great difficulty Frederick made his way down to the barber, who, though the ship's movement was a fearful combination of rolling and pitching, actually performed the miracle of shaving him.

"One has to keep going," said the barber. "If you don't work, you're lost."

He spoke and suddenly stopped, removed the razor from Frederick's throat and turned pale, if his dirty grey colour could turn a shade lighter. Frederick's face, too, still partly covered with lather, showed signs of surprise and alarm. In the engine-room the signal bell had rung loud, as a sign that the captain was sending an order down from the bridge through the speaking-tube. Thereupon the revolution of the engines had slowed down and within a few moments had ceased entirely. This event, simple enough in itself, had in this weather, about fifteen hundred miles from land, in the middle of the Atlantic Ocean, the effect of a catastrophe, not only on Frederick and the barber, but on every passenger still capable of reasoning, and even on the whole crew. One instantly observed the excitement that seized upon all at the cessation of the engines, which seemed to turn the vessel into a torpid, powerless thing. Voices cried, women shrieked, steps hurried up and down the gangways. A man tore the door open and indignantly cried, as if imputing to the poor barber the responsibility of a captain:

"Why are we standing still?"

Frederick wiped the lather from his face and, along with a multitude of questioning, groping, staggering persons, thrown now against one wall of the gangway, now against the other, hastened to make his way on deck.

"We are drifting," everybody said.

"The screw is broken."

"Cyclone!"

"Oh," said a young girl, who had dragged herself up in a dressing-gown, to Frederick, "I don't care about myself, not a bit, but my poor mother, my poor mother in Stuttgart."

"What's the matter? What's the matter?" twenty voices at the same time demanded of a steward, who was attending to his duties. He ran away, shrugging his shoulders.

Since the passengers, huddled like sheep, blocked the way to the deck at the head of the companionway, Frederick tried to get out by another way, leading a long distance through the after part of the vessel and then through a narrow corridor forward again. He walked rapidly and seemed outwardly composed, though in a state of unusual tensity, even fear.

In the second cabin Frederick's way was barred by a good-looking young man standing in front of his cabin barefoot, in his shirt sleeves and trousers. He was attempting to button his collar; but in his excitement was not succeeding.

"What's the matter?" he shouted to Frederick. "Is everybody in this cursed hole crazy? The first thing you know a stoker dies, and now there is a leak, or the screw is broken. What's the matter with the captain? I am an officer. I must be in San Francisco on the twenty-fifth of February, without fail. If it keeps on this way, I'll be in a fix."

Frederick wanted to hurry by, but the man got in his way.

"I am an officer," he said. "My name is Von Klinkhammer." Frederick also gave his name. "That's what comes of having priests on board," the young man continued, twirling the end of his moustache upward, Prussian fashion. "If there's no help for it, then the fellows ought simply to be chucked overboard. What is the captain thinking of?" he kept shouting, while an unexpected lurch of the vessel sent him plunging against the wall almost back into his cabin. "I didn't leave the service and give up a career and board this damned--"

But Frederick had run away. Now deep, intense silence prevailed throughout the vessel, which was like a dead thing; a silence, in which every now and then a step or a hasty tread on the heavy carpet in the gangway was audible. Through the thin walls came the dull, confused murmur of many voices. Doors banged, and when they opened, brief, broken sounds penetrated from the cabins, evidence of the bewilderment and alarm of their tenants. The thing that was particularly weird to Frederick in that swaying corridor, creaking like a new boot and lighted by electricity, was the incessant ringing of electric bells. In a hundred cabins at the same time, frightened persons, who had paid dear for their passage and were entitled to excellent service, were pressing the buttons. None of them was inclined to recognise the *force majeure* of the Atlantic Ocean, the cyclone, the breaking of the screw, or any other possible accident. They thought that by ringing the bells they would be giving expression to the irresistible demand for a responsible rescuer to bring them safely to dry land.

"Who knows," thought Frederick, "while they are ringing the bells down here, perhaps the life-belts are being handed out on deck, the boats are being swung out on the water and over-loaded with passengers to the sinking point."

XLI

But, thank the Lord, by the time he had finally fought his way to Ingigerd's cabin on deck, it had not yet reached that point. It was to Ingigerd Hahlstroem that an impulse had been driving him. Beside the children, for whom in a motherly way she was trying constantly to devise a new occupation, he found her father and Doctor Wilhelm.

"People's cowardice is something fearful," said Doctor Wilhelm.

"Easily said; but what's the matter?" asked Frederick.

"One of the bearings got too hot. It takes time for it to cool off."

The passengers crowded on the companionway kept calling for the captain.

"The captain has other things to do than answer silly questions," said Wilhelm.

"I think the people should be quieted and given an explanation," Frederick declared. "To me a certain amount of fear seems justifiable in the landlubber, who doesn't know anything of nautical matters and hasn't the least notion of what is happening."

"Why should they be told anything?" rejoined Wilhelm. "Even if matters are very bad, it is advisable to deceive them."

"Well, then," said Hahlstroem, "deceive them. Send stewards around to tell them everything is all right and we'll have to drown."

Shortly afterward, the captain actually did send the little army of stewards through the vessel to inform the passengers that, as Doctor Wilhelm had said, one of the bearings had got too hot, and in a short while the engines would be working again.

"Is there danger?" the stewards were asked a thousand times.

"No," was the decided answer.

To keep the air in her cabin pure, Ingigerd left the door slightly ajar; and the sight of the colossal **Roland**, as seen from her cabin, helplessly drifting in the ocean, by no means seemed to bear out the stewards' declaration.

"There is no use concealing the fact that we are scudding under bare poles," said Hahlstroem.

"We are dripping oil on the water," said Wilhelm, pointing through the opening of the door to where Pander and a sailor were lowering a bag of sail-cloth filled with oil. With the heavy seas that kept sweeping down like great mountains in motion and the fearfully boiling waves accompanying the swells, the measure seemed almost ridiculous. Each instant the dead *Roland*, constantly sending out its long-drawn signal, which sounded more like a call for help than a warning, was raised up on a plunging mountain of water, where there seemed as little prospect of safety as when it sank into the valleys. The great steamer seemed not to know where to turn. The raging waters twisted it over now on its starboard side, now on its port side. Of its herculean might, nothing remained but its unwieldy, helpless bulk. It turned about slowly, and turned back again, and all of a sudden a fearful sea, like a thousand hissing white panthers leaping from a dark green mountain ridge, dashed over the railing.

"That was bad," said Wilhelm, slamming the door shut in the nick of time. Frederick's nerves were in a state of tension, not in a mere metaphoric sense. They produced a purely physical sensation, as of violin strings too tightly drawn.

"Is it making you nervous?" asked Hahlstroem.

"Somewhat," said Frederick. "I don't deny it. A man has strength and intelligence, but can't exercise either, even when danger is imminent."

"Immediate danger?" asked Wilhelm. "No, we are not there yet. In the first place, the engines will be working again pretty soon; and secondly, even if we should really have to drift and had to resort to the sails, we could count on being perfectly easy in our minds a week from now."

"What do you mean by being easy in our minds?" demanded Hahlstroem.

"The storm is blowing from north-northwest. A ship like this never capsizes. So, in all probability, we should be carried to the Azores, where a steamer would tow us into port. Or, perhaps, we should be driven even further south, and in a week we should be anchoring in view of the glorious Peak of Teneriffe."

"Many thanks for your Peak of Teneriffe. I have to be in New York. My daughter has an engagement there. We are under obligations to be there."

"A week of uncertainty would be ruin to my nervous system," said Frederick. "I am not suited for this passive heroism. I might do more if I could be active."

"You've read the 'Leather-stocking Tales,'" said Wilhelm, ironically. "You know that the American Indians have greater respect for passive heroism. Think of the stakes on which they burn their captives to death."

"Never mind," said Frederick. "No martyr stakes for me. Were I to hear that the screw is broken and we should have to drift, my nerves couldn't stand it. I would jump into the water. That is why I am against life-preservers. I wouldn't accept one if it were offered to me ten times over. Why prolong the death agony?"

XLII

The hours passed. The grey day went down into still greyer twilight. The ear-splitting tumult of the sea never ceased. Frederick, like everybody else, had in vain awaited the moment when the engines would be working again, and the helpless ship would resume its course. Everybody, with the anxiety of despair, watched whether the intervals between the great swells would lengthen or shorten. Sometimes a superstitious illusion that he was being persecuted would take hold of Frederick. Particularly awful were the cries of the emigrants penned in the steerage, which at short intervals penetrated above on deck. They wept and wailed and shrieked to heaven for help. They were like men driven mad by fear, fury and physical pain.

Yet, as if nothing had happened, the call for dinner was trumpeted at the regular time through the gangways of the drifting vessel, through that majestic, helpless ark, lighted by electricity, which, shining through the port-holes, turned the *Roland* with its crust of ice into a fairy palace, a mournful plaything of the waves.

Frederick wondered who would have the phlegm or the courage or the desire to go to dinner. But Wilhelm cried, "Come, gentlemen," and since Rosa appeared, wet and courageous, to attend to the children, it was out of place for him to remain in the cabin, and there was nothing for him to do but join Doctor Wilhelm and Hahlstroem. The cockatoo was screeching and Ella was crying. The child was refractory. Ingigerd was trying to console her, while Rosa reprimanded her rather energetically.

"Would you like me to stay near here?" Frederick asked before leaving. "It would mean a great deal to me if you would let me be entirely at your disposal, Miss

Ingigerd."

"Thank you, Doctor von Kammacher, you will be coming again."

Frederick marvelled at the naturalness with which he had made the offer and she had accepted.

Now an unexpected change set in, which allayed everybody's excitement and went through Frederick's muscles and nerves like a soothing stream. The walls and floors of the *Roland* began to quiver faintly, a sign that her heart and pulse were beating again. It was the rhythm of its strength, the rhythm of its race to its goal. Ingigerd shouted with joy, like a child, and Frederick set his teeth. Renewed life, renewed prospects and hopes, the reassumption of system, the relaxation of his nerves made him so weak that the tears almost started to his eyes. Choking down his emotion, he stepped out on deck.

Here the scene had changed. Blithely, in all its might, the *Roland* was leaping forward again into the roaring darkness. That monstrous, seething witch's cauldron of the boiling waters was now welcome to him. Again the *Roland* was tearing breaches in dark mountains, was rising to mountain heights, and madly plunging into deep valleys; during which, for many seconds at a time, the screw would whirl wildly in the turbulent air.

Mr. Rinck was sitting on the threshold of his cabin, which was brightly lighted, smoking and petting his spotted cat.

"It's good we're under way again," Frederick could not refrain from saying as he walked past.

"Why?" said Rinck phlegmatically.

"I for one," said Frederick, "would rather be running under full steam than drifting helplessly."

"Why?" said Mr. Rinck again.

In the gangways below, even though the ship was pitching, the atmosphere was fairly pleasant and lively. Everybody seemed to have forgotten his fear. The passengers, cracking jokes and clinging to the nearest stationary thing, reeled and stumbled into the dining-room. The rattle of china near the kitchen was deafening, especially when, as frequently happened, some of the plates broke.

Frederick's clothes were pretty well soaked, and he mustered up the courage to go to his cabin to dress. Adolph, his steward, came to help him, and told Frederick of a panic that had broken out in the steerage when the engines stopped. Some of the women with their babies on their arms had wanted to jump right into the water. It was with difficulty that the other emigrants had restrained them. One of the stewards and a sailor had clutched a Polish woman by her feet just as she was taking the downward plunge.

"You can't blame these people for acting like cowards in this situation," said Frederick. "It would be strange if they didn't. Who will insist that he can stand upright when the ground beneath his feet is giving away? If a man were to say so, either he would be lying, or his lack of feeling would be so great as to degrade him below an animal."

"Yes," said the steward, "but what would *we* do if *we* were so cowardly?"

Frederick now began to deliver one of those fiery dissertations that had won him a number of youthful auditors when he was a *Privatdozent*.

"With you it is different," he said. "You are upheld, and at the same time rewarded, by the feeling that you are doing your duty. While we passengers are living in terror, the cooks have been boiling soup, cleaning fish, preparing vegetables, roasting and carving, larding venison and so on." The steward laughed! "But I assure you, at times it is easier to roast a roast than to eat it." And Frederick continued in a solemn, but for that very reason, roguish manner to philosophise on courage and cowardice.

XLIII

Dinner began, and, though the weather had by no means improved, a comparatively large number of passengers had gathered in the dining-room. Mr. Pfundner, the head-steward, with his white hair curled and arranged by the barber, if not in a braid at the back of his head, yet like a wig of the rococo period, stood, as usual, in majestic pose, before the false mantelpiece between the two entrance doors. It was the place from which he could best supervise the waiters and keep his eye on the whole dining-room.

The band was playing *Le Pere la Victoire* by Ganne. This was followed by Gillet's *Loin du Bal*. At Suppe's overture from *Banditenstreiche*, the eternal skat players came tramping into the saloon, having delayed, as usual, to finish their game. At all the tables much wine was being drunk, because it strengthened one's courage and dulled one's nerves. The passengers toasted the *Roland*. It amused them. They were all conscious of the pleasant rhythm of the great engine, to which no music in the world was comparable. Over Vollstedt's waltz, *Lustige Brueder*, the company with a sense of relief was still discussing the danger they had safely escaped.

"We hoisted distress signals."

"Rockets were shot off."

"They were already getting the life-belts and life-boats ready."

"Why, they were even dripping oil on the water."

The remarks flew about with the less restraint as neither the captain nor any of his officers were at table.

"The captain," they said, "has never left the bridge since morning."

Suddenly the port-holes were illuminated from outside. Everybody, with an "Oh!" of astonishment, let his knife and fork fall and jumped up from his seat. "A ship!" "A steamer!" all exclaimed, and crowded on deck. There, in overawing majesty, in the gleam of its thousand lights, one of the mightiest ocean liners of the time was rolling and pounding at a distance of not more than fifty yards. "The *Prince Bismarck*, the *Prince Bismarck*!" the people cried, having heard the name from the officers and crew, who had recognised the vessel. "Hurrah!" went up the full-throated cry. "Hurrah!" Frederick shouted, and so did Wilhelm and so did Professor Toussaint. Everybody who could shouted "Hurrah!"--Ingigerd and the woman physician and the woman artist. They all waved their napkins or handkerchiefs. The same shout of joy went up from the steerage, and by way of greeting the two vessels let their steam whistles thunder. They could see the passengers on the various decks of the *Prince Bismarck* waving to them, and, in spite of the noise of the tempest, could hear their faint hurrah.

The *Prince Bismarck*, a twin-screw steamer, one of the first models of its kind, had just made its record-breaking trip, in which it had crossed the Atlantic Ocean in six days, eleven hours, and twenty-four minutes. About two thousand people were now making the trip from New York to Europe. Two thousand people! That means twice as many as can fill a Berlin theatre from the orchestra to the top gallery.

The *Roland* and the *Bismarck* exchanged lively flag signals. Yet the whole grandiose vision, from the moment of its appearance to its disappearance, lasted only three minutes. In that time the seething ocean was flooded with light. It was not until nothing remained of the *Bismarck* but a dancing mist of light that its band came on deck and played. On the *Roland* they caught two or three trembling, fading measures of the national hymn, *Heil dir im Siegerkranz*. Within a few moments the *Roland* was again alone on the ocean, in the night, the tempest, and the snowstorm.

With twice as much fire, the band now played a quadrille by Karl, *Festklaenge*, and a galop by Kiesler, *Jahrmarktskandal*; and with twice as much appetite and twice as much liveliness the passengers seated themselves at dinner again. "Fairy-like!" they cried. "Glorious!" "Tremendous!" "Colossal!"--this last a favourite expression of the Germans.

Even Frederick had a sense of pride and tranquillisation. He felt a vital breath of that atmosphere which is no less necessary to the mind of the modern man than air is to his lungs.

"No matter how much we resist the thought," he said to Wilhelm, "and no matter how much I railed yesterday evening against modern culture, a sight like that must impress a man. It must go to the very marrow of his bones. It is simply absurd that such a marvellous product of secret natural forces, joined together by man's brains and hands, such a creation over creation, such a miracle has become even possible." They touched glasses. The sound of clinking glasses could be heard all over the room. "And what courage, what boldness has been built into that great living organism, what a degree of fearlessness in opposing those natural forces which man has been standing in awe of for thousands of years! What an audacious world of genius, from its keel to the top of its mast, from its bowsprit to its screw!"

"And all this," responded Wilhelm, "has been attained in scarcely a hundred years. So it signifies only the beginning of a development. Object as much as you will, science, or rather technical progress, is eternal revolution and the only genuine reform of human conditions. Nothing can hinder this development that has begun. It is constant, eternal progress, yes, progress itself."

"It is the human intellect," said Frederick, "which throughout the centuries has been lying passive and has suddenly turned active. Undoubtedly man's brains and, at the same time, social industry have entered a new phase."

"Yes," said Wilhelm, "in a certain way the human intellect was already active in ancient times, but it fought too long with the man in the mirror."

"Then, let us hope," said Frederick in confirmation, "that the last hour of the men that fight images, the swindlers, the South Sea Island medicine-men and magicians, is not far off; that all filibusters and cynical freebooters, who for thousands of years have been living by the capture of souls, will strike sail before the fast, safe ocean-going steamer of civilisation, whose captain is intellect and whose sole steward is humanity."

After dinner, Frederick and Wilhelm climbed up to the smoking-room on deck.

"It is difficult to comprehend," said Frederick, when they reached the smoky little saloon, "how a vessel can keep its course in such a stormy, pitch-black night."

At the skat table, the players were sitting, smoking, drinking whisky and coffee, and tossing the cards on the table. Everything else seemed to be a matter of indifference to them. Frederick ordered wine and continued to goad his mind into activity. His head ached. He could scarcely hold it upright on his aching neck. His eyelids ached with weariness; but when they drooped, his eyes seemed to radiate a painful light shining from within. Every nerve, every muscle, every cell in him was alert. He could not hope for sleep. How weeks in his life, months, years had passed as in the twinkling of an eye! And this evening only three and a half days had elapsed since he boarded the *Roland* at Southampton, a period with the content of years, in which seconds were eternities. Its beginning lay in the remote distance, at the conclusion of a life lived long before, on an earth from which he had parted long before.

"You're tired, Doctor von Kammacher," said Wilhelm. "So I won't invite you to the stoker's funeral on the after-deck."

"Oh, I'll come," said Frederick. He was obsessed by a stinging rage not to spare himself anything, but to taste to the dregs even the bitterest impressions of this detached, jogged and jolted fragment of a human world.

XLIV

The physicians arrived when they were sewing the stoker, Zickelmann, into sail-cloth. The bare cabin was not very brilliantly lighted by a single electric bulb. Frederick recalled his dream--how the dead stoker had been standing under the vines with the cords in his hand and had then led Peter Schmidt and himself to the Toilers of the Light. A great change had taken place in his appearance. His face was no longer of flesh, but seemed to be chiselled out of yellow wax, to which his hair, his eyebrows and beard were pasted. A faint, cunning smile seemed to be curving his mouth; and when Frederick with odd interest and curiosity scrutinised him closely, it seemed to him he was saying, "Legno santo! Toilers of the Light!"

When the dead man's face was covered up and his whole body had been sewed into the cloth in coarse stitches, the sailors bound the puppet, with difficulty keeping it in position, on a smoothly planed board, weighted with iron.

"Will such a chrysalis ever really turn into a butterfly?" Frederick wondered.

The procedure, a piece of reeling, staggering acrobatics, was less gruesome than ridiculous. Yet, though this long package might be only the mortal shell of an immortal soul, one had a sense of infinite sadness in entrusting it to the fearful solitudes of the ocean.

Since in the stormy weather it was no easy matter to throw the corpse overboard and since it was impossible to conduct ceremonies on a rolling deck constantly washed by the waves, the purser asked the few persons present--Captain von Kessel could not leave the bridge--to say a silent prayer for the soul of the dead man. They did so, and four of the stoker's mates, staggering, stopping, lurching and panting, carried the long package on deck to the railing, where at the word of command they let it slide into the sea.

When Doctor Wilhelm bade Frederick good-night, he added:

"You ought to try to go to sleep."

They parted, and Frederick hunted for a sheltered spot on deck, where he could spend the night. He wanted to look the wind and weather straight in the face, there in the glacial air, in the gloom under the pale sheen of the arc-lights fastened to the mast. He shuddered at the thought of a night in the oppressive confines of his cabin, with the closed port-hole and the hot, stale air. But that alone was not the reason which kept him chained to the deck. It was the urge, in case of danger, to be near Ingigerd Hahlstroem. And when he seated himself near the smoke-stack, with his back against the heated wall, his hat drawn low over his face, his chin in his coat collar, he suddenly laughed to himself bitterly. It was in the same position and on the selfsame spot that he had found Achleitner the night before.

There was a rushing in Frederick's ears. He observed the huge arcs that the lights on the mast described. He observed the regular onslaught of the waves, and above the seething and foaming of the water, he heard the miauing of the wind in the rigging, a wicked obstinate miauing, accompanied by the sudden spitting and leaping of a tiger. Then the sounds seemed to Frederick to be more like the pitiful whimpering of strayed children, a troop of children whom he could now distinctly discern weeping over the bier of the dead stoker. And there were the Toilers of the Light again. He immediately snatched for one to carry it to Ingigerd Hahlstroem in her cabin; but Ingigerd was dressing for her famous dance. The great spider was already hanging on the flower, weaving the cobweb in which Mara was later to entangle herself. Frederick asked for a broom. He wanted to prevent the dance by sweeping the spider away. A broom came, but in the form of a serving man, who was carrying water and pouring it out. Another man followed and a third and a fourth, until everything was flooded with rushing waters. Frederick awoke from a dream in which he was learning sorcery. The momentous word that chains the floods was still on his lips. The waves rushed. He fell asleep again. Now it was the rushing of a stream at his feet. The sun was shining. It was a clear morning. From the other shore came his wife, young, beautiful, in a dress of flowered goods, row-ing her skiff. Her full, gentle figure had the charm of the vestal virgin and the wife. From woods nearby, Ingigerd appeared in the delicacy and the adornment of her light hair and naked body. The sunny landscape, of which her pure nudity was a part, seemed to belong to the time before Adam and Eve were driven from Paradise. Frederick took his wife's hand--she was smiling on him graciously--took Ingigerd Hahlstroem's hand--she seemed to be gentle and pure and obedient--and joined them. He said to Ingigerd:

"And thou shalt walk in brightness;

I'll purge thee clean of all thy dross."

But the heavens darkened, the woods blackened, and the light of a ghostly moon rose over the trees, rushing fearfully like great waters. Frederick ran along the edge of gloomy fields, when suddenly the cry "Moira! Moira!" resounded, and a piece of the darkness severed itself from the edge of the woods and soared heavily, as if borne by mighty black pinions. It was a gigantic bird, crying, "Moira, Moira!" Frederick fled. He was struck by hideous fear, as if the fearful roc were after him. "Moira, Moira!" He drew his penknife to defend himself.

He awoke to find himself lying undressed in his berth. Someone had discovered him, as he had discovered Achleitner the night before, and had led him down to his cabin. But the cry "Moira!" which reminded him of the Moerae, the ancient goddesses of fate, still rang fearfully in his ears.

XLV

It was still long before daylight, and he fell asleep again. This time on awaking he found himself in the corridor speaking to some stewards, already at work. It slowly dawned upon him that he was clad in nothing but his night-shirt and must have been walking in his sleep. What, had he turned into a somnambulist! He was utterly disconcerted and ashamed and had to let one of the stewards help him back to his cabin.

He found his cabin covered with about three inches of water, from a leaky pipe. Crawling into bed, he squeezed himself, to keep from being tossed out, into a hollow between the boards, a method he himself had devised.

Shortly after six, he was on deck sitting on his bench, warming his hands on his hot tea-cup. The weather was frightful. The morning was of an icy dreariness unsurpassed. The fury of the sea had waxed. The falling twilight was a new sort of darkness. The roaring of the waters and the raging of the winds were deafening. Frederick's ear-drums ached. But the ship struggled on, managing to pursue its course, though slowly.

And suddenly--Frederick did not know whether to trust his hearing--above the noise of the sea rose Ariel strains, beginning solemnly and swelling serenely.

It was the chords and melodies of a church choral. He was moved almost to tears. He recollected that this dreary morning was a Sunday morning, and the orchestra, even in the midst of the cyclone, was carrying out its instructions to begin the day with devotional music. It was playing in the unused smoking-room half way up the companionway, whence the strains ascended faintly to the deck. Everything lying heavily upon Frederick's soul in chaos and struggle melted away before the seriousness, the simplicity, the innocence of this music. It brought back memories of his boyhood, of many a morning full of innocence, expectation, and anticipations of great happiness; Sundays, holidays, his father's and his mother's birthdays, when the chorus of a regimental song woke him up in the morning. What was to-day compared with that past? What lay in between! What a sum of useless work, disenchantment, recognition bitterly paid for, possession snatched after passionately and then lost, love trickled away, passion trickled away; how many meetings and hard partings; what an amount of wrestling with everything in general and in particular; how much purity of purpose dragged in the mud; how much striving for freedom and self-determination, resulting only in impotent, blind imprisonment.

Was he really a person of so much importance before God that He visited him with such bitter, refined chastisements?

"I'm wild!" screamed Hans Fuellenberg, who appeared at the entrance to the companionway. "I won't put up with it, or else I'll go insane."

Nevertheless, Hans Fuellenberg and Frederick and all the other passengers, though in the last degree exhausted, terrorized, desperate, expecting each moment to be their last, lived through the same awful strain, from hour to hour, from morning till evening, and from evening till morning again.

To most of them it seemed impossible to hold out an hour longer. Yet there were to be three days more of it, they were told, before the ***Roland*** reached New York.

XLVI

Monday brought some sunshine, but no diminution of the tempest. It was fearful. Everything on deck not nailed or riveted was removed. The cries at regular intervals piercing the struggling vessel from the steerage more resembled the bellowing of beasts under the knife of the slaughterer than human sounds. Monday night was one prolonged agony. Nobody, unless unconscious from weakness or the tortures of seasickness, closed an eye.

At dawn Tuesday morning, each first-class passenger was startled by the word, "Danger!" quietly uttered at his cabin door by a steward.

Frederick had been lying a while on his bed dressed, when his steward opened the door and according to instructions gravely pronounced the one word, "Danger." At the same time the herald of this message, as fraught with large significance as it was laconic, turned on the electric light. Frederick jumped to a sitting posture, and was annoyed by the water from the leaky pipe, which ran now from one side of the room to the other, as the vessel lurched. At first he was uncertain whether the word he had heard had really been pronounced, or whether it was an illusion of his unstrung nerves. Every night he had been torn with a jerk of his nerves from his restless dozing, only to find that the cause had been a delusive fall or a delusive cry. But now, when he distinctly heard the stewards rapping at the other cabin doors, heard the doors open, and heard the word, "Danger," repeated several times, a sensation came over him that produced a most remarkable change in his condition.

"Very well," he said softly; and, as if he had been summoned to a game that did not concern him, he carefully put on his heavy overcoat, and stepped out into the gangway.

Here there was not a soul.

"Very well," he had been thinking, "the invisible powers, whose playthings we human beings are, will now completely expose their supreme brutality."

He had not been awakened from sleep; he had been awakened and brought to his sober reason from beneath a hundred strata of dreams and sleep. Now, in that empty corridor, it again seemed to him to be a fantastic illusion of his disordered brain; and he was about to return to his cabin, when he noticed for the first time that the rhythm of the engines and the churning of the screw were neither to be heard nor felt. Suddenly he thought the great vessel was drifting in the ocean abandoned by passengers and crew, and he alone had been left behind from the general rescue. But a passenger in a silk dressing-gown reeled by, whom Frederick could question.

"What's the matter, do you know?" he asked.

"Oh, nothing," said the man. "I've only been looking for my steward. I'm thirsty. I want a glass of lemonade." He staggered past Frederick into his cabin.

"Ass!" Frederick mentally exclaimed, disgusted with himself for what he again believed was his illusion. Yet the silence weighed upon him dreadfully. Seized by a wild instinct, he could not help but suddenly rush forward, merely to be on deck.

Somebody came toward him from the opposite direction, and asked him where he was going.

"Get out of my way," said Frederick. "It's none of your business."

But the hideous, half-dressed, corpse-like creature, besmirched by the traces of seasickness, would not make way.

"Are the stewards here all crazy?" he cried.

Hard by Frederick's ear an electric bell began to hammer noisily, and the next moment the tottering phantom that barred his way was multiplied by ten, twenty, a host of similar phantoms.

"What's the matter! What's the matter! We're sinking!"

"Steward! Steward!" a voice commanded; and another, "Captain! Captain!"

"Wretched service!" a man scolded in a voice that broke. "No stewards about. What do they mean by it?" The call bells began to rage.

Frederick turned, and ran down the endless corridor to the after part of the vessel. Nobody intercepted him. He passed the windows of the engine-room. The cylinders and pistons were not stirring. From the depths of the ship, from the boilers and furnaces, a sound of rushing, splashing water penetrated above the creaking and grinding of the walls.

"Did a boiler burst?" Frederick thought, forgetting that there would have been the report of an explosion and the hiss of escaping steam.

But he hastened on without stopping, past the post office, on his way through the second cabin to the stern. In his flight it occurred to him how happy he had been in Paris when at Cook's office they had told him that by great haste he could still make the **Roland** at Southampton. Why had he been in such a fever of impatience, in such dread of missing the boat and rushing into the open arms of doom? For there was no veiling the fact that something fearful had happened to the **Roland**.

At the door of the second cabin, he encountered the barber.

"The fires are out," said the barber. "A collision. The water is pouring into the hold below my shop."

The hammering of the bells never ceased. The barber was dragging two life-preservers.

"What do you need two for?" Frederick asked, and took one and sped on.

XLVII

He reached the door leading to the after deck, but could not open it. From the position of the ship, he realized that something irretrievable had happened. On the port side, the steamer was lying high, on the starboard side, it was only ten or twelve feet above the level. As the stern was also much lower than the bow, it would have been a practically hopeless venture to clamber forward across the deck, especially with the heavy seas that were constantly sweeping it.

Willy-nilly, he must return through the mole's gallery he had traversed to the forward part of the boat.

Scarcely fifteen seconds later, when he had reached the forward entrance to the deck, at the head of the companionway leading up from the dining-room, he could not have told how he succeeded in making his way through the corridor jammed with panicky passengers without having been beaten to death, strangled, or trodden underfoot. His hands and forehead were bruised, and he was clinging to the door-post with all his might, parleying violently with Doctor Wilhelm. Doctor Wilhelm clutched him, and the two physicians, in defiance of death, climbed up to the bridge, where they huddled in the shelter of the deck-house on the port side. They saw something huge rise high up in the morning twilight and fly madly above their heads. The next instant they were drenched up to their waists, and would have been washed overboard, had they not clung to the railing with all their strength.

On the bridge it looked pretty much as usual. Captain von Kessel, apparently quite composed, was leaning forward, and the giant Von Halm was searching the ever-thickening fog with spy-glasses. The siren was howling, and rockets were being shot off from the bow. On the captain's right stood the second mate. The third mate had just received the order:

"Cut the falls. Get the boats away."

"Cut the falls. Get the boats away," he repeated and disappeared to execute the order.

To Frederick, it all seemed unreal. Moments such as this, to be sure, had entered his imagination as within the realm of the possible; but now he realised that he had never reckoned with them seriously. He knew the fact confronting him stood there inexorable; nevertheless, he was unable to grasp it in convincing reality. He was telling himself he ought to try to get into a boat, when the captain's blue eyes glanced at him, but apparently with no recognition in them. The captain's commands were uttered in his beautiful voice, remotely suggesting the clinking sound of colliding billiard balls.

"Women and children starboard."

"Women and children starboard," came like a near, word-for-word echo.

Now Max Pander stepped up to the captain. He had the noble idea of proffering him a life-belt. Von Kessel's hand found its way for an instant to his cap.

"No, thank you, my boy, I don't need it. But here--" he took a pencil from his pocket, wrote a hasty line on a piece of paper, and handed it to Pander. "Jump in a boat and, if you can, bring this greeting to my sisters."

A heavy sea swept over the port side, and a tremendous swell raised and turned and twisted the colossal vessel. Frederick in vain tried to rouse himself from the leaden indifference that had come upon him in view of the incomprehensible drama. Suddenly, he was seized with horror, but he fought it down. At no cost was he to show cowardice either to himself or to others. Nevertheless, he followed Doctor Wilhelm, who stuck close to Max Pander's heels.

"We must get into one of the boats," said Doctor Wilhelm. "There's no doubt we are sinking."

The next moment Frederick found himself in Ingigerd's cabin.

"Hurry!" he cried. "The people are already jumping into the boats."

He had left the cabin door open, and close by they could see Pander and two sailors hacking away with axes at the frozen tackles by which a life-boat was suspended.

Ingigerd asked for her father. She asked for Achleitner.

"There's no time now for you to think of anybody but yourself. It's impossible to go below deck. It would mean sure death," Frederick explained. "Get dressed! Get dressed!"

Ingigerd mutely hastened to carry out his orders. It was not until then that one of the stewards passing her cabin called in his brief message, "Danger!"

"Danger! What's the matter? Are we sinking?" she cried.

But Frederick had already picked her up and carried her over to the boat, which the next instant gave way under the axe and fell into the misty turmoil below.

"Women and children on the other side!" the third mate shouted commandingly.

His order referred not only to Ingigerd, but also to the maid Rosa, who, fiery-red with her exertions, appeared on deck dragging her mistress and both the children, with the air of a housewife loaded with purchases, afraid of missing a street car.

"Women and children on the other side!" the third mate repeated in somewhat too Prussian a manner. Fortunately his presence was now required for the next boat, over which the struggles were already commencing.

There was no time to be lost, and despite the determined resistance of two sailors, Frederick, Pander, and Doctor Wilhelm let Ingigerd safely down into the boat. In doing so, Frederick also turned somewhat too loud-voiced and Prussian. Through his iron energy, which hewed down resistance as the sailors had hewed at the life-boat tackles, he succeeded in having the children, Mrs. Liebling, and finally Rosa lowered into the boat. It was no easy matter. Frederick heard himself shouted at, roared at, and commanded, and he, in turn, shouted at the sailors, commanded, and roared. He fought, he worked, though without a gleam of hope and with the positive consciousness that the situation was beyond salvation. All was over, all was lost. If he had not thought so before, the next occurrence would have convinced him.

A second boat had been lowered, and three sailors had jumped in. It rolled from side to side and rose on a wave. About eight or nine other persons leapt for it--Frederick thought he recognised familiar figures. It filled and disappeared. As if by sleight-of-hand, the spot where the boat with the dozen people in it had been dancing turned into empty sea with mist and spray driving over it.

Slowly the dark grey of the early dawn turned into the lighter grey of the day, approaching coldly and indifferently. When the fog lifted a little, Frederick for seconds at a time had a dismaying illusion that he was in a green valley with glorious, flowery meadows, through which a snowstorm of blossoms was sweeping. But then the mountains came, driven by the ferocious spirits of the hurricane, and closed down on the valley. The heavy, glassy heights broke, and with the weight of their fluid masses, snapped away two of the ***Roland's*** masts like reeds.

With its boilers quenched, the poor wreck could no longer send up a cry for help. Its sad body was still towering upward at the bow in colossal majesty. Rockets flew, signals of distress fluttered briskly from the foremast; a futile language in that merciless raging of the elements.

In the steerage it had grown still. But from the port side came a peculiar, persistent, unbroken sound, resembling the shouting and screaming of a crowd on toboggan-slides and merry-go-rounds at a village fair. A buzzing as of swarming bees pierced distinctly through the roaring of the tempest, while above it rose the shrieking of infuriated, frenzied women. Frederick thought of his dark-eyed Deborah. She, too, was doomed. He thought of Wilke.

Bulke, the faithful valet, appeared, leading Arthur Stoss by his coat collar. Within the next few moments, Wilke also appeared. He had been drinking, and was shouting as if the whole thing were a frolic; but he was half dragging, half carrying on deck an old, wheezing working woman. Thrusting Stoss and Bulke aside, he landed her safely in the boat.

Ingigerd was clamouring incessantly for her father and Achleitner. Instead of either of these, Stoss, whom Bulke and Wilke had lowered by a rope, dropped down beside her.

About thirty feet from Frederick, a man was standing in a cabin door, carefully hooked back. With incredible calm he was smoking a cigarette and inhaling, and stroking a yellow cat on his arm.

"It looks pretty bad, doesn't it, Mr. Rinck?" Frederick said, going up to him. "Why?"

"Well, don't you think we're lost?"

Mr. Rinck shrugged his shoulders without answering.

"What's the matter? What's the matter?" somebody bellowed in his ear.

"Nothing," he said, stroking his cat.

In the meantime Bulke and Wilke had lowered Doctor Wilhelm into the boat.

"That girl down there is giving herself a sore throat screaming for her father," said Bulke.

Frederick decided, cost what it might, to take a look around below deck. Perhaps fortune might favour him; he might discover Hahlstroem and perhaps Achleitner, too, and help one or both into the boat. There was danger, to be sure, that the boat would put off before he returned.

He had worked his way as far as the unused smoking-room. It was empty. Suddenly Wilke was standing beside him.

"If you're looking for somebody, I'll help," the peasant declared.

The two together descended the rest of the companionway. The space in front of the dining-room was empty and so was the dining-room. It was tilted at an acute angle. A heap of dishes and silverware blocked the doorway.

"Hahlstroem! Achleitner!" Frederick shouted again and again.

Wilke pushed a short way down the long corridor, on which the cabins gave. But the spot closed off by the rising waters was only too clearly distinguishable.

"Come away, come away!" Frederick cried, and ran. He ran for his life. He ran in wild fear of missing the boat.

XLVIII

A moment later he was on deck, over the railing, and in the boat. The men wanted to put off. Frederick protested, and disputed loudly with the third mate, who in the meantime had entered the boat and was grasping the tiller.

He could not make up his mind to desert Wilke of the Heuscheuer, who had so courageously followed him below deck and had not yet reappeared. But now he saw him, literally sliding from the companionway entrance to the railing.

"Wilke! Wilke!" he shouted. "Jump into the boat!"

"Right away, right away," Wilke answered several times. Then he did something that Frederick tried to scold him out of doing, because it seemed so senseless and useless to everybody in the boat. He had discovered a number of life-belts and was throwing them from various points out on the water, where persons swept overboard might be struggling desperately for their lives.

The boat did not wait for him. Under the third mate's command, the sailors began to row. The sea favoured them, and soon they were more than thirty yards from the *Roland's* side.

Now they could see the spot where another vessel, or a drifting derelict, had bored the flank of the *Roland*, making a great gash near the engine-room. Since the whole of the breach was not yet under water, they could see the foaming sea streaming into the hold. Frederick thought he could hear its greedy gulping. At the sight, for all the horror about him, he felt a desire to burst into mourning for the brave warrior *Roland*, and with difficulty restrained an outcry. The fog closed in and hid the fatally wounded giant from view.

When, in a few moments, the mist cleared, the wreck had in some incomprehensible way turned. The twenty persons in the boat looked down from a dizzy height upon the after part of the deck, almost on a level with the water. They shrieked in terror, for they thought that the next instant they would be hurled down upon the mass of human beings wedged in there, swarming like ants.

Not until that moment did Frederick grasp to its full extent the catastrophe that was occurring, a catastrophe beyond human conception. All those dark little crowding ants, helplessly running up and down, were tearing at one another, hitting about, beating, wrestling, forcing their way. Groups of men and women were united in struggling knots. Some of the life-boats that had not yet been lowered seemed to have turned into dark, swaying bunches of grapes, from which every now and then a single grape dropped off and fell into the sea.

Once more the fog and spray hid the ship from view. But a sound, which Frederick did not immediately connect with the ghastly spectacle on the deck, rose above the seething and roaring of the merciless sea and the metallic clanging of the hurricane. For several seconds Frederick's thoughts were far away in a certain place near his home, a wide, marshy meadow-land, where great flocks of migrating birds stopped to rest in their passage. But it was not the chirping of joyous birds that reached his ears through the fog. It was the outcry of those human beings, who were suffering something so horrible, beyond all conception, that no human crime, he felt, could be great enough to justify such atonement. He distinctly felt how, through the excess of the hideous impression, the bridge carrying the message of his senses to his innermost soul snapped.

But suddenly the fever of the visible death struggle of eight or nine hundred innocent men after all did penetrate to his innermost soul, and wrung a cry from him, in which the whole boat load joined as by command. In that cry were fear, anguish, fury, protest, supplication, horror, wailing, cursing, and despair.

And the horror was increased by the consciousness that there was no merciful ear to listen, but only a deaf heaven. Wherever Frederick turned his eyes, he saw death. Indifferently the bottle-green, mountainous waves came rolling. In their march there was a murderous regularity, with which nothing interfered and which recognised no obstacles. He closed his eyes ready to die. Several times he felt for his parents' letters in his breast pocket, as if he needed them for passports to the land of darkness, where he was soon going. He dared not open his eyes again, because he could no longer bear to see the convulsions of the women in the boat or the hideous massacre on the stern of the *Roland*.

The sea raged. It was icy cold. The water froze on the edge of the boat. Rosa, the maid, was the only one that constantly bestirred herself to help others, the children, Mrs. Liebling, Ingigerd, and Arthur Stoss. Bulke and she vied with each other in bailing out the water in which Stoss and Mrs. Liebling were lying and which reached to the knees of the others.

What was in the meantime happening on the deck of the *Roland*, so far as Frederick caught momentary glimpses of it, did not fit in with his conception of human nature. The things he thought he saw in detail had nothing in common with those civilised, decorous ladies and gentlemen whom he had seen in the dining-room and on deck, promenading, conversing, smiling, exchanging greetings, and daintily dissecting the fish on their plates with forks. He could have sworn that he distinguished the white figure of a cook cutting his way, with a long knife, through the honourable person of a first-class passenger for whom he had cooked. Frederick was convinced he saw a stoker, a black fellow, strike a woman who was clinging to him--perhaps she was the beautiful Canadian--pick her up and throw her overboard. Some stewards, whom he distinctly recognised, were still heroically executing orders. But they got entangled in fighting groups. One of them covered with blood, struggling and shouting, helped a woman and her child into a life-boat, but the boat capsized and disappeared.

"Father! My father!" Ingigerd suddenly cried. It was only a faint breath blown away by the raging elements. She pointed, and Frederick looked where she pointed with vacant, staring eyes. Again the fog lifted and opened a sort of gap through which the sinking steamer could be seen in all its length. Somebody was standing at the railing waving a white handkerchief. It was impossible to tell who it was. But a man whom Frederick recognised as distinctly as if he were looking through a spyglass was Hans Fuellenberg, racing about like a madman, leaping with the agility of a squirrel from one point of the deck to the other.

The port-holes, making a slanting line from stem to stern, still shone with the electric lights inside. Now and then a stifled shot could be heard, as a rocket rose up into the air, making a pale line of light. But soon the gem-like gleam of the portholes was extinguished. As if the sea in its unbridled hate of man's work had been waiting for this event, it swept over the deck from the other side. That instant the waters on the near side swarmed with human beings, swimming, shrieking, and struggling.

Suddenly, no one knew how, the boat was carried close to the **Roland** again, where maddened, half-drowned, desperate men clutched at it. A hideous, bestial conflict began.

Frederick saw it all, yet without seeing it. Although it went on under his very eyes, it seemed to be happening at an infinite distance. He struck at something. It was a hand, an arm, a head, a wet monster of the deep, shrieking in a voice not human. Suddenly, pulled backwards by the merciless hands of a hidden executioner, it disappeared. Frederick saw how, with the strength of desperation, Rosa's red fists and Mrs. Liebling's and Ingigerd's little cramped fingers unloosened the hold of the hand or arm of a fellow-man from the icy edge of the boat. The sailors used their oars in a way that produced dark spurts of blood.

None in the boat noticed that the third mate disappeared, that Bulke took his place at the helm, and that in the bottom of the boat lay a long-haired young man, who gave no sign of life.

The servant, Bulke, took command. For the sake of something to do and to delay the inevitable capsizing, Frederick and Wilhelm each seized an oar and rowed with the sailors.

Minutes passed. The fog lifted. Many eternally moving mountains and valleys of water had rolled between the little boat and the wreck. Of the *Roland*, the mighty fast mail steamer of the North German Steamship Company, nothing was to be seen.

XLIX

Late in the afternoon of the same day, the captain of a sturdy little trading vessel from Hamburg sighted a boat drifting on the long, high swells. The weather was clear, and the captain made certain that the people in the boat were signalling with handkerchiefs. Within half an hour, the shipwrecked passengers of the *Roland* were with great difficulty hoisted on board the trader, one at a time.

There were fifteen persons in all, three sailors and a cabin-boy, with the well-known name of the *Roland* on their caps, two ladies, a woman evidently from the steerage, a maid, a long-haired man of about thirty in a velvet jacket, an armless man, the man who had been steering, two other men, and two children, a boy and a girl. The boy was dead.

The hardships and terrors to which the delicate child had succumbed had had almost equally dire effects upon the others. With the exception of the maid Rosa, they looked as if they had been drowned beyond hope of resuscitation. A very wet man--it was Frederick--attempted to drag an unconscious wet young woman up the gangway-ladder, but his strength failed him, and the sailors of the trader had to catch him as he tottered, take the young woman from his arms, and help him struggle up the ladder on deck, like a man whose every bone and muscle is racked by rheumatism. Attempting to speak, he could produce only an asthmatic, sibilant wheeze. On deck, he groaned, burst into a senseless, cackling laugh, and spread out his purple, frozen hands. His lips, too, were purple, and his sunken eyes glowed feverishly from a face crusted with dirt and brine. He seemed to want nothing so much as to be dried, warmed and cleaned.

He was followed by Rosa. Upon laying an unconscious little girl in the arms of the first mate, she turned back to descend to the boat again, but found the way barred by Bulke and one of the sailors of the trader, hauling up the armless actor, Arthur Stoss. He was dripping wet, his eyes were staring blankly, his nose was running, and his eyelids were red and inflamed, while the tip of his nose was waxen white. After several vain attempts to produce a sound through his chattering teeth, he finally succeeded in framing "Rum! Hot rum!"

A mutual inclination seemed to make Bulke and Rosa pull together in their rescue work like two old mates. Fairly raining water, they descended again for Mrs. Liebling, who was lying prone in the bottom of the boat in a serious condition.

"She's dead, and the boy is dead," said the sailors of the trader, and wanted first to carry up the other woman, the steerage passenger, who showed she was still alive by a rattle in her throat, fearful to hear. Rosa burst into a howl and swore Mrs. Liebling was not dead.

"She's blue," the sailors declared. "She swallowed too much water."

But Rosa would not desist, and the sailors were compelled to carry Mrs. Liebling up first.

As they were lifting on deck the unconscious woman from the steerage, still emitting the fearful rattle, one of the **Roland** sailors, whose feet were frozen and who, during the whole long, dreadful drifting about on the ocean had not uttered a sound, suddenly began to bellow in pain.

"Shut up!" said his mates. "Don't carry on like an old woman."

He was the next to be lifted on board, merely whimpering now in ineffable agony. After him came the man in the velvet jacket, who was maundering, Doctor Wilhelm, Max Pander, and the other two sailors. Lastly the little corpse of Siegfried Liebling was lifted from the boat.

When the absurdly dressed man with long hair reached deck, he performed the drollest antics. For a moment he would stand upright, chest out, like a recruit, the next instant bow profoundly, or take aim, as if hunting; and all the time he kept bawling:

"I'm an artist. I paid for my cabin. I am well known in Germany"--striking a conscious attitude--"I am Jacob Fleischmann. I am a painter, from Fuerth."

Every now and then he would writhe pitifully and vomit salt water. The water dripping from his clothes formed a pool where he stood.

Doctor Wilhelm had completely lost the faculty of speech. All he could do was to sneeze incessantly.

In the meantime, the steward of the vessel brought Frederick hot tea, and one of the sailors, who acted as barber and nurse on the vessel, attempted to restore Mrs. Liebling to life. Within less than two minutes, Frederick felt sufficiently revived to meet the demands of the occasion and assist the sailor-nurse with his Good Samaritan work.

After swallowing several glasses of brandy, Doctor Wilhelm with the help of the chief engineer, Mr. Wendler, attempted to revive Siegfried Liebling, though with small hope of success.

Mrs. Liebling, in no wise differing from a corpse, had been laid on the long mahogany table in what would have been the dining-room, had the vessel been carrying passengers. Ugly, dark, purplish patches disfigured the forehead, cheeks, and throat of the woman, who was still young and who, before the shipwreck, had been beautiful. On baring her body, they found that it, too, was marked, though less closely, with the same gangrenous spots, somewhat duller in colour. Her body was swollen. Death might have resulted from choking in a moment when she fell into a faint unobserved by any of her companions. Toward the last, there had been several feet of water in the boat, and Rosa had for some time been entirely occupied with the dying boy.

When Frederick and the sailor-nurse laid Mrs. Liebling's body face downward on the table, water flowed from her nose and mouth. Her heart was no longer beating, and she gave no sign of life. As Frederick assumed, what had happened was, that she had sunk unconscious to the bottom of the boat and had lain for some time under water. He opened her mouth, forced her gold-filled teeth apart, put her tongue in the right position, and removed mucus, which had gathered at the opening of the air-passages. While the ship's cook rubbed her body with hot cloths, Frederick tried to induce artificial respiration by raising and lowering her arms and legs like a pump-handle.

The mahogany table took up the larger part of the low, creaking saloon, the only one the vessel possessed. It was on the quarter-deck and was lighted from above. The two walls running the length of the room were formed of the mahogany doors of the twelve staterooms, six on each side. In the twinkling of an eye the deserted saloon was converted into a medical laboratory.

A common sailor had peeled Ingigerd Hahlstroem out of her clothes, and without circumstance had laid her delicate body, shining like mother-of-pearl, on a couch against the wall taking up the full width of the room. At Frederick's instruction, he rubbed her body vigorously with woollen cloths. Rosa was doing the same for Ella Liebling, who was the first to be put to bed. The steward was working away in a glow of zeal to get each of the dozen beds freshly spread, and as soon as the second one was ready, Ingigerd was laid between the warmed covers. Thanks to his faithful valet, Arthur Stoss, his teeth still chattering, was the next to be ready for bed.

Jacob Fleischmann gave his rescuers much trouble. When a sailor spoke to him kindly and attempted to undress him, he struck about wildly, and shouted in a rage, "I'm an artist!"

The steward and Bulke had to hold him fast and use main force in putting him to bed. Doctor Wilhelm abandoned his vain efforts to revive Siegfried Liebling and came with his leather case of drugs, which he had managed to save, just in time to give the painter an injection of morphine.

The sailor whose agony of pain had overcome him before he was lifted on deck had such badly swollen, frostbitten feet that his boots had to be cut off bit by bit. He clenched his teeth to keep from screaming, and merely uttered low groans until they laid him in bed; when he called for chewing tobacco.

The woman from the steerage clad in rags was also put to bed. All she could tell was that she was bound for Chicago with her sister, her four children, her husband, and her mother. Nothing of what had in the meantime befallen her seemed to have penetrated, or remained in, her consciousness.

The whole while Frederick, his upper body bared, with only the barber to help him, kept working uninterruptedly over Mrs. Liebling. It was good for him, because it made him perspire. Finally, however, his strength gave out, and Doctor Wilhelm came to his relief. He tottered into the nearest cabin, the door of which stood open, and fell face downward into the unmade bed, utterly exhausted.

L

After a time Mr. Butor, the captain of the *Hamburg*, now speeding on its way, appeared in the saloon to welcome and congratulate the two physicians, who, notwithstanding their extreme exhaustion, were still working without cease over Mrs. Liebling's body.

The room, of course, was flooded and was reeking with the sweetish-sour smell of human exhalations. The captain sent a sailor to fetch dry clothes for Frederick.

While continuing their efforts and relieving each other at intervals, Doctor Wilhelm and Frederick gave a short account of the catastrophe on the *Roland*. Captain Butor was greatly astonished. Though the weather throughout his trip had not been especially good, yet it had not been the reverse. Most of the time, as at present, it had been clear, with a stiff wind and a moderately high sea. His vessel was bound for New York with a cargo of oranges, wine, oil, and cheese from Fayal in the Azores, to which it had carried a load of agricultural implements from Hamburg.

Frederick and Wilhelm could give little information concerning the cause of the accident. Wilhelm said that shortly before six in the morning, he had been awakened by a sound like the clang of a gong. In his half-waking state, he thought it was the signal to dinner, until he remembered that on the *Roland* a trumpet blast was used to announce meals.

Frederick thought the *Roland* had probably struck a wreck or a rock. But rocks, the captain said, were out of the question. There were none in those waters, and the *Roland* could not have been carried by strong currents into a region where there were rocks, since in that event the life-boat would not have entered the course of his own vessel within so short a time. The skipper, who knew Captain von Kessel personally and had met him in Hamburg only recently, spoke of him in the highest terms, as one of the most experienced, trustworthy captains in the German merchant marine. The catastrophe, he said, was possibly the worst that had occurred in decades, if the steamer had actually sunk and not been towed into a port.

Before leaving, Captain Butor invited the two men, as soon as their task was ended, to supper at the mess table.

An hour and a half passed. The physicians were about to give up their attempts to resuscitate Mrs. Liebling, when her heart began to stir and her breast to heave. Rosa's joy was boundless. With the greatest difficulty restraining an emotional outburst, she felt the warmth return even to Mrs. Liebling's soles, which she had been rubbing unwearyingly with her palms, hard as flat-irons. The rescued woman was carried to bed and packed in hot water bottles, like a premature baby.

This great success of the physicians' efforts--it was like a raising of the dead--produced profound emotion in all that witnessed it, including Frederick and Doctor Wilhelm, who were suddenly moved to shake hands with each other.

"We have been saved," said Wilhelm. "The most improbable, the most incredible thing has actually happened."

"Yes," rejoined Frederick. "It has actually happened. It *is* absolutely the most improbable thing that has ever occurred in my life. The question is, What were we saved for?"

LI

The mess-room of the *Hamburg* was a small square cabin with iron walls, its only furniture a square table and a bench running around three sides. Once a person was seated, it was impossible to pass him; and when the officers gathered for meals, they shoved themselves into place in a certain order, the captain first.

At seven o'clock Doctor Wilhelm and Frederick appeared for supper. They found a soup tureen sending up clouds of steam and a well-constructed oil lamp over the table shedding a cheerful light. The *Hamburg* was not lighted by electricity.

The two physicians, like all victims of accidents, the objects of really touching solicitude, were assigned seats against the warmest wall, dividing the cabin from the engine-room. Captain Butor served the strong hot soup, and Mr. Wendler, chief engineer, a rotund little mariner, in an attempt to enliven the shipwrecked men, cautiously ventured a joke or two even before the roast was served. He came from

Lindenau near Leipzig, and the rest of the crew teased him for his Low German.

"Don't talk," said the captain to Wilhelm and Frederick. "Just eat, drink, and sleep."

At first they were inclined to take his advice, but in the course of the meal, after one of the sailors had served an immense cut of roast beef, and the captain had carved it, and they had washed the meat down with red wine, their spirits rose from moment to moment.

Bulke appeared at the door showing evidences of the royal banquet to which he and the sailors of the *Roland* had been treated by the sailors of the *Hamburg*. Notwithstanding his condition, pardonable enough in the circumstances, he would not go to sleep without first receiving instructions from Doctor Wilhelm and Frederick, before whom he stood in military attitude, hand to his cap, awaiting orders.

It was decided that the sailor-nurse and another sailor of the *Hamburg* should go on night duty, since all the men from the *Roland* needed rest and sleep.

Though Frederick's and Doctor Wilhelm's spirits rose visibly, they never referred to the sinking of the *Roland*. It was too tremendous a thing, too dreadful, too near for any of the survivors, except the sailors, to speak of it without intense emotion. It was like a dull weight on their souls. Whatever Wilhelm and Frederick said related merely to their difficulties in the life-boat, or to the trip on the *Roland* before it overstepped that moment in eternity which determined its awful fate.

"Captain," said Frederick, "you don't know how astonishing it is to be raised from the dead. Conceive a man who has taken definite leave of everything that was dear to him in life, who has felt the rattle in his throat, and received extreme unction, and death, death itself, has settled on his flesh and limbs. I still feel death in my joints. And yet I am sitting here in safety, in the pleasant lamplight, almost as in a circle of friends and relatives. I am sitting in the cosiest home, with the difference that I still cannot get myself to look upon you"--they were the captain, the engineer, the boatswain, and the first mate--"as something so insignificant as mere men."

"When we sighted the *Hamburg*", said Wilhelm, "I had just made my last will and testament. You see I don't give myself up for lost as quickly as my friend, Doctor von Kammacher. When your ship gradually grew from the size of a pinhead to the size of a full-grown pea, all of us who could, screamed at the top of our voices.

We nearly burst our throats screaming. And when your **Hamburg** attained the size of a walnut, and we realised we had been sighted, your ship flamed in my eyes like a huge diamond or ruby, and to me the east from which you came shone more brilliantly than the west, where the sun was still shining above the horizon. All of us howled like watch-dogs."

"It will always be a miracle to me," Frederick resumed, "that such an evening as this could follow such a morning. I have let days slip past, by the hundreds, holding no more in them than minutes. But in this one day, a whole summer has passed, and a whole winter. I feel as if the first violet had followed directly upon the first snow."

Wilhelm told of how excited the sailors had been in Cuxhaven because Catholic priests had boarded the **Roland**. Then he mentioned a dream his old mother had had the night before he was to sail. A child of hers that had been born many years before and had lived only a day, appeared to her as a grown-up man and warned her not to let him make the trip.

"She begged me not to go," he said, "but, as I am an enlightened man, I simply laughed at her for her fears."

Once launched upon the boundless sea of superstition, beloved by sailors, the men went on to recite cases they knew of prophetic dreams, of forebodings fulfilled, and the appearance of dying or dead men. This suggested his friend's last letter to Frederick. He drew his portfolio from his waistcoat pocket, where it had remained throughout his perilous trip, and passed the letter around.

They read the passage, "In the vivid, flashing orgies of my nocturnal dreams, you are always tossing in a ship on the high seas. Do you intend to make an ocean trip?" Of course, it excited not a little astonishment, and it was with some thrills that they read: "Should it be possible for me, after the great moment, to make myself noticeable from the Beyond, you will hear from me again."

Captain Butor asked with an incredulous smile, yet eagerly, whether his friend had indeed made himself noticeable from the Beyond.

"This is what happened to me in a dream. Judge for yourselves. I don't know," said Frederick, in a voice still hoarse and barking. It was unlike him to go on and relate, as he did, the dream that had been greatly occupying his thoughts, which began with the landing in a mystic port and ended with the Toilers of the Light. He described his friend, Peter Schmidt, and declared that Peter had sent his astral self half way across the Atlantic to greet him. He spoke of 1492, of Columbus's flag-ship, the **Santa Maria**, but chiefly of his meeting with Rasmussen in the form of an old chandler, giving a detailed description of the remarkable ship in the shop window, the shop itself, and the chirping of the goldfinches. He drew out his note-book and read aloud what the mysterious chandler had said to him:

"It was precisely thirteen minutes past one on the twenty-fourth of January when I drew my last breath."

"Whether that is true," Frederick concluded, "remains to be proved. So much is certain--if there is anything about this dream that isn't the illusory work of my imagination--my soul grazed the boundaries of the world beyond, and I received a hint of the catastrophe to come. As to the **Roland**, my friend, Peter Schmidt, showed me a ship in the harbour with a tremendous hole in its side and said it had brought in a great many people,--which would mean, it had transferred them to the world beyond. In regard to my rescue, my disguised friend, Rasmussen, said I should soon celebrate the four hundredth anniversary of 1492 with Peter Schmidt in New York. But dreams are froth and foam. I fancy it would not be difficult to explain all this rationalistically, from psycho-physiologic causes."

Before the little family circle of the **Hamburg** broke up for the night, they touched glasses again with great gravity, even solemnity.

LII

Frederick awoke the next morning from an eleven hours' sleep, for which he was indebted chiefly to a dose of veronal. Doctor Wilhelm had undertaken to do whatever was necessary during the night for the sick passengers of the **Roland** and had persuaded Frederick, whose more delicate constitution was in the utmost need of rest, to take the drug. The sun was shining brightly into his tiny cabin. Through the slat door, he heard the sound of voices speaking calmly and the cheerful clatter of plates and dishes. At first he recalled nothing of the previous day's events, and thought he was on the fast mail steamer, **Roland**. But he could not reconcile the change in his cabin with the idea he had formed of his room on the **Roland**. In his bewilderment he reached out from bed and knocked on the mahogany slats of the door. The next moment Doctor Wilhelm's face, lively and refreshed, was bending over him.

"With the exception of the woman from the steerage, all our patients had a good night," the *Roland's* doctor said, and went on to give a report of each case. It was not until he had nearly ended his account that he noticed the difficulty Frederick was having to explain his surroundings. Wilhelm laughed and recalled some incidents. Frederick started up and clapped his hands to his temples.

"A void," he exclaimed. "A whirl of impossible things is going round in my brain."

Shortly after, he was sitting at breakfast with Doctor Wilhelm, eating and drinking. And yet not a word was said of the sinking of the *Roland*.

Ingigerd Hahlstroem had awakened and fallen asleep again. The barber and sailor-nurse, Flitte by name, had locked her door. Arthur Stoss was still lying abed with his door open and was cracking jokes in the best of spirits, while his trusty valet, Bulke, fed him or handed him food to take with his feet. From the ring of his falsetto voice one would have judged that the horrors he had survived were nothing but a series of comic situations.

"This business," he said, leaving his original subject and dropping a few highly flavoured oaths, "is going to cost me one thousand American dollars. I shall not be able to keep the first days of my engagement in New York." In good English he cursed the whole German Hansa, especially the *Hamburg*. "The wretched little herring keg! At the utmost it doesn't make more than ten knots an hour."

Fourteen hours of peaceful sleep brought the painter, Jacob Fleischmann of Fuerth to his senses. He had his breakfast served in bed, rang the call-bell, gave orders, and kept the steward dancing attendance on him. The others could hear him loudly reiterate again and again that though the loss of his oil-paintings, sketches, and etchings, which he had intended to sell in America, was irreparable and beyond compensation, yet the steamship company was unquestionably liable, and as soon as he reached New York, he would take to haunting the company's office, until they paid him full damages. They were to find out who and what he was.

Rosa, happy and eager, though with eyes red from crying, passed to and fro between her mistress's cabin and the dining-room table, carrying now one thing, now another, to Mrs. Liebling, who was still whining reproachfully. It had been agreed to keep Siegfried Liebling's death a secret from her, an easy thing to do since she had declared she was not yet strong enough to see the children. Yet it was remarkable how the dead woman had revived. When Frederick after breakfast paid her a professional visit, he found she had only a dim recollection of having been unconscious. She had had glorious dreams, she said, and when she realised she was to be awakened, had felt so regretful that she tried to resist the summons back to earthly life, back from the wondrous isle, the veritable paradise, in which she had been.

Mrs. Liebling was beautiful. She complained of pains, and at Frederick's bidding bared her body. He found it marked with blue spots, the result of the rough tossings in the life-boat, which had left him, too, bruised and wounded in various places and with frozen toes and fingers.

"My dear Mrs. Liebling," he said, "put up with your slight discomfort. We were all dead, and we have undeservedly been granted a second life."

Shortly before ten o'clock, Captain Butor entered the dining-room, shook hands with the gentlemen, asked how they had slept, and told them that all night the men on the bridge had redoubled their vigilance on the chance of discovering more survivors of the *Roland*. Since the wind was still from the northwest, it was possible that the *Hamburg* might chance on the wreck, in case it had not sunk.

"As a matter of fact," he said, "we did sight a derelict at one o'clock, but there were absolutely no persons aboard. It was an older wreck and a sailing vessel, not a steamer."

"Perhaps it was the *Roland's* murderer," said Doctor Wilhelm.

The captain asked the two physicians to come to the chart-room where they and the sailors of the *Roland*, who were already awaiting him, were to give him the vouchers he needed for his brief report to be submitted to his company's agent in New York in regard to the picking up of the castaways. A sort of audience was held, during which nothing new concerning the tremendous disaster was revealed.

Pander showed the scrap of paper with the pencilled message that Captain von Kessel had asked him to take to his sisters. All were greatly moved on reading the few hastily scrawled words. The incident revealed what a wrench the hearts and nerves of even the seamen had undergone. At the mention of this or that person or incident, Pander and the three sailors burst into hysterical tears. When asked whether they thought the *Roland* would remain above water over the day, all said "No." One of the sailors, who from the first warning of danger to the boarding of the *Hamburg*, had gone about his heavy duty with the same grit, the same matter-of-course manner, scarcely uttering a word, concluded each of his statements with: "Captain, it was like on Judgment Day."

At the conclusion of the audience, Frederick felt a great need to be alone for a while. "It was like on Judgment Day," followed him. Yes, it was like on Judgment Day! The horrors of the cruellest judgment could not exceed those amid which the victims of the shipwreck had perished. Strange, the evening before, Frederick had still been able to laugh; to-day he felt as if the gravity of his being were turned to brass and had laid itself about him, not like an iron mask, not like a leaden cloak, but rather like a heavy metal sarcophagus.

He knew a man, an architect verging on middle age, who had been on the island of Ischia during the last great earthquake there. The architect and some very dear friends were sitting together over a bottle of wine when the calamity was ushered in by the roll of subterranean thunder. A moment later the ceiling and floors burst, and an abyss swallowed up five or six persons, men and women, full of hope and joy in life. He himself remained on the brink of the abyss unscathed. Though years intervened, there was still not a clod of earth, not a rock, no matter how adamantine, on which he could set foot with his old confidence; there was no wall or ceiling that he did not seem to see falling on his head and crushing him. Groping along the walls of houses on the street, terror would seize him. Open places made him dizzy, and not infrequently a passerby seeing his helplessness would lead him like a blind man across the city square.

Frederick felt that the sinking of the *Roland* had left him with a gloomy heritage, a black compact cloud-mass brooding menacingly in the spaces of his soul. With all his will, he had to overcome a shudder when something like a flash of lightning darted from the cloud and illuminated the horror he had witnessed, as if it were still present to his eye.

Why had the powers revealed Judgment Day to him, not as a vision, but as an actuality? Why had they showed such partiality as to let him and a few others escape perdition? Was he, the tiny ant, which was susceptible of such titanic terrors, important enough to assume the guidance of things for himself, to fulfil a loftier purpose for good or evil? Had he transgressed? Was he deserving of punishment? But that wholesale massacre was too fearful, too vast a thing! It was ridiculous to attribute to it a pedagogic purpose for the discipline of one minute human existence. Indeed, he felt how the large generalness of the event had almost entirely dislodged everything personal. No! Nothing but blind, deaf and dumb powers of destruction had been at work.

Yet, in facing the elemental tragedy of the human race, the inexorable gruesomeness of the powers, in looking into the eyes of death, he had acquired knowledge that turned something in his being into the hardness of the hardest rock. What was the sense of such a disaster if the eternal goodness ordained it? And where was the power of eternal goodness, if it was incapable of hindering it? Nothing remained but to strip oneself bare of all pride and dignity and grovel in the dust before the great unknown, a humble, will-less slave, completely at its mercy.

LIII

While on the *Roland*, time had crawled at a snail's pace, the hour hand of the clock on the *Hamburg* travelled twice around its face with surprising rapidity. During that interval, the two ladies remained in bed, though the weather, which was clear and moderate, permitted being on deck. In Mrs. Liebling the consequences of the strain manifested themselves in periodic attacks of great excitement and fear accompanied by violent palpitation; in Ingigerd Hahlstroem, in healthy sleepiness, which made the administration of morphine in her case unnecessary. Neither of the women developed fever. But the sailor whose feet were frozen and the woman from the steerage had a high temperature. The immigrant in her delirium wanted to jump from bed, and, at the physicians' request, Captain Butor appointed one of the well sailors from the *Roland* and a sailor from the *Hamburg* to relieve each other in keeping constant watch over her.

Each time Frederick went to look after the poor creature, he felt himself assailed by the temptation to save her forever from the moment of awakening. From her own lips, while she had still been conscious, he had heard of all the relatives she had probably lost on the *Roland*, her husband, three sons, and a daughter-ranging from seven to eighteen years of age--a sister and her mother. At first her fevered fancy occupied itself with the shipwreck, her husband, children, and sisters. Later she seemed to become a child again, reliving her life in her parents' home. Swallows' nests, a cow, a goat, a meadow, in which there was a haystack roofed to keep off the rain, figured as important things.

"Would that she passed away in those illusions!" thought Frederick.

Arthur Stoss, transported up-stairs by his faithful Bulke, and Jacob Fleischmann strolled about on deck, or reclined in the steamer chairs, which even the trading vessel possessed. Stoss needed some massaging and patching up, and while the physicians were busy with him, he crowed and cawed in his most jovial manner:

"I always say you can't destroy weeds. Tanned leather is impervious to salt water. I am like an ant which can spend a week under water without dying."

Thanks to Rosa's unwearying care, Ella Liebling escaped with nothing but a bad cold. Looking very pretty and saucy in her own clothes, which had been cleaned and dried, the little maiden pried about in every nook and cranny of the vessel. The skipper granted her a free pass to his bridge, the engineers to the engine-room. She was even admitted into the great tube of the propeller-shaft. She was everybody's pet, and all soon became acquainted with her mother's position in the world and manner of life.

When Ingigerd, after about fifty hours of rest in bed, finally appeared on deck, wrapped in Frederick's overcoat, the passengers and crew fairly celebrated the event. The exquisite creature, who had lost her father, was regarded with the same masculine pity by all the men on board. Pander, the gallant cabin-boy, converted himself into her shadow. He made a stool for her feet from an empty box of smoked sprats, and while she sat talking to Frederick, he stood off at a short distance ready to receive her orders. Even Flitte, sailor and barber and nurse, who was supposed to give all who needed him equal attention, ran hither and thither for her sake with special zeal.

The call for Flitte was the one most frequently heard on the *Hamburg*. The undersized little man from Brandenburg, whom a love of adventure had changed from a barber-surgeon into a sailor, unexpectedly experienced a triumph of his personality. Now it was Mrs. Liebling who summoned him, now Ingigerd, now the sailor with the frozen feet, now Fleischmann, now Stoss, and even Bulke and Rosa--Rosa, who for several hours during the day made herself useful in the contracted little kitchen, which was ruled by a shrewd old cook. The physicians, too, had, of course, constant use for him; and it was the most natural thing that he should become a man of importance in the eyes of even his idolised captain, whom, in the ordinary course of things it was his duty to shave. He was well aware of this, and since, moreover, pity had fanned into a lively flame his old inclination for nursing, he outdid himself in self-sacrificing deeds for the sick, both by day and night. Frederick asked him the same question he had asked each member of the *Roland's* crew:

"Would you rather be a seaman than anything else?"

And Flitte was the first that without hesitation answered, "Yes."

LIV

The unexpected arrival of the little troupe of peculiar passengers on the *Hamburg* in mid-ocean produced a flutter of excitement in both captain and crew. It was a feeling of mingled solemnity and gaiety. For the benefit now of the captain, now of the boatswain, or the first mate, or the cook, or the engineer, the physicians had to repeat again and again the account of how they had been sighted and rescued. It was a story that never grew stale, and from the eagerness with which the *Hamburg's* crew listened to the oft-told tale, the physicians realised that even to those old sea-dogs the event was a miracle. None of them, in all the years they had been sailing the high seas, had ever fished up such booty.

"When Captain Butor had me look through the spy-glasses," Wendler would say, "his face was the colour of green cheese. And when I thought for a moment that I made out a boat and the next second heard the captain say, 'Look sharp, there are people in it,' I felt my knees getting weak."

In telling of his impressions when the boat entered, and immediately disappeared from, the field of his spy-glasses, the captain invariably declared that he had suddenly been beset by a paralysed feeling in his feet, and rubbed the glasses, and began to search again. He was on the point of leaving the bridge, since he could not get another view of that strange little flyspeck on the ocean and decided it was an allusion, when it occurred to him that for reasons of general security he had better scan the entire circle of the horizon. This time he looked backwards. Instantly he had the *Hamburg* stopped and turned, because he had sighted the boat a second time and it was now decidedly nearer. The first mate, too, on looking through the glasses saw it was a boat and that it contained passengers. Wendler was called on deck. When he peered through the glass, he distinguished white cloths waving.

"When my boys found out what was doing," said Captain Butor, "they began to carry on like lunatics. I had to use some of my sea-lingo on them. They wanted to dive over the railing into the sea, and swim to the boat."

*   *   *   *   *

Ingigerd was lying stretched out in her comfortable steamer chair, and Frederick was sitting on a camp-stool in front of her. On the *Roland*, when the sense of danger began to thicken, a feeling of ownership in regard to Ingigerd had taken hold of Frederick and never left him. Doctor Wilhelm and, as a result of his influence, everybody on the *Hamburg* looked upon Frederick as the romantic rescuer and lover of the little dancer. All were conscious of witnessing the development of a romance especially sanctioned by Divine Providence, and looked on with interest and respect. Ingigerd's attitude to Frederick was that of tacit docility, as if she, the obedient ward, recognised in him her natural guardian.

The air was fresh, the motion of the sea was easy. Suddenly, after a long spell of silence, which Frederick had imposed upon her, Ingigerd asked:

"Was it really nothing but chance that brought us together on the *Roland*?"

"There is no such thing as chance, or, rather, everything is chance, Ingigerd," was his evasive answer.

Ingigerd was not satisfied, and did not desist until she learned the causes and circumstances that had led Frederick to board the unfortunate *Roland* at Southampton.

"So for my sake," she said, "you came within a hair's breadth of losing your life. Instead, you saved my life."

This brief conversation cemented the bond between them more firmly.

In the survivors, with the exception of Frederick and Ingigerd, the consciousness of their newly acquired life soon assumed exuberant forms. Scarcely two days lay between them and the sinking of the *Roland*, yet these very people, who had undergone the brutal terrors of that awful event, abandoned themselves to the greatest gaiety. Arthur Stoss probably had never before shot off such an incessant fire of jokes and jibes, and probably never before had set such an audience a-laughing as the captain, the first mate, the boatswain, Wendler, the ship's cook, Fleischmann, Doctor Wilhelm, and even Mrs. Liebling, Rosa, Bulke, and the sailors of the *Roland* and the *Hamburg*.

Fleischmann involuntarily and unconsciously danced to the tune that Stoss in perfect good humour intentionally piped. It was most amusing when the man with black locks, dressed in a black velvet suit saturated with salt water, swaggeringly passed judgment upon Adolf Menzel, Boecklin, Liebermann, and other celebrated German masters. In expanding his theories of painting, he always used his lost treasures as examples. Stoss never wearied of getting the caddish genius to describe his paintings, the loss of which in Fleischmann's opinion was the worst disaster connected with the sinking of the *Roland*. The form that Doctor Wilhelm's teasing of Fleischmann took was, when Ingigerd was not present, to make him describe his rescue in detail. In the artist's brain, it was an event in an eminent degree glorifying to himself. All the sorry incidents had completely passed from his mind, including the fact that Rosa, Bulke and Ingigerd had pulled him out of the waves howling like a wet poodle.

The sum at which he estimated the loss of his pictures and which he intended to demand of the steamship company was a matter of general knowledge, like the price of stocks and bonds, within two and a half days jumping from eight hundred dollars to six thousand. There was no telling to what amount it might soar.

Fleischmann had contrived to get some writing paper on the *Hamburg*, and industriously set to work to caricature everybody on board. Thus, he often bestowed his company unbidden upon Frederick and Ingigerd, who had no need of anybody else in the world. That would ruffle Frederick's temper.

"I am surprised," he once said to him, by no means amiably, "that after so solemn an event, you are capable of such superficial trifling."

"A strong character!" said Fleischmann, laconically.

"Don't you think," Frederick continued, "that Miss Hahlstroem may be annoyed by your constantly looking at her?"

"No," said Fleischmann, "I don't think so."

Ingigerd took Fleischmann's part, thereby heightening Frederick's ill humour.

LV

Shortly after, just as Wendler, who was off duty, passed by with a chess-board under his arm, Frederick was summoned to Mrs. Liebling. Of the two physicians, he was the one that had inspired her special confidence, why, he did not know.

"Doctor von Kammacher," said Doctor Wilhelm, with a swift side glance at Ingigerd, "you've cut me out again."

At least once every twenty minutes Mrs. Liebling called for Flitte and at least once every hour Frederick von Kammacher had to sit beside her on the edge of her bed. Strangely enough, it did not occur to the young scientist to take amiss the jokes that Doctor Wilhelm and the others aimed at him on that account. He was really sorry for the poor woman and was unaffectedly ready to be of service to her.

They had not yet informed her of Siegfried's death, but, now that only Ella kept coming to her, a suspicion had arisen in her mind. Flitte and Rosa, when she begged them to go fetch Siegfried, always returned without him, and when pressed, gave as the reason that the boy was sick.

"What is the matter with my dear, sweet Siegfried?" she cried, wringing her hands, when Frederick entered her cabin. The next moment she fell back on her pillow and lay rigid, pressing her hands to her eyes.

"O my God! O my God!" she exclaimed in impotent denial of the truth. Without waiting for what Frederick had to say, she began to cry quietly, in genuine grief.

On returning to the deck half an hour later, Frederick found the fat little engineer and Ingigerd playing chess together.

"The painter and I have made Miss Hahlstroem laugh three times already," cried the engineer.

"I know where you were, Doctor von Kammacher," Ingigerd said. "Does she know the truth now?"

"Yes," Frederick replied. "I hope she will be quieter now."

Ingigerd wanted to go down to Mrs. Liebling. Tears came to her eyes, and revealed, as with a ray of light shining inward, what she refrained from saying, that she who had lost her father was most fitted to share the grief of a mother who through the same misfortune had lost her son. Frederick was indignant that Ingigerd had been told, and used all his authority to prevail upon her not to visit Mrs. Liebling for the present.

LVI

The next day at about noon Doctor Wilhelm and Frederick helped Mrs. Liebling on deck. Her appearance there made a gruesome impression upon those who had not seen her since she had been dragged, a lifeless corpse, from the boat to the *Hamburg*. The sailors, though most solicitous to read Ingigerd Hahlstroem's wishes from her eyes, even before they were conceived, kept at a distance from Mrs. Liebling and cast shy glances at her, as if still in doubt whether she was a real human being. If the sea gives up its dead, why should not little Siegfried emerge from his death chamber?

Mrs. Liebling, wrapped in blankets and a coat belonging to the captain, was placed in a comfortable position on the other side of the deck from Ingigerd, because she wished to be alone. For a long while she looked across the expanse of the quiet sea. Then she said to Frederick, whose company she had requested:

"It's strange that I feel merely as if I had had a dreadful dream--just a dream-- that is the strange thing. No matter how hard I try, I cannot fully convince myself, except when I think of Siegfried, that my dream reflects an actuality which I experienced."

"We mustn't indulge in vain broodings," said Frederick.

"I know," she continued without looking at him, "I know I didn't always do what is right, but if *I* deserved to be punished, Siegfried did not. Why did I escape?" After an interval of silence, she began to speak of her past, of conflicts with her husband, who had deceived her. Hers had been one of those loveless matches which are contracted in the customary business fashion. She told Frederick that she was an artist by nature, Rubinstein, for whom she had played when she was eleven years old, having prophesied a great future for her. "I don't know anything about cooking or children. I was always terribly nervous. Still, I love my children. If I didn't, would I have been so obstinate in trying to win them from my husband? I pledge you my word, Doctor, if I could change places with Siegfried, you would find me ready at any moment."

Frederick made all sorts of consolatory remarks, some of which were not wholly superficial; for instance, what he said of death and resurrection and the great atonement that every form of death, even mere sleep, involves.

"If you were a man, I should recommend Goethe. I should say to you, 'Read over and over the beginning of the second part of *Faust*.'

'Then the craft of elves propitious

Hastes to help where help it can.'
or the passage beginning:

'The fierce convulsions of his heart compose;

Remove the burning barbs of his remorses,
And cleanse his being from the suffered woes!'
Doesn't what we went through give you a sense of expiation and purification?"

"I feel," said the woman who had arisen from the dead, "as if my former life were far, far away, as if, since the sinking of the *Roland*, an impassable mountain were lying between me and my past. But leave me now, Doctor. You are bored. Don't waste the precious time you owe your pretty friend on me."

As a matter of fact, Frederick preferred to talk to Mrs. Liebling rather than to Ingigerd. If he was bored, it was with Ingigerd, not with Mrs. Liebling.

"Oh," he said, "never mind. Ingigerd Hahlstroem always has company. She doesn't need me."

"My mother urged me," said Mrs. Liebling, "not to take the children, but to leave them with her. Had I obeyed, Siegfried would still have been alive. She has a perfect right to reproach me severely. And how can I face Siegfried's father? He did what he could to keep the children back. He wrote to me and sent friends and his attorneys."

"With 'if' and 'hadn't I,' you can't undo what has been done. The event is too general, too titanic, to be thought of in such a way. It is too fearful to be considered with reference to a single individual and his puny fate. What happened had to happen, whether or not we believe in predestination. We human beings must not have feelings so petty as to allow mere chance to play a role in this event."

Frederick could not make up his mind to speak of his dream, in which Rosa figured as jumping from the boat with Siegfried in her arms and escaping to the white marble quay of the wonderful Columbus port, where he had been received by Peter Schmidt and where the **Santa Maria** was slowly crumbling away. Since there were things in his dream that gave support to a belief in predestination relieving the mind of self-blame, his telling it might have soothed Mrs. Liebling's troubled conscience; but Rosa had remained alive, Siegfried alone was dead. Besides, though Frederick was constantly revolving the dream in his soul and kept recalling Hamlet's words, "There are more things in heaven and earth, Horatio, than are dreamt of in your philosophy," he did not want to strengthen Mrs. Liebling's superstition, which showed itself in a predisposition for table-tipping and patience-playing.

On walking to the other side of the deck, after a rather prolonged absence, he was greeted with a shout.

"Hullo, father confessor!" they cried.

"Come be seated, my saviour," said Ingigerd, looking considerably better and brighter than the day before.

Frederick turned slightly pale, but did as he was bidden and said in a tone that did not harmonise with the good humour of the group:

"Mrs. Liebling was Rubinstein's pupil. I haven't met another woman on this trip to whom it is so well worth the while to talk."

"All due respect to you, a matter of taste," said Doctor Wilhelm.

"Let him alone. My saviour is displeased," said Ingigerd.

It was evident that occasionally she stood in awe of Frederick.

LVII

Aside from little tiffs between Ingigerd and Frederick, the spirit on board the *Hamburg* was generally good-humoured, even jolly. The weather remained clear, and the place of terror already lay eight hundred miles behind in the ocean. Each minute carried the passengers of the *Roland* farther along in their newly acquired lives. The ladies were feasted from the cargo of tropical fruit in the hold of the vessel, which had a carrying capacity of some two thousand register tons. Often the men for Ingigerd's amusement would use the oranges for playing ball. The Atlantic Ocean about the *Hamburg* seemed a very different thing from that awful, treacherous sea which had swallowed the *Roland*. It lay like a wave-tossing heaven under the steamer, and gave it a gentle rocking motion, by no means unpleasant. There was majesty in the course of even the plain little trader, painted black above the water-line and red below. Compared with that mechanical marvel, the *Roland*, it was like a comfortable old stage-coach, and could be depended upon to make its ten knots an hour with a great show of speed. Captain Butor in all seriousness declared the castaways had brought him good luck. The moment they appeared, the old man of the sea turned as peaceful and serene as an octogenarian English rector.

"Yes," said, Stoss, "but your old English rector first filled his belly with a few hecatombs of human lives. Stop, look, listen! Don't be too quick to trust him. When he's done assimilating, he'll have a still better appetite."

Up to the very end of the trip, though there was a corpse on board and the woman from the steerage was still very sick, the atmosphere on the *Hamburg* lost none of its festal character. The bridge was free territory. Ingigerd was usually to be seen there in the daytime playing chess with Wendler, or looking on while Frederick won one game after the other from the engineer. Naturally enough, the entire crew, by no means exclusive of Captain Butor, felt profound satisfaction because of the booty they had recovered on the high seas, each wearing an air of evident pride in the catch. Had the exalted feelings that swelled the hearts of all on board the gallant freight coach, the *Hamburg*, been transferred into od-rays, the steamer would have sailed up New York Harbour surrounded, even at high noon, by an aureole of its own radiance.

There was betting as to the number of the pilot-boat that would come to meet the *Hamburg*, when suddenly it appeared hard by, with the number "25" decipherable on its sail. Arthur Stoss had won. Almost choking with laughter, he raked in a considerable sum, and Jacob Fleischmann envied him with comically obvious greed.

The close companionship with his fellow-passengers on the small steamer, the compulsion he was under to listen to their jokes and to the superficial, reiterated tale of the disaster made Frederick inwardly impatient. Unlike the others, he had not yet recovered his old relation to life. His soul was numbed. He had lost his feeling for the past, his feeling for the future, even his passion for Ingigerd. The moment of the catastrophe seemed to have snapped all the threads that bound him to the events, men, and things of his former life. Whenever he looked upon Ingigerd, he felt an oppressive consciousness of responsibility. In these days it almost seemed as if the girl in her predominatingly soft, serious mood were awaiting the declaration of his love.

"You all want to have fun with me," she once said, "but nobody wants anything serious of me."

Frederick did not understand himself. Hahlstroem was no longer living, Achleitner had had to pay the penalty of his undignified, dog-like love, and the girl, shaken and refined to the depths of her being, was wax in his hands. Often he would look at her to find that her eyes had been fixed upon him in a long, grave, meditative gaze. Then he would seem to himself a very sorry sort of person, and was compelled to admit that he who had once wished to overwhelm the girl with the infinite riches of a passionately loving soul, was a bankrupt, groping with empty hands in empty pockets. He ought to speak, ought to open the sluices on the other side of which the flood of his passionate love must have gathered and risen high; but all the waters had trickled away, all the sources had dried up. To mask the aridity of his soul, he adopted his old method of a curt, dictatorial manner.

LVIII

It was the fifth of February, about thirteen days after the **Roland** had left Bremen, and twelve after Frederick had boarded the **Roland** at the Needles in the Channel, when the pilot took the guidance of the **Hamburg**. Compared with the length of the **Fuerst Bismarck's** record-making passage, this was an extremely long time. But how inconceivably brief it seemed to him when he recalled all he had experienced in that period, both in his waking and sleeping hours. On the **Hamburg**, he no longer dreamed at night. A mighty blast had swept his soul clean and denuded it of all images.

Shortly before ten o'clock in the morning of the sixth of February, Captain Butor, standing back of Ella Liebling, who was sitting under the telescope merrily kicking her thin legs, spied land. It was a tremendously stirring moment when the news was carried to the passengers. The steward that called it into Frederick's cabin and the next instant disappeared little realised how his brief announcement, "Land!" affected the stranger. Frederick closed the door, shaken by great, hollow, toneless sobs coming from the depths of his being.

"Such is life," went through his heart. "Did not a steward on a gloomy, horrid night call 'Danger!' into my cabin, like the shouting of a death sentence into the cell of a poor sinner by both the judge and the hangman? And now comes the peaceful piping of the shepherd's reed, while the thunder is still rolling." It was not until his sobbing ceased that he felt a thrill of bliss, as if life were again drawing near in triumph. A flash of feeling set him afire, as when a vast army approaches with music playing and banners flying, an army of invincible brethren, among whom he is safe at home again. Never before had life come rolling toward him in waves so strong or colours so shining. One must have been cast very, very deep down in darkness and confusion to learn that there is no more glorious sun in all God's heavens than the sun that shines upon our earth.

The other passengers from the **Roland** were each in his own way affected by the call of "Land!" Mrs. Liebling was heard to cry for Rosa and Flitte.

"By Jove, you rascal," said Arthur Stoss to his faithful Bulke, "by Jove, we'll feel the land under our soles again after all."

Doctor Wilhelm peeped into Frederick's cabin.

"Congratulate you, Doctor von Kammacher," he said. "The land of Christopher Columbus and Amerigo Vespucci has been sighted. We enjoy the advantage of having no trunks to pack."

Suddenly the fat little engineer, Mr. Wendler, was peering over Doctor Wilhelm's shoulder.

"Doctor," he cried, wringing his hands with a comic air of helplessness, "you must come right on deck. Your ward is crying her eyes out." He referred, of course, to Ingigerd.

She was still crying when Frederick reached deck. His attempts at consolation did not touch her. He had never before seen her cry, and the state she was in, so like the one from which he himself had scarcely emerged, aroused his pity and sympathy, which, however, were rather of a paternal sort, untinged by his former passion.

"I am not to blame," she suddenly said, "that my father lost his life. I am not even responsible for Mr. Achleitner. I did my best to dissuade him from making the trip."

Frederick stroked Ingigerd's hand.

"All due respect to Achleitner, but if I mourn single victims of that fearful night, I first think of the heroes of the **Roland**, Captain von Kessel, his mate, Von Halm, and all those picked braves who really died like great men fulfilling their duty. They are a loss to the world. At the first sight of them, I, in my innocence, actually believed the Lord would never permit their destruction."

LIX

The **Hamburg** had left behind the vast solitude of the ocean, broken only at long intervals by single far-off ships, and was already making its way through waters lively with a large number of steamers and sailing craft, leaving, and making for, the port. Now the lighthouse at Sandy Hook was visible.

Though Ingigerd as well as Frederick could not still the fluttering of their shaken souls, they were fascinated by the changing pictures of the entrance to the harbour. It was an amazing spectacle. Surprise followed surprise. Each second brought a new sensation.

A gigantic White Star liner came gliding toward them slowly, to the accompaniment of its brass band. It was starting out on the passage that the ***Hamburg*** was just concluding. Passengers swarmed like ants on the majestic vessel's decks, giving an impression of gaiety and festivity. What knew they of the thing awaiting them, perhaps, out there on the ocean? When they looked down upon the little ***Hamburg***, with its few passengers on deck, they had not the least inkling of the greatness, the fearfulness of the event of which those few puny persons were the sole surviving witnesses.

The emotion that filled the ***Roland's*** passengers with restlessness and excited them as with fire and tears when the ***Hamburg*** entered New York Harbour and steamed up through the Lower Bay toward the Narrows, was both a farewell to home and to the dangers of the sea and a greeting to solid land, to a stable human civilisation. This was the known, the usual, the mother's lap from which they had sprung and in which they had grown until the time came for them to start out upon their spiritual life's journey. It was also that without which the individual even today is helpless against the powers of nature.

Thus, they experienced a sort of home-coming, mingled with a peculiar dream-like feeling, that they were arriving on a strange planet, after having been ferried across Stygian currents on a Charon's raft. Out there, on the ocean and over the ocean, hovered a gruesomeness of solitudes, in which the human being, himself seeing everything, remains unseen, unknown, forgotten by God and the world. To be happy in his heated, clustered ant nests, man can and must forget the murderous in those watery transitional realms--man, that insect-like being whose sense organs and intellect are capacitated for the knowledge of his vast isolation in the world, but for nothing beyond that knowledge.

Sailing vessels passed one another, steamers blew their whistles, flocks of gulls swooped down on the water for fish, or darted hither and thither in the fresh breeze. Another great ocean greyhound, of the Hamburg-American line, neared them at Norton Point. The huge structure was propelled forward quietly and surely, as by some mysterious force. The gong summoning the passengers from the promenade deck to the dining-room could be distinctly heard.

"At this moment," said Frederick, drawing his watch from his pocket, "it is quarter of six in Europe, and still dark."

Captain Butor exchanged flag signals with the quarantine station. The ***Hamburg*** came to a standstill to receive health officers on board. After prolonged negotiations, in the course of which the physicians were called upon to give detailed information, the sick woman from the steerage and, with Mrs. Liebling's consent, Siegfried's corpse were taken from the ***Hamburg***. Frederick saw to it that Mrs. Liebling remained in her cabin and was spared the too painful scene. Within half an hour, the gallant ***Hamburg*** was steaming at full speed through the Narrows into the magnificent Upper Bay.

Long before it appears, travellers are always on the lookout with spy-glasses for the Statue of Liberty, the gift of the French nation. Even Frederick, when he beheld the goddess towering up from the water on her star-shaped base, did homage to her in his thoughts. From the distance at which he saw her, she did not look so gigantic. She seemed to be sending him a beautiful message, rather of the future than of the present, a message that found its way to his heart and, even in the strange mood he was in, expanded his breast.

"Liberty!" The word may be misused, yet it has not lost any of its magic or promise.

LX

And now, suddenly, the world seemed to Frederick to have gone mad. The ***Hamburg*** was entering the narrow harbour, the basin surrounded by skyscrapers, veritable towers of Babel, and alive with numberless grotesquely shaped ferry-boats. The scene, perhaps, would be a ridiculous monstrosity, were it not so truly gigantic. In that crater of life civilisation bellows, howls, screeches, roars, thunders, rushes, whizzes and whirls. Here is a colony of white ants, whose activity is staggering, bewildering, stupefying. It seemed inconceivable that in that intricate, raging chaos, a single minute could pass without a collision, or a collapse, or a killing. How could one possibly pursue one's own affairs quietly amid that shrieking, that hammering, that clanging, that mad uproar?

During these last moments together, the involuntary passengers of the ***Hamburg*** had become as one in heart and soul. Frederick had not lost his cash in the disaster, and he persuaded Ingigerd Hahlstroem not to reject his services during her first days on land. All agreed not to lose sight of one another in New York. Naturally enough, there had been much lively, genuinely heartfelt leave-taking and well-wishing for more than an hour before the ***Hamburg*** was secured to the dock.

The dithyrambic noise of the mighty city, where millions of men were at work, exercised a renewing, transforming influence. It was a whirlpool into which one was drawn unresistingly. It suffered no pondering, no immersion in an unalterable past. Everything in it urged and impelled forward. Here was the present, nothing but the present. Arthur Stoss seemed already to have one foot planted on Webster and Forster's stage. There was much parleying in regard to Ingigerd's appearance in theatre. She and Stoss had been engaged for the same time, which was already past. With the uncertainty in her heart as to her father's fate, she said she could not possibly dance; while Arthur Stoss declared if he got there in time, he would appear for his number that very evening.

"I've already lost two evenings," he said, "at a round five hundred dollars an evening. Besides, I must work, I must get among people."

He advised Ingigerd for her own advantage to do the same, and cited instances of persons who had not allowed the greatest griefs to keep them from the exercise of their calling. He knew of a scholar, he said, who delivered his lecture while his wife was dying, of a clown who cracked his jokes on the stage, though his wife had eloped with another man and his heart was bleeding.

"That's our profession," Stoss continued, "and not only our profession, but everybody's profession--to do his duty, whether with liking or disliking, whether with happiness or with anguish in his soul. Every man is a tragi-comic clown, although he doesn't pass for one, perhaps, as we do. To me it is a triumph, after what I have gone through, to stand on the stage this evening without trembling, among three thousand sensation-seeking spectators, and shoot the middle out of an ace."

By degrees Stoss fell more and more into a lively strain of boasting, which, though not disagreeable, utterly lacked wit. "If you haven't anything better to do," he said, turning to the physicians, "you might come to Webster and Forster's and see me cut my capers. Work! Work!"--this was meant for Ingigerd--"I very much wish you would make up your mind to dance. Work is medicine, work is everything. To lament the past is of no use. Besides," he said, turning serious, "don't forget, stocks in us are booming. Actors must not reject such an opportunity. Just wait and see how we'll be surrounded by reporters the moment we set foot on land."

"How so?" said Frederick. "Don't you suppose that all the details of the sinking of the *Roland* have been telegraphed to New York from quarantine? Look at those great skyscrapers, that one with the cupola is the *World* building. We have already gone to press, and millions of newspapers have spun us out, in the greatest detail. The next four or five days there won't be a man or woman in New York who can vie in celebrity with the survivors of the *Roland*."

Amid similar talk, the *Hamburg* reached its pier, and leave-taking began in earnest. It was truly remarkable to see what emotion suddenly seized these people, who at bottom were strangers to one another. Mrs. Liebling wept, and Frederick and Doctor Wilhelm had to submit to her overflowing kisses of gratitude. Rosa kissed Bulke; she kissed Doctor Wilhelm's and Frederick's hands again and again, amid veritable howls. It goes without saying that the ladies also exchanged endearments. Praises were bestowed upon Flitte; and Captain Butor and Wendler, in fact the entire crew of the *Hamburg*, were extolled as brave, noble rescuers. The physicians and Stoss called the sailors of the *Roland*, "Our dear comrades! Our heroes!"

It was agreed that all should meet again, and Doctor Wilhelm made an appointment with Captain Butor, Wendler, and even the tattered painter, Fleischmann, for noon of the day after next. The place chosen for the meeting was the Hoffman House bar. From there, they would go together on a jaunt through the city.

Poor Jacob Fleischmann, the painter, was somewhat perplexed by the mad city, and turned rather mealy-mouthed. He could not speak English, he had little cash, and he had lost his only capital, his paintings. He tried delicately, though with evident anxiety, to attach himself to the men with whom fate had thrown him, and they did not withhold the support he sought. They agreed to look out for him. Even Arthur Stoss proffered his services and good advice.

"Should you have trouble with the company's agent," he said, "call on me, and I'll introduce you to my friend, the owner of the *Staats-Zeitung*."

PART II

I

A few moments later Frederick felt the solid pier beneath his feet. His brain reeled lightly. The crowd on the pier cheered and hurrahed. In that shouting, shrieking, roaring, swaying mass of humanity, he and Ingigerd, who was clinging to his arm, seemed exposed to the danger of another sort of drowning. Suddenly he found himself confronted by a little Japanese, or someone whom at first glance he took to be a Japanese, and heard him saying:

"How d'ye do, Doctor von Kammacher? Don't you know me? How d'ye do, Doctor von Kammacher? Don't you know me?" several times in rapid succession.

Frederick tried to recall the man to his memory. He scarcely knew who he himself was, with those cheers thundering in his ears, with hands on all sides shaking his hands, and newsboys flourishing newspapers behind him and above him and under his very nose.

"Don't you know me, Doctor von Kammacher?" the Japanese repeated, grinning.

"By Jove," cried Frederick, "now I recognise you. You are Willy Snyders. How do you come to be here?"

While studying several semesters in Breslau, Frederick had eked out his income by tutoring a boy, a rather desperate case, whose father, a furniture manufacturer, paid handsomely for his son's private lessons. Frederick's pupil turned out to be a good-hearted chap, an amusing scapegrace, who soon became his devoted slave. It was this scapegrace, now a full-grown man, that Frederick recognised in the jolly Japanese.

"How I come to be here? I'll explain later," said Willy, his nostrils dilating with the joy of seeing his teacher again. "The first thing is, have you already engaged rooms, and shall I slip you past that damned lot of reporters? Or do you want to be interviewed?"

"For heaven's sake, no! Not for the world."

"Then stick close to me," shouted Willy. "A cab is waiting for us, and we'll drive straight to our folks."

Frederick introduced Ingigerd.

"I must first see this young lady safe to a hotel. And even then I can't leave her entirely alone."

Willy instantly took in the situation, but it did not change his plans.

"Miss Hahlstroem can stop with us, too. She will be far more comfortable than in a hotel. The only question is, can she put up with Italian cooking?"

"I don't anticipate any difficulties from your macaroni and spaghetti *al sugo*," said Frederick, who read Ingigerd's willingness in her eyes. "So I'll follow your lead as you followed mine years ago."

"All right! Forward, march!" Willy's joy in his booty was patent.

When they left the pier, they saw Stoss still surrounded by reporters, working his jaws with incredible rapidity, as he discoursed upon himself and the role he had played in the sinking of the *Roland*. They were about to enter their cab after their flight, through the crowd, when an elderly gentleman, panting breathlessly and perspiring, despite the nipping wind, stepped up to Ingigerd Hahlstroem with, "I beg your pardon, but I come from Webster and Forster." He took off his hat and wiped the inside band with his handkerchief. "I was told--I was told--I came in a carriage--a carriage is waiting--" He stopped, too exhausted to continue.

"Miss Hahlstroem cannot possibly appear this evening."

"Oh, Miss Hahlstroem looks very well!"

"See here," said Frederick ready to flare up.

Webster and Forster's agent put his hat back on his bald pate.

"It would be the greatest mistake if Miss Hahlstroem were not to dance tonight," he said. "I was commissioned to provide her with money and anything else she needed. There's my carriage. Rooms have already been engaged for her at the Astor."

Frederick grew angry.

"I am a physician," he snapped, "and as a physician, I tell you Miss Hahlstroem will not dance to-night, nor for several nights."

"Will you make good to Miss Hahlstroem her financial loss?"

"What I shall do in regard to that is neither your nor Webster and Forster's business."

Frederick thought he had disposed of the matter, but the agent became offensive.

"Who are you, sir? My dealings are with Miss Hahlstroem exclusively. What right have you to mix in this affair?"

"I don't think I could dance to-night," Ingigerd interposed.

"You will lose that feeling as soon as you step on the stage. The manager's wife gave me a letter for you. Her maid is at the Astor with everything you need. She is entirely at your disposal."

"Our Petronilla is a jewel, too," Willy Snyders interjected. "If you tell her what you need, Miss Hahlstroem, she'll have it for you in five minutes." With the insistence of a seducer, he helped Ingigerd into the cab.

"Very well, then," said the agent emphatically, "you are breaking a contract, and I warn you of the consequences. I will have to ask you for your address."

Willy Snyders shouted a number on 107th street. The agent jotted it down in his note-book.

The cab with Ingigerd, Frederick, and Willy in it was transported from Hoboken to New York in the usual way, jammed in between other carriages and trucks on the ferry-boat. A newsboy on the ferry handed into the cab a copy of *The Sun*, with whole columns already describing the disaster. The authors of the information were probably the health officers and Captain Butor. When Willy Snyders began to speak of the *Roland*, Frederick checked him with a nod toward Ingigerd; but she had of herself noticed the report in the paper and asked if they had been the first to bring the news to New York.

"The *Roland* was overdue more than three days," Willy explained. "We were already beginning to be alarmed. Finally the passenger list from Bremen was published, and soon after your name, too, Doctor von Kammacher, appeared in the newspapers, your father in the meantime having cabled that you left Paris to catch the *Roland* at Southampton. I never lost faith that nothing but the wretched weather was delaying you, and I inquired at the steamship company's office every day. It was there that I learned of the sinking of the *Roland* and the arrival of the *Hamburg* with the first rescued passengers on board, with you among them." Noticing Ingigerd's sudden pallor, Willy added vivaciously, with apparent conviction, "A lot of others must surely have been rescued."

The amount of traffic, as indicated by an endless number of ferry-boats, tugs, and steamers of every sort, was immense. The ferry-boats, black with people, resembled floating towers of Babel, above which rose an iron something like a pump-handle, seesawing up and down with the invisible pistons.

When the boat lay fast in the slip, there was a great thundering as the vehicles all began to move at the same time to the accompaniment of a tramping mass of humanity.

"This city," Frederick thought, "is obsessed by a craze for money making." The idea was suggested to him chiefly by the advertisements staring on all sides, those shrill, over-spiced, over-charged asseverations, compared with which the same thing in Europe was delicate as a violet, innocent as a newborn babe. Wherever he turned his eyes, gigantic placards glared at him, gigantic letters, gigantic, garishly coloured pictures, gigantic fingers and hands pointing to something. Twenty negroes carrying bill-boards, a carriage drawn by twelve horses harnessed like circus horses passed by. It was a shrieking, greedy war of competition, waged with every conceivable means, a wild, shameless orgy of acquisitiveness, but for that very reason not lacking in a certain greatness. There was no hypocrisy about it. It was honest in its outspokenness.

The cab stopped at a telegraph office, and Frederick cabled to his father, "I am safe, sound, and well;" Ingigerd to her mother in Paris, "I am safe. Papa's fate uncertain." While Ingigerd was writing, Frederick took the chance to tell Willy Snyders that she had probably lost her father in the wreck.

Several times newsboys thrust a paper under Frederick's nose, calling out the great sensation, "All about the sinking of the *Roland*! All about the sinking of the *Roland*!" In large, catching headlines he read: "The *Roland* leaves Bremen. Slight accident compels her to return. *Roland* starts on trip again. Constant storms. Dead man on board. Nine hundred drowned. Heroic conduct of a servant-girl. Doc-

tor Frederick von Kammacher performs miracles of bravery." Frederick started, reflected, but could not recall anything of the sort. "Child dies in life-boat. Captain
Butor of the **Hamburg** sights castaways. Report of survivors. Arthur Stoss, champion armless marksman, helped into life-boat by faithful valet," and so on. It was an
invaluable supply of fresh, sensational, gratuitously obtained material, to be served
for a week in generous portions to readers in both the old and the new worlds.

The cab rolled up Broadway, that main thoroughfare of New York stretching along for miles, with two apparently unbroken chains of street-cars moving by
each other. At that time the cars were propelled by an endless cable travelling in
a conduit under the roadway. The traffic all along Broadway was enormous, and
the contrast was the more surprising when the cab, after traversing another lively
street, turned into a deserted-looking side street, where almost country-like quiet
prevailed.

The cab came to a halt, and Willy Snyders helped Ingigerd out. The travellers
found themselves in front of a low one-family house with a flight of outside steps,
differing in no wise from the other houses on the block, which were all built on the
same plan, of exactly the same height, of exactly the same width, and with absolute
similarity of detail. Frederick had observed such architectural monotony only in
workingmen's houses in Germany, while here it was the mark of a fairly aristocratic
section.

Twilight had already fallen when Frederick and Ingigerd at length found privacy in their rooms. The rooms, plainly furnished and scrupulously clean, were
lighted by electricity and heated from a furnace in the cellar; and the floors were
not laid with wood, but paved with red bricks. Petronilla, the old Italian housekeeper, took Ingigerd in charge, looking after the smallest of her wants with touching motherliness. The two said what was necessary to say in a mixture of Italian and
English. After showing Ingigerd to her room and seeing that she was provided with
everything, Petronilla stepped out into the hall to call a maid, who was working in
another part of the house. Frederick heard her, and put his head out of the door to
inquire after Ingigerd.

"The signorina dropped on the couch without undressing and fell right asleep,"
she said.

Frederick feeling somewhat uneasy went with Petronilla to look after Ingigerd, and found that she had merely succumbed to a leaden sleep. Her constitution, after weeks of over-exertion and abuse, was asserting its rights. Petronilla and the maid undressed her and put her to bed, all unconscious, though now and then opening wide her shimmering sea-green eyes.

II

Frederick washed and went down-stairs to the basement with Willy Snyders. Here there was a tidy little dining-room with a table set for eight. As in the other rooms, the floors were of brick, and the walls half-way up were hung with burlap. Where the burlap ended, a narrow shelf ran around the entire room, set with all sorts of household utensils, chiefly *fiaschi* of wine in straw cases. Like everything else about the place, the napery was exquisitely clean.

Willy in the meantime had in his droll, lively way fully informed Frederick of the character and purpose of this extremely comfortable house. It was leased by a group of German artists, whose main prop was a sculptor of twenty-eight by the name of Ritter. Willy lauded Ritter as a genius. He had entered upon a career in the New World most remarkable for a man of his age. Among his patrons were the Astors, the Goulds, and the Vanderbilts; and he had received most of the orders for exterior sculpture work on the buildings of the Chicago Exposition. Willy called Ritter "a devil of a fellow," and praised him for his "smartness."

In a corner of the dining-room, in the halls and on the stairway landings, were reproductions of Ritter's works. Willy extolled them to the skies; Frederick honestly admired them. The large bas-relief in the corner of the dining-room represented a group of singing boys, for which Ritter, probably at the suggestion of his customer, a Vanderbilt or an Astor, had used the famous relief of Luca della Robbia as a model. In style, nobility and freshness, his work surpassed anything then being done in Germany.

Another sculptor partaking of the benefits of the club-house was a friend of Ritter, who helped him with his work. Like Ritter, Lobkowitz was a native Austrian. The fourth member of the group was Franck, a painter from Silesia, an impecunious eccentric, upon whose talents his comrades placed an extremely high estimate. It was Willy Snyders the kind-hearted who, soon after a chance meeting with his fellow-Silesian, dragged him from his wretched quarters, not without much coaxing, and transferred him to the club-house.

"Wait and see the way that lunatic Franck is going to behave," said Willy in his peculiar voice, in which there was a blending of the guttural and nasal tones of American English with the Austrian German accent of his friends. "He snaps like a mad dog. He's enough to make you split your sides laughing--that is, if the perverse creature comes at all and doesn't have dinner served in his room."

As a matter of fact, Franck was the first to enter the dining-room. Willy's tongue kept wagging, while the eccentric merely shook hands limply with Frederick and said nothing. Though the three were countrymen, Franck's appearance--like Willy, he was wearing evening dress--added a touch of embarrassment where there had been perfect unconstraint; and though Willy had lent Frederick a suit, and a tailor had already been ordered, Frederick expressed regret at not being appropriately dressed.

"Yes, Ritter's a great stickler for form," Willy observed. "Every evening we have to present the appearance of at least attaches to an embassy."

Petronilla entered and explained in wordy Italian that the poor, dear, sweet little signorina had fallen asleep in bed and was breathing quietly and regularly.

"You could shoot off a cannon, bum! bum! Outside her window, and she wouldn't wake up," she said. Then holding out a newspaper, she asked whether the gentlemen had heard of the sinking of the *Roland* and the few survivors. When Willy, with his dilating nostrils and his characteristic half-serious, half-comic expression, introduced Frederick as one of those survivors, she burst into a noisy laugh, which vastly amused two of the three Silesians. When convinced that Willy was not teasing, she stared at Frederick speechlessly, burst into tears, and kissed his hands. Then she ran out.

Soon after, Lobkowitz entered, a tall, quiet man. He had heard of Frederick's recent experience, and greeted him with simple cordiality.

"Ritter has just come in his cart," he said.

They looked out of the window. Frederick saw an elegant two-wheeled dog-cart with a handsome coachman in black livery preparing to drive off, while a thoroughbred grey, feeling the tightening of the reins, was rearing and plunging in the shafts.

"The coachman," said Willy, whose lack of reserve and extreme indiscretion his friends accepted good-naturedly, "is a ruined officer of the Austrian army. He ran away from his gambling debts. I don't know whether he got out of the army or was put out. At any rate he is of invaluable service to Ritter. He tells him to the dot how he must dress for luncheons and dinners, for tennis and golf and riding and driving; how to manage a four-in-hand, when to wear a black chimney-pot or a grey one, what colour gloves to wear, what sort of necktie, what sort of cuff links, what sort of stockings. In short, he tells him all the things a man has to pay attention to in order to succeed here in high life."

At this point Bonifacius Ritter, whom fortune had favoured in America beyond his most extravagant expectations, now entered, young, brisk, handsome, amiable as Alcibiades. Frederick was instantly carried away by his manner, radiating bonhomie, naivete, joy in life, and simple heartiness. The atmosphere of the New World had imparted ease and fire to the flabby amiability of the Austrian.

Dinner was served, and over genuine Italian soup, conversation was soon in full swing. Willy Snyders, as commissary, poured the wine. It was evident how proud he was of Bonifacius Ritter and what satisfaction it gave him to present his quondam teacher to such friends and such a home in this foreign land. The company thawed; and by the time the maid in white cap and apron had finished serving, the four had all touched glasses with Frederick on his and his protegee's rescue. A short pause of embarrassment followed, which Frederick interpreted as a demand for a statement regarding himself. His pale scholarly face still showed deep traces of the hardships he had undergone.

"I came over," he said, "to continue some studies with a friend which he and I began years ago. You know him, Willy. He is Peter Schmidt, the physician, in Springfield, Massachusetts."

"He's in Meriden now, an hour's ride from Springfield."

"Yes?" said Frederick, "I assumed he was still in Springfield. But no matter. While I was in Berlin and Paris, I conferred with some scientists, friends of mine, before boarding the **Roland** at Southampton. Everybody told me the **Roland** was one of the best vessels. To my astonishment, I met the young lady who is now enjoying your hospitality. She was going to the United States with her father. We were fortunate. We got into the life-boat perfectly quietly, before the panic broke out, but we had to leave the young lady's father behind. I forgot to say I had already become acquainted with Hahlstroem and his daughter in Berlin. Thus, fate brought us together, and I consider myself responsible for Miss Hahlstroem, both as a physician and a human being. She is an artistic wonder. She is a dancer."

Willy Snyders gave a witty account of the attack of Webster and Forster's agent; and the conversation turned on art in general and on American art in particular.

"Millions of dollars annually," said Bonifacius Ritter, "are spent upon all sorts of art objects, an enormous sum on paintings alone. At the same time, there is a class of persons here of Puritanic descent to whom any kind of art is the abomination of the arch-enemy. For instance, there is an association of pious pillars of society, an association of vandals, invested with certain civic rights, whose object is the abolition of filth and the maintenance of chastity. To that end it recently broke into one of the famous clubs of the New York *jeunesse doree* and destroyed a number of irreplaceable art treasures, masterpieces, among them even a Venus by Titian."

"And the relation of the amateurs here," said Lobkowitz, "to their artistic possessions is very funny. You should see how they place their paintings. The "Crucifixion" by Munkaczy is displayed in a department store in Philadelphia. The Goulds have Rembrandts in their extremely comfortable bathrooms. Of course, I have nothing to say against good pictures hanging in hotel halls and stairways. The largest bar-room in New York has the whole Barbizon school--Millets, Courbets, Bastien-Lepages, and Daubignys--hanging over the bar."

"My sole reason," said Franck, "for going there every day for my whisky and soda."

Ritter, Snyders and Lobkowitz burst out laughing.

Franck had the looks of a gypsy; so that two more un-European types, as Frederick said to himself, than he and Willy Snyders were scarcely conceivable. Though a year older than Frederick, Franck, small-boned and youthfully slim, seemed to be seven or eight years younger. He was forever shoving from his eyes a pitch-black lock, which promptly fell over his forehead again to the top of his nose. He drank heavily and kept smiling. He smiled, while the others laughed as he expounded the relation of art to whisky.

A sense of security such as he had not experienced in years came over Frederick. He had always felt drawn to artists. Their conversation, their camaraderie never failed to exercise a charm over him. Now was added the fact that here, where he had counted upon a chilly foreignness and complete isolation, he had been ardently expected, had been welcomed with open arms by such a circle. In the midst of their merry toasting and informal dining, informal despite their evening dress, Frederick every now and then asked himself whether the awful experiences he had gone through had really occurred. Was he actually in New York, three thousand miles away from old Europe? Was not this his home? Within the past ten years in his own country had he ever felt even nearly so comfortable and at home as here? How life came surging toward him! Each minute a new wave rolling to his feet--to him who had undeservedly escaped with his bare existence from almost universal perdition.

"I thank you from the depths of my heart, gentlemen and countrymen," he said, "for the hospitality you show me. I don't deserve it." He raised his glass, and they all touched glasses with him. Suddenly, to his own surprise Frederick expanded in a wave of frankness, calling himself a shipwrecked man in two senses of the word. "I have gone through much in my past; and were not the sinking of the **Roland** so fearfully tragic, I should feel inclined to look upon it as a symbol of my former life. The Old World, the New World. I have taken the step across the great pond, and already feel something like new life within me.

"I don't know just what I shall do." He did not realise he was contradicting himself. "I shall certainly not practise medicine or take up my profession as a bacteriologist. Possibly I shall write books. What sort of books I don't know. One of the things I think of a great deal is the restoration of the Venus of Milo's body. I have already completed in my mind a work on Peter Vischer and Adam Krafft. But for all I know, I may merely write on the use of artificial manure. For I am thinking of buying some land, felling trees, and living a retired life, farming and raising cattle. Then again, I may write nothing but a sort of romance, the romance of a whole life, which may turn out to be something like a modern philosophy. In that case, I should begin where Schopenhauer left off. I mean the sentence that is always going around in my head from **Welt als Wille und Vorstellung**: 'Something lurks behind our existence which is inaccessible to us until we shake off the world.'"

The discourse of the young scholar, passing through his belated period of storm and stress, was listened to respectfully. His reference to artificial manure produced a burst of merriment, and when he ended, his audience applauded.

"Shaking off the world, that's something for Franck, Doctor von Kammacher. Tell him, Franck, how you came to America," said Willy.

"Or about your tramping on foot to Chicago," said Lobkowitz.

"Or," said Ritter, "your adventure in Boston, when two policemen, strangely mistaking your condition for a tremendous jag, took you on a drive in the patrol wagon to the lock-up."

"It's very good they did," said Franck, smiling and tossing the lock from his forehead. "I should certainly have caught a cold if they hadn't."

To Frederick's puzzlement, every one of Franck's utterances was greeted by a shout of laughter.

"Franck is a genuine genius," whispered Willy to Frederick, while filling a glass with Chianti, "and the greatest eccentric in the world. Franck," he cried, "didn't you come to America without a cent of money?"

"For what does one need money?" Franck rejoined, at great leisure, with a naive smile.

"Didn't you come over as a stoker?"

"Ye-e-es," said Franck, "I was engaged as a stoker."

"But you didn't do any stoking?"

"No, I didn't have the muscle for it."

"But what did you do on the ship?" asked Lobkowitz.

"I? I sailed on the ocean."

"Of course. But you were engaged to work. You must have done something to earn money."

"I played sixty-six with the first mate."

Finally Franck's story was extracted from him. It was by painting the portrait of the head-steward that he had lived so handsomely on the steamer and had landed on American soil with fifty dollars in his pocket, though a day later not a cent of the fifty dollars was left.

"Money's a nuisance," said Franck.

III

Up to this point a wholesome-looking waitress, in white cap and apron, had been serving. Now the Italian cook himself, Simone Brambilla, came in to bring on the dessert and cheese and inquire whether the dinner had been to the gentlemen's taste. The familiarity between masters and cook, who spoke Italian together, testified to the best relations between them. This little fragment of the artists' Italy in America enlivened them all, bringing back memories of the days they had spent in Italy, the days that signify the heyday of their youth to all German scholars and artists.

"Now then, strike up a tune, my boy!" Willy suddenly ordered the cook, "Signor Simone Brambilla, you will please perform for us now! And *cantare*. Understand? *Ma forte* not too *mezza voce*!" He took a mandolin from the sideboard and pressed it into the chef's arms.

"Signor Guglielmo e sempre buffo," said the cook.

"That's it--buffo, buffo," cried Franck, striking the table with his fist. His smile had already turned somewhat idiotic, and he seemed to think "buffo" meant "to sing."

"Cosa vuole sentire?" asked Brambilla.

"'Addio mia bella Napoli,'" suggested Willy, "or anything you like, Mr. Brambilla."

"What does 'like' mean?" asked Franck. "I have heard the word so often."

"Would you believe," Willy said to Frederick, "that that ox has been here over a year and doesn't know a word of English?"

"'Deutschland, Deutschland ueber alles!'" Franck began to sing.

"Goodness gracious!" said Willy. "His toothache has begun to bother him again."

"'Ich weiss nicht, was soll es bedeuten,'" sang Franck.

"But I do!" cried Willy. "Silentium! When Franck begins to sing and Lobkowitz to yawn and Ritter empties his first glass on the table-cloth, we'll soon be lying stretched out under the table."

The cook had seated himself decorously and was holding the mandolin in position. With his cap of white linen and his white linen jacket and apron, he cut a droll figure among those correctly dressed young men. Willy Snyders poured some *vino nero* for him into a tumbler, and he struck a few notes by way of prelude, though hesitating to interrupt Franck and begin. He kept his face, glowing from the kitchen fire, turned toward Franck with an expression of courteous waiting and politely besought him in Italian to keep on singing. Finally, since Franck, instead of answering, arose, gave him a comically commanding look, and waved his fork like a baton, he began, striking up an accompaniment with a catching rhythm, which titillated his auditors' nerves. He was an excellent singer and a master-hand at playing the mandolin. He gave those well-known street-ballads which one hears everywhere in Italy, especially in Naples: "Addio mia bella Napoli," "Funiculi Funicula," "L'altro ieri a Piedigrotta," "Margherita di Parete era sarta delle signore," and also more serious songs, such as the languishing "Ogni sera di sotto all' mio balcone sento cantar una canzon d' amore."

The cook's melodies undoubtedly charmed back his home to him, though in colours less glorious and alluring to himself, perhaps, than to the artists, whether they had been in Italy or not. Frederick leaned his head back and closed his eyes. The dining-room was filled with the fumes of cigars and cigarettes, and the electric bulbs shone as in a mist. Frederick's thoughts carried him far, far away. His arm hung at his side limply, while a Simon Arzt cigarette burned to a stump between his fingers--throughout his adventures, his silver cigarette case had remained safe in his pocket.

Before his inner vision rose the coasts and blue gulfs of Italy, the brown Doric temples of Paestum and the cliffs of Amalfi, Sorrento, and Capri. He was standing on the Posilipo. He was with Doctor Dorn in the loggia of the zoologic station for deep-sea researches, which Hans von Marees had decorated. In Rome, Frederick had sat over many a bottle of wine with Hans von Marees and Otto, who died while working on the Luther Memorial in Berlin. He saw himself in the famous Est Est Cafe in Rome, or visiting the malaria patients in the hospital on the Capitol, or promenading in the sunshine on Monte Pincio with a deaf and dumb sculptor, with whom he then went to an afternoon concert. He had laughed because the artist explained that he did not hear the music with his ears, but felt it, or rather felt the drum alone, in his belly.

In that period of his life, Frederick had been undergoing a crisis. But a little more and his preoccupation with Goethe's "Italian Journey," his intercourse with the artists, and the vast number of his impressions of sublime art would have turned him aside from science. But one day he chanced to meet Mrs. Von Thorn and her daughter Angele. He became engaged, and there was no question now of a change of profession. Angele was beautiful, and those days, when he read aloud to her chapters from Goethe, or inspired and inspiring passages from Winckelmann, or recited Hoelderlin, or held forth to her on the masterworks in the Vatican, were full of never-to-be-repeated romantic asininity. They bought engagement rings of a jeweller on the Corso. Where was his ring? He had removed it from his finger, and, like all his other possessions, it had gone down forever in the cabin of the *Roland*.

Frederick again felt that sensation of hot waves rising from his breast to his eyes. This time the emotion was a soft one, a feeling of reconciliation, of mourning over lost illusions. The second epoch of his life, if a second epoch were really to develop from this beginning, was not like the first, full of innocence and based upon illusions. Frederick was sorry for himself. He was moved almost to tears. For it is an all-too strong faith, an all-too certain hope in happiness that finally bring disillusionment.

It was in one of the intervals of clapping and applause punctuating the end of each of Brambilla's songs, that Petronilla came in and whispered something to Willy Snyders, which caused Willy in turn to whisper to Frederick, who immediately jumped up and left the room. Willy went with him.

Despite Petronilla's protestations, a gentleman and a stately, rather gorgeously dressed lady had forced their way into Ingigerd's room. Frederick and Willy arrived just as the lady was trying to wake Ingigerd and raise her up in bed.

"For Heaven's sake, child," she kept saying, "wake up for a second."

Frederick and Willy recognised Webster and Forster's agent and immediately expelled him to the hall, talking to him in whispers, but none the less energetically. They told him a few forceful things, which he received with a shrug of his shoulders. When they asked the lady by what right she had forced her way in, she said she was the proprietor of one of the largest New York theatrical agencies and had negotiated the contract between Webster and Forster and Ingigerd Hahlstroem's father, who had received a thousand dollars in advance.

"Time is money, especially here in New York," she declared. "Even if Miss Hahlstroem cannot dance to-night, she must begin to think of to-morrow. I should be willing to accommodate her, but this is only one of a hundred cases that I have to look after. And if Miss Hahlstroem is to appear to-morrow, she must go with me this very minute to"--she mentioned the Gerson of New York--"so that they can work on her costume over night. The establishment is on Broadway, and a cab is waiting in front of the door."

The lady said all this in Ingigerd's room, intentionally refraining from lowering her voice. Several times Frederick and Willy interrupted to ask her to moderate her tones.

"Miss Hahlstroem will not dance at all," said Frederick, finally.

"Indeed?" said the agent. "Then she'll be involved in a very unpleasant law suit."

"Miss Hahlstroem is a minor," said Frederick, "and her father, with whom you concluded the contract, probably lost his life in the sinking of the *Roland*."

"And I," said the agent, "don't want to lose a thousand dollars for nothing."

"Miss Hahlstroem is sick."

"Very well, then I'll send my physician."

"I myself am a physician."

"A German physician, I suppose," she said. "The only physicians that count for us are Americans."

Perhaps this American woman, equipped with a masculine intellect, masculine energy, and a masculine voice would have put through her will, had not Ingigerd's heavy sleep defied all the noise about her, even the shaking to which she had been subjected. At length Frederick displayed a degree of determination so unambiguous that the agent had to recede from her position and temporarily withdraw from the field. Besides, Willy hit upon an idea, the far-reaching significance of which Frederick did not realise until later. He declared that if the agent did not desist, he would notify the Society for the Prevention of Cruelty to Children, since Miss Hahlstroem was not yet seventeen years old.

"Gentlemen," said the lady, evidently taken aback and coming round a bit, "remember that both Webster and Forster and myself have been spending enormous sums on advertising for four weeks. I reckoned on a tour as far as San Francisco. Now that Miss Hahlstroem happens to be one of the survivors of the **Roland** and has lost her father besides, she has become the sensation of the season. If she were to appear now, she could return to Europe in three months with fifty thousand dollars over and above the sum contracted for. Would you be responsible to Miss Hahlstroem for such an enormous loss?"

After the agent and her escort had left, Willy Snyders confirmed what she had said about the amount of advertising that had been done. For weeks all the billboards, all the building scaffoldings, every empty barrel where building was going on were covered with posters announcing "Mara, or the Spider's Victim." Sometimes they displayed a life-size figure of a dancer, represented as almost a child still, a sort of albino with red rabbit's eyes and streaming saffron-yellow hair. A spider, with a body the size of a small balloon, was crouching behind its web. The poster was by Brown, the most talented poster-painter in New York.

"You can see those posters everywhere on the streets still," said Willy Snyders. "That's why it seems so funny to think I always stared at them quite unsuspecting; and now Miss Ingigerd and you are in this house. Life concocts crazy plots. I assure you, when I looked at those posters, I thought of everything else in the world but you, Doctor von Kammacher. And little did I divine that they would ever be of more significance to me than the advertisements of any ordinary vaudeville."

When Frederick and Willy returned to the dining-room, the chef was gone, and Lobkowitz and Franck were engaged in the time-worn dispute, whether Raphael or Michael Angelo is the greater. Willy gave a humorous, though indignant account of the battle of the Amazons that had just taken place and how Webster and Forster wanted to insist on Miss Hahlstroem's appearing that very night. The artists' chivalry was aroused. They declared unanimously that they would refuse to give up their lovely ward, even if all New York were to come and besiege them.

Frederick looked at his watch. It was a few minutes past ten. The last thing Arthur Stoss had said on parting occurred to him, "At half past ten to the dot, I shall be on the boards behind the footlights." Frederick told the artists about Arthur Stoss; and Willy Snyders, the man of initiative, proposed that they go together to Webster and Forster to see the armless actor's performance.

IV

Ritter lent Frederick one of his evening suits, which fitted him to perfection, and within less than half an hour the company was sitting in a box at Webster and Forster's. The enormous hall, in which smoking and drinking were allowed, was full. Willy estimated that there were about four or five thousand people present. A number of immense arc-lights shone in the tobacco smoke like frosty, white moons.

When Frederick and his friends entered, a woman and a slim toreador were dancing. The music was of an exciting nature, and the character of the performance and the performer immediately took the artists captive. The dance was an eccentric mixture of drollness, innocence, and wildness. When watching the toreador, Frederick felt as if he were in an arena at Seville; when watching the girl, as if he were near the Gulf of Corinth, or on one of the islands of the Cyclades. He promptly decided to leave Spain and follow the lovely dancer to her home in Greece, where she was his Chloe and he, her Daphnis. Old shepherds sat tippling in a pine grove dedicated to Pan. From the highland meadows he looked down upon the far off Ægean Sea beating noiselessly against the rocky coast-line.

The music of the orchestra turned into the piping of Pan, while Webster and Forster, the heavy fumes, the air vitiated by the exhalations of five thousand people no longer existed. The pure breath of spring was rustling in the pines. The shepherdess was dancing as she had learned to dance from the droll caperings of the goats or, by natural inheritance, from great Pan himself. It was a dance of young, wild, bubbling joy in life.

"The origin of all music," thought Frederick, "is dance and song in one and the same person. The feet compel the rhythm that the throat voices; and if the dancer herself does not sing, she hears music different from the music to which she is dancing, and if she dances without an accompaniment, we who behold her hear her music nevertheless. The melodies I hear in this girl's dancing are comparable in their bucolic innocence to the things of the same sort that Mozart, Beethoven and Schubert wrote. They have exorcised the vulgar muse from this vulgar place, banishing her to a remote distance."

The dancer was a Spaniard. She made little leaps in the air and tossed her head archly, as if for her own joy, unconscious both of the audience and the toreador, who sometimes picked her up and held her aloft. Her dancing was innocent, entirely free from sensuality. At the conclusion of her performance, Frederick and his friends clapped madly, while the vast audience gave very scanty signs of applause.

"Caviar to the general," said Frederick.

When she disappeared in the wings, a lackey in red livery stepped on the stage and set a number of small seats at regular distances from one another. It was not until he had left and returned again with a pea-rifle and a violin that Frederick recognised the brave private, Bulke. The next moment Stoss appeared. A frantic outburst of delight, threatening never to end, greeted him. He wore a jacket and knee-breeches of black velvet, a lace jabot, lace cuffs, black silk stockings, and buckled pumps of patent leather. His yellowish hair was brushed straight up all around his large head. His pale face, with its broad cheek bones and broad flat nose, was turned to the audience with a professional smile. The applause refused to end, and the armless trunk made a moderately profound bow.

Frederick saw the same man helpless, drenched with water, crouching under the seats of the life-boat; and he recalled with what murderous determination the sailors, Bulke, Doctor Wilhelm, and he himself, as well as the women, Rosa, Mrs. Liebling, and Ingigerd, had prevented the boat from capsizing. What an unreal contrast between the past and the present! And why was Stoss receiving such homage?

The psychology of certain mass demonstrations has yet to be written. What could the applause have been intended to signify? "We are grateful to God that he rescued you. This you have accomplished, you poor armless man, that hundreds, though they had two arms, perished, while you are privileged to appear on the stage this evening as if nothing had occurred. We must enjoy ourselves; and it is better that you who entertain and amuse us with your thousands of tricks should have been saved than any Tom, Dick, or Harry. Besides we want to reimburse you for all the troubles you have been through. What is more, because of your skill and because of your rescue, you are a lion whose worth has increased twofold."

The turbulence continued. The man the audience so honoured was fairly drowned in a sea of applause. At last a man in evening dress stepped from the wings and made signs that he wanted to speak. Silence fell, and he announced that Arthur Stoss, the world's champion, would say a few words. The next instant Stoss's sharp, clear boyish voice rang through the theatre reaching even the hindmost seats.

Frederick caught expressions here and there, "My dear New Yorkers," "hospitable Americans," "the hospitable shores of America," "Columbus," and "1492." He heard Stoss say that on the bill-boards one read "1492," the year in which modern America was born. He distinguished phrases such as "navigare necesse est, vivere non necesse," "through darkness to light," and so on. Stoss's speech utterly lacked inspiration.

"Noah's ark," he said, "has not yet become superfluous. Two-thirds of the earth's surface is still covered with water. But if a vessel here and there is swallowed up in the flood, the ark of humanity cannot sink, since God has set his rainbow in the heavens. The ocean is the cradle of heroism, it is the unifying, not the dividing element."

The name of Captain von Kessel resounded in the hall. Frederick saw the dead hero tossing about in the great black waters under a starless heaven. Above the performer's shrill voice, he heard the captain's voice saying:

"My brother has a wife and children. He is an enviable man, Doctor von Kammacher."

Frederick was roused from his recollections by the frantic applause that greeted the conclusion of the brilliant speech.

Arthur Stoss now seated himself on one of the seats, and Bulke, the hero and life saver in red livery, laid a violin on another and proceeded to draw off his master's shoes. Stoss's feet were clad in black stockings leaving his toes bare. With the toes of his right foot, he took the bow and with his left foot, deftly rosined it; a spectacle that sent a whisper of astonishment rippling through the audience. The orchestra struck up Bach's "Prelude," to which Stoss played Gounod's "Ave Maria." The tones he produced were beautiful, and the vast crowd was enraptured. Remembering the awful disaster, they were transported into a sentimental, religious mood. Frederick shuddered with disgust. The sinking of the ***Roland*** was being exploited.

It was a relief when Stoss finally took up the pea-rifle. Bulke in the part he now played aroused as much admiration in Frederick and the artists as Stoss, if not more.

While his master shot off the rifle, he stood at a distance of fifteen feet, with total unconcern holding up cards for Stoss to aim at. Stoss put a hole through the middle of the card every time.

V

When he awoke rather late the next morning, Frederick was astonished to find everything about him standing still. The bed was not pitching, the glasses and water basin were not rattling, the floor was not sloping downward, nor were the walls tumbling on his head. The grey light of a cloudy winter day coming through the window by no means made an unpleasant or cheerless impression.

He rang, and Petronilla appeared. The young lady, she said, had awakened, looking well and rosy, and had already breakfasted. She handed him a note from Willy Snyders, saying exactly where he could be found at different times during the forenoon and that he would be back for lunch at quarter past twelve.

Frederick took the second bath he had had within twelve or fourteen hours. They had laid out fresh underwear and several perfectly new suits of Bonifacius Ritter's for him to choose from; and he sat down to breakfast a "newborn" man. Petronilla herself brought in breakfast. While serving, she told him everybody, even all the servants, had gone out. She left the room, and returned a few moments later to ask if there was anything else he wished.

"Nothing, thank you."

She then requested permission to go out for about an hour and a half to purchase various trifles for the signorina. Soon after, Frederick saw the excellent housekeeper, all muffled up, step from the front door into the wet, almost deserted street.

After he had made this observation, he became uneasy, lit a cigarette, screwed his right eye meditatively, and bit his lips. The house was empty. For that reason his heart was audibly knocking against his ribs. Again the fantastic incalculableness of life struck him as so remarkable. An occasion, a condition such as this he had scarcely hoped to reach in weeks, or even months, certainly not in the wild welter of New York. From the noise of the steamer and the city, from the rushing and roaring of the Atlantic Ocean, he was suddenly plunged into the silence of the grave.

It affected him with a sense of desertion and oblivion. In that city of four million inhabitants, each man was strenuously pursuing his own affairs, or was harnessed into an iron yoke of duties, which deafened and blinded him to everything beside the path he had to tread.

Frederick looked at his watch. It was twelve minutes past ten. His uneasiness increased. He was unable to sit still. Each nerve, each cell of his body was touched and excited by invisible forces storming upon him from all sides. A force of this nature, penetrating walls, floors and ceilings, has been called by various names. We speak of magnetism, of od, of electricity. As for electricity, Frederick just then had a peculiar experience of it. He was trying to find composure in front of the open fireplace; and whenever he touched metal with the tongs, crackling little sparks shot out. Everything in the room seemed to be charged. If he merely ran his finger tips lightly over the rug before the hearth, there were little flashes and reports, like the crack of a tiny whip.

"There they are," he thought, smiling, "the Toilers of the Light." And while he racked his brain to recall in what book of fairy tales he had read of those diminutive elves, the dream he had had on the **Roland** occurred to him. "Toilers of the Light, what are you doing?" he asked several times, and snatched after the sparks, as one snatches after flies in a fit of impatience and boredom. It seemed to him that countless numbers of those little children of Lucifer were pricking his blood like so many dancing stars. Even the air was filled with stars. They clogged his breathing. He arose and walked out into the hall.

As he paced up and down there for a while, undecided what to do, making as little sound on the bricks as possible, he looked into the kitchen, which, like the dining-room, was in the basement, and convinced himself that it was empty. Then he softly ascended the marble steps to the next floor, where he tried with all his might to check the rise of a passion almost robbing him of his senses. In that endeavour he entered the library, a room comfortably furnished and well equipped with appurtenances for reading and writing. The walls were covered with views of ancient Rome and engravings by Piranesi. But neither the city of the Tiber nor the grave of Cecilia Metella, nor the Colosseum, nor the Temple of Vesta in Tivoli had the power to engage his real attention.

He was out in the hall again, though hesitating still whether to mount to the first story. For a while he stood uncertain, clinging with both hands to the wooden post of the balustrade, his head sunk on his hands, and his whole body shivering as in a chill. Then he raised his head. His eyes were fixed. He seemed a different person.

In that moment Frederick comprehended the passionate speech of his body, and sanctioned its demands. The thing that now came to the fore, despite all the grief that had been gathering in him, despite all his spiritual conflicts, his bitter mental convictions and self-condemnations, despite his repugnance, his horror, his compassion and his hesitating and delaying, the thing that came to the fore was the suppressed, unsatisfied demand of his body. In the silence of the morning in that strange house, it suddenly assumed an elemental, indomitable force. It would have overridden the firmest will opposing it. But Frederick's will did not oppose it. His clear, firm intention approved it, strengthened it, and made its power invincible. He entered Ingigerd's room. She was sitting at the open fireplace in a dressing-gown of Petronilla's purchasing, and was drying the masses of her long, light hair.

"Oh, Doctor von Kammacher!" she cried in slight alarm, and fixed her shimmering sea-green eyes upon the man standing there with eyes almost closed, breathing heavily, incapable of uttering a word. As by hypnotic influence, a helpless look of self-abandonment, of complete melting away spread over her face.

The sight of her expression robbed Frederick all the more of self-control. At last the time had come to extinguish the fires tormenting him in one wild, greedy draught. With the hoarse cry of a beast and the fury of a man dying of thirst, he plunged deep into the slowly, slowly cooling waves of love.

VI

It was nearly eleven o'clock when Petronilla returned. She was accompanied by an errand boy and a fair-haired young man, who was not dressed with the elegance of the residents of the club-house. His feet were heavily shod. While waiting in the hall he waved a wet umbrella with his sinewy left hand and a worn felt hat with his right hand, whistled very skilfully, and paced noisily to and fro in long strides, as if entirely at home in the place.

Petronilla summoned Frederick. With an almost passionate outcry of welcome, the one of the two men ran up the stairs, two steps at a time, and the other down the stairs twice as fast. They kissed and shook hands vigorously.

Frederick's early visitor was Peter Schmidt, of whom he had dreamed on the *Roland*. He had read Frederick's name in the newspaper among the survivors and had come from his home in Meriden, several hours' ride from New York, to see his old friend. The paper also gave Frederick's address, the reporters having got hold of it through his connection with the celebrity, Ingigerd Hahlstroem.

The first question Frederick asked after the storm of greeting had subsided, was, "I say, old boy, do you believe in telepathy?"

"Telepathy? Not a bit," replied the Friesian, and laughed a mighty laugh. "I am scarcely thirty, and sound in mind and body. I'm not an idiot. I hope no Mr. Slade has turned your head like old Zoellner's in Leipzig. Have you come over to preside at a theosophical or spiritualistic meeting? Then good-bye to our friendship, old fellow."

This was the familiar tone to which the friends were accustomed from their university days. It was infinitely refreshing to both to hear it again. No conventions of any sort divided them. Their relations were free of everything that hampers association in later years.

"You've been through a thing or two," his friend said, when Frederick confirmed the newspaper account of his having witnessed the sinking of the *Roland*. "I believe you're a married man and have children and are living in Germany, and as an avocation are doing scientific work, while practising medicine as a vocation. You were thinking of everything else in the world but a trip to America, which never had any charms for you."

"Isn't it weird," said Frederick, "how one suddenly finds oneself in a place one never dreamt of, arriving there in ways most unforeseen and at a time most unforeseen? And doesn't it seem as if the life we lived eight years ago, which was so chokefull of actuality, of real living, had all of a sudden turned to nothing?"

Peter Schmidt proposed, since they were both peripatetic philosophers, to take a walk through the streets of New York. Frederick went to consult Ingigerd. He found that for the next few hours she would be completely taken up with dressmakers. All she said was that she hoped to see him again at luncheon. Soon after, the two friends were walking along the asphalt paths of Central Park, swept clean of snow, under the bare, snowy trees between snowy lawns, while the mad city around them filled the air with a hundred-tongued Dionysiac uproar.

Though there had been an interruption of eight years in their intercourse, they took up the threads of conversation as if they had parted only half an hour before. Within a short time, each had told the other the most important facts of their lives during those eight years. Frederick for his account of himself had to go back to the date of his marriage, the notice of which he had sent to Peter Schmidt. Without departing from the truth, he related his story with a certain fancifulness, and though stating facts, mingled in psychological effects and spiritual crises. He did not refrain from telling how he had been uprooted and torn this way and that. The first and final achievement of his former life, he said, was that he had acquired the will to resignation, though the tone of his voice, as a result of his morning's experience and his meeting with his best friend, was fresh and vigorous, by no means tinged with the drab of resignation.

Peter Schmidt's account of himself, in contrast, was very brief. All he had to report was that his marriage had remained childless and his wife, a physician, over-whelmed with a sort of midwife practice, had to fight against the climate and was sick with longing for her father and mother and her Swiss mountains.

Nostalgia, Frederick suggested, was probably the universal ill from which all Germans in America suffered. The Friesian refused to admit it, and Frederick observed in unchanged form that characteristic in his friend which made of him at once the well-informed practical man of affairs and the undismayed ideologist. As ideologist, he hoped for the best for humanity's future in America, for that reason refusing to admit that a large number of the inhabitants of the United States had not yet struck root, spiritually speaking, in the land of liberty.

A newsboy with a heavy pack of papers, seeing the Germans laughing and talking and gesticulating in the Park, which at that hour was not much frequented, came toward them, holding out a paper. Peter Schmidt, who had always been a great devourer of newspapers, bought several.

"There you are," he said, unfolding one of the immense sheets. "The *Roland*, the *Roland*, and still the *Roland*, columns and pages of the *Roland*."

Frederick clutched at his head.

"Was I really on the ***Roland***?" he exclaimed.

"Very much so, it seems," said Schmidt. "Here you are in black type. 'Doctor Frederick von Kammacher performs miracles of bravery.' And here they have a picture of you."

The artist of ***The World*** had with a few strokes dashed off a young man, the replica of a million others of his kind, descending into a life-boat on a rope ladder from the top deck of a half-submerged steamer and carrying on his back a young lady wearing nothing but a shift.

"Did you really do it?" asked Peter Schmidt.

"I don't think so," said Frederick. "I must admit the details of the accident are not very clear in my mind any more." Frederick stood still, turned pale, and tried to recollect. "I don't know," he said, "what is most fearful about such an event, the things that really occurred, or the fact that one gradually digests it and forgets it." Still standing in the middle of the path, he continued: "What strikes a man hardest is the absurdity of it, the stupid senselessness of it, the superlative brutality. We know nature's brutality in theory; but to be able to live, we must forget it in its real extent, in its gruesome actuality. The most enlightened modern man somehow and somewhere in his soul still believes in something like an all-beneficent God. But such an experience gives that 'somehow' and 'somewhere' an unmerciful drubbing with iron fists. And I have come from the sinking of the ***Roland*** with a spot in my soul deaf and dumb and numb. It has not awakened to life yet. The brutalisation is so extreme that while it is still fresh in one's mind, one would as soon express belief in God or man or the future of humanity or in a Utopia, or anything else of the sort, as give utterance to something that one knows to be a vile deception. What is the sense of our sentimentalising over man's dignity, his divine destiny, when such fearful, inane injustice is wrought upon innocent persons and cannot be undone?"

Frederick turned very pale. He was seized by a violent attack of nausea. His lids opened wide, his eyes popped with a curious expression of horror. He trembled slightly, and in some alarm clutched impetuously at his friend's arm. His brain reeled dully as he felt the ground beneath his feet beginning to heave.

"I have never had anything like this before," he said. "I think the accident has left me with something."

Peter Schmidt led his friend to a bench, which fortunately happened to be close by. He saw it was a nervous attack. Frederick's hands turned numb, cold sweat broke out on his body, and he suddenly fell over in a faint. When he awoke, it took some time for him to recognise his surroundings. He said things meant for somebody else. He thought he saw his wife, then his children, and then his father in full uniform. When he regained complete consciousness, he implored his friend to keep the incident a secret. Peter Schmidt promised he would.

"My opinion is," he said, "that your over-wrought, over-taxed nerves are in revolt. They are taking revenge and at the same time curing themselves."

"Though I have inherited the strongest constitution from both my father's and mother's sides," said Frederick, "yet, from last summer on, I have been assailed by so many things that I have long been expecting a collapse. I know this will not be the last attack. I should have cause for rejoicing were the condition not to become chronic."

"Oh," said Schmidt, "you may have two or three more attacks, but if you live quietly for a few months, they may never recur again."

In coming out of his swoon Frederick, as he himself said, returned from a trip around the world. He had travelled through the axis of the earth to the antipodes, which actually did hang head downward.

"I felt as if I had been dead and had come back to life," he said, trying to give his friend a conception of the remarkable state through which he had passed. "It was not like being asleep. During the first part of my dreams, I felt as if I had been something like a block of granite for hundreds of years. On awaking I stood in the shadow of the deepest abyss. I saw subterranean landscapes, gigantic caves, heavens of stone, enormous Adelsberg grottoes. Something lifted me up. The only thing I can compare it to was the way a diver must feel who slowly, slowly rises to brighter and brighter regions from ten thousand feet below the surface of the sea. I felt as if I were forcing myself up out of the grave. I re-lived my whole conscious life from my babyhood up to this very day. You can imagine what a medley it was of nurses, military expeditions, cramming for examinations, confirmations, birthdays, marriages, sick-beds and death-beds. At the end I went through the whole sinking of the *Roland* again. And when you called me, I heard you in spite of my paralysed condition, but I saw you coming out of an inn on the quay of the little harbour where Columbus's flag-ship was slowly decaying."

"All right, all right, Friedericus Rex," Peter Schmidt soothed him. Friedericus Rex had been Frederick's nickname at the university. "Never mind," Peter continued, in a tone clearly revealing that he took Frederick's dreams to be a symptom of his over-wrought nerves. "Don't think of it, don't think of anything, old man. Let your ganglion cells rest."

Frederick assured Peter that he felt like one newly arisen to a new world and had rested better than he had for years. While they walked on together, Peter Schmidt tried to speak only of the mechanical, physiological causes of the attack. After a while, the friends regained their old liveliness and began to talk of other things. From now on, Peter Schmidt was careful never to mention the sinking of the *Roland* in Frederick's presence.

VII

"We are near Ritter's studio," Schmidt said. "If you like, we might drop in for a while."

Frederick agreed, again begging his friend not to refer to his nervous attack.

"It was very astute of me, or of the wire-puller above us, to postpone my fit until the very moment you were with me," he said.

Several times within the next few hours, Schmidt had occasion to be struck by Frederick's evident belief in predestination and the superstition that clung to him from his crossing of the Atlantic.

The street that Bonifacius Ritter's studios were on adjoined Central Park. In the first room, a man in a round paper cap of his own making was at work taking a plaster cast of a man. His cap and his smock and trousers, or as much of his trousers as showed from under his smock and above his slippers, were covered with hardened daubs of clay. Death-masks, casts of antique statues, and anatomical studies of the human body, in whole or part, hung on all the walls. When the workman left the room to announce the visitors the model, whose upper body, nude to the hips, showed the brawny development of an athlete, began to speak to Frederick and Peter.

"What won't a man do to earn his bit of daily bread!" he said. "I am from

Pirna"--he pronounced it "Berna," speaking in a round Saxon dialect--"and I tell you, it's no joke for fellows like me in this damned New York. At first I earned my living as a professional strong man. Then my boss failed, and I had to give up my outfit, my iron bars and my weights and everything I needed for my job. I can carry twelve hundred pounds on my stomach."

Ritter sent word asking the gentlemen to come to his private studio. They passed through a room in which a stately young lady was working without a model at an almost completed portrait bust in clay. In the next room, three or four marble-cutters were making a great noise hammering and chiselling imperturbably, without glancing up, at marble blocks of various sizes. From this room, a cast-iron circular stairway led up to a narrow skylight studio, where Bonifacius Ritter received Frederick and Peter.

It was a delight merely to behold the young master in his slimness and elegance. When the men entered, he removed his left hand from the pocket of his light smock, tossed away his burning cigarette, and greeted them with evident pleasure, blushing like a girl. He ushered them into a small room adjoining, lighted by a single window of antique stained glass from a French church. The low ceiling was coffered in weathered oak, and the walls were panelled in wood to a height of about six feet. A heavy oak table with benches on three sides took up nearly half the length of the room. The front of the room was partially blocked up by a genuine Nuremberg stove with the precious Delft tiles of antique green glaze testifying to the wonderful old potter's art. Willy Snyders had chanced upon the beautiful Renaissance piece in a shop near the wharf, and had succeeded in buying it for Ritter for only one hundred dollars.

"Here's a comfortable corner of the Fatherland," said Ritter. "Willy planned it all, collected all the stuff, and attended to the entire furnishing."

The university student in Frederick, the thorough German in him was surprised and delighted. Though the room looked like the cell of a St. Jerome, or, better still, the study of an Erasmus, it nevertheless resembled in its least details the dim sanctum of a German **Weinstube**, and all the more so when a young man in a blue apron, a stone-cutter's helper, who might equally well have been a wine-cellar keeper, brought in a bottle of old Rhine wine and several coloured hock glasses.

The wonderful poetry of their student days long past descended upon the friends. Frederick was still in a state of excitement and irrational recklessness. He pinned his faith to the moment, ready to stake his yesterday and his morrow upon it. The twilight of the room brought back memories of youthfully blissful times. He had found his old friend again and a new friend of the same warmth of temperament and of the same German ways, far from the old home. Settling himself snugly in the corner by the window, like a man intending to take his ease in a restaurant, he touched glasses with the others and uttered an exclamation of rapture.

"You'll never get me to budge from this corner, Mr. Ritter--though," he added, "I should first like to see your works."

"No hurry about that," said Ritter gaily, at the same time bringing an album bound in pigskin, in which he asked Frederick and Schmidt to write their names. Then he opened a very practical closet reaching to the floor, one of Willy's contrivances, and took out a carved wooden figure, a German Madonna by Till Riemenschneider. The sweet oval of her lovely face was not so much that of a Madonna as of a real German Gretchen.

"Willy Snyders told me," Ritter explained, "that he bought it from a rascal of a New York customs official, a man of German extraction, whose father had been a cabinet-maker in Ochsenfurt. The figure comes from the town-hall there and had been taken to the cabinet-maker for repair. He substituted another freshly painted figure, which the good folk of Ochsenfurt greeted with joy as the original greatly beautified and rejuvenated. Thus, Willy Snyders. I am not responsible for the version," he concluded laughing. "But one thing is certain, it's a genuine Riemenschneider."

The lovely statue by the Wuerzburg master radiated a vivid charm, which with the spell of the small room, decorated with such tender affection for old memories, and the greenish-golden sparkle of the Rhine wine in the hock glasses, brought back the German home in all its deep-seated force and beauty--a beauty, it is true, unintelligible, and therefore non-existent, to the average German of to-day.

"Once I followed up Tillman Riemenschneider's works," said Ritter. "I started at Rothenburg ob der Tauber, and went down the valley of the Tauber past Kreglingen, and so forth, as far as Wuerzburg. I am confident of recognising every piece of his at first glance, especially his Madonnas. They have almost completely cast off the Gothic, and no other sculptor in wood of his time knew so well how to treat the peach bloom of a woman's skin or the charm of a woman's face and body. His women are the pick of the lovely girls of Wuerzburg and its surroundings. Each one is adorably beautiful. Here is Veit Stoss." He took a portfolio from a shelf filled with portfolios. "Veit Stoss is superior to Riemenschneider in force of temperamental expression; he has capacities in his passions that make him superior, or at least equal, to Rembrandt." Ritter spread before them several reproductions of the master, showing the seriousness and sorrow inspiring all his works. "Nevertheless," he said, "Riemenschneider holds his own against him for the very reason that he differs from him so absolutely."

"The obstinate resistance of the Gothic," said Frederick, "the nightmare condition of mediaeval Christianity, its fearful revelling in pain, its ardour for suffering had to give way to the clear, healthy vision of a burgher. The atmosphere clears, the garments acquire a natural flow of line, erring flesh begins to blossom forth--"

"Tillman Riemenschneider's portraits are unsurpassed by any works, ancient or modern, unsurpassed, I say, by the very best," Ritter reiterated.

Willy Snyders entered with a great bluster. He had come directly from his work in the offices of an interior decorating firm.

"I say, Ritter," he said, shaking hands with the men, "if you think I'm not thirsty, you're very much mistaken." He examined the bottle. "The deuce! Without me to help him, the wretch taps one of the twenty bottles of Johannisberger with which a Chicago pork packer presented him when he made a portrait of his humpbacked daughter. Well, now that one is gone, another may as well follow. Gentlemen, isn't this a jolly place for little carousals?" Pointing to the Madonna from Ochsenfurt-on-the-Main. "Isn't she a smart little body? She certainly is not by Pappe. I myself collect nothing but Japanese works." The fact seemed quite to accord with his appearance. "I'm nothing but a poor dog now, but inside of four or five years I intend to have the wherewithal, and the collecting of things Japanese will proceed by electricity. There's no race that can compete with those fellows in art. But now I want to tell you something." He turned to Ritter. "With your kind permission, I'll go call Lobkowitz and, what is more, I'll call Miss Eva. Just now, as I passed through her room, she told me she would like to meet the hero of the *Roland*." Without awaiting an answer, he left the room; and within a few moments Lobkowitz, who collaborated with Ritter, and Miss Burns, the pupil, appeared.

After the conventional greetings were over, the little Madonna was used as a welcome occasion for starting conversation again, which had begun to lag a bit on the entrance of the newcomers. Willy held the statue, a little less than three feet high, against different panels of the wall to see how it looked for permanent placing there. A spot was finally chosen, and the Madonna was fastened to it temporarily.

The stone-cutter's helper brought another bottle of the heavy, expensive wine, more hock glasses, large Delft plates, and a mountain of sandwiches. Though Frederick and Peter had declared they must end their too lengthy visit, a fresh wave of conviviality swept over the company and held them on. A half hour passed, and another half hour, and a whole hour, and still the new friends were sitting over their German wine and still they were discussing that inexhaustible theme so dear to all of them, German art.

"It is an eternal shame," said Frederick, "that the spirit which created the art of the old Greeks cannot be united with that profound German spirit, an entirely new spirit, which characterises the works of Adam Krafft, Veit Stoss, and Peter Vischer."

"Doctor von Kammacher," Miss Burns asked, "have you ever done any work in sculpture?" Miss Burns spoke a correct German. Her father was a Dutchman, her mother a German, and when her parents settled in London, she was only a child of three.

"Doctor von Kammacher exudes talent at every pore," said Willy, answering in Frederick's place. "I can testify to it." Willy Snyders' passion for collecting had manifested itself while he was still a boy. Among his treasures had been some copies of so-called "beer gazettes," humorous sheets got up to be read at German students' merrymaking. The copies in his possession contained sketches by Frederick, both of a humorous and serious character.

"I exude talent?" Frederick exclaimed, blushing. "Never, Willy. I beg of you, Miss Burns, don't believe that enthusiast of a schoolboy. If I really have talent, those sketches of mine in beer gazettes wouldn't prove it. As a matter of fact, I once did do some work in art. Why should I deny that, like all silly children of between sixteen and twenty, I dabbled in painting, sculpture, and literature? Once my father had to bring me to reason because I was all afire for going on the stage. Later, I wanted to throw everything to the winds to enter politics and revolutionise society by working for a party which has never even existed, a German-Social party. I leave you to judge how flighty I was and how much talent I had for art. But I love art, with a love stronger, I think, now than ever before, because everything in the world beside art has become problematical to me. I would rather have carved a wooden Mary like this"--indicating the statue by Riemenschneider--"than have been Robert Koch and Helmholtz rolled into one. Of course, I am speaking purely subjectively. I know how great Koch and Helmholtz are, and I have the profoundest admiration for both."

"See here! See here! What's the matter with us, Friedericus?" cried Peter Schmidt, jumping to his feet. Though the artists had great fondness and respect for Peter Schmidt and went to him for advice, yet, whenever he was with them, a violent discussion invariably arose whether art or science deserves precedence in the field of human culture, Peter, of course, championing the cause of science. "If you were to throw that wooden statue into the fire," he said, "it would burn like wood. Neither the wood nor the immortal art infusing it resists fire. And once it burns to ashes, it can, of course, be of no significance to the world's progress. The world is full of marvellous gods and mothers of God, and so far as I know, they never cast a single ray of light into the night of the darkest ignorance."

"I'm not saying anything against science," Frederick declared laughing, "I am merely speaking of a very unsettled man's love of art. So be at ease, Peter."

"If sculpture really attracts you," said Miss Burns, who had given her exclusive attention to Frederick, "why don't you begin right away to model here under Mr. Ritter? Begin to-morrow."

"I can't say I know very much about wood-carving," said Ritter, gaily. "However, I am entirely at Doctor von Kammacher's disposal."

"I cannot leave my little Madonna, my wooden Mother of God," cried Frederick, flushed with the wine, rising and holding up his glass. The others followed his example, laughing; and they drank to the little Madonna, each with a secret thought linking Frederick's outburst with the girl in the club-house. The glasses rang, and Frederick continued rather daringly: "I wish it had been granted me to do with divine intelligence and human hands, as Goethe said, what the animal man can and must do with the animal woman." He made a cup of his hands as if to dip up water. "I feel my Madonna in the hollow of my hands like a homunculus. She is alive there. The palms of my hands are warm. They are a golden shell. Conceive my Madonna to be a hand's breadth high, of live ivory, and imagine some rosy flecks here and there on her. Imagine her robed in the garments that Godiva wore, that is, nothing but her hair of flowing sunbeams, and so on, and so on." Frederick began to improvise poetry.

"Said the master: 'Come into my workshop.'
And he took, like unto the Creator,
God! in both his hands a little image,
And his heart with mighty throb vibrated.
'As thou seest it, once I saw it living.'
And so on, and so on.

Over my hands
Flowed golden wavelets,
Cool, sweet lips and--

I'll say no more. I'll merely add that I should like to carve that Madonna in German linden-wood and give her all the colours of life itself, and then die, for all I care."

Frederick's enthusiastic outburst was received with great applause.

Eva Burns was a beautiful young woman of over twenty-five years, imposing and perhaps somewhat masculine in appearance. Her German was rather hard, suggesting to a hypercritical person that her tongue was too thick for her mouth, like a parrot's. Her abundant hair was parted in the middle and drawn over her ears. Her figure was broad, stately, and perfectly formed. While Frederick spoke, and even after he had done speaking, she looked at him with searching interest in her large, intelligent, meditative eyes. Finally she said:

"You really ought to try to do it."

Eva Burns was one of those knowing, companionable women that are always welcome and never disturbing in a company of men. Her eyes and Frederick's eyes met, and the young scholar answered her in a tone of mixed raillery and gallantry:

"Miss--Miss--"

"Burns," Willy helped him, "Miss Burns from Birmingham."

"Miss Burns from Birmingham, you said something of great significance. On you be the blame if the world is impoverished by the loss of a poor physician and enriched by the addition of a poor sculptor."

It had grown dark, and they lighted three large candles of the finest bee's wax in the chandelier above the table.

"I have no objections," Schmidt several times interjected in the debate, "I have no objections to your trying to help toward the evolution of sublimer types by means of divine intelligence and human hands; for all I care, by means of divine intelligence alone, that is, by means of reason. The very same, if you will allow it, is the object, the ultimate object, of the science of medicine. A day is coming when artificial selection among human beings will be obligatory." The artists burst out laughing, but Schmidt continued unabashed. "And another day, a still more beautiful day, is coming when persons like ourselves will be considered like, well, let us say at the utmost, the African Bushmen."

VIII

The candles had almost burned to the bottom when the little company decided it was time to break up. It was a half holiday, the stone-cutters had stopped work sooner than usual, and the other rooms were dark and deserted. The artists used the stumps of the candles to light the company about. In passing through the first studio, Lobkowitz partially uncovered pieces meant for the Chicago Exposition, colossal plaster casts and models in clay representing commerce, manufacture, agriculture and the like. They threw enormous shadows on the walls and ceiling.

"You can't get results in art from large figures," said Ritter, though the statues were full of animation, and there was something prepossessing in them.

"Everything for the anniversary of 1492, everything for the Chicago Exposition," said Willy. "A Viking ship is coming over from Norway. The last descendant of Christopher Columbus, a knock-kneed Spaniard, is to be passed around for show, a tremendous humbug, always an acceptable dish to the Americans. Ritter owes this big order to his monkey-like quickness. The building commission applied to various sculptors, and Ritter sent them sketches for all the statues before the other artists had even wet their clay."

"I was working in my little studio in Brooklyn," said Ritter, "and for forty-eight hours in succession I didn't take my hands out of clay. These figures don't bother me in the least. After the Exposition they won't exist except in photographs."

"That's the way the Americans are. Please, Ritter, do give us a Washington memorial. Perhaps you have a Washington memorial ready-made in your waistcoat pocket."

"No, but by eight thirty-five this evening I will have one for you."

"He can do it, too," said Willy, patting his idol. "That is why he fits so well into the United States of America."

The men now entered Ritter's real workshop. Here there were pieces very different in spirit. While the large figures for the Chicago Exposition showed traces of commercialism, here everything was thoroughly artistic. A companion piece in clay to the bas-relief in the club-house, a group of singing girls not yet completed, was standing on a heavy scaffolding. It showed the same noble qualities that Frederick had observed in the relief of the singing boys. Had these works been displayed in Germany, they would undoubtedly have been epoch-making. A bust of an old woman had some of the traits of Donatello. Everything in the room testified to the facility with which the youthful master created. There was a long decorative frieze in clay, putti with goats, dancing fauns, maenads, Silenus on his donkey, a procession of bacchantic figures celebrating the vintage and reproducing all the bacchic joyousness, the drunkenness, of men and women vintagers, as they cut and trod the grapes and drank the wine. Another uncompleted work in clay was the figure of a middle-aged Neptune at a fountain, looking with a jolly smile at a huge fish in his hands. There was a completed plaster cast of St. George, frankly inspired by its glorious model, the St. George of Donatello in the National Museum in Florence. In all these works, Ritter had struck a happy medium between the Greeks and Donatello and created a style fully expressing his own personality, yet showing permissible dependence upon his predecessors.

The pieces in this room were without exception meant for the country residence of an American Croesus, who had taken a tremendous fancy to the young sculptor and his work and jealously tried to keep his creations from straying into another's possession. He looked upon himself as a Medici of the nineteenth century. His marble palace in extensive grounds on Long Island had already swallowed up millions of dollars, though meant as a residence merely for himself, his wife, and his only daughter. No one but Ritter was to do the statuary and sculptural decorations for his house and garden, and he was to have free play. What commissions are given in America! Were talents as easy to create in "our country" as dollars, there would be a second Renaissance even greater than the great Italian Renaissance.

Frederick was fairly intoxicated by the young man's singular good fortune. What he particularly admired was the union of success and merit. When he compared the abundance of these works, tossed off apparently as in play, and the young man's cheerful evenness of temper with his own torn, distracted existence, a feeling came upon him that he had never before had, the feeling that he was an outcast, a feeling of discouragement and helpless defeat. While the light of the candles glided over the creations of the man who had infused form and soul into the formless clay, a voice within him kept saying:

"You have frittered away your existence, you have wasted your days, you will never retrieve your loss."

And the voice of envy, of bitter reproach against a nameless being asked why he had not been permitted to find a similar path and follow it in time.

Ritter's life had received a wrench in Europe. Some brutal mishap while he was serving in the army had made him revolt and later desert. Now, after seven years in America, he was compelled to admit that the wrench had been indispensable for transplanting the sapling to the soil best suited to its growth. In the new surroundings, Ritter's nature developed simply, harmoniously and symmetrically, like a tree with plenty of space and sunlight. Fate atoned for the lack of military subordination in the young prince from genius-land by granting him a surplus of superordination.

Suddenly Ritter said to Frederick:

"I understand Toussaint, the Berlin sculptor, was on board the **Roland**."

Peter Schmidt had warned the artists in an aside not to touch upon the disaster, telling them his friend was very nervous and a reference to the accident might have a bad effect upon him. But his warning had been forgotten.

"Poor Toussaint," Frederick said, "hoped to find mountains of gold here, though, you may say, he was nothing but a fancy-cake genius."

"And yet I assure you," said Lobkowitz, "there was something grand about him as a man. In spite of his success, he was always poor. He suffered from having a wife who was too fond of society and from having to associate with the persons who bestowed favours upon him and were so much richer than himself. That dandyism of his was not natural. Had he reached America, he would probably have ignored his wife and become an entirely different man. All he wanted to do was to create, to work. What he loved best was to be perched on a scaffolding, with shirt sleeves tucked up, among first-rate workmen. Once he said to me, 'If you should happen to see a mason resembling me in New York, sitting on the pavement eating his lunch and drinking a can of beer, don't hesitate to believe I am that mason, and don't pity me. Congratulate me.'"

"Another one," thought Frederick, "who kept the best part of himself hidden beneath the conventional foppishness of his time; another one who, like me, may always have been trying in vain to reach a definite decision between being and seeming."

IX

Ritter's dog-cart was waiting in front of the door. He suggested that Frederick and Schmidt drive down in it to the railroad station, where Schmidt was to get the train back to Meriden. The two men squeezed in beside the Austrian horse-trainer, valet, or whatever Ritter's coachman was. The trotter went off at a swift gait, and again the wild, noisy phantasmagoria of the streets of the new Babylon went flashing by Frederick's eyes.

Ritter had introduced his coachman as Mr. Boabo. He wore a small round hat of brown felt, brown gloves, and a short brown jockey's overcoat. His chin was heavy, his nose finely chiselled, and his moustache dark and downy. He was a handsome man, or lad, since boyish naivete still predominated in his expression. He was about the same age as Ritter. While guiding the magnificent grey through the medley of cabs, trucks, and street-cars, he smiled faintly, as if delighted by it all.

Notwithstanding the city's excesses of architecture and engineering, its distinctive characteristic was unimaginativeness. The hurry and bustle, "business," the chase after the dollar had lashed the technical arts on to audacious attempts; for example, the skyscrapers, or the elevated railroad, with its unfenced tracks high overhead, its trains thundering along incessantly in two directions, winding sharply about the corners like an illuminated snake, and writhing into streets so narrow that a person in one of the upper stories of the houses can almost touch the coaches with his hands.

"Madness, lunacy!" Frederick exclaimed in his amazement.

"Not altogether," said Schmidt. "Back of it all is a very sane, unscrupulous practicality, riding down every obstacle in its way."

"It would be hideous were it not so tremendous," Frederick shouted above the din.

The newsboys were still calling the wreck of the *Roland*.

"What is that? What was that?" thought Frederick. "I am wallowing in life. How does that story concern me?"

A congestion of traffic compelled the grey to come to a halt. He champed on his bit, tossed his head, sending flecks of foam flying from his mouth, and looked about as if to try the heart and reins of the young Austrian officer with his heroic, fiery eyes. During the compulsory pause, Frederick had a chance to observe how sheafs of newspapers were being consumed by the pressing, crushing, jostling throngs.

"The cow gobbles grass, and New York gobbles newspapers," Frederick thought. And heaven be praised! In *The World* that Schmidt bought of a boy, who at risk of his life had threaded his way to the cart, there were fresh sensations taking precedence of the *Roland*--"Explosion in a Pennsylvania mine. Three hundred miners cut off." "Fire in a factory in a thirteen-story skyscraper. Four hundred working-girls perish in the flames."

"After us the deluge," said Frederick. "Coal is dear, wheat is dear, oil is dear, but men are cheap as dirt. Mr. Boabo, don't you think our civilisation is a fever of a hundred and six degrees? Isn't New York a mad-house?"

But the handsome youth, after the fashion of Austrian officers, put his hand to his cap with inimitable grace, while a decided smile, a smile of happiness, played about the corners of his mouth, and his answer by no means expressed assent.

"Well, I love life. Here one really lives. When there is no war in Europe, then it is wearisome," he said, speaking in English, which most clearly proved how distant his relation to the old continent was.

At the station, when they were standing on the platform beside the train, Schmidt said to Frederick, wringing his hand impetuously in his German way:

"Now, old fellow, you must soon come to see me in Meriden. Meriden is a small place, and you can recuperate there better than here."

"I'm not altogether a free agent," Frederick replied with a faint, fatalistic smile.

"Why not?"

"I have obligations. I am tied down."

With the indiscretion of intimacy, Schmidt asked:

"Has it anything to do with the wooden Madonna?"

"Perhaps it is something of the sort," Frederick replied. "The poor little thing lost her father, her natural protector, and as I had a share in her rescue--"

"Then there was a girl in a shift, and a rope ladder!"

"Yes and no. I'll tell you more about it some other time. Now just take my word for it, there are times when all of a sudden in a most surprising way, one finds oneself saddled with complete responsibility for a fellow-creature."

Peter Schmidt laughed.

"You mean, if a woman steps up to you in a crowded city street and asks you to hold her baby a moment, and never comes back for her baby?"

"I'll tell you everything some other time."

The train with its long, elegantly built coaches began to move slowly, though no signal of any sort had been given, no whistle or bell or word of command. Without the least to-do, it slipped out of the station wholly disregarded. Peter and Frederick were the only persons taking leave of one another in this crowded train bound inland. Peter mounted the steps, and again shook hands with Frederick.

"I hope to see you soon again," each said to the other warmly.

X

When Frederick returned home, he learned that a number of reporters and other persons had been there inquiring for him. Webster and Forster's agent had given his address, Frederick deduced upon seeing among the reporters' cards one of Arthur Stoss's. There was also a letter from an impresario, a German of the name of Lehmann, who, failing to find Frederick in, had left a pencilled note asking whether, and under what conditions, Frederick would be prepared to deliver a medical lecture in New York, Boston, Chicago, and later other cities, in which lecture he was each time to touch upon the sinking of the *Roland* and weave in some of his impressions of the event.

"What else?" thought Frederick, disgusted, though he had to admit that he had actually become famous.

Through Petronilla he sent word to Ingigerd to ask whether it would be agreeable to her to receive him. Petronilla returned with the message that Ingigerd would see him in a quarter of an hour. "Signor Pittore Franck is with her," the housekeeper added; which piece of information sent the blood rushing to Frederick's head; and though it had been his intention to wash and change his clothes, he scarcely waited for Petronilla to conclude her message, and dashed up-stairs three steps at a time. He knocked on Ingigerd's door loudly. No one said "Come in." Nevertheless he opened the door and entered and saw the gypsy painter sitting at Ingigerd's side. On the table under the electric bulbs, lay a large sheet of paper, on which Franck was sketching with a soft pencil what Frederick on stepping nearer saw to be hasty designs for costumes.

"I said in a quarter of an hour," said Ingigerd slowly, making a wry face.

"I'll come whenever I choose to," said Frederick.

Franck, rising without the least air of haste or confusion, greeted Frederick with perfect cordiality and walked to the door.

"I don't want to disturb you. Good evening, Doctor von Kammacher," he said with a grin betraying some delight in Frederick's annoyance.

"Rigo!" Ingigerd called after him. "You promised to come again to-morrow morning."

"What's that boy doing in your room, Ingigerd?" Frederick demanded some-what roughly, in evident anger. "And 'Rigo'? What does 'Rigo' mean? Are both of you out of your wits?"

Though this tone of his must have been new to her, it seemed agreeable to her, for she said very humbly:

"Well, why did you stay away so long?"

"I'll tell you later. But as matters now stand between us, I forbid your striking up such friendships. If you want to do something for the fellow, present him with a comb and a nail brush and a tooth-brush. Besides, his name isn't Rigo but Max, and he's a seedy sort of chap, absolutely dependent upon his friends."

In his moments of jealousy, it was easy for Ingigerd to put Frederick to shame.

"It makes no difference to me," she said, "whether a man is poor or rich, whether he dresses like a dude or a tramp. Rigo intends to paint my portrait, and I'm looking forward with pleasure to being his model."

"His model? You won't be his model. I'll see to that," said Frederick. "But please explain how you hit upon 'Rigo'? Why do you call him 'Rigo'? Tell me."

"His mother was a gypsy, and when he was a child, some respectable people took him into their family."

"Do you believe that? Franck's friends say he lies every time he opens his mouth."

"I'm not a father confessor. He may lie for all I care."

Frederick did not reply.

Ingigerd was still sitting at the table. With gentle ardour he pressed his lips to her head, loosened the ribbon tying her hair at the nape of her neck, and plunged his fingers deep into the wave of flowing gold.

"Where were you?" the girl asked. Frederick told her of Peter Schmidt and the exhilarating afternoon in Ritter's studio.

"I don't like that sort of thing," she said. "How can people drink wine?"

The thought passed through Frederick's mind that the girl's remarks were rather flat and failed to echo the things he had been telling her.

About an hour later Frederick asked Willy to help him find a boarding house where he and Ingigerd could live, or Ingigerd could live alone without his protection.

"You must realise," Frederick explained, "that no matter how unprejudiced you and your friends may be, it won't do to let a young lady remain permanently in a bachelors' club-house."

Willy did realise the impropriety of the situation; and that very same evening he found an excellent place for her with friends on Fifth Avenue.

The next morning, after the men had left the house, Frederick again fell under the spell of a strange excitement that led him to Ingigerd's room. This time, however, it was not a wave of passion, but a storm of desire for self-purification.

"Ingigerd," he said, "fate has brought us together. I am sure you, too, feel that in spite of all the appalling events we underwent, something like predestination was at work." Frederick now told her, as he had fully planned to do, the story of his past. It was a complete confession. He spoke of his youth and marriage, spoke with all possible forbearance and love of his wife. "There was no hope for her ever getting well again. I have nothing to reproach myself with in regard to her, except that I was a man merely of good intentions and imperfect achievement. But I may not have been the right husband for her in so far as I could not give her the repose of spirit that she needed and I myself lacked. When the collapse finally occurred and other misfortunes--they seldom come singly--and in addition I suffered disappointments outside my family life, I had great difficulty in bearing up. I hate to speak of it, but it is the truth--before I saw you, I picked up a revolver more than once for a very definite purpose. Life weighed upon me like lead. It had turned stale and tasteless. The sight of you, Ingigerd, and, strange to say, the wreck, which I experienced not only symbolically but in actuality, taught me to value life again. You and bare existence--the two things I saved from the wreck. Once more I stand on terra firma. I love the soil. I should like to fondle it. But I am not yet secure, Ingigerd. I am still sore, without and within, you know. You have suffered a loss, I have suffered a loss. We have beheld the other side of existence, the unforgettable gloom. We have looked into the pit. Ingigerd, shall we cling to each other? Will you come to a man torn and distracted, lashed by scorpions, to a man who is greedy to-day and surfeited to-morrow, to a man who longs for peace and repose, and be peace and repose to him? Could you for my sake give up all that has until now filled your life, if I for your sake leave behind me everything that has wasted my existence? Shall we both begin afresh, on a new basis, simply and without any false glamour, and live and die as plain country persons? I will be tender with you, Ingigerd." Frederick hollowed his hands and held them as he had done when speaking of the Madonna. "I will--" He broke off and cried: "Say something! Just tell me the one thing, Ingigerd! Can you--can you become my comrade for life?"

Ingigerd was standing at the window looking out into the fog and tapping the pane with a pencil.

"Perhaps, Doctor von Kammacher," she said finally.

"Perhaps!" Frederick blazed up. "And Doctor von Kammacher!"

Ingigerd turned and said quickly:

"Why do you always fly into such a temper right away? How do I know if I am suited to your needs and desires?"

"It is merely a question of love," replied Frederick.

"I like you. Yes, I do like you, but whether my feeling for you is love, how can I tell? I always say that so far I haven't loved anything but animals."

"Animals!" cried Frederick von Kammacher. He felt mortally ashamed. Never, it seemed to him, in his whole life had he so degraded himself.

XI

A few moments later there was a knock at the door, and a man in a long over-coat and brown kid gloves, carrying a silk hat in his fat hand entered.

"Excuse me," he said, "I presume this is Miss Hahlstroem?"

"Yes. I am Miss Hahlstroem."

"My name is Lilienfeld--manager of the Cosmopolitan Theatre." He handed Frederick his card, which announced that he was also manager of a variety theatre and impresario in general. "I obtained your address from Mr. Stoss, the armless marksman, you know. I heard you had had some unpleasantness with Webster and Forster, and I said to myself, I must go and call on the daughter of a good old friend of mine. I knew both your father and mother." Mr. Lilienfeld, in tactfully subdued tones, wound up his rather lengthy address with delicate expressions of sympathy and his personal sorrow at Hahlstroem's death.

Ingigerd being helpless as a child in business matters, Frederick had taken it upon himself to represent her, and he used the pause in the impresario's speech to put in a word. The man's personality was by no means displeasing to him, and his presence for several reasons was highly welcome.

"Owing to the state of her health, Miss Hahlstroem was unable until now to appear in public. I as her physician am responsible for her refusal to dance, but Webster and Forster used such rough methods of coercion both through intermediaries and through the mail that Miss Hahlstroem of her own accord decided in no circumstances to dance under their management."

"Never!" explained Ingigerd. "Absolutely never."

"Besides," Frederick continued, "their terms are miserable. We have received letters offering three and four times as much."

"Exactly what was to be expected," declared Lilienfeld. "Pardon me if I give you a bit of advice. In the first place, be perfectly easy in your mind about Webster and Forster's attempts to intimidate you. For various reasons the contract with Mr. Hahlstroem is legally invalid. It so happens that I have pretty accurate information regarding the terms of the divorce between your father and mother. They themselves told me, and what is more, my brother was counsel for your father. Your mother was made your legal guardian. Your father had no right to make a contract for you. You ran away. You went with your father because you were devoted to him body and soul and the relation between you and your mother may not have been quite so pleasant. I do not hesitate to say you acted wisely, very wisely. Your father's training has made a great artist of you."

"Thank you," Ingigerd laughed, at the mere memory of her training involuntarily protesting against her artistic education. "For hours at a time, while he sat in a chair comfortably smoking his meerschaum, I had to dance for him without a stitch of clothing on and perform all sorts of contortions and acrobatic feats on a rug. In the afternoon he would play the piano and I would have to go through the same thing all over again."

"Your father was a positive marvel as a trainer. He put two or three international stars on their dancing legs, if you will permit the expression. He was the dancing master of two worlds and"--the impresario laughed significantly--"many other interesting things besides. But to stick to the matter in hand--if you want, your contract with Webster and Forster is null and void." He paused for an instant and began again, this time addressing himself more to Frederick. "I do not deny that I am a business man--always within the limits of gentlemanliness--and I should like to ask you a question, Doctor von Kammacher. Is it your intention to let Miss Hahlstroem dance at all again, or have you and she decided that she is to retire to private life?"

"Oh, no," said Ingigerd very decidedly.

Frederick felt something like cold iron enter his soul. He seemed to himself to be a sword-swallower unable immediately to extract the steel from his body.

"No, we have not," he, too, said, "though I for my part should like Miss Hahlstroem to give up the stage because she has a delicate constitution. But she maintains she needs the sensation of it. And when I see the offers she receives, I do not know whether I have the right to persuade her against her will."

"Don't, Doctor von Kammacher, don't!" cried Mr. Lilienfeld. "Miss Hahlstroem, Doctor von Kammacher, let me take up the cudgels for you against Webster and Forster--bloodsuckers, I tell you--and they've insulted the lady, besides. I assure you, they are the source of a lot of vile rumours about her."

"Mention names," said Frederick, turning white. "I shall have no difficulty, I fancy, in finding a second, and I hope the same code of honour holds for gentlemen here as in Europe."

"Tush--tush!" The impresario lifted his fat hands in pacification, and it seemed to Frederick as if the business man's round head, set low between his shoulders, were trying to make signs to him, as if he were winking his eyes furtively and were suppressing a broad smile, unexpectedly upsetting his business zeal and gravity. "You make entirely too much of it." He looked Frederick straight in the face in a peculiar way with a significant expression in his large round eyes. Then he continued: "For an engagement of twenty evenings in cities to be decided upon, I offer you one hundred and fifty dollars more per evening than anybody else has yet offered you, the engagement to begin inside of four days. If you are agreed, we can go to the lawyer this minute."

Within less than half an hour Frederick and Ingigerd were standing in a huge elevator, which was to take them to the fifth floor of a New York City office building. Ingigerd was the only woman in the elevator, and it pleased her that for her sake the nineteen gentlemen in the car held their hats in their hands.

"If you have never before seen such a thing," Lilienfeld said to Frederick, "the offices of a big American lawyer will astonish you. This is a law firm, two partners, Brown and Samuelson; but Brown's a nincompoop and Samuelson is the whole thing."

The offices of the famous New York lawyer, Samuelson, were partitioned off with wood and ground glass from an immense hall, a writing factory, in which there was a horde of assistants working typewriters. Samuelson made the impression of a man of nearly forty. He was not very tall, had a bad, pallid complexion, and wore a short, pointed beard. The clothes of this man, whose share of the firm's income was estimated at three hundred thousand dollars a year, though of the correct cut, were by no means new; in fact, they were rather shabby, and his entire appearance suggested that he was scarcely a model of American cleanliness. He spoke in a very low, thick voice, as if suffering from a sore throat.

Within less than fifteen minutes, the contract between Lilienfeld and Ingigerd had been concluded, a contract, which owing to the fact that Ingigerd was a minor, was no more valid than the contract with Webster and Forster. Samuelson showed that he was informed of all the details of the case of Hahlstroem *vs.* Webster and Forster. When the question of their demands arose, he merely smiled with an air of great disdain and said:

"We will quietly lie low and let them make the advance."

When Ingigerd and Frederick were sitting alone together in a closed cab on the way home, he put his arms about her passionately.

"If you dance on the stage, Ingigerd, I'll go out of my mind. I feel as if you and I and our love would be exposed in the pillory. If it were I instead of you, it would not be half so hard to stand."

The poor young scholar began again to pour out before the little vampire all the anguish he had been suffering, this time with hot kisses and embraces.

"I am a drowning man. If you do not hold your hand out to me I shall sink forever. You are stronger than I am. You can save me. The world is nothing to me. What I lost is nothing, was nothing and will always be nothing to me, if only I can exchange it for you. Come with me, and you shall be all in all to me, the one thing of significance in my life."

"You are not weak," the girl whispered with a dying-away look in her eyes. She breathed heavily, her narrow lips parted, and that fatal, seductive smile spread over her languishing face, like a mask.

"Take me! Run away with me!"

For a time they were silent as the cab rolled along easily on its rubber tires.

"They can wait a long while for you, Ingigerd," Frederick at length said. "To-morrow we shall be with Peter Schmidt in Meriden."

But she laughed. Yes, she laughed at him, and Frederick clearly saw he had melted her body, not her soul; or a soul was a thing this girl did not possess.

The cab came to a halt in front of the club-house. Frederick seemed to have lost his speech. Without saying a word, he escorted Ingigerd to the door, pressed her hand, and returned to the cab. He chose a place at random, and called to the coachman to drive him there.

XII

Frederick crouched in a corner of the cab. In a passion of shame, he called himself the vilest names. He removed his slouched hat, which he had not yet replaced by the New York chimney-pot, wiped the sweat from his brow, and beat his fist against his forehead.

"My poor father! Within a month, I shall probably be no more nor less than the official kept man of a prostitute. Everybody will know me and pay homage to me. Every German barber in New York will tell his patrons who my father is, and who I am, and what I live by, and whom I am running after. I shall become that worthless little fiend's lap dog, her monkey to perform tricks for her, her procurer. The German colonies in every city, large or small, that we visit will behold in me a typical example of the loathsome degree to which a scion of the German nobility can sink, into what a cesspool of vice a man who was once a good man, husband, and father can descend."

While being bowled rapidly down Broadway, Frederick, in his state of intro-spection and shame, looked blindly upon the houses as they glided by. Suddenly he started up from his crouching position. The sign of the Hoffman House had struck his eye and recalled the appointment the men on the **Hamburg** had made. He consulted his watch, and found it was just about the time they had set, between twelve and one. He called to the driver, but before the horse could be brought to a stop, the cab had rolled some distance beyond the hotel. Frederick got out, paid the coachman, and in a few moments was inside the well-known New York bar-room.

He saw a long bar, marble slabs, marble wainscoting, polished brass, polished silver, shining mirrors, on which there was not the smallest speck of dust, very many shining glasses, empty glasses, glasses with straws sticking in them, and glasses partially filled with bits of ice. Bar-keepers in spotless white linen prepared the famous American drinks, innumerable in variety, with a dexterity bordering on art and a stolidity out of which nothing could shake them.

The wall behind the bar was studded within reaching distance with an array of gleaming polished metal taps; back of the bar were the passageways to the pantries and kitchen. Oil paintings hung above the taps and doorways. Over the heads of the business men standing or leaning at the bar, with derbies or silk hats shoved back from their foreheads, Frederick saw a delicious woman's figure by Courbet; sheep by Troyon; a bright seascape with clouds by Dupre; several choice pieces by Daubigny, sheep on a dune landscape, a pool reflecting the full moon hanging low over the horizon and two cud-chewing oxen; a Corot--a tree, a cow, water, a glorious evening sky; a Diaz--a pond, old birches, light reflected in the water; a Rousseau--a gigantic tree in a storm; a Millet--a pot with turnips, pewter spoons and knives; a dark portrait by Delacroix; another Courbet, a landscape; a small Bastien-Lepage, a girl and a man in the grass with a great deal of light; and many other excellent pictures. He was so fascinated that he almost forgot his recent experience and his purpose in coming.

In his complete absorption, he was only vaguely annoyed by a rather loud group, whose boisterous laughter and restlessness contrasted sharply with the quiet demeanour of the other guests. Suddenly he felt a hand on his shoulder, started, looked around and met the eyes of a man whose bearded face seemed coarse and unfamiliar. Cocktails and other good drinks had shot his peony complexion with a bluish tinge.

"What's the matter?" the stranger said. "Don't you know me--Captain Butor?"

Captain Butor, the man to whom Frederick owed his life! And now he also recognised the other members of the noisy group. There were Arthur Stoss and his valet, Bulke, in inconspicuous black livery, sitting a little off from the others. There were Doctor Wilhelm, and the painter Jacob Fleischmann, and Wendler, the *Hamburg's* engineer, and two sailors from the *Roland*, wearing new suits and caps. They had already been engaged on another steamer of the same line and had been presented with a fair sum of money.

The men all greeted Frederick like an old friend. Arthur Stoss, for the benefit of a New York gentleman, was retailing his old story, that he intended in a short while to give up touring and retire. He made frequent loud references to his wife, evidently considering it very worth while to publish as widely as possible the fact that he, the man without arms, actually possessed a wife.

"I have met with the most tremendous success this time," he said. "Last night the audience stormed the stage and lifted me on their shoulders to the tune of '1492,' the song they sing every evening in the Metropolitan Theatre."

"1492"--wherever he turned his eyes, on the streets and open squares, Frederick read advertisements of the ballad, a product of the vaudeville stage, in which the discovery of America, four hundred years after the landing of Columbus, was interpreted in the patriotic sense of the new nation that had since arisen.

"Well, Doctor von Kammacher, how are you?" asked Doctor Wilhelm. "How have you spent your time?"

"Oh, so, so," Frederick replied, shrugging his shoulders. He did not know how he came to frame this summary dismissal of a time so rich in content. Strange to say, here on land, in the Hoffman bar, little or none of his former impulse remained to entrust confidences to his fellow-physician.

"How's our little girl?" Doctor Wilhelm inquired, smiling significantly.

"I do not know," Frederick returned with an expression of cool astonishment, and added: "Whom do you mean?"

As his answers to all their inquiries were equally curt and stiff, it was impossible to start a conversation. He himself in the first few minutes did not understand why he had come. It was extremely disturbing to him that the other men in the bar-room recognised the group as the survivors of the *Roland*. Stoss by himself, the man without arms, the well-known marksman, would have been conspicuous.

Stoss could drink holding a glass between his teeth; but he was not touching liquor to-day. Nevertheless, he was in a treating mood, a circumstance by which Captain Butor, Wendler, Fleischmann and the sailors profited to toast one another freely. Nor did Doctor Wilhelm require much urging.

In an undertone he informed Frederick that *The Staats-Zeitung* in its issue of the morning before had opened a collection for Fleischmann, and a sum had already come in such as the poor fellow in his whole life had probably never before seen. At last Frederick laughed, and heartily. He understood why Fleischmann was drinking heavily, with so determined a manner, and why he was puffing himself like a turkey.

"What do you think of that stuff, Doctor von Kammacher?" he asked, pointing to the paintings and snorting disdainfully. "To call such stuff art! Millions and millions are spent on getting those things over from France. They palm the trash off on the Americans. I'll wager that if one of us Germans in Munich, Dresden, or Berlin were to do no better than that, or that"--he pointed at random to several pictures--"we'd put him in the A B C class."

"Perfectly true," said Frederick, laughing.

"Just you wait," cried Fleischmann. "I'll show the Americans a thing or two. German art--"

But Frederick ceased to listen. His only impression after the lapse of some time was, that in the meanwhile Fleischmann had misused the same words, "German art," an endless number of times. Turning to Doctor Wilhelm he said unblushingly:

"Do you remember the way this howling dog, this creature laughing like a lunatic, rose up out of the waves beside our boat?"

Captain Butor and Wendler, who had been laughing mightily over something, now stepped up with brimming eyes, as if they deemed the time had come to be serious for a few moments in the company of the two physicians.

"Did you hear, gentlemen, that Newfoundland fishermen have sighted corpses and floating fragments of the *Roland*?" said Captain Butor. "Life-preservers from the *Roland* have also been found. The corpses and fragments are said to have been washed on a sand reef, where a lot of sharks and birds are hovering and swarming. The fishermen say the sharks and birds are what first attracted their attention."

"What is your opinion, Captain?" asked Doctor Wilhelm. "Do you think anybody from the **Roland** beside ourselves will turn up dead or alive?"

As to living persons, the captain would not commit himself.

"It may be," he said, "that one or two of the life-boats were carried farther south and entered calm waters. Only, in that case, they were not in the course of the large steamers, and they may not have met a vessel for three or four days. Derelicts, fragments, and corpses are usually carried south by the Labrador Current until they meet the Gulf Stream, which carries them to the northeast. If they turn northward with the Gulf Stream at the Azores, they may soon reach the coast of Scotland."

"Then there is a chance," said Frederick, "that our magnificent Captain von Kessel may still find a grave in some Scotch potter's field."

"We poor captains," said Butor, who looked more like a German horse-car conductor than a captain. "They ask us to command the sea and the storm, like our Lord Jesus Christ, and if we cannot, we have the choice of drowning in the ocean or hanging on land."

Arthur Stoss joined them, and said:

"Do you remember when the **Roland** began to sink, were the bulkheads shut down?"

Frederick reflected and said, "No, they weren't."

"I am of the same impression," said Stoss. "The sailors declare they know nothing about it."

"We carried out whatever orders we received," said the sailors.

Fleischmann put in his word:

"The bulkheads were not closed down. I never saw the captain, and I don't know what sort of man he was. But the bulkheads were not closed. My place was next to a family of Russian Jewish emigrants. We felt an awful shock, and a crashing and crunching as if the ship had run against a great rock. The panic broke out immediately. All lost their heads and went clean out of their minds. We were hurled against one another and against the walls. Here you can see how I was bruised." He rolled up his sleeves. "There was a dark girl belonging to the Russian Jewish family who saw to it that time should not hang heavy on my hands during the trip." Doctor Wilhelm looked at Frederick significantly. "She wouldn't let go of me. She was hoarse from screaming. Finally, all she could do was pant. She hung on to me, and, as I said, kept panting, 'Either you'll go down with me or you'll save me.' What could I do? I really had to give her one over her head."

"Yes," said Wendler, "what is a man to do in a case like that? Here's to you, gentlemen!"

All touched glasses. Frederick turned pale, and the others laughed heartily.

"By the way, Doctor von Kammacher," said Stoss, "I just thought of that Hahl-stroem girl. Really, you ought to persuade her to come to an agreement with Webster and Forster. If you keep her from dancing, you will be interfering with her future."

"I?" queried Frederick. "What an idea! What business is it of mine?"

Stoss, without heeding him, continued:

"Webster and Forster are, as a rule, very decent. But their influence and connections are incalculable. Woe to the man or woman that incurs their displeasure."

"I beg your pardon, Mr. Stoss, but you may as well spare your breath. I am by no means the girl's guardian. Nor am I at all fitted to be a trafficker in men or girls."

"Oh, oh, oh! Why so severe?" said Stoss. The others, including Doctor Wilhelm, chimed in; which only heightened Frederick's brusqueness. "Don't you know there's lots of money in that little witch just now? As the American business man says, 'There's money in it.' Don't forget we're in the dollar land, where you can't rest until the ground has been completely exhausted and the last nugget of gold has been extracted."

Frederick was outraged. He felt like taking his hat and running away. In his present mood, he could scarcely conceive why he had come to meet these people. To turn the conversation and give vent to his spite and ill humour, and also for a nobler reason, he suddenly began to speak of the maid, Rosa, denouncing the American newspapers for having said almost nothing of the heroic girl.

"It would be of far more importance to me to do something for her than for any other woman. I'm not a man to bargain and haggle; but if a collection was made and they did not collect for Rosa, then they neglected a true heroine of the *Roland*."

"What do you mean by that? What do you mean?" Fleischmann demanded somewhat rudely, afraid of losing his booty.

Here Bulke intervened.

"Remember, Mr. Fleischmann, Rosa was the first to see you. If Rosa hadn't dragged you out of the water--she's as strong as a bear--the rest of us in the boat might merely have struck you over the head with our oars and let you sink."

"You're talking nonsense, you numskull," said Fleischmann, withdrawing and turning toward the wall with the pictures. "I keep seeing nothing but those two moonstruck oxen." He referred to one of the wonderful Daubignys.

Frederick paid and took leave, declining, as politely as he could, their proposition that they all lunch together.

XIII

When alone on the street, Frederick felt some disgust with himself for lacking humour. Were those innocent men to blame if he happened to have rasped nerves? Since it was Frederick's way, as soon as he perceived that he had done a wrong, to set resolutely to work to undo it to the full extent of his ability, he decided, after coming to the conclusion that the fault had been his, to lunch with his shipmates after all. He had been walking about eight minutes. He now turned back, accelerating his pace, and within five minutes the sign of the Hoffman House was again in sight. Broadway as usual was crowded, and the two endless chains of yellow cable cars with short spaces between were perpetually moving by each other. It was cold and windy. There was a great din and bustle on the streets, and into the din and bustle Frederick saw his friends of the **Roland** and the **Hamburg** step from the bar. As he was about to wave to them, he slipped and stumbled on a piece of fruit on the pavement.

"Don't fall, Doctor von Kammacher!" a woman's voice cried. "How do you do?" On regaining his equilibrium Frederick found himself face to face with a beautiful, dignified young lady hidden behind a veil and wearing a fur hat and coat. He slowly recognised Miss Eva Burns. "I'm in luck," she said. "I very rarely come to this part of the city. It just so happened that I had to buy something near here, and I am on the way now to my restaurant. I always take my meals in a restaurant, because I loathe boarding-houses. By chance, too, I am later than usual. A little lady whom you know, Miss Hahlstroem, visited the studio with Mr. Franck and kept me three quarters of an hour longer than I am accustomed to stay."

"Do you take your meals alone, Miss Burns?"

"Yes," she said, somewhat taken aback at the abrupt question. "Does that seem strange to you?"

"Oh, no, not at all," Frederick hastened to assure her. "The astonished expression on my face was merely due to my stumbling and to this unexpected meeting with you. The reason I inquired whether you eat alone was because I wanted to ask you if you had any objections to my lunching with you."

"I should be very glad if you were to, Doctor von Kammacher."

The stately couple attracted much attention from passers-by. Frederick was tall and rather broad and carried himself well, and his hair and beard may have gone rather too long without the application of the shears. Eva Burns was almost as tall. She was a brunette, suggesting in her face and figure, which bore no resemblance to the wasp-like figures of the American women, a race and type more in accordance with the Titian ideal of feminine beauty.

"Would you mind waiting here a minute?" Frederick asked. "You see those people over there getting into the car? Some of them God in his inscrutable ways destined to be fellow-passengers of mine on the *Roland*, the others my rescuers. I should not like to meet them again." When the little company was safely aboard the car on the way to Brooklyn, he said: "I am profoundly grateful--" and stopped.

"Because you were rescued from those men in the car?" Miss Burns laughed.

"No. Because I met you, and you rescued me from them. I admit I am ungrateful. There's that captain--when I saw his ship come steaming toward us from across the waters and saw him standing on the bridge, he seemed to me to be an instrument of God, if not an archangel. Awe-inspiring repose, solemn, awe-inspiring grandeur rested upon him. He was not *a* man, he was *the* man, the saviour man, and beside him there was none. My soul, all of our souls, clamoured for him, worshipped him. But here he has dwindled into nothing but a good, commonplace little workman. On the trip, Stoss's liveliness was a relief. Now, in the treadmill of his daily occupation, he has turned from the finer thoughts of his leisure moments. Duty, while deepening Captain Butor and temporarily converting him into a useful, even an important personage, acts as a leveller on Stoss. Stoss merely seemed to partake in the life on the sea, while in actuality concerned with nothing but himself. And there's my colleague, the ship's surgeon. I was completely upset to find what an empty vessel he is. I really thought he was more interesting." As if sluices in his being had been opened wide, Frederick began to speak freely of the shipwreck, to which he had never before more than merely alluded.

"What particularly frightened me to-day was the fact that a man can, as it were, digest an oak-tree twice within less than forty-eight hours. I keep discovering myself in the act of doubting the wreck of that giant steamer, every corner of which was familiar to me. I saw something, but I am so infinitely remote from it that I still cannot grasp it. I am only just beginning to feel the ship coming to life in my soul. Four or five times within the past twenty-four hours, I experienced the whole accident over again. Last night I started up actually bathed in cold sweat, and did not know where I was. The confusion on board, the tooting of the distress signals, the bloody, distorted faces, the floating human limbs, all was so frightfully appalling. If I keep on seeing such visions, I'll go down with the *Roland* again.

"It may be morbid to feel as I do. A man in my condition may say to himself, 'Go down and stay down, if once you have sunk.' But those people who got into the car do not even say that, Miss Burns. The whole thing has gone down for them once for all. They have digested the whole of the *Roland* and everything that happened to the hundreds of human beings it was carrying. They have digested the whole affair and almost forgotten it. That ability of theirs, enviable though it may be, insults my general humanitarian instincts. It is loathsome to me. And their clumsy phrases revealing the indifference, the obtuseness of their souls make me shudder. In their eyes I see that calm selfish sense of their own security to the damage of another person's security which is at the bottom of a murderous madness that I myself experienced. Those men are cold men, they are murderous men. And a brutal state of self-defence but slightly veiled and suppressed is their permanent state."

"Your friends, it seems to me, must have behaved very badly," Miss Burns said, laughing.

To this Frederick could not truthfully assent. He merely repeated:

"The way I feel about it is that they have taken the ship between their teeth, the ship with all its timber and iron and its immense human cargo, and chewed it to a pulp, and swallowed it down without leaving a trace behind." He removed his hat and ran his fingers through his hair.

"If you really do wish to lunch with me, Doctor von Kammacher, you must not have high-flown notions, like Mr. Ritter," said Miss Burns halting in front of a tidy little restaurant.

They entered a low room with a red brick floor and panelled walls and ceiling. Owing to the enormous timber resources of their country, the Americans make a very free, though refined use of wood. The clean little room was frequented by German barbers, riding-masters, coachmen, and clerks. An inexpensive lunch and the usual American drinks were dispensed at the bar. The corner where the proprietor sat was decorated with a small collection of sporting pictures, well-known jockeys with their horses, acrobats, and baseball champions. Something in his appearance suggested that at night he had different customers to deal with than in the daytime, that his athletic figure--he was neatly dressed, but in his shirt sleeves--was meant to inspire respect in his clients. Frederick still suffered from too much breeding, and he was secretly astonished that Eva Burns ventured into such a place.

"You are late, Miss Burns. Aren't you feeling well?" inquired the host, with an immobile mask-like seriousness of expression.

"Oh, yes, Mr. Brown. I'm always all right," Miss Burns answered brightly. "Bring me my regular lunch. But the gentleman, I am afraid, will not be satisfied with it. Perhaps you have something special for him?"

Frederick, however, insisted upon ordering the very same as Miss Burns.

"I give you fair warning," she said when they were alone, "I really don't think you will be satisfied with my diet. I never eat meat, I want you to know, and you surely do."

Frederick laughed. "We physicians," he said, "are also coming more and more to give up a meat diet."

"I think it is horrible to eat meat," said Miss Burns. "I have a handsome fowl in my garden. I see it every day, and then I go and cut its throat and eat it up. When we were children, we had a pony which had to be killed, and the people in the East End ate it." She drew her long kid gloves from her hands without removing them from her arms. "People eat dogs, too. I adore dogs. But the worst thing is the frightful, endless shedding of blood which human meat-eaters deem necessary for their preservation. Think of all the butchers in the world, think of those immense slaughter-houses in Chicago and other places where the machine-like, wholesale murder of innocent animals is constantly going on. People can live without meat. It isn't indispensable to their welfare."

She said all this in a tone of seriousness tinged with humour, speaking a correct, though somewhat laboured German.

"For various reasons," Frederick said, "I still hesitate to form a definite opinion in regard to meat-eating. As for myself, I can do very well without meat, provided I have my steak regularly every day for lunch and my roast beef for dinner."

Miss Burns looked astonished, then laughed merrily.

"You are a physician," she cried. "You physicians are all animal torturers."

"You refer to vivisection?"

"Yes, to vivisection. It's a shame, it's a sin. It's a horrible sin to torture innocent animals to death just for the sake of adding a few days more to the life of some commonplace person."

Frederick did not reply, being too much a man of science to concur in her opinion. Miss Burns detected this, and said:

"You German physicians are horrible men. When I am in Berlin, I am in a constant state of dread that I shall die unexpectedly and before my relatives can prevent it, I shall be taken to your dreadful laboratories for dissection."

"Oh, then you have been in Berlin, Miss Burns?"

"Certainly, I have been everywhere."

The conversation now turned on Berlin. Miss Burns spoke of it glowingly, because it offered the greatest opportunities for hearing good music and seeing good plays.

"I have a number of friends among the Berlin professors and artists. One of them is a Polish pianist. He brings back money by the bushel from his American tours. He owns an estate near Cracow, and has asked me to visit him there. Unless I accept his invitation sooner than I expect to, I shall not see Berlin again for a long time."

The host served the lunch, consisting of baked potatoes, cabbage and fried eggs. Though at any other time this would scarcely have satisfied Frederick, he ate with a hearty appetite and, like Miss Burns, drank American ice-water.

Miss Burns's manner in talking was thoroughly unconstrained and sprightly. She had observed that the foundering of the **Roland** was still too vivid in Frederick's thoughts, and bearing Peter Schmidt's warning in mind, purposely turned the conversation away from it. But Frederick, for some reason dissatisfied with himself for his criticism of his fellow-passengers, tried several times to revert to the shipwreck. His whole demeanour showed that something was gnawing at him and tormenting him.

"We speak of a justice imminent in the plan of the world. But why was such a pitiful collection of men saved, while hundreds of others drowned? Why did that splendid Captain von Kessel drown? I shall never forget him. Why did all those splendid picked men of the crew of the **Roland** drown? Why and for what purpose was I myself saved?"

"Doctor von Kammacher," said Miss Burns, "yesterday you were an entirely different man. You were full of brightness and life; to-day you are all gloom. I think you are wholly wrong in not being simply grateful for your good fortune. In my opinion, you are not responsible either for the quality of those who were rescued, or for your own rescue, or for the number of those that sank. The creation was planned and executed without regard to you, and you have to accept it as it is. After all, to accept life is the one art the practice of which is really of permanent use."

"You are right," said Frederick, "only I am a man. Besides I inherit a most unnecessary instinct for ideal rather than practical activity. 'The time is out of joint,' says your Danish Englishman, Hamlet. 'O cursed spite that ever I was born to set it right.' I cannot get rid of that absurd megalomania. To make matters worse, there is the Faust in me that sticks in every good German who thinks anything of himself. 'I've studied now Philosophy and Jurisprudence, Medicine,' and so on. As a result, a man has all the more chances of being disillusioned at every turn, and so would rather pledge himself to the devil. Strange to say, the first thing the devil usually prescribes is a blonde Gretchen, or something like her."

Miss Burns remained silent, and Frederick felt himself under the necessity of continuing.

"I don't know whether it is of interest to you to learn something of the remarkable adventures of a German scholar and ideologic bankrupt."

Miss Burns laughed and said:

"A bankrupt? No, I don't think you are a bankrupt. Of course, whatever concerns you and whatever you wish to tell me is of interest to me."

"Very well," said Frederick, "we'll see whether you are right. Conceive a man who, until he was thirty years old, was always going the wrong way, or if not that, then, at least, the trips he took, no matter along what way, always ended precipitately in a broken shaft or a fractured limb. That I escaped the real catastrophe, the shipwreck, is really most peculiar. Nevertheless, I think my ship has been wrecked and I with it, or I and my ship are in the midst of foundering. For I see no land. I see nothing solid or firm anywhere near me.

"I was kept in a military school until I was ten years old. The desire came upon me to commit suicide, and I was punished for insubordination. There was no fascination for me in being prepared for a great carnage. So my father, though it meant that he had to give up his pet idea, took me away from the school, and I went through the much-discussed humanistic *Gymnasium*. My father is a passionate soldier. I became a physician, but I had scientific interests outside of my profession, and I devoted myself to bacteriology. Broken shafts and fractured limbs again. Good-bye to medicine and bacteriology. It is scarcely likely that I shall ever work in those fields again. I married. Beforehand, I had reared, as it were, an artificial structure of the whole matter of marriage--a house, a little garden, a wife and children, children whom I intended to educate in a freer, better way than most people do. I practised in a poor country district, being of the opinion that I could do more real good there than in Berlin West. 'But, my dear boy,' everybody said, 'with your ancestral name, your income in Berlin could be thirty or forty times larger.' And my wife absolutely objected to having children. From the very moment she knew a child was coming until its birth, there was one desperate scene after the other. Life became a veritable hell to us. It was no rare thing for us, instead of sleeping, to argue the whole night through, from ten o'clock in the evening until five the next morning. I would try mild persuasion and comfort, I would urge every conceivable argument softly and loudly, violently and gently, wildly and tenderly. My wife's mother, too, did not understand me. My wife was disillusioned, her mother was disillusioned. She saw nothing but craziness in my avoiding a great career. Then there was this--I don't know whether it occurs in all young marriages--each time before the child was born, we quarrelled over all the minutiae of its education, from infancy to its twentieth year. We quarrelled over whether the boy should be educated in the house, as I wished, or in the public schools, as my wife wished. I said, 'The girl shall receive instruction in gymnastics.' My wife said, 'She shall not receive instruction in gymnastics.' And the girl was not yet born. We quarrelled so violently, that we threatened each other with divorce and suicide. My wife would lock herself into a room and I would beat against the door, because I was frightened and dreaded the worst. Then there were reconciliations, the consequences of which were only to increase the miserable nervous tension in our home. One day I had to put my mother-in-law out of the house as a way of securing peace. Even my wife realised that it was necessary to do it. We loved each other, and in spite of all that happened, we both had the best intentions. We have three children, Albrecht, Bernhard and Annemarie. They came inside of three years, one very soon after the other, you see. My wife had a nervous tendency which these births brought to a crisis. After the very first child was born, she had an attack of profound melancholia. Her mother had to admit that Angele had been subject to similar attacks from childhood up. After the last child was born, I took her on a two months' trip in Italy. It was a lovely time, and her spirits actually seemed to brighten under the happy sky of Italy. But her sickness progressed below the surface. I am thirty-one years old and have been married eight years. My oldest boy is seven years old. It is now"-- Frederick reflected a few moments--"it is now the beginning of February. It was about the middle of October last fall when I found my wife in her room slashing to tiny bits a piece of not exactly inexpensive silk which we had bought in Zuerich and which had been lying in her drawer more than four years. I can still see the costly red stuff, that is, as much of it as had not been cut, and a loose mountain of patches lying on the floor. I said, 'Angele, what are you doing?' And then I took in the situation. Nevertheless, I cherished hopes for a time. But one night I awoke and saw my wife's face close above me with a ghastly far-away look in it. At the same time I felt something at my throat. It was the very pair of scissors with which she had cut the red silk. 'Come, Frederick,' she said, 'get up and dress. We must both go to sleep in a coffin of linden-wood.' It was high time to tell her relatives and mine and convoke a family council. I might have protected myself, but it was dangerous for the children.

"So you see," Frederick concluded, "it was not very far along the road of marriage that I travelled with my talent for life. I want everything and nothing. I can do everything and nothing. My mind has been over-loaded, and yet has remained empty."

"You certainly did go through a hard time," said Miss Burns simply.

"Yes," said Frederick, "you are right, but only if you use the present tense instead of the past and if you fully gauge the extent to which the trouble with my wife has been complicated for me. The question is, am I to blame for the course that my wife's mental suffering took, or may I acquit myself of all blame? All I can say is, that the suit in this case, in which I myself am plaintiff, defendant and judge, is still pending, and no definite decision has yet been rendered.

"Now, Miss Burns, do you see any sense in the Atlantic Ocean's having refused to take me of all the persons on board the *Roland*? Do you see any sense in my having fought like a madman for my mere existence? Do you see any sense in my having struck some unfortunate creatures over the head with my oars because they nearly capsized our boat? I struck them so hard that they sank back in the water without a sound and disappeared. Isn't it vile that I still cling to life and that I would rather do anything than give up this botched and bungled existence of mine?"

Though he had spoken in a light conversational tone, Frederick was pale and excited. It was long since the plates had been removed, and Miss Burns, perhaps to avoid a painful answer, asked:

"Shall we take coffee here, Doctor von Kammacher?"

"Whatever you will, to-day, to-morrow, and forever, provided I do not annoy you. I am a gloomy companion, I fear. I fancy there is no other person in the world troubled with such petty egoism as I am. Think of it, my wife locked up in an asylum is occupied every moment of the day with proving her own selfishness, weakness, unworthiness and wickedness toward me. Because she is so unworthy, as she says, and because I am so great, so noble, so admirable, they have to watch her all the time, I am told, to keep her from inflicting injury upon herself. A very pleasant fact to be conscious of, isn't it, Miss Burns, and haven't I good reason to feel proud?"

"What you need," said Miss Burns, "is rest. I never thought--I beg your pardon for saying so--that a man who outwardly makes the impression of such strength can possess such a wee, trembling soul. What you ought to do now, I should think, is simply cover up your past as much as possible. All of us have to do some covering up in order to be fit for life."

"But I am altogether unfit," said Frederick. "This minute I am feeling strong, because I am with someone in whose presence, for some reason or other, I can wash myself in clean water--excuse me, I am speaking euphemistically."

"You ought to concentrate on something, you ought to work," said Miss Burns. "You ought to make yourself physically tired to the point of exhaustion."

"Oh, my dear Miss Burns," cried Frederick, "how you overestimate me! Work! I am no better than a tramp. The thing I thought to cure myself with was laziness, idleness. Here I sit in a land discovered and conquered as a result of the tremendous will power of the Europeans, with my oars gone, my rudder gone and my last bit of free will. It is this that distinguishes most men of to-day from the men of that time."

Coffee was served, and for a while Frederick and Miss Burns stirred the sugar without speaking. Then Miss Burns asked:

"How did you come to lose your free will, as you say?"

"Theridium triste," said Frederick and suddenly recalled the simile of the spider that Doctor Wilhelm had used in reference to Ingigerd. Miss Burns, of course, did not understand him; but Frederick broke off, and though she questioned him, refused to explain. She promptly withdrew her question, saying she thought it was quite right and good for him if the conversation lost its German philosophic cast and descended to the level of a superficial person like herself.

"I advise you," she added, "no matter how sharply you may criticise yourself for having travelled so many roads without reaching the end, to strike out into a new road, and do so quite cheerfully. Confine yourself to something that makes an equal demand on your hands, your eyes and your brain. In short, return to your old love and try your hand again on sculpture. Perhaps in a few months you will be the creator of a world-famous Madonna in polychrome wood."

"You are mistaken in me," Frederick rejoined. "I do nothing but blow soap bubbles. Leave me to my illusion, that there is a great artist in me awaiting the moment of self-expression and development. What I am really much more fitted for is to be Mr. Ritter's coachman, or valet, or at best his business manager."

XIV

Miss Burns took out her little purse, refusing to let Frederick pay for her, and they stepped out again into the busy streets.

"By Jove," said Frederick, whose manner when in the hurly-burly changed completely, "what a lot of stuff I have been chattering! I deserve to be punished for trying your patience to such an extent. I must have bored you horribly."

"Oh, no," she said, "I am accustomed to such conversations. I have associated with artists for many years."

"Do you mean to impugn my truthfulness, Miss Burns?" Frederick asked in some alarm.

"No, but I think," she said calmly, with almost masculine firmness, "that if nature makes us suffer through something, she does not intend us to suffer again and again from the same thing. It seems to me the Creator had a definite intention in always and everywhere placing night and sleep between day and day."

"Not always and not everywhere," Frederick observed, thinking of the difficulty he had had for many nights in snatching a few hours' sleep.

At a street crossing Miss Burns stopped to wait for a car to take her back to the studio.

"Look at that," said Frederick, pointing to six similar placards of gigantic dimensions, which represented Mara, the Spider's Victim, in screaming colours. A green stripe was pasted slantwise on each placard, announcing that the dancer had been suffering from the consequences of the shipwreck, but that she would appear at Webster and Forster's the next day for the first time in America. Above the advertisement on the same wall were seven or eight full-length pictures of Arthur Stoss larger than life-size.

"Your little friend invited Mr. Ritter to a rehearsal in a theatre on Broadway day after to-morrow. It was not Webster and Forster's," said Miss Burns. Frederick explained what had happened in connection with Mr. Lilienfeld, though he himself had not known of the intended rehearsal.

"I feel nothing but pity for that girl," he said lightly. "As a result of a strange combination of circumstances, I feel I am responsible for her. She lost her father, who was all in all to her, since she is not on good terms with her mother."

"Indeed?" said Miss Burns. "Why, this very morning in a short conversation in the studio, she told me something very different."

"She did!" exclaimed Frederick.

"She told me that in many ways her father had been a fearful burden to her. In the first place, she had to earn money for him, and then he tyrannised over her terribly."

"Well," said Frederick, somewhat confused, "it is perhaps the essence of perversion that a person feels compelled to hoodwink people by doing things and making statements the very reverse of what is natural and what is to be expected. Miss Burns, I wish, I heartily wish, you would look out a little for that poor creature drifting about without anybody or anything to guide her."

"Good-bye," said Miss Burns, hailing a car. "Come and start work in the studio as soon as possible. As for your little friend, she is too self-willed. In fact, she has an iron will. There is no holding her, or leading her, that would keep her from doing anything she had once made up her mind to do."

When the car had carried Miss Burns off into the stream of New York traffic, Frederick, strangely enough, had a fleeting sense of forlornness, to him a novel sensation. Feeling inclined to taste it to the full, he continued to walk the streets alone, choosing his way at random. For the first time after speaking so freely to a comparative stranger, he did not regret his conduct. Again and again he went over in his mind his first meeting with Miss Burns in the studio, her manner during the lively carousal, when they discussed the wooden Madonna, his second meeting with her on the street, her upright carriage, her proud eyes, her imposing appearance in the little cosmopolitan restaurant. Without intending to, she undeniably dominated her surroundings, and that merely as a result of her naturalness. It had given Frederick secret pleasure to watch her eat and drink daintily, yet heartily, without any airs or graces, and systematically dissect her orange and peel her apple. Eating and drinking was to her a noble, legitimate and also inevitable act, not to be disposed of lightly beneath a foolish masquerade. When Frederick recommended Ingigerd to her guidance, he did so because he himself had experienced a beneficent influence from her remarks, dictated by a beautiful intellect, and from the glance of her straight, honest, scrutinising eyes.

"At the risk of making myself ridiculous," he said to himself, "I will go to Ritter's studio to-morrow morning, bury my hands in the clay, and try to reconstruct my life again from the bottom up out of moist clay."

XV

At about ten o'clock the next morning Ritter himself gave Frederick a very glad, bright welcome to his studio, and assigned to him a small room opening on Miss Burns's room. Miss Burns proposed that he begin by copying a plaster-cast of the arm of the Saxon athlete.

Frederick for the first time handled the moist clay fraught with so much significance, the clay out of which the gods made man and man in turn has made gods. As a result of the hours he had spent in Rome with sculptor friends, watching them work and observing each movement of their fingers, he accomplished his task with great ease, to his own astonishment and Miss Burns's admiration. His anatomical knowledge and medical experience also stood him in good stead. Shortly before completing his course as a medical student, he had for a time entertained the idea of publishing an anatomy for sculptors, and with this in view had made a number of drawings which won the favour of real connoisseurs.

After Frederick had worked feverishly with his shirt sleeves rolled up for three hours, the athlete's muscular arm began to take shape clearly, and he felt a sense of satisfaction wholly novel to him. In working he completely forgot who he was, and where he was. When Willy Snyders came in, as he usually did on his way from his work to luncheon for the purpose of saying "how-do-you-do" to Bonifacius Ritter and art, it seemed to Frederick that he had been awakened from a dream and called back to a strange life.

"I am sorry to have to leave work and go to lunch. Lunch is really a very disturbing thing," he confessed.

When Ritter entered, they all laughed heartily at his genuine passion for sculpture.

"When I return to Europe," he said, "I must immediately make portraits of my three children."

Miss Burns and Willy Snyders had actually made Frederick proud by their praise, though in Ritter's presence they turned silent awaiting the master's verdict.

"You must certainly have modelled in clay before," said Ritter. Frederick could honestly deny that he ever had. "Well," Ritter rejoined, "then you have handled your material like a man who has art in his blood. To judge by this first attempt, it seems to me you have merely been waiting for the clay and the clay has been waiting for you."

"We'll see," said Frederick, and added, "Unfortunately there is a serious drawback. The saying is that all beginnings are difficult. My former experiences lead me to believe that with me the reverse is generally true. As a rule I win the first and second round of chess, or cards, or billiards, and lose in the end. I succeeded at first in my practice and my bacteriological researches. If I write a book, only the first and second chapters are worth anything."

The artists refused to believe this, though there was a grain of truth in what he said. Nevertheless, Frederick left the studio with them in a healthier frame of mind than he had been in for years.

But his spirits departed in a measure after he had spoken with Ingigerd Hahlstroem in the club-house. The girl listened unsympathetically, if not ironically, to his account of his new occupation. Ritter, Willy and Lobkowitz were secretly outraged at her disdainful remarks, especially since they observed that Frederick was still entangled in the girl's meshes, body and soul.

She told him he must go to Webster and Forster and insist on their withdrawing a notification which they had sent to the Society for the Prevention of Cruelty to Children. Since her new contract with Lilienfeld meant the loss of the money that she was worth to them, they wanted revenge, at least, and were going to put a spoke in their competitor's wheel. Ingigerd, beside herself with rage, told Frederick that in the morning she had had a brief rehearsal in the theatre, and a representative of the Society for the Prevention of Cruelty to Children had announced his intention of attending the rehearsal the next day. She was bent upon letting her light shine in New York and receiving twofold homage, the homage of pity and the homage of admiration. Besides, she did not want to lose the money in prospect. If she were prevented from appearing in New York, there was no chance for her anywhere in the United States.

It was useless to oppose the girl's obstinate will. Whether or no, to his unspoken disgust, Frederick had to perform messenger and handy-man services for the little star. He rushed from Webster and Forster to Lilienfeld, from Lilienfeld to the attorneys, Brown and Samuelson, from Second Avenue to Fourth Avenue, from Fourth Avenue to Fifth Avenue, finally to knock at the door of Mr. Garry himself, the head of the Society for the Prevention of Cruelty to Children, and represent to him Ingigerd Hahlstroem's position, which was, that by preventing her appearance, the society would expose her to material want in a strange country. Mr. Garry refused to receive Frederick.

Fortunately for him, Willy Snyders the good-hearted, in order to make things as easy as possible for him, sacrificed himself by obtaining an afternoon's leave of absence from work. His saucy, healthy humour, his jolly remarks on New York conditions helped Frederick through many unpleasant moments.

Frederick was happy when the next morning came and he could go at his modelling again. His brain, whirling with the rattle and clatter of New York, could spend itself in his passionate occupation, which employed both his eyes and his hands. He deemed himself fortunate for being genuinely unpractical and not having to take part in that gruesome horse-racing and sack-racing and target-shooting, that crawling and dancing and jumping for the sacrosanct dollar. The very breath of that frenzied life tore the garments of his soul into shreds, as it were, while this simple occupation of modelling the details of the athlete's arm, was healing to his soul. He was conscious of it. Now and then Miss Burns came in to inspect his work and exchange a few words with him. He liked this. Her companionable presence soothed him and even made him happy. Her figure, her gestures, her conversation seemed to be the very essence of firmness and repose, and her self-sufficiency always aroused Frederick's silent admiration. When he told her how perceptibly his new work acted as a sedative upon him, she replied that she had had the same experience, and if he did not fly off at a tangent but remained steadily at the work, he would feel the good it did him even more.

XVI

Ingigerd Halstroem had "invited" the artists to her rehearsal at twelve o'clock. When they gathered in Miss Burns's room--beside Frederick, there were Ritter, Lobkowitz, Willy Snyders, Miss Burns, and the gypsy-like painter Franck, who carried a portfolio and sketching material--there was a certain solemnity in their manner.

It was a clear day and the streets were dry, and they decided to walk to the theatre. On the way Ritter told Frederick of a little country house he was building for himself on Long Island. Frederick had already heard of it through Willy Snyders. It was to be a rather pretentious building, with gardens and stables and barns. Ritter was erecting it according to his own ideas and plans. He discussed the beauties of the Doric column. It was the most natural of column forms and therefore the most suitable for any surroundings. That was why he had used it in his villa. For his interiors, he had partly followed Pompeian models, and there was to be an atrium. He spoke of a little figure, a gargoyle, which he intended to place over a square fountain.

"In these things, which offer the jolliest possibilities, artists nowadays are very unresourceful," he said. "We have naive German examples in the *Gaensemaennchen*, the *Maennicken Piss*, and the *Tugendbrunnen* in Nuremberg. One of the best classic examples is the drunken Silenus of Herculaneum. Water when combined as a mobile element with immobile works of art, can run, trickle, dash, splash, spray, bubble up, or rise up in a splendid jet. It can hiss and sputter and foam. From the drinking bottle of the drunken Silenus in Herculaneum it must have popped. I have had a plaster-cast model made of the little Pompeian figure of Narcissus at the spring in Naples. It is exquisitely beautiful. I am going to place it somewhere in my villa. My gardens will reach down to the seashore, and I intend to have a landing-place for boats, with marble steps and balustrades and sculpture work."

While walking in the cold sunny air next to the slim, elegantly dressed sculptor, listening to his Greek fantasies, Frederick's heart beat mightily against his ribs.

Whenever the thought arose in his mind that here, in this new country, after everything that had happened, he would again see Ingigerd Hahlstroem dance her dance, he felt that he was no longer equal to the trial. The forces of his soul that had remained healthy were already rising in rebellion against anything that might increase the power of the little demon. Nevertheless, he was so intimately connected with her, that the public exhibition of her charms tortured him, and he suffered from the anticipation of her great success. Yet while dreading it, he fervently desired it.

The theatre was dark and empty when Ritter and his following entered. They could scarcely see and had to grope their way after the young man that led them to seats in the parquet. Gradually, their eyes grew accustomed to the darkness, and they could distinguish the vast windowless cave, with its rows of seats, its galleries and painted ceiling. The air, smelling of dust and decay, lay heavily on Frederick's lungs. There were recesses in the great grotto that made the impression of gloomy holes for coffins. Some of them were hung with grey canvas, and canvas lay spread over the whole parquet, with the exception of a few rows left free for seats for the visitors. The stage curtain was up, and the only lighting on the stage came from a few incandescent lamps with weak reflectors, which cast only a narrow circle of light, which widened somewhat as the visitors' eyes learned to be content with the faint illumination.

None of the men had ever before seen an empty unlighted theatre, and they felt cramped and oppressed. For no special reason, they lowered their voices in speaking, and sat there in the expectant mood in which people always await the beginning of a performance.

No wonder that Frederick's heart throbbed more and more turbulently. Even Willy Snyders, who was not easily shaken out of his composure and was always inclined to make sarcastic remarks, was silent and adjusted his glasses on his nose. He sat with his mouth open and his nostrils dilating. When Frederick's eye happened to fall upon him in his unwonted state of self-forgetfulness, he was amused by the comic appearance of his black Japanese head.

After a number of tense minutes had passed and nothing had yet occurred, the artists were about to unburden their feelings in questions and remarks, when the silence was suddenly broken by a tramping of feet, and the stage resounded with a loud, though dull and by no means melodious voice. It was the impresario Lilien-feld, in a long overcoat, his hat pushed back on his neck. He was scolding violently and flourishing a cane. The vision tickled the artists' risibilities. It was all they could do to keep their laughter within the limits of courtesy.

Lilienfeld roared and called for the porter, and thundered unmercifully at a charwoman happening to stray on the empty stage.

"Where's the carpet, where are the musicians, where is that good-for-nothing of a fellow who attends to the reflector? I expressly ordered him to be here at twelve o'clock. Miss Hahlstroem is standing back there and can't get into her dressing-room."

A voice from the parquet--it came from the young man that had guided the art-ists to their seats--several times attempted a timid "Mr. Lilienfeld, Mr. Lilienfeld." Finally Lilienfeld caught the sound and, holding his hand to his ear, stepped to the edge of the stage. Forthwith a shower of curses, which had ceased for an instant, descended upon the lad, with reinforced severity. The reflector man came and re-ceived his dose of furious rebukes. A man in a silk hat pushed in three musicians, carrying a tom-tom, a cymbal and a flute.

"Where's the flower? The flower! The flower!" Lilienfeld now shouted into the parquet, when a hesitating "I don't know" came from somewhere. Lilienfeld disap-peared, crying "Where's the flower? Where's the flower?"

"Where's the flower? The flower! The flower!" was taken up in endless echoes here and there, above and below, from the wings, on the stage, and now from the last rows of the parquet--a circumstance which only increased the artists' inclina-tion to titter.

A few more lights were turned on, and a remarkable, great red paper flower was set on the stage. Lilienfeld, now better satisfied, reappeared and entered into a conversation with the three musicians.

"Have you studied the dance I told you to?" he demanded, humming the tune and stressing the accented parts to impress it upon them. "Now then," he said, "let's hear what you can do." He raised his bamboo cane like a conductor's baton and said commandingly, "Well, begin."

And the musicians began to play that provoking, passionate melody, that bar-baric music, now dull and suppressed, now loud and screeching, which, ever since it first began to excite his nerves, had pursued Frederick night and day. He thanked heaven that the darkness helped conceal his emotion. It was that hard, convulsive motive conjuring up the demons which had been the beginning of his obsession in the **Kuenstlerhaus** in Berlin. Over and again those sounds had lured him and led him on.

What was this strange Ariel's intention with him? At whose bidding was he acting when he assailed his victim with inner storms and almost let him perish in a real storm on the seas? Why did he prick Frederick's flesh with this music? Why did he cast its inseverable hempen cords about his throat and limbs? How was it that after so tremendous an eternal tragedy had been enacted out there on the cosmic solitudes of the ocean, after the waters had unmercifully swallowed so vast a number of men, loving life--how was it that this music had remained untouched and unweakened, that it had here resumed its fantastic devilishness? Frederick felt as if new cords were biting into his flesh and tightening about his throat. Something like the anguish and frenzy of a bull with a lasso about its horns came over him--a bull whom a cruel power will misuse for a senseless, bloody show in the arena. Frederick did not hit about him. He did not run away, and yet he came near doing both. His head, it seemed to him, was wrapped up heavily in thick sail-cloth. He must do something finally to rid himself of that enforced blindness. He must look straight in the face of his grotesque opponent--Prospero or Caliban?

"There is no doubt," Frederick felt, while the music tortured and harrowed him, "that men seek madness, they seek it again and again. They are fond of madness. Was not madness the leader of those men who first made the impossible possible and crossed the ocean, though they were neither fish nor fowl?"

In Skagen in Denmark there is a sight worth seeing. In the dining-room of a small inn there are painted figureheads of foundered vessels saved from the wreckage. The hand of madness has unmistakably touched all those wooden men and women with their painted faces and clothes. They look forward into the distance, where they seem to see something beyond all. Their noses quiver in the air on the scent of gold and foreign spices. In some way or other they have come upon a secret and have lifted their feet from their native land to tread the air and pursue illusions and phantasmagoria and discover new secrets in the trackless salt waste. It was by such that El Dorado was discovered. It was such that have led millions and millions of men to their destruction.

And Ingigerd Hahlstroem, who shortly before had been his painted Madonna of wood, now became Frederick's ecstatic figurehead. He saw her high above the waves on the prow of a phantom sailing ship, bent forward with open mouth and wide eyes, her yellow hair falling straight down from both sides of her head.

The music ceased, and Ingigerd Hahlstroem stepped on the stage. She was wearing a long blue evening cloak over her costume.

"Mr. Lilienfeld, I think it is rather stupid to change the name of my number from 'Mara, the Spider's Victim' to 'Oberon's Revenge,'" she said very dryly.

"Miss Hahlstroem," said the impresario, nervously, "please, for heaven's sake, leave that to me. I know the audiences here. Besides, I have reasons for choosing another title. I want to avoid a damage suit by Webster and Forster. Please begin, Miss Hahlstroem. We have to hurry." Mr. Lilienfeld clapped his hands and called to the musicians to strike up.

Again those provoking strains, immediately upon which Mara danced in, like a naked elf floating in the air. While flying in wide circles about the flower, as yet unseen, she resembled a fabulous, exotic butterfly in her transparent veil shot with gold. Willy Snyders called her a naiad, Ritter a moth. Franck said nothing, merely keeping his eyes fixed upon the transformed girl.

The moment came when with her eyes closed, like a somnambulist, she sniffed the perfume and began to seek its source. In that seeking, there was both innocence and maddening wantonness. A fine quiver went through her body, like the quiver of a moth in its sultry love-play. At last she smelt of the flower itself, and her sudden rigidity showed that she had perceived the great spider on it.

As Frederick knew, she did not always represent the horror, the numbness of fright and the flight in the same way. The artists all admired the change of expression on the dancer's sweet face, where faint distaste gave way to violent repulsion, fright and stark horror. As if a great hand had tossed her, she flew to the outer limits of the circle of light.

But a force compelled her to return to the flower. Mara no longer followed sweet scents. The hideous venomous creature in the flower's calyx drew her against her will, struggling wildly. Her lids were no longer closed. It was with clairvoyant eyes that the little thing went to meet her doom.

"Strange," thought Frederick, "if her father really conceived the idea of this dance himself. In that case he may have divined his daughter's fate with greater insight and love than he is credited with. As she herself admitted, she is sometimes more irresistibly drawn by what is ugly than by what is pure and beautiful; and the dance follows a logical course leading on pitilessly to tragedy."

The new phase of the dance began, in which the dancer looks at the spider again, takes it to be harmless, and laughs at herself, as it were, for her fears. Ingigerd portrayed this with inimitable grace, innocence and merriness.

After passing through a state of pleasant repose, the fight with the imaginary threads enmeshing her limbs began. At this point, the door opening on the parquet creaked on its hinges, and a tall, stately, noble-looking old man was ushered in. He carried his hat in his hand. His hair was silvery grey, and his clear-cut face was clean shaven. He was a gentleman, "every inch of him." The young man who had led the stranger in, dashed out again, and the gentleman seated himself near the door by which he had entered. Director Lilienfeld appeared and, turning and twisting like an eel around the awe-inspiring old man, officiously begged him to be seated in one of the front rows.

The gentleman, Mr. Garry, President of the Society for the Prevention of Cruelty to Children and many other organisations, declined with a wave of his hand and fixed his attention upon the performance. Ingigerd had been confused by the creaking of the door, the arrival of a new spectator, and the mumbled greeting of her impresario. She stopped dancing.

"Keep on! Keep on!" cried Lilienfeld. But the girl stepped to the edge of the stage.

"What's the matter?" she inquired.

"Nothing, nothing at all," the director assured her, all impatience.

Ingigerd called for Doctor von Kammacher. Frederick, who was reminded of his father by the old gentleman and had been looking at him with respect, was not a little startled when he heard his name echo through the theatre. It was fearfully painful and humiliating to him to have to step up to the platform and speak to Ingigerd. She bent down and told him to go "sound that old guy from the Society and try to bring him around."

"If I am not allowed to dance, I will jump from Brooklyn Bridge, and you can go fishing for me where my father is," she cried.

Amid convulsive jerkings of her body, throttled by the spider's threads, Ingigerd ended what was apparently her life, though in reality nothing but her dance. Lilienfeld introduced Frederick to Mr. Garry. The stiff old descendant of the Pilgrim Fathers, who had come over in the *Mayflower* and founded the New England States, measured Frederick with a cold, penetrating glance of his steely grey eyes, a glance hostile as a cat's and as capable, it seemed to Frederick, as a cat's to see in utter darkness. Mr. Garry spoke very quietly, but what he said scarcely aroused hopes that his attitude would be tolerant.

"Evidently," he said after Lilienfeld had got done with an eager harangue, "evidently, the girl's father has already misused her for low purposes, and evidently, the child's education has been neglected. The creature is to be pitied for not having been taught even the commonest notions of feminine shame and decency. Unfortunately," he added in a cold, haughty manner, which in advance robbed any statements in controversion of their force, "unfortunately we have as yet no law to prevent such revolting performances, which grossly offend public sentiment and morality." He scarcely seemed to comprehend Lilienfeld's arguments, assuming without question that Lilienfeld must know how vile he and his profession were in the eyes of every gentleman and that Lilienfeld in his, Mr. Garry's, eyes was entitled to but one epithet, "vermin."

His inadequate English prevented Frederick from taking an important part in the conversation. Nevertheless, he ventured to mention the necessity under which Ingigerd was of earning her own living. Mr. Garry instantly silenced him with the old question:

"Are you the girl's brother?"

Mr. Garry left the room, and Lilienfeld cursed and stormed against the miserable hypocrisy of those old-fashioned Yankees and Puritans.

"I have my strong suspicions," he said, "that an injunction will be issued preventing Ingigerd Hahlstroem from appearing in public. I owe the whole cursed business to Webster and Forster."

When Frederick went to fetch Ingigerd in the dressing-room, he found her in tears.

"I have nobody but you to thank for this," she cried in a fury. "Why couldn't you let me dance the first day under Webster and Forster, as Mr. Stoss and everybody else advised?"

"Ingigerd," said Frederick, "I had to look out for your health."

"Stuff and nonsense! You took the whole matter into your hands. You acted illegally, against my expressed wish, when you chased Webster and Forster's agent away from the cab when we left the steamer."

Frederick was disgusted. Mr. Garry had made his father's personality more vivid to him than it had been for weeks. Although his father would never have expressed and carried out his views in the same form as Mr. Garry, yet his opinions, as Frederick very well knew, were akin to the Yankee's. Indeed, even in Frederick's soul, many of the same notions, implanted by birth and education, remained unshaken. For the first time since he had fallen under Ingigerd's spell, he realised that he was inwardly independent of her. The one question that still troubled and occupied him was how to rid himself outwardly as well as inwardly from the degrading liaison. Without fully admitting it to himself, he had suffered a disenchantment in Ingigerd's dance; to judge by which, the demon's spell was broken. This time that alluring seductive dance had seemed inconceivably empty. Nor was his compassion aroused to nearly the same extent as formerly.

Franck, the gypsy painter, burst in. He behaved like a madman. His enthusiasm, which somewhat improved Ingigerd's temper, was of the sort that stammers and stutters and cannot find the words to express itself. Frederick looked at him in disgust, but the next moment started when he recognised in his behaviour the marks of his own former obsession. Ingigerd let the painter take her hand and cover it with wild, passionate kisses, which travelled from her wrist to her elbow, a demonstration that seemed to her to be perfectly natural and quite in order.

"I wish you would go visit Mr. Garry again and try to influence him with pleas and threats and money," she said to Frederick.

"That would be foolish and useless," Frederick declared; whereupon Ingigerd wept.

"The only friends I have," she wailed, "are friends that exploit me. Why isn't Achleitner here? Why did Achleitner have to lose his life, and not somebody else? Achleitner was my real friend. He knew how to go about things in the world, and he was rich and unselfish, too."

XVII

The very next day the injunction was issued, restraining Ingigerd Hahlstroem from dancing in public. The girl conducted herself wildly. Lilienfeld said the time had come to place the matter before the Mayor of New York. In order to protect Ingigerd from slander and from being sent to an orphan asylum, Lilienfeld, who was married but had no children, offered her a refuge in his own home on 124th Street near Lenox Avenue. Whether she wanted to or not, Ingigerd had to accept.

The morning after Ingigerd's departure to Mr. Lilienfeld's home, when Frederick sat in front of his modelling in a new smock of unbleached linen of Miss Burns's buying, he experienced a sense of relief on Ingigerd's account. A burden had been lifted from him. Her change of home had removed a part of the responsibility from his shoulders and made a break in the feeling he had had of their belonging to each other.

After the rehearsal, Ingigerd was much discussed in the studio. Ritter had expressed to Miss Burns and his friends a desire to make a model of the dancing girl for a bronze statuette. Miss Burns told Frederick of his wish. But Frederick, who was still regarded somewhat in the light of Ingigerd's guardian, assented unwillingly.

"You see, Miss Eva," he said, "I am really the last person in the world to stand in the way when beautiful things are to be created. But I am only a man, and if Ritter were to use Miss Hahlstroem as a model here, where only one or two walls would separate us, that would mean an end to my peace of soul." Miss Burns laughed. "You may well laugh," he said, "but I am a convalescent, and relapses, you know, are worse than the sickness they follow."

A week passed, in which Frederick carried on a remarkable, but not, as yet, victorious warfare. He worked in the studio daily, and Miss Burns became his confidante. From his own mouth she learned what she had already observed, that he was languishing in the chains of an unhappy passion. Without ever interfering in his spiritual struggles unless he positively demanded it of her, she gave him advice as a good friend and comrade.

"Every time I see Ingigerd, or go out with her, or spend any time at all with her," he said, "I feel outraged and bored. I have firmly made up my mind not to go back to her."--A resolution frequently broken a few hours after it was made.

Miss Eva was so long-suffering that Frederick never felt compelled to drop the theme of Ingigerd Hahlstroem. The girl's soul was turned inside out and back again.

One day Ingigerd said to him:

"Take me, seduce me, do with me whatever you will, Frederick. Be strict, be cruel with me. Lock me up. You are the only man I want to have anything to do with me any more." Another time she said beseechingly: "I want to be good, Frederick. Make me good."

But the very next day she again subjected her friend and protector to unpardonably vile treatment. The fact was, she already had a following of men, running errands for her, attending to her affairs, thinking for her, and paying for her.

The thing that Frederick could not wean himself from was that sweet, fair, frail, pathetic body. Yet he was determined to wean himself.

One day Ingigerd came to sit for Miss Burns for her portrait. Frederick placed a revolving stand in front of her and also tried to model the blonde Madonna in clay. Even Ritter had a mass of clay for modelling a bust of her prepared on a revolving stand, and the master entered into rivalry with his pupils. Miss Burns's purpose in arranging these sittings was not easily fathomed. The result was, however, that the very severe study of his idol's features had a remarkable effect upon Frederick.

The flatness of her forehead, her eyebrows, the setting of her eyes, the turn of her temples, the shape of her ears and the twist they took where they joined her head, her nose as narrow as the dull edge of a knife, her nostrils, the oldish-looking nasolabial line, the depressions at the corners of her mouth, her beautiful yet brutal chin, her unbeautiful throat, with the washer-woman's pit in it--all these traits had a very sobering effect upon Frederick, sapping from his imagination every bit of its strength to beautify or palliate. Perhaps Miss Burns knew what results from such strenuous, such persistently logical observation of an object. In some ways it has the same effect as blood-letting. That is why the artist must bleed to death unless new sources of illusion always open up to him.

Moreover, in the long sittings, to which Ingigerd submitted from vanity, she betrayed the narrowness, the attenuation, the barrenness of her mind. In contrast with Miss Burns, Frederick perceived in Ingigerd with fearful clearness that incompleteness which is eternally rudimentary. Once she brought a letter from her mother in Paris and read it aloud. For about a quarter of an hour, it actually seemed to torture her. It was serious, severe, full of concern, and not unloving. Her mother referred sorrowfully to Hahlstroem's death, and asked Ingigerd to come and live with her in Paris. She told her of a woman in New York, the wife of a German barber, with whom it would be eminently suitable for her to remain until she returned to Europe. She even mentioned the steamer she should take.

"I am not wealthy," she wrote. "You will have to help me with my work, Ingigerd, but I will try to be a mother to you in every respect,"--here came the apodosis--"if you make up your mind to change your mode of life."

There was hard, stupid, even savage hatred in Ingigerd's commentaries on this and other parts of her mother's letter.

"I am to go to her and repent," she mimicked, "because the Lord has so miraculously saved me. Mamma should be the first to repent. I am not going to be such a fool as to turn myself into a dressmaker. Always to receive orders and listen to sermons from mamma! I am not bothered about myself so long as I am not under somebody's thumb."

And so she went on, without the least hesitancy retailing the ugliest intimacies in the life of her parents.

XVIII

The Mayor of New York appointed the twenty-fifth of February for a hearing in the City Hall, at which Lilienfeld and his attorneys, Brown and Samuelson, and the Society for the Prevention of Cruelty to Children were to present their arguments for and against the injunction restraining Ingigerd Hahlstroem from dancing in public. Mrs. Lilienfeld dressed Ingigerd up in "smart" clothes, put her in a cab, and in the capacity of chaperone drove down to the City Hall with her. Frederick, upon whose presence Ingigerd had insisted, had gone ahead in another cab with Lilienfeld.

"This is the situation," Lilienfeld explained as they drove through the length of the cold, grey, dreary city. "At present New York is in the control of Tammany. At the last elections the Republicans were defeated. Ilroy, the Mayor, is a Tammany man. The word Tammany is derived from an Indian sachem, Tamenund, who figures in Cooper's Leather-stocking novels. The party leaders have silly Indian names and titles. But don't be deceived by all that romantic Indian nonsense. The members of Tammany Hall are mighty practical. The Tammany tiger is an animal not to be trifled with in the great New York sheepfold. I think we may feel pretty sure, though not absolutely certain, of having the Tammany tiger, and therefore the Mayor, with us in this matter. Mr. Garry is a Republican, a deadly enemy of Tammany Hall, and it would give Ilroy the greatest satisfaction to deal a neat little blow at him and that idiotic institution, the Society for the Prevention of Cruelty to Children. But his term is nearly expired, and as he would like to be elected again, it is politic for him to make a few concessions to the Republicans. Well, we'll see. We have to wait and see."

The cab rolled down Lenox Avenue through Central Park and along Fifth Avenue, past the Metropolitan Museum, the Lenox Library, the millionaire residences, and St. Patrick's Cathedral. Below Fiftieth Street it turned into Broadway, where Lilienfeld pointed out the buildings of interest, Madison Square, and the Hoffman House, the gathering place of the Democrats. Finally they reached the City Hall Park, in the centre of which stands the City Hall, a marble structure with a cupola and a portico. In the portico the gentlemen awaited the ladies.

While walking to and fro, Frederick suddenly felt someone tugging at his coat. He turned and saw a pretty, stylishly dressed little girl.

"Why, Ella Liebling, where do you come from?"

Ella courtesied and said:

"I am out with Rosa. There she is."

Frederick turned and saw Rosa standing on the steps.

"Good morning, Doctor von Kammacher," she said.

Frederick introduced Ella to Mr. Lilienfeld. "Ella was in the shipwreck. Here you have additional proof of the tremendous physical power of resistance of the so-called weaker sex."

"Good morning, little girl. Is it really true that you were in that awful shipwreck?"

"Yes, indeed," came the unabashed answer, spiced with a dash of childishly coquettish pride, "and my brother was drowned."

"Oh, poor child," said Lilienfeld. His manner was abstracted. Evidently his mind was on the speech he might be compelled to deliver before the Mayor of New York. "Excuse me," he said suddenly to Frederick, and moved a few steps away to make a hasty, nervous perusal of his notes, which he had written on a slip of paper and had taken from his pocket.

"My mother was dead, too, but came back to life again."

"How's that? How's that?" asked Lilienfeld, raising his gold spectacles slightly from his nose and peering at her from under them.

Frederick explained how they had had to work over Mrs. Liebling for several hours before they succeeded in resuscitating her.

"If in this world honours were awarded according to merit," Frederick added, "then that simple servant-girl there"--he pointed to Rosa--"ought to receive greater honour as a hero of two worlds than Lafayette. She performed miracles. She never thought of herself, but only of her mistress, Mrs. Liebling, of the two children, and the rest of us."

Frederick went to Rosa and shook hands with her. When he inquired for Mrs. Liebling, she turned red as a peony.

"Mrs. Liebling is very well," she said, and promptly burst into tears, having been reminded of little Siegfried. When she dried her eyes, she told Frederick that she and a German consul, without Mrs. Liebling, had attended to all the formalities of the burial and that she had been the only one to see the little corpse laid away in the Jewish cemetery.

"Oh, why did you stop trying to revive Siegfried so soon? I begged and begged you to go on. There was still life in him. He would have come to," she wailed.

Here a stranger joined them. It was not until he was quite close that Frederick recognised in the correctly clad man the valet of Arthur Stoss.

"Doctor von Kammacher," said Bulke, "Rosa cannot get it out of her mind. Can't you make her understand that it isn't right always to be going over and over such a thing and that she ought to forget it? It couldn't be worse if she had lost a boy of her own. I want to tell you, Doctor von Kammacher, Rosa and I are engaged to be married."

"You are certainly to be congratulated, Mr. Bulke. I am delighted to hear it."

"As soon as I can get away from Mr. Stoss and Rosa can get away from Mrs. Liebling, we are going back to Europe. Before I entered the navy, I was a skilled butcher. My brother in Bremen wrote to me that there was a little meat and sausage and steamer supply business to be had there. We both have some money saved up. So why shouldn't we try it? You can't go on working for strangers forever."

"I quite agree with you," said Frederick.

The marksman's valet held out his hand to Rosa, whispered "Mrs. Liebling's coming," and left. The same instant Ella ran off calling, "Mamma."

Mrs. Liebling was coming through the park, walking beside a gentleman. From her costume, befitting the wife of a Russian prince of the royal house, it was evident that she had already found the opportunity to replace her wardrobe. Frederick shook hands with her and remembered the mole under her left breast and several other marks on the lovely body, which he had so ruthlessly worked like a machine to restore the breath to it.

She introduced him to her companion, a dark, thick-set, elegantly dressed man, who eyed Frederick with a suspicious, repellent expression.

"Curious," thought Frederick. "This microcephalous creature thinks I am his enemy, whereas he ought to know what he owes me. There I toiled and travailed and sweated to raise the dead. I considered myself a highly moral instrument of Providence, and after all, I was working for nothing but the pleasure of a sleek, consequential Don Juan."

Mrs. Liebling, who had already been in Boston and Washington, was perfectly delighted with America.

"What do you think of the New York hotels? I am living at the Waldorf. Aren't they magnificent? I have four rooms in the front. Such quiet, such luxury, such beautiful pictures! You feel as if you were in the Arabian Nights. Doctor von Kammacher, you positively must go to Delmonico's. What has Berlin, or even Paris, to compare with it? You can't find a restaurant like Delmonico's or hotels like New York hotels in Europe."

"Possibly," said Frederick, quite dazed.

"Have you been in the Metropolitan Opera House yet?"

Mrs. Liebling continued to put similar lively interrogations, to which she demanded small responses from Frederick, supplying most of the answers herself.

He thought of Rosa and Siegfried and had time to inspect and reinspect the signor's brand-new patent leather shoes, the straight creases down his trousers, his watch chain, his diamond scarf pin, his monocle, his high hat, and his expensive fur coat.

"What have you got to do with our famous tenor of the Metropolitan Opera Company?" Lilienfeld asked Frederick, when he returned to the portico with a "Whew!" of relief. Frederick did not understand, and Lilienfeld repeated the same Italian name that Mrs. Liebling had mentioned in introducing the signor to Frederick. He was astonished that Frederick did not know what a world-renowned star this new friend of Mrs. Liebling's was.

XIX

The meeting had so clearly put before Frederick the tragi-comedy of existence that his sense of humour was stirred and he was capable of taking the painful situation less seriously.

The cab with the ladies drove up. Simultaneously half a dozen reporters stepped into the lobby. Frederick, to his surprise, observed that most of them were on a rather free and easy footing with Ingigerd, and shook hands with her familiarly. She looked very dainty and pretty.

Her rather numerous body-guard, which now included Mr. Samuelson and his assistant, were ushered into the audience chamber, a lofty wainscoted room with bay windows. When they entered, they saw Mr. Garry's tall figure already seated at a long table near the empty chair that the Mayor was to occupy. He was dressed in black, almost like an English clergyman, and the theological spirit of the Puritan shone from his face. Yet there was too much worldly acumen, too much cold determination in his impressive features for a clergyman. He held his eye-glasses in his hand and now and then turned over the pages of his notes. Mr. Samuelson and Mr. Lilienfeld took seats on the other side of the Mayor's chair, without greeting him. The rest of the space about the table was occupied by a few clerks, the reporters, and other persons interested, among whom sat Frederick, Lilienfeld's wife, prepossessing and stately, and Ingigerd Hahlstroem, the *casus belli*.

The Mayor entered by a high folding door a few feet behind his chair. He was an Irishman, somewhere between forty and fifty, wearing a smile of mixed shrewdness and embarrassment. Though he did not go through the formality of a greeting, there was a touch of courteous affability in the glance he cast about the room.

One of the reporters at the bottom of the table whispered to Frederick:

"Miss Hahlstroem's case is going to come out all right. Everybody is of the firm opinion that the Mayor is going to give that old hypocrite a jolt." As a matter of fact, the Mayor's manner toward his honourable neighbour on the right was too cordial to presage good. Silence was ordered, and the session began. The Mayor called upon Mr. Garry to speak.

The old gentleman arose in all his height, with a gravity and self-assurance seldom seen except in eminent statesmen. Frederick was fascinated. He could not remove his eyes from him and almost regretted that his speech, according to the reporter, was doomed to failure in advance. As for Frederick's feelings in regard to the real issue, when he listened to the voice of his passion, he did not desire Ingigerd's appearance in public. But for some time he had learned to silence that voice, and he had no objections if his cure were to be accomplished as the result of a severe operation. He felt certain that for Ingigerd to receive permission to dance in public would mean a definite verdict in his own case.

Mr. Garry first set forth clearly and succinctly the aims of his society, citing a number of cases to show how children are maltreated, how their health is ruined in industry, commerce and on the stage.

Here a reporter whispered in Frederick's ears:

"He should sweep before his own door. He's a Wall Street man and employs a whole lot of children in his chemical works in Brooklyn. He is a merciless exploiter."

Mr. Garry went on to explain that these abuses had necessitated the organisation of the Society for the Prevention of Cruelty to Children. The society made it its duty to interfere only in cases in which the maltreatment could be actually proved. Such a one was the case in hand.

"For several years," he said, "New York has been overrun by a peculiar sort of freebooters." He laid emphasis on the word freebooters. "There is a connection between this phenomenon and the increasing atheism in our country, the increasing irreligion, and the craving for pleasure and dissipation, which always goes hand in hand with irreligion. This growing immorality, this festering corruption in our midst is the wind that fills the sails of those pirates. The disease is not of American origin. It has come to us from the dens of vice in the large European cities, London, Paris, Berlin, Vienna. It is an epidemic the spread of which must be arrested, and to that end we must put a curb upon the freebooters who spread the infection and continue to bring it in from abroad."

Lilienfeld, red as a lobster with rage, fidgeted on his seat.

"In the opinion of these men, circumventers and despisers of the laws of the land, the United States is here merely for their purposes, to allow them to sow disease and rake in the dollars. They are not good American citizens, these peculiar Europeans. They are not citizens at all." Mr. Garry pronounced every word with hard correctness. "That is why it is a matter of perfect indifference to them if our religion, our customs, our morals are destroyed. They are unscrupulous birds of prey, and once they have filled their crops, they return with their spoil to their haunts in Europe. The time has come when Americans should take thought and repel the invasion of such parasites."

While the old jingo made these cutting remarks, speaking with an unshaken front, proudly, hitting straight out from the shoulder, Frederick unwearyingly watched every movement of his hard, noble old face. The anthropologist and the newly awakened sculptor in him were equally stirred. When comparing the "freebooters" to birds of prey, Garry himself had resembled a bird of prey. His expression was like an eagle's. He stood with his back to the windows, but with his head turned slightly to one side, and when he spoke of the birds filling their crops, it seemed to Frederick that his light-blue eyes paled to a whitish sheen.

Garry now came down to the subject of Ingigerd.

"By God's will a tremendous shipwreck has occurred, an appalling event, wholly calculated to turn men's thoughts to repentance." He interrupted himself to say it was useless to go into more details on this point, since those who did not know how to respect such a visitation from God were beyond redemption. "It has not been proved that the girl who survived the shipwreck is over sixteen years of age. I propose to place her in a hospital, have one of the steamship companies transport her back to Europe as soon as possible, and consign her to her mother, who lives in Paris. She should be placed in the care of a physician and under guardianship. She has been trained to do a certain dance, during which she falls into a pathologic condition not unlike an epileptic fit. She turns stiff and rigid as a block of wood, her eyes start from her head, she plucks at her clothes. Finally, she falls into a faint and loses consciousness of her surroundings. Such things do not belong on the stage. It would be an outrage, an insult to public opinion to reproduce this hospital scene in a theatre. I protest against it in the name of good taste, in the name of public morality, in the name of American decency. It is not seemly to drag that poor unfortunate child before an audience and shamelessly exploit her misery, merely because the shipwreck has placed her name in everybody's mouth."

Mr. Garry seated himself. He had pronounced his last words with sharp emphasis. Mr. Samuelson, Lilienfeld's counsel, turned pale and arose instantly. The reporters moved up closer and leaned forward, cocking their ears to catch every word of the famous lawyer. He began in a very faint voice. Frederick as a physician saw he was suffering from chronic laryngitis, probably having exchanged his sound larynx for his millions. Samuelson's delivery, his way of pleading were well known. At first he would spare himself, in order later to take his auditors by storm in a violent outburst of passion.

When the violent outburst of passion came, it did not fulfill the expectations either of Lilienfeld, his client, or the reporters, or Frederick. It was very noticeable that his indignation was forced, that it did not flow from a natural source, but from a bottle standing long uncorked. His iron will compelled him to simulate a feeling that he owed it to his client to display. In fact, the tired, harassed man, with his small, pointed beard and his worn, dirty-looking skin, was remarkable merely as a victim of his profession. Even in that capacity he was not so imposing as pitiable. Unfortunately, he was most pitiable when he gave the whip and spurs to that jaded little charger, the Rosinante of his eloquence, to ride down his opponent.

Mr. Garry and Mr. Ilroy, the Mayor, looked at each other significantly. They seemed to wish to return good for evil and come to the help of this knight of the sorry figure on his hack all skin and bone, which at the end of the attack fell and broke his legs.

Lilienfeld could not restrain himself. He turned crimson. The veins of his forehead swelled. The time for remaining silent had ended and the time to speak had come. Since the man with the hundred typewriters and the millions was unequal to the task, Lilienfeld had to take the reins in his own hands. From the mouth of the dumpy, bull-necked impresario, the words came pouring with irresistible momentum, with elemental force, as from the crater of a volcano.

Now it was Mr. Garry's turn to suffer in silence the thrusts and blows that rained down on him from his opponent. The old gentleman was not spared. He had to swallow many disagreeable statements about the exploitation of children in certain factories in Brooklyn, about Puritan hypocrisy, about drinking water in public and wine in secret. He was told he was a member of that narrow-minded caste hating art, culture, and life itself, and seeing devils with cloven hoofs and long tails in authors like Shakespeare, Byron, and Goethe.

"Such people," Lilienfeld said, "are always trying to turn back the hands on the clock, a most revolting sight in this so-called land of freedom. There is very little hope of success in trying to turn back the hands on the clock. The days of Puritan prudery, the bothersome Puritan conscience, Puritan orthodoxy, and Puritan intolerance have passed, never to return. There is no stemming the tide of time, or the tide of progress, or the tide of culture. But the forces of reaction, threatened in their mediaeval management of things, have begun a cowardly guerilla warfare, a series of petty, cowardly, miserable, meddlesome tricks."

And now Lilienfeld handed back to Mr. Garry what Mr. Garry had given Mr. Lilienfeld.

"If there really is a pest in America, its seat is in the Society for the Prevention of Cruelty to Children. The society is the very breeding-place of the epidemic, in so far as there is an epidemic in the land. It is ridiculous in Mr. Garry to maintain that Europe is a plague-boil. Europe is the mother of America. Without the genius of a Columbus--we are at this very moment celebrating Columbus's discovery of America--without the genius of a Columbus and the constant influx of powerful intellects from Germany, England and Ireland," here he winked an eye at the Mayor, "the United States would be a dead and dreary land."

After thus moving heaven and earth and sea for the little dancer's sake, Lilienfeld exposed the base intent of his competitors, Webster and Forster, in denouncing him to the Society, and indignantly repudiated Garry's assertion that he, Lilienfeld, was an exploiter. His competitors, perhaps, were exploiters.

"See how good the conditions are under which Miss Hahlstroem is filling her engagement with me. There is my wife. In some respects she has been a mother to the girl. She is taking care of her in our own home, and the girl is in good health. She has a dancer's physique. It is a piece of bare-faced impudence to impugn the girl's honour. She is not a degenerate. She is not a neglected child. On the contrary she is simply a great artist."

Lilienfeld had left his highest trump for the last.

"Mr. Garry," he shouted so loud that the lofty windows rattled, "Mr. Garry called me a foreigner, a freebooter and the like. I object most decidedly. I am as much an American citizen as Mr. Garry. Mr. Garry, do you hear I am an American citizen?" For certain reasons Lilienfeld had had himself naturalised only a month before. "Mr. Garry, do you hear I am an American citizen?" he cried several times in succession, directly addressing the old jingo and leaning far across the table. "Mr. Garry, do you hear I am an American citizen? Mr. Garry, I am an American citizen, and I will have my rights like you."

That was the end. The wheezing in Lilienfeld's chest, as he seated himself, breathing heavily, was distinctly audible. There was not the faintest quiver in Mr. Garry's face.

After a rather lengthy pause, during which there was profound silence, the Mayor spoke. His words came out quietly, in his customary manner of mild embarrassment and shrewd affability, which rather became him. His decision was exactly what the political augurers, judging by the constellation in the ascendant, had prophesied. Ingigerd was granted the right to dance in public.

"The young lady, according to the decision of physicians called upon to testify, has been declared sound in body. There is no occasion to doubt that she is over sixteen years of age and no reason for preventing her from earning her livelihood by the exercise of an art which she has already practised in Europe."

The reporters grinned at one another significantly. The secret hate of the Irish Catholic toward the native Puritan of English descent had broken through the surface. Mr. Garry arose and shook his enemy's hand with cold dignity. Then he walked away, drawn up to his full height. His other adversary, of a very different nature from the Mayor, did not succeed in darting in his face his look of hate, also of a very different nature from the Mayor's; for Mr. Garry's eyes did not rest upon Lilienfeld for the fraction of a second.

Everybody crowded about Ingigerd, overwhelming the girl, the impresario and his wife with congratulations. In her joyous excitement Ingigerd's small face beamed sweetly. She looked very lovely. It was something to her heart's desire, this struggle to possess her carried on, as it were, before the eyes of two continents. Indeed, the extreme importance to which her person had attained almost humbled her a bit; but her pride and pleasure every now and then showed in her glances, even in the glances she sent Frederick. The men fairly courted her and did homage to her. Had a princess of the royal blood come along at that moment, their attention could not have been diverted for an instant from the little dancer, whom the delight, even gratitude shining in her face made very attractive.

Lilienfeld immediately invited all the reporters to luncheon. Mr. Samuelson declined the invitation, pleading an urgent appointment in the Court House. This may have been a pretext, for Frederick noticed, not without peculiar sympathy, that he was suffering under the consciousness of his failure. The poor man, so famous and influential, but now totally disregarded, was extremely grateful when Frederick, descending the City Hall stairs beside him, said a few words of appreciation of Samuelson's presentation of the case, though he actually felt no appreciation.

To excuse himself from taking part in the luncheon, Frederick said he had several business engagements. Nevertheless he had to promise Ingigerd that he would return in time for the demi-tasse.

XX

Frederick crossed the park to the main Post Office, a huge building, in which twenty-five hundred clerks and officials worked. Here he despatched a telegram, and then turned back into the noise of the streets, where the people, bending their heads before a cutting wind, ran about in hurrying swarms. The unceasing traffic, the cars and cabs and trucks, produced a deafening din. Frederick drew out his watch. It was half-past twelve, the exact time at which Miss Burns was wont to take her modest lunch in the little restaurant near the Grand Central Station. Frederick hailed a cab and drove to the restaurant. If on this occasion Miss Burns had failed to be lunching there, he would have been sadly disappointed. But there she was, happy as usual to see the young German scholar.

"Miss Burns," he cried, seating himself beside her, "you see in me a man who has been dismissed from prison, from a reformatory, from an insane asylum. Congratulate me! I am at last a free and independent agent again." He was blissful, exultant. "I have the appetite of three men, the humour of six men, and good spirits enough to cheer Timon of Athens out of the blues. I am totally indifferent to the future. So much is certain--no Circe has power over me any more."

Miss Burns congratulated him and laughed heartily.

"What happened?" she asked.

"I will tell you all about the tragi-comedy in the City Hall some other time. First I have to prepare you for dreadful news. Set your teeth, Miss Eva, and listen--you are going to lose me."

"I, you!" she laughed. Yet she was somewhat taken aback, and a dark red came and went on her face.

"Yes, you are going to lose me," Frederick repeated. "I just sent a telegram to Peter Schmidt in Meriden, and to-morrow morning at the latest I shall leave you. I shall leave New York, go to the country, and turn farmer."

"Oh, I really am sorry if you are going away," said Miss Burns, turning serious, though without the least trace of sentimentality in her voice.

"Why should you be sorry?" Frederick cried gaily. "You will come out to see me. The man you have until now known me to be has been nothing but a dish-rag. Perhaps, when you come to visit me in the country, you will discover that I am good for something after all. I really think I see land in the distance now. I feel I still have sound bones in my body. To take an illustration from chemistry. A salt solution vigorously stirred by the spoon of God Almighty begins to crystallise. Something in me is struggling to crystallise. Who knows whether, when the clouds that surround and penetrate the solution precipitate, the result of all the storms in the glass will not be a new, solid piece of architecture. Perhaps the evolution of a Teuton does not stop at the age of thirty. In that case the crisis may come just before the attainment of settled manhood, the crisis which, to all appearances, I have just safely passed through, and which, in any circumstances, I should have had to pass through."

Frederick now gave a brief account of the audience in the City Hall, the comic clash of two worlds in Garry's and Lilienfeld's speeches, which he called *tant de bruit pour une omelette*.

"The Mayor's decision," he said, "in opening up to Ingigerd the career for which she was so anxious, has opened up to me the way to a new life, a life all my own. It was almost like a physical sensation to realise that the Mayor's verdict decided my case, too."

He described Garry and told how, despite the opposition in their views, the descendant of Cromwell's followers, whom Charles I persecuted and executed, had impressed him and made him think. Undoubtedly his harsh, severe dealings had been dictated by purely humanitarian sentiment for Ingigerd's welfare, because of the frailty of her body and still more the frailty of her soul, all in accordance with the narrow-minded principles of a traditional belief, of which he was a credulous follower. As for Lilienfeld, did not victory in the struggle to possess Ingigerd body and soul mean money to him?

"Garry may really have been a hypocrite, yet wasn't Lilienfeld a hypocrite, too, when he spoke openly of Ingigerd Hahlstroem's honour and chastity? I looked up in alarm, and I saw a grin glide like a malicious shadow over the rows of reporters. Doesn't falsehood blossom everywhere? Doesn't hypocrisy flourish equally on each side of every contest? Isn't it a matter generally taken for granted?"

Frederick, as always, was feeling very comfortable in Miss Burns's company. Her presence always gave him, spiritually speaking, a sense of neatness and order. A man could tell her everything, and her replies straightened things out, instead of muddling them, steadied things and gave them a mooring, instead of tossing them about tempestuously. But he was not so well satisfied by her manner as usually, she not seeming sufficiently pleased with his release. He did not know whether he should attribute this to lack of sympathy or to secret doubts.

"I came to you, Miss Burns, because I do not know anybody to whom I would rather speak of this new phase of my life. Tell me frankly, was I right in doing what I did, and do you understand how a man feels when he is no longer in the chains of a senseless passion?"

"Perhaps I do," said Miss Burns, "but"--

"But what?"

Miss Burns did not reply.

"What you mean is, you cannot be certain of the convalescence of a man like myself. But I assure you, I will never sit in an audience watching that girl publicly expose her body. Still less likely am I to follow her to the four corners of the globe, through all the music-halls in the world. I am rid of her! I am free! I will prove to you that I am."

"If you were to prove it to yourself, it might be of some value to you," said Miss Burns.

But he much preferred to prove it to her.

"Perhaps you think it is a whim in me or a piece of foolishness. Yet, the way I am constituted, it is practically impossible for me to do anything for my sake alone. Your sympathy would act as a stimulus to keep me to my resolution." He drew from his pocket a letter from Peter Schmidt, saying that near Meriden there was a frame house that would be suitable for Frederick. Evidently his plan to retire to rural solitude was by no means a recent one. "When I come to myself in the quiet of the country, and I have reason to hope I will come to myself, you will hear from me. From time to time the world learns of a man of about thirty who suddenly disappears, leaving his family, his wife and his children in ignorance of his where-abouts. Sometimes he is a statesman, sometimes a young professor in a university, sometimes a mayor in good standing with all the citizens of his town, sometimes a rich business man enjoying the respect of the community. He leaves most un-ceremoniously, without concerning himself for the affairs of importance, even of extreme importance, that he may have to attend to the next day, perhaps the very next hour. He obeys the iron impulse to throw off the entire world, his next of kin, his dearest friends, and be alone with himself, so alone that he passes into oblivion and may even count as dead. It is a similar state, though perhaps not so pathologic in its character, a state conditioned rather by strokes of fortune, that has uprooted me. Don't forget, all social connections signify an immense consumption of nerve force and attach a person to his surroundings by a thousand threads and fibres. Ingigerd Hahlstroem is not the only one that is enmeshed and throttled in a spider's web. Every now and then all of us have to pant for air and tear away wrappings. Then the moment comes when we no longer do the thing that has been well considered, the thing that convention has established, but the very thing that has not been considered, that takes heed of nothing, the purely instinctive thing. Call it what you will, fermentation, folly, passion, shipwreck, storm. Whatever it may be, the fact is, all at once a man again feels the desire for life expanding his lungs."

Frederick now drew from his pocket the photographs of his three children, which his father and mother had sent along with their letters. In their great happiness that he had escaped drowning and was safe and sound, his parents had completely forgotten their solicitude for him.

Miss Burns took a friendly interest in the pictures and found a word of praise for each child. There was some discussion, pedagogic and non-pedagogic, of the characteristics of the little people. Frederick again spoke of his wife, this time without any critical reflections, dwelling only on her good and lovely and excellent qualities, really native to her.

The meal was over. Frederick had eaten heartily of the vegetarian dishes. He rose, shook hands warmly with Miss Burns, and thanked her for having listened so patiently. He left hastily, and jumped into a cab in order to keep his promise to Ingigerd Hahlstroem to come before luncheon was over at Lilienfeld's house.

XXI

The Lilienfelds lived in a one-family house, an exact replica of the other houses on the same block on 124th Street. Frederick found the company drinking coffee in a reception-room on the first floor, richly furnished with oriental rugs, expensive lamps, Japanese vases, and fine, dark, highly polished walnut furniture. The shades were drawn, and the electric bulbs of a gorgeous chandelier imparted a certain splendour to the room. The air was heavy with the smoke of Lilienfeld's strong imported cigars, at which the reporters were puffing away comfortably.

Ingigerd, smoking a cigarette, was reclining in an easy-chair surrounded by the reporters. Her hair was hanging loose about her shoulders and down her back. Altogether her appearance was not prepossessing. Since she looked impossible dressed as a grown lady in long skirts, she wore schoolgirl clothes and was tempted to furbish herself up like a tight-rope dancer with ribbons, openwork stockings, and white shoes.

When Frederick von Kammacher entered the room, she blushed slightly, and held her hand out to him indolently. Unfortunately, this hand had short, ordinary fingers, probably the plebeian heritage from her mother, her father having had long, beautiful hands. Frederick was at least a head taller than anybody in the room and was distinguished from the other gentlemen by his air of good breeding. He kissed Mrs. Lilienfeld's hand, German fashion, and begged her pardon for having come so late.

The subject of discussion, of course, was the hearing in the City Hall. Lilienfeld ran about, offering the reporters cigars and cordials, so importunate in his hospitality as not to shrink from sticking long Havanas into their coat pockets and cigarettes into their cases. There was design in this. Every now and then he would take a reporter aside to force upon him information regarding Ingigerd's past, her birth, her rescue, her father, her European success, and the way in which her talent had been discovered. It was a rather garish mixture of truth and fiction. Lilienfeld knew that this story of her life would appear in the New York newspapers that very same evening in connection with the report of the audience in the City Hall. He had brewed the concoction according to his own recipe from various details that he had heard, and he felt certain of its effectiveness.

Ingigerd looked very tired. But she had received orders to be as lavish as possible with her amiabilities so long as a single reporter remained in the house. Frederick felt sorry for her. He saw that her severe professional duties had begun.

Mrs. Lilienfeld was a calm, refined woman of nearly forty, with a look of suffering on her face, yet extremely attractive. She was dressed with tasteful simplicity. One got the impression that her husband worshipped her blindly and was accustomed to act, or to refrain from acting, according to a scarcely perceptible glance from her soft, grave eyes. For all his noisiness the bull-necked man, coarse, brutal, sensual, was like a timid child before her.

She devoted herself for a while to Frederick, who felt he had found grace in the lady's eyes and that for some reason she wished to be helpful to him in leading him away from the aberrations of his passion. Had he not had a sense of security in the firmness of his decision, he might perhaps have given more serious attention to her searching questions, which showed that she had done some thinking about him.

Her method was far from flattering to Ingigerd. With an infinitely disdainful smile, she called the girl, who was chattering nonsense to a circle of flirtatious reporters and was overwhelmed with their tokens of approval, "a mechanical doll with a light head of porcelain filled with sawdust."

"A good plaything," she said, "a plaything for a man, an article of merchandise, but nothing more. She may be worth money, but she is not worth anything else. She is not worth more than any piece of emptiness, any trifle, or knickknack."

Ingigerd, moved perhaps by a little wave of jealousy, came up and asked Frederick, without suspecting the significance the question had in his eyes, whether he had packed his things.

"Not yet. Why should I pack my things?"

"Mr. Lilienfeld," she said, "has made a contract for me for two evenings a week in Boston. You must get ready and go to Boston with me day after to-morrow."

"To the ends of the world," said Frederick lightly, "to the ends of the world, dear lady."

She was contented, and gave Mrs. Lilienfeld a look of satisfaction.

XXII

Frederick was greatly relieved when the festivity at Lilienfeld's house was at last a thing of the past. With Willy Snyders' help, he had succeeded in getting together a few effects, and he spent part of the afternoon arranging them. In the evening the artists, who had grown very fond of their guest and were sorry to lose him, gave him a farewell dinner at the round table.

For a long time Frederick had not felt so serene and at peace with himself and the world as that afternoon. After he had got his baggage ready, Willy Snyders, who had been waiting ever since Frederick's arrival to show him his collection of Japanese art objects, invited him to his room. It was a small room on the top floor, cluttered up with a mass of antiques. He first placed before Frederick a number of Japanese sword-guards, tsubas, as the Japanese call them, small elliptical pieces of metal, about which a man's hand can easily reach. They are decorated with figures in slight relief, partly of the same metal as the ground, partly damascened, or inlaid with copper, gold, or silver.

"A tiny object, tremendous labour," Frederick observed, after more than an hour spent in admiring the wonderful workmanship of pieces in the Kamakura and Namban styles, pieces by members of the Goto family extending over centuries, of the Jakushi family, and the Kinai family; pieces of the Akasaka school and the Nara school; pieces from Fushimi in the fifteenth and sixteenth centuries, from Gokinai and Kagonami; glorious sword-guards in the maru-bori, maru-bori-zogan, and hikone-bori styles; pieces of the Hamano family, and so on. Who can boast a prouder aristocracy than Goto Mitsunori, who lived at the end of the nineteenth century and could trace his descent back through a line of sixteen ancestors, all great masters in the art of sword-decorating, a glorious race of craftsmen, inheriting not only the life, but also the skill of their fore-fathers.

And all the things portrayed on those small oval tsubas! The cloven turnip of Daikoku, god of fortune. The god Sennin creating a man by his breath. A shining full moon and flying geese. Wild geese flying over reeds. The moon rising from between snow-clad mountains, an oval of iron, gold and silver, no larger than a man's palm, yet suggesting the vast reaches of a moonlit night.

Frederick and Willy both marvelled at the lapidary style of this metal work, in which the artist with the finest understanding of his art displayed a wealth of composition within the smallest space.

One of the tsubas represented a tea pavilion behind a hedge. In the spacious landscape was a waterfall, sky and air, perfectly depicted by holes in the iron, that is, by nothing. Others represented the hero Hidesato vanquishing a monster on the bridge of Seta; the sage Lao Tsze on his ox; Senno Kinko, a pious man, riding on his golden-eyed carp, absorbed in a book; the god Idaten, pursuing an oni, or devil, who had stolen Buddha's pearl; a bird prying open a Venus's shell with his bill; a golden-eyed octopus or cuttlefish; the sage Kiko leaning from the window of his house, reading a scroll by moonlight.

Willy, endlessly resourceful and allowing nothing to daunt him, had ferreted this collection out of a restaurant in the Five Points district, a restaurant of viler repute than even the neighbourhood it was in. A Japanese had left the tsubas with the proprietor of the den as pledge of the payment of his bill, but had disappeared without ever returning to redeem his pledge. Scarcely a day passed that Willy did not visit a junk shop on the Bowery, or in the Jewish quarter. Peering with his fearless, fiery eyes, which always wore an expression of mingled astonishment and indignation, he ventured into the worst sections of the city, even into the obscurest opium hells of Chinatown. His confident manner and round spectacles, he told Frederick, caused him to be mistaken for a detective; which stood him in good stead in making his purchases.

In one shop in Chinatown, belonging to a fat Chinese usurer, Willy for very little money came into possession of a quantity of Japanese prints. These were the next things he showed Frederick. There were most of Hiroshige's views of Lake Biwa; there were the thirty-six views of Fujiyama by Hokusai. One of the most exquisite showed remnants of snow left on the mountain and a brownish red sun setting in a cold sky with fleecy clouds. There were Shunsho's and Shigemasa's illustrations of the book, "Mirror of the Beauties of the Green Houses," Yedo, 1776, and Shunsho's illustrations of "The Book of Sprouting Weeds." Frederick called one of Hokusai's prints "the golden poem of summer." It was a deep-blue heaven with Fujiyama to the left and golden grain beneath, persons sitting on benches, heat, radiance, joy! One of Hiroshige's prints he dubbed "the great poem of the moon." On wide, moist, melancholy meadows, scant-leaved trees, like weeping willows, their branches drooping in the mirror of an idly flowing stream, barges loaded with turf passing by, a floating bridge propelled by Japanese raftsmen, the water blue in the evening twilight, a great, pale moon, veiled by pale, bloody tints, rising above the distant edge of the melancholy plain.

In addition to his tsubas and prints, Willy had a collection of so-called netsuke, some in boxwood, some in ivory, small, dice-like carvings, representing with remarkable animation all sorts of real and fantastic scenes.

Among the finest of Willy's possessions was a Japanese figure carved in wood not more than a foot high, a woman selling oysters. Each least detail was most precisely rendered. It was the attempt of a more recent Japanese master to portray feminine beauty. In this one rare instance he had succeeded, having produced one of those precious objects adapted to make thieves of their lovers.

Willy, who mingled in American sporting circles, had also found occasion to collect a few Indian curiosities. He showed Frederick the feather adornment of an Apache chief, a wampum belt, Indian knives and bows and arrows. He had made the acquaintance of Buffalo Bill, the famous hunter, and some Indian chief and cowboys in his troupe, men in whom natural instincts are combined with a Barnum and Bailey business sense, and real excellence with the actor's vanity. Willy's especial friend, whom he had been very eager for Frederick to meet, was a well-known acrobat who had jumped from the Brooklyn Bridge into the East River.

"Willy," said Frederick, "since you have so profitably employed your time in America, you won't be going back to Europe empty-handed."

"The devil!" replied Willy. "What else is to be got out of this damned country?"

XXIII

The next morning Frederick went down alone to the train. He had taken final leave of his friends the night before, telling them expressly not to let his departure interfere with their day's routine. After placing his luggage in a wire basket hanging over one of the red plush seats in a coach which was one of a train of six or seven similar coaches, long and elegantly built, he returned to the platform. All of a sudden the whole little colony of artists appeared, with the master-sculptor at their head--in corpore, as college students say. Miss Burns, too, had come, like the rest of them, carrying three of those purplish-red, long-stemmed roses with deep green leaves which were not yet being grown in Europe.

"I feel like a prima donna," Frederick said, really touched, as he took the roses from each.

The platform and the train were as quiet as a cemetery, as if there never were arrivals or departures between friends. But here and there, the face of a traveller, aroused by the "temperamental" chatter of the Germans, peered from behind the window-panes of the train to look curiously upon the little rose procession. Finally, without a signal, or a word from any official, the train started to move, as if by chance.

Soon the group of artists in the station receded. There stood Bonifacius Ritter, dignified and elegant, waving his handkerchief. There was Lobkowitz, friendly and serious, Willy Snyders the good-hearted, Franck the gypsy painter, and, last but not least, Miss Eva Burns. Frederick felt that with this moment, an epoch of his life had come to a close. He was conscious of what he owed these fellow-countrymen and kindred spirits for their warmth and hospitality, and of what he lost in losing them. Nevertheless, after the strange way of man, he was in a state of joyous excitement because his future, in a real and in a metaphoric sense, had been set in motion.

At first the train rolled for some time through a dark tunnel under the city, then through an open cut between high walls of masonry, and finally it burst into a wide, free landscape. So this was America's real face. Only now, after the noises of the Witches' Sabbath, the turmoil of the great invasion, had somewhat subsided, Frederick breathed the true breath of the virgin country's soil.

Observing that all the passengers in the coach stuck their tickets in their hat bands, Frederick did the same, and then turned his eyes on the fields and hills clothed in their white winter garments. To the young man, uprooted from his native soil, there was a happy, stimulating mystery in this landscape, which in the light of the winter sun so closely resembled his birthplace. The alien surroundings all spoke to him of his home. He could have jumped from the car and taken the snow in his hands, not only to look upon it, but to feel that it was the very same snow which as a schoolboy he had rolled into balls for bombarding his playmates. He felt as a spoiled child feels which is torn from its mother's arms and thrown upon a heartless world of strangers and, after a long period of anguish, unexpectedly meets a sister of his mother in a dreary country far, far from home. He feels the blood-tie, he feels how like he is to her and she to him, how surprisingly, how delightfully she resembles his mother, feature by feature.

At last, it seemed to Frederick, the great Atlantic Ocean was really behind him. Though he had landed in New York, he felt that until now he had not planted his feet firmly on the ground. Great well-established mother earth, the breadth and extent of her solidity, which he beheld again after so long a separation, at last set bounds in his soul to the fearful expanse and might of the ocean. Mother earth was a good and great giantess who had cunningly snatched the lives of her children from the giantess ocean and had put everything on a firm, everlasting basis with a hedge of safety all around.

"Forget the tumbling waters, forget the ocean, strike root into the soil," a voice within Frederick spoke; and while the train rolled smoothly and faster and further inland, he had a sense of being on a blissful flight.

Frederick was so lost in meditation that he started when someone without saying a word took the ticket from his hatband. It was a cultivated-looking man in a simple uniform, the conductor, who punched the card, said not a word, moved not a muscle of his face, and travelled from seat to seat, performing the same operation and always returning the punched tickets to the men's hats, which they kept on their heads. Nobody paid the least attention to him. Frederick smiled when he thought of Germany, where every train was received with the clanging of a bell and set in motion with three soundings of a gong, amid the general uproar of the officials, who bellowed like a horde of Apaches; and where the conductors demanded the tickets from the passengers with much rough, awkward ceremony.

The whirring of the wheels made a pleasant accompaniment to his thoughts. He was enjoying his flight, which signified anything but shame and disgrace. In his complete absorption, he discovered himself picking little threads from his clothes, like a spider's cobweb, and he observed how with each minute he drew his breath more freely. Sometimes it seemed to him that the wheels of the tremendous express train were not turning swiftly enough on their axles, and that he himself ought to put his hands to the wheels to hasten on the new health-giving impressions and place them behind him like thin curtains, so that the partitions dividing him from that dangerous, fatal magnet which he had left behind should grow denser and denser.

In New Haven, where the train halted for a short time, a negro with sandwiches and a boy with newspapers passed through the train. Frederick bought one of the papers, and found the whole disaster of the *Roland* warmed up over again in connection with the sensational reports of the hearing in the City Hall. On that bright winter day his mood was too gay and peaceful to suffer the appalling impressions of the sinking of the vessel and its drowning mass of humanity to revive in his soul. To be sure, he had had absolutely no right to escape, and he was still somewhat ashamed that the regnant powers had preferred him to so many innocent brothers and sisters. On that account, there had been a time when he would have given back his life in a passion of embittered pity and glowing indignation; for there was no sin great enough to justify that horrible, brutal drowning on the seas and no merit great enough to justify escape from it. But on this winter day, on his flight from New

York, his rescue filled him with nothing but sincere gratitude. Captain von Kessel and the many others that had gone down with the **Roland** were dead and so were removed from all pain and suffering. Everything about Frederick this day breathed an atmosphere of convalescence and reconciliation.

All the way from New Haven to Meriden he regaled himself with the sketch of Ingigerd's life that appeared in the papers. He could scarcely keep from laughing. Lilienfeld displayed a positively poetical, exuberant imagination. Though Ingigerd's father was of German parentage and her mother a French Swiss, Ingigerd figured as the scion of a noble Swedish family, and the body of a relative of hers was reported to be resting in the Riddarholms-Kyrka in Stockholm. The impresario well knew that Americans are fascinated by a single drop of royal blood.

"Poor little thing!" thought Frederick, as he folded up the newspaper. Then, at the sudden realisation of what tremendous import the "poor little thing" had until that moment been to him and others, he clapped his hand to his brow and muttered, "That's over and done with, that's over and done with," and swore several oaths at himself.

XXIV

Peter Schmidt was at the train to meet Frederick, who was the only passenger getting off at Meriden. The little station was empty, but near by was the hurry-scurry of the main street of this country town of about twenty-five thousand inhabitants.

"Now," said Schmidt, "all's well. No more New York dissipation. We'll sound different chords here in Meriden. My wife sends her regards. She could not come to meet you because she had to look after some patients. If you like, we might lunch together and afterwards drive out in a sleigh to take a look at the little house I found for you in the country. If it suits you, you can rent it at a very low figure. In the meantime you can take a room at our hotel here, which the whole city is proud of."

"Oh," said Frederick, "I have a wild longing for solitude. I should prefer to spend the very first night beneath my own roof far, far from the madding crowd of

Meriden."

"Very well," responded Schmidt, "the man that owns the house is a good friend of mine, a druggist. His name is Lamping, a pleasant Dutchman. He'll be satisfied with any arrangements we make; and if you decide to take the house, everything can be settled with him in fifteen minutes."

The two men went to the hotel, where they were served with a rather tasteless meal in surroundings comfortable and luxurious far beyond European notions. Schmidt left Frederick alone for a while and in a few moments sent a bell-boy to announce that the sleigh was waiting outside. To Frederick's astonishment he found his friend sitting alone in a pretty, two-seated sleigh reining in a fiery chestnut.

"I congratulate you on this tidy little conveyance," he said.

Peter laughed and quickly dispelled Frederick's illusion, that the immaculate little vehicle with the horse and harnessings were his own. He had merely hired it without a driver, a frequent practice in America.

"In fact," he joked, "I shall be quite content if we get there without being pitched out into the snow. I confess, I have never in my life driven a horse."

"Ah," said Frederick with chuckling satisfaction, "it is not for nothing that my father is a general. Let me drive."

Frederick's luggage was placed in the sleigh, he jumped in, caught up the reins, the chestnut reared, and off they dashed, with a deafening jingle of the sleigh-bells. Their way lay along the main street, a broad, bustling thoroughfare.

"Is this the sort of horse they usually have here?" asked Frederick. "The beast is positively running away. If we come out of this crowded street without broken limbs, it will be God's doing, not mine."

"Let him have his way. Every day there are one or more runaways here. What's the difference if it's our turn to-day?"

But Frederick reined the horse in so tightly, that he actually succeeded in pulling him up just as the Boston-New York express thundered by on a line of railroad tracks crossing the street not safeguarded by gates or fence. Frederick wondered how it was that a multitude of children, workmen, gentlemen in high hats, ladies in silk dresses, horses, dogs, trucks, and carriages were not mangled to a pulp and dashed against the walls of the houses lining the tracks. The horse plunged and reared and shot forward over the rails behind the last coach, sending clods of ice and snow flying in Frederick's and Peter's faces.

"The devil!" snorted Frederick. "Now for the first time I observe that form of madness which is specifically American. If you fall under the wheels, you fall under the wheels. If you want to take a drive, be your own coachman. If you break your bones, you break your bones. If you break your neck, you break your neck."

Farther along on the same highway Frederick for the first time saw an electric street car, then still unknown in Europe. The brilliant sparking at the meeting of the trolley and the overhead wire was to him a new, stimulating phenomenon. The posts holding up the wire were all shapes, thick and slender, bowed and slanting, so that the whole made a promiscuous impression, though the coaches were of a pleasing shape and glided along with great rapidity.

They had passed the more frequented and dangerous section of the city without an accident and had reached the open country. The houses grew lower and farther apart. Before the chestnut with his jingling bells lay an endless stretch of unblocked roadway, with excellent tracks for the sleigh worn into the snow. The valiant American could speed to his heart's content.

"How strange!" thought Frederick. "Here I am riding in a sleigh and driving a horse, things I have not done since I was a boy."

Stories of sports and incidents that he had not thought of for ten years or more occurred to him. How his father's accounts of hunting expeditions and sleighing mishaps had set them all laughing when the family was cosily gathered together in one room on a winter evening.

During that brisk, refreshing drive Frederick's heart was rejuvenated. The happiest years of his boyhood were as vivid to him as yesterday--thrilling, romantic rides by night, when the same sound of sleigh-bells scared the silence of sleeping forests and filled the boy's soul with pictures of midnight attacks, romantic murders, and strange devilish phantoms. In the dazzling brilliance of the snowy fields, breathing in the pure, bracing air, mere existence became unspeakable bliss. Sitting there in that dainty sleigh Frederick was inclined to look on life as a pleasure drive.

Suddenly he turned pale and had to hand the reins over to Peter Schmidt. In the jingling of the sleigh-bells his ear caught something like the insistent hammering ring of electric bells. It was an illusion of his hearing, but it filled him with rising horror, and a shiver went through his whole body. By the time Peter Schmidt, who instantly observed the change in his friend, had brought the horse to a stop, Frederick had already mastered his nervous attack. He did not admit it was the sinking of the **Roland** that had unexpectedly announced its presence again. He merely said that the noise of the bells had irritated his nerves beyond endurance. Fortunately, the spotless expanse of Lake Hanover was already close by and the little house on the other shore already visible. So the two men descended from the sleigh. Peter Schmidt, in silence, removed the bells from the harness and hitched the horse to the branch of a bare tree. They crossed the frozen lake on foot, making for the solitary house under its heavy covering of snow.

Peter ascended the front door steps, which resembled great bolsters of snow, and opened the door.

"To judge by the way it looks now, the house is scarcely habitable in winter."

"Oh, yes it is," Frederick declared.

Having been built for summer use only, it had no cellar. On the ground floor there was a little kitchen and two other rooms; in the attic a bedroom as large as the two down-stairs rooms together. In the attic room Frederick immediately decided to build his nest for an indeterminate length of time. He scouted Peter's considerations in regard to household service.

"I feel," he declared, "as if this house had been waiting for me, and I for the house."

XXV

The very next day he took up his abode in his lonely refuge on Lake Hanover, which he alternately dubbed his Diogenes tub, his Uncle Tom's Cabin, and his retort. It was no Diogenes tub, because the two friends brought wood and anthracite coal for a little American stove in the bedroom, which gave quite a good deal of heat and made a cosey appearance with the glow of the burning coal visible; and because the kitchen and pantry contained everything that is necessary for life, and a little more. Frederick refused to have anybody share his quarters with him or help with the housework. As he said, he wanted to settle his accounts and take his trial balance, and the presence of another person might be disturbing to that process.

After Peter Schmidt disappeared in the distance and the sound of the sleigh-bells had died away and Frederick felt he was quite alone in that wide American landscape wrapped in the night's darkness, it was a supreme moment for him. He returned into the house, closed the door and listened. He heard the crackling of the wood in the small kitchen stove. Taking the candle that had been left standing on one of the lower steps in the hall, he went up-stairs, where the warmth and the dusky glow of his little American stove rejoiced him. He lit a lamp, and after arranging his toilet articles on an unusually long, bare dresser, he settled himself beside the lamp in a comfortable bamboo chair. He was filled with a mysterious sense of rich, deep delight.

He was alone. Outside, lay the clear, silent winter's night, the same that he had known in the home of his childhood. The things he had hitherto experienced were no more, or as if they never had been. His home, his parents, his wife, his children, the girl that had drawn him across the ocean, everything that had happened to him on his trip were nothing more in his soul than magic lantern pictures.

"Is life," Frederick asked himself, "meant to be nothing more than material for dreams? So much is certain, my present condition is the sort that leaves an everlasting effect. We should not be unsociable, but we have still less right to leave this state uncultivated, which is the basic state of man's personality, in which he is most natural and undisturbed and stands face to face with the mystery of life as though it were a dream."

During the past months, he had led a life full of incidents of the extremest contrasts. He had been alarmed, excited, menaced. His own anguish had been submerged in the anguish of others, and their pangs had only increased his own. From the ashes of a dead love, the flames of another passionate illusion had flared up. Frederick had been driven, pursued, lured on, led about in the world, without a will of his own, like a puppy on a strap--without a will of his own and with his senses departed. Now at last his senses had returned. And the senses return when the life that has been lived in an unconscious state becomes material for dreams to the mind in a conscious state.

Frederick took a sheet of paper, dipped a new American pen in a new inkwell of fresh ink, and wrote: "Life: Material for Dreams."

He rose and again went about arranging his Robinson Crusoe household to suit his fancy. He piled up books that he had got in New York, little Reclams and other volumes, among them a copy of Schleiermacher's translation of Plato, which he had borrowed from Peter Schmidt. In front of an old Dutch sofa covered in leather, which Lamping, the druggist, had brought over from Leyden, his birthplace, stood a large, round table. Frederick covered the table with a green cloth and arranged the long-stemmed roses that the artists had given him in plain glass vases, placing Miss Burns's roses by themselves. Before Peter Schmidt had left, he and Frederick had taken a cup of coffee together. Frederick now washed and cleared away the utensils, loaded a revolver that Schmidt had lent him, and placed it beside the inkstand on his writing table. Next he took from his trunk a more peaceable instrument, a Zeiss microscope, examined all its parts, and set it up. It was the microscope that he had selected years ago in Jena for his friend, Peter, when he was leaving for America. Here was a remarkable meeting with the old instrument.

There were more things that Frederick had to do. He had to take apart a seaman's clock, put it together again and hang it on the wall. It was an antique that he had come across that very day and secured at a low price along with some furniture. To his joy the old grandfather began to tick away at a proper, dignified pace on the wall at the foot of the bed. There it was to remain in its brown case about three feet long until, as Frederick inwardly vowed, he would return it to its home in Europe, Schleswig-Holstein, for which it was pining. When Frederick lay on his bed, he could see the yellow brass pendulum gleam back and forth behind a small glass door. The dial was a curiosity. It was painted in garish colors in a primitive style and represented a chubby-cheeked sun wearing the Island of Heligoland as a crown. Below the face, little metal sailing vessels connected with the clockwork swayed back and forth in the same sober rhythm as the pendulum. This was designed to make the tempest-tossed seafarer doubly sensible of the comforts of a solid hearth.

"When was it," Frederick pondered, "that I listened to Mr. Garry's cutting remarks, Mr. Samuelson's unsuccessful attack, and Lilienfeld's wild sally against Puritan intolerance--a low, hypocritical battle ostensibly fought for the salvation of a soul; in reality nothing more than the clapperclawing of crows over a helpless hare. When was it? It must have been years ago. But no, it was only last night that Ingigerd appeared in public for the first time. So it cannot have been longer ago than day before yesterday."

He had already received her first letter. He had laughed over it heartily, and yet it had moved him. She was furious and complained bitterly of his breach of faith. In one and the same breath, she said she had been dreadfully deceived in him and had seen through him the very moment she laid eyes on him when he came up to speak to her after her dance in Berlin. In one sentence she tore his character to shreds, in the next sentence urged him to return.

"I celebrated a tremendous triumph to-day. The audience lost their heads. After the performance Lord ---- came up to congratulate me. He is a handsome young Englishman, who is living over here because he had a falling out with his father. But when the old man dies, he will inherit the title of duke and millions."

"This story," Frederick thought, "is either a true story or a concoction. If a concoction, then I have reason to assume that the little girl wants to make me jealous and so has not lost interest in me. But the story need not be an invention, either wholly or in part. For if an invention, it will undoubtedly become a fact within three or four days, or, at the utmost, within a week. Some rich rascal will come along and buy her."

Frederick shrugged his shoulders. He no longer felt the slightest impulse to be the girl's protector, knight and saviour, or the faintest solicitude for her probable fate.

The next morning he awoke in a shiver, though the stove had retained some heat and the sun was shining into the room brightly. He took his gold watch from his pocket--a possession that had escaped drowning with him--and ascertained that his pulse was beating more than a hundred times a minute, which is too much for a healthy man. But he paid no attention to his condition, got up, washed all over in cold water, dressed, and prepared his breakfast, by no means feeling like an invalid. Nevertheless he was aware he ought to be cautious, knowing that now, when the tension and excitement had relaxed, his body might have to confess to its consumption of capital and file a petition in bankruptcy. Sometimes, without a warning to one's strength, the body overcomes the severest hardships as if the thing were mere child's play; and all goes well so long as the stimulated body is in motion. It works on its surplus energy, and as soon as the will and the tension relax, it collapses.

XXVI

Shortly before ten o'clock Frederick was in his friend's consultation room. The walk to Meriden on the brisk winter day had done him good.

"How did you sleep?" asked Schmidt. "You know, you superstitious people maintain that what you dream the first night in a strange place will come true."

"I hope not," said Frederick. "My first night was rather insignificant, and things passed helter-skelter through my brain."

He said nothing of a dream he had had, in which he heard the ringing of the electric bells on the ***Roland***. Though he fought against the impression, it obstinately transported him back to those horrid moments of the shipwreck. Little by little this illusion of his hearing had become Frederick's cross. Sometimes he feared it might be a species of aura, which he, as a physician, knew not infrequently announces an attack of severe illness.

The consultation rooms of the two physicians were separated by the waiting-room, which they used in common. Mrs. Schmidt, whom Frederick had met the day before, came over and, greeting him parenthetically, asked her husband to help her with the examination of one of her patients, a woman of about twenty-seven, who shortly before had married a workman holding a good position in one of the Meriden factories. The woman complained of an upset stomach. Mrs. Schmidt suspected cancer of the stomach.

Both Schmidt and his wife asked Frederick to join them in the examination. They found the patient smiling as she lay stretched on the table. Her smile changed to an expression of astonishment when she saw the two gentlemen. Mrs. Schmidt introduced Frederick as a famous German physician.

"I just spoiled my stomach a little," the woman, who was pretty and well dressed, said in excuse for the trouble she was giving. "My husband will laugh at me and scold me if he hears I ran to a doctor."

Frederick and Peter confirmed Mrs. Schmidt's diagnosis, and Mrs. Schmidt told the candidate for the grave, who was so gay and unsuspecting, that she might have to undergo a slight operation. She inquired kindly for her husband and her child, who had come into the world three months before with her help, and the woman gave ready answers in the best of spirits. Peter took it upon himself to acquaint her husband the very same day with her condition.

During the next week, Peter drew his friend more and more into his practice. Frederick found a certain grim attraction in it. It was a strange treadmill, set in a world of everlasting suffering and dying, in a subterranean stratum of life, having nothing in common with that deceptive existence of a comparatively happy superficiality which he had been able to lead in New York. The Schmidts were doing hard service requiring the utmost self-renunciation. They received no greater compensation than enabled them to obtain sufficient food, clothing and shelter to be able to continue in that service. Though Peter Schmidt was not a Socialist, his practice was almost exclusively confined to the working class. Most of the two doctors' clients were poor immigrants with large families, who toiled laboriously in the Britannia-metal factories to keep the wolf from the door. Their fees were extremely low, and in half the cases Peter, true to his views of life, did not collect them.

The section of the city in which their office was located was dismal beyond parallel. A factory with its offices took up a whole block. Though Frederick was well acquainted with the corrosive sublimate and carbolic acid smell of consultation rooms, he nevertheless had difficulty in concealing the depressing effect the Schmidts' home had upon him. It was dark and gloomy, and the street noises came in directly from the windows. In Germany, a city of thirty thousand inhabitants is dead. This American city of twenty-five thousand inhabitants raced and rushed, rang bells, rattled and clattered and raved like mad. Nobody had a moment's time. Everybody hurried past everybody else. No question of joy in life here. If a man lived in Meriden, he lived there to work. If a man worked in Meriden, he worked for the sake of the dollars that had the power finally to free him from that environment and introduce him to a period of enjoyment. Most of the people, especially the German and Polish workmen and tradesmen, saw in the life they were compelled to lead a temporary, provisional existence, a condition the bitterness of which was intensified when return to the home country was cut off by sins committed in the past or by expulsion and banishment. From psychologic interest, Frederick had entered into conversation with patients in the waiting-room and had already learned of sad cases of men having been ejected from their country and left without a home.

Mrs. Schmidt was a Swiss. She had a broad German head, straight, finely chiselled nose, and a figure like the figures of the women of Basel that Holbein painted.

"She is much too good for you," Frederick teased Peter. "She ought to be the wife of a Duerer, or still better, the wife of the wealthy Ratsherr Willibald Pirkheimer of Nuremberg. She was born to preside over a comfortable patrician household, with closets and chests full of linen and heavy silk and brocade garments. She should go to sleep every night on a bed three yards high covered with silk spreads. She should have twice as many hats and fur garments as the town council allows the wealthy. Instead of that, poor soul, she studied medicine, and you let her run around to every Tom, Dick, and Harry with her little bag of ill omen."

As a matter of fact, the ugliness of her surroundings and the strenuousness of her occupation, which opened up no vista of hope and usually robbed her of four nights' sleep in a week, had made of Mrs. Schmidt an embittered person suffering from homesickness. What aggravated matters was that she was dominated by an obstinate sense of duty and that dogged insistence on saving characteristic of the Swiss. Since her parents' letters strengthened her in her notions, she was not to be shaken in her resolve not to return home until after a certain sum had been laid aside, and of this there was no immediate prospect. Whenever Peter, saddened to see his wife withering away from overwork and nostalgia, proposed that they return to Europe, she would become very hard, cutting and bitter. But when she had a free hour in which to talk to Frederick and her husband of the Swiss mountains and mountain climbs, she revived visibly. There, in the musty office, or in the physicians' private rooms, arose the glorious vision of Sentis, in the face of which Mrs. Schmidt had been rocked in her cradle. The conversation, of course, turned on Scheffel's "Ekkehard," the chamois reserve, Lake Constance, and St. Gall. They recalled memories of a Rigi tour, a tour up from Lake Lucerne at Fluelen to Goeschenen, from Goeschenen to Andermatt, from Andermatt up over the Rhone glacier and down to the wonderful Grimsel Hospice, with its clear icy-cold lake, which lies in a rocky funnel, like the entrance to the kingdom of shades. One looks about to see if Charon's raft is not waiting. Mrs. Schmidt said she would rather be the dirtiest shepherdess on Sentis than a physician in Meriden.

"Very well," cried Peter, "we will cross the ocean again and settle in Berne or

Zuerich." As always when Peter Schmidt made this proposition, Mrs. Schmidt's face took on an expression of hard, hostile determination. It did not escape Frederick's notice.

Everything Mrs. Schmidt said testified to her humanity and her clear, serious, sympathetic insight. What a pity she had forgotten how to laugh! What a pity she was not Ratsherr Willibald Pirkheimer's stately, respected wife, surrounded by his healthy children! Her broad shoulders and hips, her long, thick hair required the soft curves of a body blooming in happiness, sunlight and wealth. As it was, her face, though she was only twenty-seven years old, was fearfully worn and anxious, and her shabby clothes hung carelessly on her angular figure. Nevertheless, Frederick perceived the beauty even in her neglected appearance.

Naturally Peter Schmidt, the blond Friesian, also suffered under these conditions, but not to such an extent as to be shaken in his peculiar, deep-seated idealism. It was his idealism, never for an instant forsaking him, that raised him above all momentary hardships. This very fact, it seemed to Frederick, only added to his wife's vexation. From certain remarks of hers, he could tell that it would have been more pleasing to her had Peter cared more for his own advancement and less for the advancement of humanity at large. No man possessed firmer belief than he in the triumph of good, and no man rejected religious beliefs with greater horror. He was one of those who disavow the Garden of Eden and declare the next world to be a myth, yet are firmly convinced that the earth may be developed and will develop into a paradise and that man may be developed and will develop into the divinity of that paradise. Frederick, too, had an inclination for Utopias, and his friend's notions had a revivifying effect upon him. When accompanying him on his professional visits, or skating on the little Lake of Hanover, or conversing with him in his Diogenes tub, hope came back to him; but when his friend left, hope forsook him.

But Peter Schmidt was no vain Utopist. He had a solid basis for his ideals, and endeavoured to realise them in practice. Frederick knew no one so well versed in the natural sciences, political economy, and medicine; and since he also had very accurate knowledge of the geography and history of the important countries, his survey of political conditions was enviably broad. When twenty years old, he had upheld the pan-Germanic ideal. Now, at thirty, he wrote anonymous editorials, which received much attention, advocating the coalition of America, Germany and

England, while strongly objecting to the Russian policy in Germany that originated with Bismarck. The theme that the friends chiefly discussed in those days may be summed up in the names of Marx and Darwin, or either of them. In Peter Schmidt a sort of adjustment, or rather fusing, of the fundamental tendencies of those two great personalities was in process, though the Christ-Marxian principle of the protection of the weaker gave way to the natural principle of the protection of the stronger; and this mirrors the result of the profoundest revolution that has ever taken place in the history of mankind.

"If, with that tough Friesian skull of yours," Frederick once said to him, "you succeed for twenty years in propagating the idea of artificial selection as applied to man, and if the idea of race hygiene, of a teleologic improvement of human types is sufficiently spread, it will undoubtedly be fruitful of practical results some day. That is, a fresh, healthy, vigorous stream of blood will flow through our veins and tend more and more to counteract the increasing marasmus that is enfeebling the race."

XXVII

The first week Frederick regularly took his midday meal with the two physicians in a boarding-house. Towards dusk he always returned to his Diogenes tub, usually on foot.

The next week he did not visit his friends so often, why, he himself did not know. He slept badly. Again and again the electric bells haunted his dreams. Even in his waking hours, he easily took fright, a condition to which in former times he had been a perfect stranger. If a sleigh with bells actually did pass the house, he was sometimes so alarmed that he trembled. That he should hear his own breathing in the silence of his room did not surprise him; but it perturbed him strangely to listen to it. Sometimes he had chills. As a physician he kept a clinical thermometer, and on several occasions ascertained that he had some temperature. These circumstances disquieted him. He seemed to be living in an atmosphere producing mild shocks and alarms, which he tried in vain to dispel. Once, when he was starting off to lunch with Peter Schmidt, a disinclination to leave his room and lack of appetite kept him back. Another time it was complete exhaustion that turned him homeward again when he was half way on the road to Meriden. He could scarcely drag himself back to the house. His friends never learned anything of these secret experiences of his. It did not seem odd to them if now and then he should prefer to remain alone under his own roof.

Over him came creeping a strange life, growing ever stranger. The world, the sky, the landscape, the country, everything that fell within his vision, even the human beings he met changed. They moved away. Their affairs took on a remote, alien character. Indeed, his own affairs underwent a change. They had been taken from him. Somebody had led them aside for a time. Later, perhaps, he would find them again, provided the goal of his altered condition remained the same as his former goal.

At length Peter Schmidt became observant of his friend's retired existence. When he expressed his solicitude, Frederick repulsed him somewhat brusquely. Even his friend had grown remote. He betrayed nothing of that oppressive atmosphere of alarm in which he was enclosed. Curiously, there was a secret fascination in it, which he was loath to share with any one and so have it disturbed.

On a starless, pitch-black night, he was sitting, as usual, in his lonely house at his desk beside his lamp, when it seemed to him that someone was bending over his shoulder. He was holding his pen in his hand over a pile of disordered manuscript pages, absorbed in profound thought. He started and said:

"Rasmussen, where do you come from?" He turned and actually saw Rasmussen sitting reading at the foot of his bed wearing the Lloyd cap in which he had come from his trip around the world.

"How tremendously interesting!" he thought, and carefully studied the apparition from head to foot. He could see where the stuff of his jacket and the lining joined. He could distinguish the buttons on his waistcoat, and noted that the last one was off. Rasmussen was holding a clinical thermometer in his hand with the manner and attitude of a nurse who is passing unoccupied time at the patient's bed reading.

Frederick noticed that solitude heightens the visionary character of existence. Without a companion, a man is always condemned to intercourse with spirits. In his hermitage Frederick had merely to think of someone to see him in person, talking and acting as in life. This inflammability of his imagination did not alarm him. He had given George Rasmussen's apparition cool, careful observation. Nevertheless he was aware that his spiritual life had entered a new phase.

Before going to bed he went down-stairs to lock up the house. To his great astonishment, as he opened the door of one of the rooms to close the shutters, he saw by the light of his candle another phantom as distinct as the first. He congratulated himself upon no longer having to depend upon mere hearsay in regard to this psycho-pathologic phenomenon. At the table four men were sitting playing cards. One of them was looking on. The men had rather coarse red faces, were smoking cigarettes and drinking beer. They seemed to be business men. Suddenly Frederick clapped his hand to his forehead. From the brand and the bottle, he recognised the beer that had been served on the *Roland*, and these men were those eternal drinkers and card players who had been in everybody's mouth on the *Roland*. Shaking his head over the remarkable fact that they should be sitting in his own house, he returned up-stairs to his warm room.

The daytime, in which he did a great deal of out-of-door work, even though by himself, had a wholesome effect upon him and brought him back to reality. On the whole, his opinion of his own condition remained sound. Nevertheless, as the sickness came creeping over him stealthily, he failed to notice it. It seemed natural to him that he should reckon with the apparition of Rasmussan sitting at the foot of his bed and the four men playing skat in one of his down-stairs rooms as with realities. In the instinct to counteract the physical crisis, which in a dull way he felt was approaching, he resorted to exercise. But even while skating on the lake, which he himself had swept clean of snow, dreams, he found, gradually threw their veil over him, and he associated with men and things that were not of the lake or of its snowy, solitary banks.

Many Indian legends are connected with the lake and the little stream, the Luinnipiac, which empties into it. One day Frederick skated miles up the stream to follow it to its source. On the way he was accompanied by a hovering shadow, the corporeality of which he never for a moment doubted. It resembled the stoker Zickelmann who had died on the *Roland*, not the Zickelmann that he had seen lying stretched out a corpse in the stoke-hole, but the Zickelmann he had seen in his dream.

The shade of the stoker told him that five engine-men, thirty-six stokers, and thirty-eight coal-passers had sunk with the *Roland*, a number far greater than Frederick had thought.

"The harbour where you landed in your dreams," he told Frederick, "was the Atlantis, a submerged continent. The Azores, the Madeira Islands, and the Canary Islands are the remnants of that continent."

When Frederick found himself leaning over a hole such as foxes make, seriously hunting for a way to the Toilers of the Light, he came to his senses and laughed at himself.

From day to day, aye, from hour to hour, the creations of his disordered brain assumed more and more fantastic forms. Rasmussen was always sitting on his bed, the four passengers of the *Roland* were always playing skat in the lower room, and the sick man went about his house conversing in whispers with all sorts of invisible men and things, unconscious for hours at a time of where he was. Sometimes he thought he was in the house in which he lived when a practising physician, at other times, in the home of his parents. As a rule, he was on the deck, or in the saloons of the *Roland*, crossing the ocean to America.

"Why," he said to himself, shaking his head, "after all, the *Roland* did not sink."

After midnight he would get up from bed and take the wrapping from a mirror hanging on the wall, which he had covered up because he was not fond of mirrors. He would hold the candle close to the glass and frighten himself by making grimaces, which distorted his features beyond recognition. Then he would talk to himself, asking questions and listening to answers, and hearing questions and giving answers. Some of this was utterly irrational, some perfectly rational. It showed that he had investigated one of the obscurest, most awful psychic problems, the sickness of men who are haunted by their doubles. He jotted down a note:

"The mirror has made man out of the animal. Without the mirror, no I and no you. Without an I and a you, no thought. All fundamental concepts are twins, beautiful and ugly, good and evil, hard and soft, sorrow and joy, hate and love, cowardice and courage, jest and earnest, and so on."

The image in the mirror said to Frederick:

"You have divided yourself into you and me before you could distinguish the separate characteristics of your being, which acts only as a whole. That is, you divided yourself before you could divide yourself. Until you saw yourself in a mirror, you saw nothing of the world."

"It is good to be alone with my image in the mirror," thought Frederick. "I don't need all those distressing concave and convex mirrors which other people are. This condition in which I am is the original condition, and in the original condition one escapes the distortion to which other people's words and glances subject one. The best thing is to be silent or to speak with oneself, that is, with oneself in the mirror."

Frederick kept this up until one evening, when he was returning from a walk in the neighbourhood, he opened the door of his room and saw himself sitting at his desk. He stood still and rubbed his eyes, but the man continued to sit there, though Frederick tried to drive him away with a sharp look as a ray of light dispels a cloud of fog. He was filled with horror, and at the same time a wave of hate swept over him.

"You or I!" he cried, quickly grasping his revolver and holding it to the face of his double. Hate confronted hate. It was not twin love and hate, each confronting the other.

The mirror had been an illusion.

XXVIII

Peter Schmidt had a serious operation to perform for a fibroid tumour. Knowing that Frederick had witnessed Kocher perform the same operation in Berne and had repeatedly been successful with it himself, he called upon him for help. The patient was a native Yankee farmer, forty-five years of age. His son, a lad of nineteen, drove out in a sleigh to fetch Frederick.

At the appointed time Frederick entered the office, very pale, but outwardly calm. Nobody suspected what a tremendous amount of will power he had to summon to keep his self-control. Like a boy saying his A B C's, he kept repeating to himself:

"I am Frederick von Kammacher. This is Peter Schmidt. This is his wife, and this is the patient."

When he looked about the room, he saw other persons, the shades of those he had met within the last few days and on his trip across the ocean. But he pulled himself together and swore to himself--even in the moment of greatest danger he had not prayed--and saw that the unbidden guests in the room were also swearing.

The farmer was sitting in the waiting-room. The physicians consulted with one another, and Peter Schmidt and his wife urged Frederick to do the operating. His head was a-whirl. He was hot, he trembled, but his friends detected nothing. He asked for a large glass of wine and went about his preparations without speaking. When Mrs. Schmidt brought the wine, he drank it down in one gulp.

Mrs. Schmidt led the old farmer in. They had agreed that she was to do the washing and administer the anaesthetic. She adjusted him on the operating table, bared his body, and washed it thoroughly. Then Peter Schmidt shaved the hair away from his armpit. The physicians exchanged only brief words and signs. It was a matter of life and death. Success hung by a thread.

The torpor and composure of a somnambulist had come upon Frederick, who with his shirt sleeves rolled up was ceaselessly washing his arms and hands and brushing his finger nails, all at the bidding of a will not his own. He was acting in a state of will-lessness, of auto-suggestion. Yet it was with perfect lucidity and due deliberation that he selected the necessary instruments from the doctor's closet.

The anaesthetic was taking effect. Peter handed the instruments to Frederick, who once again carefully and coolly examined the morbid spot, found that the tumour might already have progressed too far, but nevertheless, with a firm, sure touch, cut into the mass of living flesh. He kept cursing at the insufficient light. The room was on the ground floor with the windows giving directly upon the main street with its heavy traffic. Contrary to expectation, the tumour lay deep, extending between the large nerve bundles and blood vessels in the inner portion of the brachial plexus. It had to be removed with a scalpel, a very ticklish operation because of the proximity to the thin-walled great vein, which at the least incision sucks in air and produces instant death. But everything went well. The large hollow wound was stuffed with antiseptic gauze, and at the end of three-quarters of an hour the farmer, with the help of his son, was carried unconscious into a hospital room on the other side of the hall and laid in bed.

Immediately after the operation, Frederick said he would have to telegraph to Miss Burns, who intended to visit him the next day, telling her not to come. But the words were scarcely out of his mouth, when a boy brought a cable message from Europe for him. He opened it, said not a word, and asked the farmer's son to drive him straight back home. He shook hands with his friends and took leave without referring to the contents of the message.

The drive in the sleigh beside the farmer's son through the snowy landscape was very different from the drive he had taken with Peter on his arrival two weeks before. This time he himself was not driving; what was worse was the absence of the earlier feeling that he had regained mastery over himself and renewed joy in life. He feared his last moment had come. The country he was in, the place he was driving to, the fact that he was sitting in a sleigh, these things he realised only intermittently. Though the sun was shining in a cloudless sky upon a dazzling white earth, he felt for minutes at a time that he was being drawn forward into utter darkness to the accompaniment of sleigh-bells. The farmer boy noticed nothing, except that the famous German physician was taciturn and extremely pale.

Frederick had never been in greater need of all his will power. But for his iron self-control, he would have gone stark mad and jumped with a shout from the sleigh dashing along at full speed. He knew a telegram was lying crumpled in the right-hand pocket of his fur coat; but each time he tried to recall what was in the telegram, it seemed that a hammer kept knocking at his head, dulling his senses. The grateful country boy had no inkling that close beside him was sitting a man who had to exert superhuman strength not to succumb to an attack of raving madness. As a matter of fact, the boy was in danger of a maniac's clutching him by the throat and drawing him into a life and death struggle.

At his door Frederick shook hands with the farmer's son and groped his way into the house through midnight darkness. The boy's few words of thanks went down in a rushing and roaring of vast black waters. The sleigh-bells began to jingle again and never ceased, turning into that infernal ringing that had become firmly fixed in Frederick's head since the shipwreck.

"I am dying," he thought when he reached his room. "I am dying, or else I am going crazy." The clock on the wall came into his vision and receded again. He saw his bed and clutched for the post.

"Don't fall," said Rasmussen, who was still sitting there with the thermometer in his hand.

But no, this time it was not Rasmussen. It was Mr. Rinck, with his yellow cat in his lap, the man who had been in charge of the mail on the *Roland*.

"What are you doing here, Mr. Rinck?" Frederick roared.

The next moment he was at the window in the light of the dazzling sun, which radiated, not light, but raven-black darkness, like a hole in the heavens pouring out night. The wind suddenly began to moan and howl about the house. It whistled derisively through the door cracks, like the jeers and taunts of a mob of rowdies. Or was it Mr. Rinck's cat miauing? Or was it children whimpering in the hall? Frederick groped about. The house quivered and was thrown from its foundations. It swayed to and fro. The walls began to snap and crack like wickerwork. The door flew open. The rain and hail whipped in. A sudden gust of wind lifted Frederick from his feet. Somebody cried "Danger!" The electric bells raged and mingled with the voices of the storm.

"It's not so! It's a lie! The devil is hoaxing you. You will never set foot on American soil. Your hour is come. You are at the Judgment seat. You are going to perdition."

Suddenly silence set in. Something unheard-of was about to happen, something far worse to see perhaps than to experience. Frederick wanted to save himself. He tried to gather his things together, but he had no hat. He could not find his trousers, his coat, or his boots.

Outside, the moon was shining. In the bright light, the storm was raging. Suddenly, like a wall broad as the horizon, the sea came rolling up. The ocean had risen over both its banks.

"Atlantis! The hour has come," thought Frederick. "Our earth is to be submerged like Atlantis of old."

He ran down-stairs. On the steps he caught up his three children and realised it was they who all the time had been whining and whimpering in the hall. He carried the smallest one on his arm and led the other two by the hand. At the front door, they saw the dreadful tidal wave sweeping nearer and nearer in the ashen light of the moon, carrying along the ship, which was a steamer rolling and pounding fearfully in the waters. The whistles were blowing frightfully, sometimes in a prolonged blare, sometimes in abrupt toots, one after the other.

"It's the **Roland** with Captain von Kessel," Frederick explained to the children. "I know it. I was on the ship. I myself went down with that superb steamer." He heard shots being fired from the struggling vessel. Rockets hissed up towards the moon and burst in the sombre grey of dawn, dazzling his eyes. "All's over," he said to the children. "All those fine, brave men are doomed to rot in the water."

And picking up on his arm now one of the children, now another, and losing them and finding them again, he began to run to save their lives from the flood. He ran, he raced, he jumped, he fell down. He protested against having to sink after all, though he had already been rescued. He swore, he ran, he fell, and scrambled to his feet, and ran and ran, with a hideous fear in his breast, a senseless fear such as he had never before experienced. When the wave overtook him, fear changed into soothing peace and calm.

XXIX

The next morning, with the same train by which Frederick had come, Miss Burns arrived in Meriden. She went directly to Peter Schmidt's office to inquire for him, having expected to find him awaiting her at the station. Peter told her of the operation Frederick had performed the day before.

"It was a mighty difficult job, I tell you," said Peter Schmidt, "and he covered himself with glory. He intended immediately afterwards to send you a telegram telling you not to come. But just as he was about to go, he himself received a cablegram."

"Well, now that I am here," said Miss Burns in her sprightly way, "I shall not allow myself to be turned down in such an offhand manner. I don't intend to visit Rome without seeing the Pope."

Three quarters of an hour later the two-seated sleigh drawn by the spirited chestnut, with whose peculiarities they now knew better how to deal, reached Uncle Tom's Cabin on Lake Hanover. Peter, who was anxious to bring Frederick news of the farmer and tell him he had not developed fever, drove Miss Burns out. They were amazed at the condition in which they found things, and, as they mounted the stairs, freely exchanged criticisms without lowering their voices. The door to Frederick's room was slightly ajar. They walked in. He was lying stretched on his bed, still wearing the fur coat in which he had left the office after the operation. He was unconscious, mumbling in a delirium, evidently very ill. Peter Schmidt picked up the cablegram lying on the floor. He and Miss Burns felt that in the circumstances they were justified in learning its contents. What they read was:

Dear Frederick, news from Jena. In spite of the greatest care Angele
passed away yesterday afternoon. Take the inevitable with composure.
Keep yourself well for your loving old parents.

For a week Frederick hovered between life and death. The powers of darkness, perhaps, had never grappled for him so greedily. For a week his whole body was like something about which tongues of fire lick and roar, ready to consume it and send it up into the air, like a puff of smoke.

Peter Schmidt, of course, brought all his medical skill to his friend's service. Mrs. Schmidt, too, did whatever she could for him. Miss Burns felt it was predestination, not chance, that had brought her to his side at so critical a moment, and instantly decided not to leave until he was entirely out of danger. She engaged a woman attendant and a man to go on errands by day and night.

The terrible frenzy in which Frederick had been the night before was apparent from the way in which things had been thrown about. The glass of his seaman's clock on the wall was broken, and dishes were shivered to bits. Peter Schmidt's diagnosis was typhoid fever. The first two days and nights he did not leave Frederick's side, except when his wife took his place. The paroxysms repeated themselves. Memories of the shipwreck still tormented him, and at certain hours he would tell his attendants, whom he did not recognise, to look in a corner of the room, where, he said, a black spider, the size of a bowling ball, was lying in wait for him. Peter and his wife with extreme caution applied all the means at a physician's disposal to reduce his temperature; but the third day passed, and still it did not fall below 105.8 deg.. Peter grew graver and graver. Finally, however, the fever curve showed declinations, and by the end of a week its downward course remained pretty constant.

Frederick looked like a pale, empty, incombustible husk, inside of which a great auto-da-fe had taken place. What a wild orgy salamander-like creatures must have been holding behind his sweaty forehead. Countless times, by the most different methods, Angele murdered Ingigerd and Ingigerd Angele. His father, the general, fought a pistol duel with Mr. Garry, Captain von Kessel acting as second and measuring the distance. Doctor Wilhelm kept rising again and again from beneath the raging chaos in his soul. Ten or twenty times he brought him a human embryo wrapped in paper, and said:

"To live is good. Not to live is better."

Hans Fuellenberg had to leave his hiding-place and join in the gruesome, grotesque dance to death. Sometimes it seemed as if a puff of burning air swept all these figures into an oven to destroy them forever.

Something like the dizzy movement of the sea kept tossing up and down. He was carried aloft--his consciousness left him. He sank deep down--again his consciousness left him. He flew--he lost his sense of ponderosity. High on the crest of this cosmic, immaterial swell, he suffered constantly from nausea. In his lucid moments he said to himself:

"The ocean does not wish me to be saved. It kept me alive just to display the full extent of its powers and draw me down from my security."

He had dreams of tremendous cosmic proportions, showing he had images of a might and power far exceeding the sane, normal strength of conception, with no precedent for them in experience. Even when the life-boat with its small load of castaways, shrieking, praying, or unconscious, was dancing on the great broad swells of the heavy, mineral ocean, Frederick had had no such feeling of the microscopic minuteness of his personality.

At the end of the first week he recognised Miss Burns and began to understand what she had done for him. He smiled with difficulty and made signs with his hand lying limply on the bedspread.

It was not until the end of the second week, the twenty-sixth of March, that the fever left him entirely. He spoke, slept, had vivid dreams. In a tired voice and sometimes with a touch of humour, he told of the wild things that had passed through his brain. He expressed desires, showed gratitude, inquired for the farmer on whom he had operated, and smiled when Peter told him the wound had healed promptly and the farmer had driven out to bring some guinea-fowls for bouillon.

Miss Burns's management of the household was exemplary. Such considerate, ever-ready ministrations as Frederick received do not fall to the lot of many men. Physicians like Peter and his wife are not, of course, prone to prudery. Neither was Miss Burns, with her strong arms and sculptor hands, which were accustomed to modelling from life. Though her manner was calm and composed, there was secret passion and a strong maternal instinct in her nursing. She seemed to have found her true vocation.

At her bidding Peter sent cablegrams to Frederick's parents, keeping them informed of his condition, and notifying them when he was pronounced out of danger. With the request that it be held for him until his health was restored, she returned a thick letter from the general written before Frederick was taken ill, correctly assuming that it contained details of his wife's tragic end. She knew that by keeping the letter, she might be tempted to betray its existence to the sick man and would then find it too hard to prevent him from reading it. At the beginning of the fourth week, she received a letter from the old general, in which he thanked her and the two doctors from the depths of his heart for all they had done for his son.

"I may tell you," he wrote, "that poor Angele did not die a natural death. At the institution, they knew she needed the strictest watching, but, unfortunately, even with the greatest care, there are moments when a patient is not observed. It was one of those moments that Angele seized to take poison, one of the poisons that are frequently used and are not kept under lock and key."

The snow had melted away. Slowly, slowly Frederick adjusted himself to life again. There was a mildness in him like the mildness of nature outside his window. It was a surprisingly sweet experience. The world seemed to be granting him indulgence. Lying on his clean bed, with the little pewter sailing vessels on the old seaman's clock ticking to and fro, he had a sense of security and, what is more, a sense of rejuvenation, of having expiated and received pardon. From torrid black clouds, a storm had come with thunder and lightning to cleanse the air. It was still rumbling on the distance horizon, farther and farther away, never to return again, leaving behind in the weak man a rich, full, peaceful joy in life.

"A cure of force, a violent eruption and revolution has purged your body of all poisons and putrid matter," said Peter Schmidt.

XXX

"A pity no birds are singing," Frederick said one day to Miss Burns, who had opened his bedroom window wide.

"Yes," said Miss Burns, "it is a pity."

"Because," Frederick went on, "you say it is already greening on the banks of Lake Hanover."

"What does that mean--'greening'?" asked Miss Burns, who did not know the German word he had used. He laughed.

"It means spring is coming, and spring without the singing of birds is a deaf and dumb spring."

"Come to England. There's where you hear birds."

"You come to Germany, Miss Burns. There's where you hear birds," Frederick mimicked his friend's drawl.

When the time came for him to sit up for a while, he refused.

"I don't want to get out of bed. I feel too comfortable lying here," he declared.

Soon after the fever left him, he ceased to feel ill, and for the last week they had been bringing him books, entertaining him with stories and anecdotes of the neighbourhood, and reading the papers to him, all in moderation, of course. They divined his wishes from his eyes. His microscope was put beside his bed, and he set seriously to work to examine specimens from his own body, an occupation that brought many jests down on him. The horror of his illness had turned into a diversion, a pleasant subject of study.

It was not until he had left his bed and was sitting in a comfortable chair wrapped in blankets that he inquired whether a letter had not come from his parents. Miss Burns told him his father had written and recounted those things in his letter which she knew would please Frederick and ease his mind. She was astonished to hear the pale convalescent say:

"I am convinced poor Angele took her own life. Well," he continued, "I have suffered what I had to suffer; but I will not reject the hand that I feel is graciously extended towards me. By that I mean," he added, thinking from the expression in

Miss Burns's eyes that she did not understand him, "that for a' that and a' that, I am glad to be restored to life and confidence in life."

One day, while Miss Burns was telling of some eminent men in different countries with whom she had become acquainted, mild complaints escaped her, showing she had suffered disenchantments.

"In a year," she said, "I am going back to England, to some village, and devote myself to the education of neglected children. The sculptor's profession does not satisfy me."

"How would you like this, Miss Burns," said the convalescent, with a frank, roguish smile, "wouldn't you like to educate a rather difficult big child?"

Peter and Eva had agreed not to mention Ingigerd Hahlstroem's name. But one day Frederick handed Miss Burns a piece of paper with a verse written in lead pencil in a trembling hand.

"To whom does this refer?" he asked.

"Have threads been spun? No, there were none!
We were so chill, so small and lone.
Have we to higher regions gone?
To give the key Peter was not prone.
I saw the sacramental stone
And laid my hallowed hands thereon.
Alas! the bread and wine were gone.
With dazzling radiance all things shone,
'Twas base deceit; I was undone."

Miss Burns was touched to see that his thoughts were still engaged with the little dancer. On another occasion he said to her:

"I am not fitted to be a physician. I am incapable of making the sacrifice to humanity of pursuing an occupation that depresses me so. I have a riotous imagination. Perhaps I could be a writer. But I am determined to become a sculptor. While I was sick, especially at the end of the second week, I remodelled all the works of Phidias and Michael Angelo. Don't misunderstand me, Eva. In becoming a sculptor,

I am no longer ambitious of distinction. I shall merely be rendering homage to the greatness of art. While remaining a faithful workman asking nothing for myself, I may in time succeed in mastering the nude form sufficiently to produce at least one good piece."

"You know I have confidence in your talent," said Miss Burns.

"Then, what do you think of this plan, Miss Eva? The income from my wife's estate is about five thousand marks, enough for the education of my three children. I receive an annuity of three thousand marks. Do you think we five could end our days in peace in a little house with a studio, say, near Florence?"

Miss Burns's answer to the weighty question was a hearty laugh.

She was intimately acquainted with the artistic disposition and so, perhaps, was actually well fitted to educate adult children. She had been the good friend and comrade of two or three great artists in France and England, and had a soothing way of entering into the work, the interests, and the experiences of such extraordinary men. Neither of her parents had been an artist. Her father had been a plain business man. Yet both had possessed that veneration and love of art and artists which is almost as rare as the creative gift. In the museum at Birmingham, there were pictures by Burne-Jones and Rossetti and a collection of drawings, the gift of her father while still a prosperous man. She herself was not convinced that she had an imperative calling to art. Her passion was to be useful to art in serving artists. This was not the first time, and Frederick knew it, that she had acted the part of the good Samaritan. She was always ready to sacrifice herself in order to help artists out of every sort of difficulty.

"I have no desire to be a Bonifacius Ritter," said Frederick. "A great collection of studios, with works turned out by wholesale, no matter how excellent they may be, does not suit my disposition. What I want is a workshop opening on a garden, where I can pick violets in winter and break off branches of evergreen oak, yew, and laurel. There, in peace and quiet, hidden from the world, I should like to devote myself to art and culture in general. The myrtle, too, would have to blossom again within my garden wall, Miss Burns." Miss Burns laughed and paid no attention to the allusion.

She thoroughly approved of his plans from her own healthy point of view.

"There are enough people," she said, "who are born physicians and men of action, and there are far too many entering those careers and jostling one another out of the way."

She spoke of Ritter with sympathy, yet in a tone of superiority, and smiled with benignant understanding upon his naive penetration into the regions of the Upper Four Hundred.

"Life," she said, "when it is eager to hurry on with a show of vivacity, demands credulity, love of pleasure, ambition. I, myself, before my father lost the greater part of his fortune, got to know high life in England through and through. I found it insipid and boresome."

When Frederick was able to stand alone and walk and go up and down stairs, Miss Burns left for New York to complete the work that she had begun in Ritter's studio, wishing to finish it before the middle of May, when she intended to return to England to straighten out some legal matters in connection with a small inheritance from her mother, who had died two years before. She had already engaged passage on the *Auguste Victoria* of the Hamburg American line. Frederick von Kammacher let her go without protest. He did not try to detain her. He profoundly admired the girl who was so strong and stately; and he had conceived of his future existence as a state of lasting companionship with her. There was Dutch and German blood combined with the culture and polish of the Englishwoman. Wherever she settled down, wherever she busied herself, she produced the cosey charm of the English home. She was healthy and, as Frederick had to admit, very beautiful. He did not detect the faintest symptom of the thing he most dreaded, feminine hysteria.

"I should like to have a comrade like her for life," he thought. "I should like her to be the mother of Angele's children."

XXXI

Frederick grew better daily. It seemed to him as if he had been ill for more than a decade. His body was not undergoing a process of evolution but of rebuilding from fresh young cells. The same thing seemed to be happening to his soul. The burden that had been weighing upon his spirits, the restless thoughts that had constantly been circling about the various shipwrecks in his life had departed. He had thrown off his past as one discards a cloak which the wind and weather, thorns and sword thrusts have torn and worn. Memories, which before his illness had forced themselves upon him unbidden in the awful guise of actual presence, no longer recurred to him. To his astonishment and satisfaction he observed that they had sunk forever on the other side of a remote horizon. The itinerary of his life had brought him to a province wholly new and novel. He had passed through a fearful process of fire and water and had come out cleansed, purified and young. Convalescents always grope their way into their newly granted lives, like children without a past.

The American spring had come early. Suddenly the weather turned hot. In that part of America the transition from winter to summer is very abrupt. In the pools and lakes, the bullfrogs croaked in rivalry with the high, clear shrilling of the other American frogs. Now came that unendurable combination of heat and humidity which Mrs. Schmidt so dreaded. She suffered fearfully during the summer, when she continued with her hard work just as in winter.

Frederick began again to accompany Peter Schmidt on his professional rounds, and sometimes the friends took long excursions into the country. They fell back into their old habit of revolving problems and pondering the destinies of mankind. To his friend's astonishment, Frederick did not display his old incisiveness in debate, whether in attack or defence. There was a cheerful placidity about him which took the keenness from any hope or fear of a universal character upon which they touched in their discussions.

"How do you account for it?" asked Peter Schmidt.

"I think I have well earned the precious right merely to breathe, and I think I appreciate it. What I want to do for the time being is smell, taste, and enjoy. An Icarus flight does not suit my present condition, and with my newly awakened tender love for the superficial, you will scarcely find me ready to dig laboriously into the depths. I am now a bourgeois. I am done with my former state," he concluded, smiling.

Peter Schmidt, as a practising physician, expressed his satisfaction with this mood of Frederick's.

"To be sure," he said, "you will change again."

"Time will show, but I think not," rejoined Frederick.

Indian lore had a fascination for Peter Schmidt. He liked to go to certain spots in the hilly country to which history or legend attaches stories of the conflicts between the first white colonists and the Indians, and remain there a long time, mentally living over again the experiences of the fur trappers and the tenacious wrestling of the settlers for possession. Sometimes, in a wave of warlike feeling, he would draw his revolver and shoot at a mark. Frederick was no match for him as a marksman.

"The blood of the old German adventurers and colonists is flowing in your veins," he said. "A finished civilisation, over-ripe and over-refined such as ours, really does not suit you. Where you ought to be is in a wilderness with a Utopia hovering above."

"The world is still not much more than a wilderness," said Peter. "It will be quite a while before the structure of our cosmic philosophy will stand on a solid foundation. In short, Frederick, much remains to be done."

"Like the Lord God, I shall knead human beings from wet clay and inspire them with a living breath."

"Stuff and nonsense!" said Peter Schmidt. "Making dolls like that leads nowhere. You are too good to be doing it. You belong on the ramparts, in the front ranks of the battle line, my dear boy."

"I for my part," said Frederick, smiling, "have stipulated an armistice for the next few years. I want for once to try to get on with what the world is able to offer. I want to disaccustom myself as much as possible from reflection and dreams."

Frederick felt it was his duty to persuade his friend, both for his own and for his wife's sake, to return to Europe.

"Peter," he said, "the Americans have no use for a man like you. You cannot recommend patent medicines, nor can you by administering small doses keep a man chained to his bed for two months when you can cure him with quinine in a week. You have none of those characteristics which in the eyes of the average American make an aristocrat. From the American point of view you are a simpleton, because you are always ready to sacrifice yourself for every poor dog that strays your way. You ought to return to a land where, thank the Lord, the aristocracy of the spirit, the aristocracy of ideas is still a match for that other aristocracy. You ought to return to a land that would consider itself defunct and buried were the men of science and art no longer to represent the flower of its inhabitants. There are enough Germans here without you who are breaking their necks to forget the language of Goethe, the language their mothers taught them. Save your wife. Save yourself. Go back to Germany, go to Switzerland, go to France, go to England, go anywhere you will, but don't remain in this tremendous industrial corporation, where art, science, and true culture are, at present at least, wholly out of place."

But Peter Schmidt wavered. He loved America. And if, Indian fashion, he laid his ear to the ground, he already heard the festive music being rehearsed below ground that is to be played on the great day of a universal renaissance.

"All of us," he said, "should first be Americanized and then become neo-Europeans."

One of Frederick's favourite walks was to the suburb of Meriden where the Italian wine-growers settled. You could hear the men singing with their voices warm as the sunlight, the women calling the children with that cry of theirs pitched in octaves. You saw brown men binding the vines, and on Sundays you heard them talking and laughing, while the ***boccia*** balls rolled with dull thuds over the well-trodden soil in the open fields where they played. Those voices and sounds were piercingly sweet and familiar to Frederick.

"You may kill me for saying so, but I am, and will remain, a European."

His homesickness grew stronger and stronger. He went about singing such passionate praises of Europe to his friends that he entangled them in the web of his feelings, and finally melted away even Mrs. Schmidt's rigid resistance.

A surprising change came over her. She forgot her exhaustion, she moved briskly, she laughed again, and began to make all sorts of plans for a future in Europe.

The farmer upon whom Frederick had operated fairly persecuted him with gratitude. He expatiated upon how he had always relied upon God and how a man always can rely upon God, and how God on this occasion had sent him the right man at the right time. Frederick now realised the profound motive that destiny had had in sending him on his fearful trip.

In a morbid disinclination to learn of his comrades on the sea trip, Frederick avoided reading newspapers. One day Ingigerd Hahlstroem accompanied by a distinguished looking American by no means in his prime got off the Boston train and went directly to Peter Schmidt's office. She introduced herself and asked whether

Frederick von Kammacher was still in Meriden. Before he was taken ill they had exchanged letters. Later she had had no time to write because she had been making a rapid tour of the whole United States. She knew nothing of his illness. Peter Schmidt and his wife, though they had an instinctive habit of always telling the truth, a habit which interfered with their success in life, now deliberately, shamelessly, boldly told a bare-faced lie.

"Frederick has returned to Europe. He took a White Star steamer, the **Robert Keats**," they told Ingigerd.

Without informing anyone, Frederick had engaged passage on the **Auguste Victoria** for the same crossing as Miss Burns. Peter and his wife wanted to go by a slower, less expensive steamer. They were all in a glorious state of impatience. Once more the ocean became nothing but a small pond across which their yearning lightly swung a bridge.

At that time a sentimental song was being sung in all the theatres in America, entitled "Hands Across the Sea." Every bill-board, fence and barrel bore "Hands Across the Sea." Frederick went about humming "Hands Across the Sea." Whenever he saw "Hands Across the Sea," his soul was stirred by a rich, beautiful melody.

But there was one thing that still prevented Frederick from enjoying complete serenity of spirit. A single thought kept haunting him. Should he express that thought by word of mouth or by letter? He constantly wavered between the two impulses. Not a day passed that he did not make ten decisions, one way or another, until one Sunday chance came to his rescue in the form of Willy Snyders and Miss Eva Burns, who had come to Meriden on an excursion. When he saw the lovely girl, dressed in light summer clothes, coming towards him with a smile, he realised that "Shall I?" or, "Shall I not?" had until then played an important role in his deliberations. But now that question was decided.

"Willy," he cried beaming, "do what you will, go wherever you will, stay wherever you will, amuse yourself as best you can, and at supper we'll all meet at the hotel." He grasped Miss Eva's hand and drew her arm in his, and she went off with him, laughing. Willy was greatly amazed, but he, too, burst out laughing and said in his comic fashion:

"Oh, in that case I certainly am **de trop**."

When Frederick and Eva returned in the evening, to the handsome dining-room of the Meriden Hotel, a delicate charm, a tender warmth hovered about them, making them younger and comelier. Their friends observed it. To their own surprise, these two human beings had been penetrated by a new element and a new life. Though they had been steering towards it, neither of them had had a divination of it even a short time before. That evening champagne was drunk.

A week later the little colony of artists saw Miss Burns and Frederick off on the *Auguste Victoria*.

"I am going to follow you soon," Willy bawled as the steamer began to move from the pier.

Every day on board the steamer was a Sunday to Frederick and Eva. The afternoon of the third day the captain, never suspecting that he was speaking to one of the survivors of the *Roland*, said:

"It was hereabouts that the *Roland* went down about three months ago."

The sea was smooth, like a sky eternally cloudless. Dolphins were sporting in the waters. The night following that afternoon, a glorious night, became Frederick's and Eva's wedding night. In blissful dreams they were carried over the place of horror which was the grave of the *Roland*.

At the quay in Cuxhaven, Frederick's parents were awaiting him with his children. He saw nothing but his children. He held them, all three of them, in his arms for a whole minute. They laughed and chattered and clung to him wildly. Eva approached them, and everything was self-understood.

After all could get their breath again, Frederick made several obeisances and laid both hands on the ground, while looking into Eva's eyes. Then he arose and held up his finger to command silence. From the broad stretches of the fields with their young crops came the thousand-throated trilling of the larks.

"This is Germany, this is Europe! What of it, if after an hour like this, one should sink?"

The captain of the *Auguste Victoria* passed by and greeted Frederick.

"Do you know," said Frederick in his overflowing spirits, "do you know, I am actually one of the survivors of the *Roland*?"

"Indeed!" said the captain, adding, as he walked away, "Yes, we always cross the same ocean. I hope you have a pleasant trip, Doctor von Kammacher."

The Codes Of Hammurabi And Moses
W. W. Davies

QTY

The discovery of the Hammurabi Code is one of the greatest achievements of archaeology, and is of paramount interest, not only to the student of the Bible, but also to all those interested in ancient history...

Religion   **ISBN:** *1-59462-338-4*   **Pages:132**

MSRP $12.95

The Theory of Moral Sentiments
Adam Smith

QTY

This work from 1749. contains original theories of conscience amd moral judgment and it is the foundation for systemof morals.

Philosophy   ISBN: *1-59462-777-0*   **Pages:536**

MSRP $19.95

Jessica's First Prayer
Hesba Stretton

QTY

In a screened and secluded corner of one of the many railway-bridges which span the streets of London there could be seen a few years ago, from five o'clock every morning until half past eight, a tidily set-out coffee-stall, consisting of a trestle and board, upon which stood two large tin cans, with a small fire of charcoal burning under each so as to keep the coffee boiling during the early hours of the morning when the work-people were thronging into the city on their way to their daily toil...

Pages:84

Childrens   ISBN: *1-59462-373-2*   *MSRP $9.95*

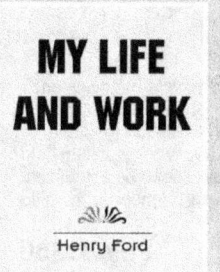

My Life and Work
Henry Ford

QTY

Henry Ford revolutionized the world with his implementation of mass production for the Model T automobile. Gain valuable business insight into his life and work with his own auto-biography... "We have only started on our development of our country we have not as yet, with all our talk of wonderful progress, done more than scratch the surface. The progress has been wonderful enough but..."

Pages:300

Biographies/   ISBN: *1-59462-198-5*   *MSRP $21.95* www.bookjungle.com *email: sales@bookjungle.com fax: 630-214-0564 mail: Book Jungle PO Box 2226 Champaign, IL 61825*

The Art of Cross-Examination
Francis Wellman

QTY

I presume it is the experience of every author, after his first book is published upon an important subject, to be almost overwhelmed with a wealth of ideas and illustrations which could readily have been included in his book, and which to his own mind, at least, seem to make a second edition inevitable. Such certainly was the case with me; and when the first edition had reached its sixth impression in five months, I rejoiced to learn that it seemed to my publishers that the book had met with a sufficiently favorable reception to justify a second and considerably enlarged edition. ..

Pages:412

Reference   **ISBN: *1-59462-647-2***   *MSRP $19.95*

On the Duty of Civil Disobedience
Henry David Thoreau

QTY

Thoreau wrote his famous essay, On the Duty of Civil Disobedience, as a protest against an unjust but popular war and the immoral but popular institution of slave-owning. He did more than write—he declined to pay his taxes, and was hauled off to gaol in consequence. Who can say how much this refusal of his hastened the end of the war and of slavery ?

Law   **ISBN: *1-59462-747-9***   **Pages:48**

MSRP $7.45

Dream Psychology Psychoanalysis for Beginners
Sigmund Freud

QTY

Sigmund Freud, born Sigismund Schlomo Freud (May 6, 1856 - September 23, 1939), was a Jewish-Austrian neurologist and psychiatrist who co-founded the psychoanalytic school of psychology. Freud is best known for his theories of the unconscious mind, especially involving the mechanism of repression; his redefinition of sexual desire as mobile and directed towards a wide variety of objects; and his therapeutic techniques, especially his understanding of transference in the therapeutic relationship and the presumed value of dreams as sources of insight into unconscious desires.

Pages:196

Psychology   **ISBN: *1-59462-905-6***   *MSRP $15.45*

Dream Psychology
Psychoanalysis for Beginners

Sigmund Freud

The Miracle of Right Thought
Orison Swett Marden

QTY

Believe with all of your heart that you will do what you were made to do. When the mind has once formed the habit of holding cheerful, happy, prosperous pictures, it will not be easy to form the opposite habit. It does not matter how improbable or how far away this realization may see, or how dark the prospects may be, if we visualize them as best we can, as vividly as possible, hold tenaciously to them and vigorously struggle to attain them, they will gradually become actualized, realized in the life. But a desire, a longing without endeavor, a yearning abandoned or held indifferently will vanish without realization.

Pages:360

Self Help   **ISBN: *1-59462-644-8***   *MSRP $25.45*

The Rosicrucian Cosmo-Conception Mystic Christianity *by Max Heindel*   ISBN: *1-59462-188-8*   **$38.95**
The Rosicrucian Cosmo-conception is not dogmatic, neither does it appeal to any other authority than the reason of the student. It is: not controversial, but is: sent forth in the, hope that it may help to clear...   New Age/Religion Pages 646

Abandonment To Divine Providence *by Jean-Pierre de Caussade*   ISBN: *1-59462-228-0*   **$25.95**
"The Rev. Jean Pierre de Caussade was one of the most remarkable spiritual writers of the Society of Jesus in France in the 18th Century. His death took place at Toulouse in 1751. His works have gone through many editions and have been republished...   Inspirational/Religion Pages 400

Mental Chemistry *by Charles Haanel*   ISBN: *1-59462-192-6*   **$23.95**
Mental Chemistry allows the change of material conditions by combining and appropriately utilizing the power of the mind. Much like applied chemistry creates something new and unique out of careful combinations of chemicals the mastery of mental chemistry...   New Age Pages 354

The Letters of Robert Browning and Elizabeth Barret Barrett 1845-1846 vol II   ISBN: *1-59462-193-4*   **$35.95**
by Robert Browning and Elizabeth Barrett   Biographies Pages 596

Gleanings In Genesis (volume I) *by Arthur W. Pink*   ISBN: *1-59462-130-6*   **$27.45**
Appropriately has Genesis been termed "the seed plot of the Bible" for in it we have, in germ form, almost all of the great doctrines which are afterwards fully developed in the books of Scripture which follow...   Religion/Inspirational Pages 420

The Master Key *by L. W. de Laurence*   ISBN: *1-59462-001-6*   **$30.95**
In no branch of human knowledge has there been a more lively increase of the spirit of research during the past few years than in the study of Psychology, Concentration and Mental Discipline. The requests for authentic lessons in Thought Control, Mental Discipline and...   New Age/Business Pages 422

The Lesser Key Of Solomon Goetia *by L. W. de Laurence*   ISBN: *1-59462-092-X*   **$9.95**
This translation of the first book of the "Lernegton" which is now for the first time made accessible to students of Talismanic Magic was done, after careful collation and edition, from numerous Ancient Manuscripts in Hebrew, Latin, and French...   New Age/Occult Pages 92

Rubaiyat Of Omar Khayyam *by Edward Fitzgerald*   ISBN:*1-59462-332-5*   **$13.95**
Edward Fitzgerald, whom the world has already learned, in spite of his own efforts to remain within the shadow of anonymity, to look upon as one of the rarest poets of the century, was born at Bredfield, in Suffolk, on the 31st of March, 1809. He was the third son of John Purcell...   Music Pages 172

Ancient Law *by Henry Maine*   ISBN: *1-59462-128-4*   **$29.95**
The chief object of the following pages is to indicate some of the earliest ideas of mankind, as they are reflected in Ancient Law, and to point out the relation of those ideas to modern thought.   Religion/History Pages 452

Far-Away Stories *by William J. Locke*   ISBN: *1-59462-129-2*   **$19.45**
"Good wine needs no bush,' but a collection of mixed vintages does. And this book is just such a collection. Some of the stories I do not want to remain buried for ever in the museum files of dead magazine-numbers an author's not unpardonable vanity..."   Fiction Pages 272

Life of David Crockett *by David Crockett*   ISBN: *1-59462-250-7*   **$27.45**
"Colonel David Crockett was one of the most remarkable men of the times in which he lived. Born in humble life, but gifted with a strong will, an indomitable courage, and unremitting perseverance...   Biographies/New Age Pages 424

Lip-Reading *by Edward Nitchie*   ISBN: *1-59462-206-X*   **$25.95**
Edward B. Nitchie, founder of the New York School for the Hard of Hearing, now the Nitchie School of Lip-Reading, Inc, wrote "LIP-READING Principles and Practice". The development and perfecting of this meritorious work on lip-reading was an undertaking...   How-to Pages 400

A Handbook of Suggestive Therapeutics, Applied Hypnotism, Psychic Science   ISBN: *1-59462-214-0*   **$24.95**
by Henry Munro   Health/New Age/Health/Self-help Pages 376

A Doll's House: and Two Other Plays *by Henrik Ibsen*   ISBN: *1-59462-112-8*   **$19.95**
Henrik Ibsen created this classic when in revolutionary 1848 Rome. Introducing some striking concepts in playwriting for the realist genre, this play has been studied the world over.   Fiction/Classics/Plays 308

The Light of Asia *by sir Edwin Arnold*   ISBN: *1-59462-204-3*   **$13.95**
In this poetic masterpiece, Edwin Arnold describes the life and teachings of Buddha. The man who was to become known as Buddha to the world was born as Prince Gautama of India but he rejected the worldly riches and abandoned the reigns of power when...   Religion/History/Biographies Pages 170

The Complete Works of Guy de Maupassant *by Guy de Maupassant*   ISBN: *1-59462-157-8*   **$16.95**
"For days and days, nights and nights, I had dreamed of that first kiss which was to consecrate our engagement, and I knew not on what spot I should put my lips..."   Fiction/Classics Pages 240

The Art of Cross-Examination *by Francis L. Wellman*   ISBN: *1-59462-309-0*   **$26.95**
Written by a renowned trial lawyer, Wellman imparts his experience and uses case studies to explain how to use psychology to extract desired information through questioning.   How-to/Science/Reference Pages 408

Answered or Unanswered? *by Louisa Vaughan*   ISBN: *1-59462-248-5*   **$10.95**
Miracles of Faith in China   Religion Pages 112

The Edinburgh Lectures on Mental Science (1909) *by Thomas*   ISBN: *1-59462-008-3*   **$11.95**
This book contains the substance of a course of lectures recently given by the writer in the Queen Street Hail, Edinburgh. Its purpose is to indicate the Natural Principles governing the relation between Mental Action and Material Conditions...   New Age/Psychology Pages 148

Ayesha *by H. Rider Haggard*   ISBN: *1-59462-301-5*   **$24.95**
Verily and indeed it is the unexpected that happens! Probably if there was one person upon the earth from whom the Editor of this, and of a certain previous history, did not expect to hear again...   Classics Pages 380

Ayala's Angel *by Anthony Trollope*   ISBN: *1-59462-352-X*   **$29.95**
The two girls were both pretty, but Lucy who was twenty-one who supposed to be simple and comparatively unattractive, whereas Ayala was credited, as her Bombwhat romantic name might show, with poetic charm and a taste for romance. Ayala when her father died was nineteen...   Fiction Pages 484

The American Commonwealth *by James Bryce*   ISBN: *1-59462-26-8*   **$34.45**
An interpretation of American democratic political theory. It examines political mechanics and society from the perspective of Scotsman James Bryce   Politics Pages 572

Stories of the Pilgrims *by Margaret P. Pumphrey*   ISBN: *1-59462-116-0*   **$17.95**
This book explores pilgrims religious oppression in England as well as their escape to Holland and eventual crossing to America on the Mayflower, and their early days in New England...   History Pages 268

QTY

The Fasting Cure *by Sinclair Upton*
ISBN: *1-59462-222-1* **$13.95**
In the Cosmopolitan Magazine for May, 1910, and in the Contemporary Review (London) for April, 1910, I published an article dealing with my experiences in fasting. I have written a great many magazine articles, but never one which attracted so much attention... New Age/Self Help/Health Pages 164

Hebrew Astrology *by Sepharial*
ISBN: *1-59462-308-2* **$13.45**
In these days of advanced thinking it is a matter of common observation that we have left many of the old landmarks behind and that we are now pressing forward to greater heights and to a wider horizon than that which represented the mind-content of our progenitors... Astrology Pages 144

Thought Vibration or The Law of Attraction in the Thought World
ISBN: *1-59462-127-6* **$12.95**
by William Walker Atkinson
Psychology/Religion Pages 144

Optimism *by Helen Keller*
ISBN: *1-59462-108-X* **$15.95**
Helen Keller was blind, deaf, and mute since 19 months old, yet famously learned how to overcome these handicaps, communicate with the world, and spread her lectures promoting optimism. An inspiring read for everyone... Biographies/Inspirational Pages 84

Sara Crewe *by Frances Burnett*
ISBN: *1-59462-360-0* **$9.45**
In the first place, Miss Minchin lived in London. Her home was a large, dull, tall one, in a large, dull square, where all the houses were alike, and all the sparrows were alike, and where all the door-knockers made the same heavy sound... Childrens/Classic Pages 88

The Autobiography of Benjamin Franklin *by Benjamin Franklin*
ISBN: *1-59462-135-7* **$24.95**
The Autobiography of Benjamin Franklin has probably been more extensively read than any other American historical work, and no other book of its kind has had such ups and downs of fortune. Franklin lived for many years in England, where he was agent... Biographies/History Pages 332

Name	
Email	
Telephone	
Address	
City, State ZIP	

☐ **Credit Card**   ☐ **Check / Money Order**

Credit Card Number	
Expiration Date	
Signature	

Please Mail to: Book Jungle
PO Box 2226
Champaign, IL 61825
or Fax to: 630-214-0564

ORDERING INFORMATION
web*: www.bookjungle.com*
email*: sales@bookjungle.com*
fax*: 630-214-0564*
mail*: Book Jungle PO Box 2226 Champaign, IL 61825*
or PayPal *to sales@bookjungle.com*

Please contact us for bulk discounts

DIRECT-ORDER TERMS

**20% Discount if You Order
Two or More Books**
Free Domestic Shipping!
Accepted: Master Card, Visa,
Discover, American Express

www.ingramcontent.com/pod-product-compliance
Lightning Source LLC
Chambersburg PA
CBHW081145020726
47504CB00009B/2000